THE SHATTERED AND THE SOULLESS

THE HORUS HERESY®

Book 1 – HORUS RISING
Dan Abnett

Book 2 – FALSE GODS
Graham McNeill

Book 3 – GALAXY IN FLAMES
Ben Counter

Book 4 – THE FLIGHT OF THE EISENSTEIN
James Swallow

Book 5 – FULGRIM
Graham McNeill

Book 6 – DESCENT OF ANGELS
Mitchel Scanlon

Book 7 – LEGION
Dan Abnett

Book 8 – BATTLE FOR THE ABYSS
Ben Counter

Book 9 – MECHANICUM
Graham McNeill

Book 10 – TALES OF HERESY
edited by Nick Kyme and
Lindsey Priestley

Book 11 – FALLEN ANGELS
Mike Lee

Book 12 – A THOUSAND SONS
Graham McNeill

Book 13 – NEMESIS
James Swallow

Book 14 – THE FIRST HERETIC
Aaron Dembski-Bowden

Book 15 – PROSPERO BURNS
Dan Abnett

Book 16 – AGE OF DARKNESS
edited by Christian Dunn

Book 17 – THE OUTCAST DEAD
Graham McNeill

Book 18 – DELIVERANCE LOST
Gav Thorpe

Book 19 – KNOW NO FEAR
Dan Abnett

Book 20 – THE PRIMARCHS
edited by Christian Dunn

Book 21 – FEAR TO TREAD
James Swallow

Book 22 – SHADOWS OF TREACHERY
edited by Christian Dunn and
Nick Kyme

Book 23 – ANGEL EXTERMINATUS
Graham McNeill

Book 24 – BETRAYER
Aaron Dembski-Bowden

Book 25 – MARK OF CALTH
edited by Laurie Goulding

Book 26 – VULKAN LIVES
Nick Kyme

Book 27 – THE UNREMEMBERED EMPIRE
Dan Abnett

Book 28 – SCARS
Chris Wraight

Book 29 – VENGEFUL SPIRIT
Graham McNeill

Book 30 – THE DAMNATION OF PYTHOS
David Annandale

Book 31 – LEGACIES OF BETRAYAL
edited by Laurie Goulding

Book 32 – DEATHFIRE
Nick Kyme

Book 33 – WAR WITHOUT END
edited by Laurie Goulding

Book 34 – PHAROS
Guy Haley

Book 35 – EYE OF TERRA
edited by Laurie Goulding

Book 36 – THE PATH OF HEAVEN
Chris Wraight

Book 37 – THE SILENT WAR
edited by Laurie Goulding

Book 38 – ANGELS OF CALIBAN
Gav Thorpe

Book 39 – PRAETORIAN OF DORN
John French

Book 40 – CORAX
Gav Thorpe

Book 41 – THE MASTER OF MANKIND
Aaron Dembski-Bowden

Book 42 – GARRO
James Swallow

Book 43 – SHATTERED LEGIONS
edited by Laurie Goulding

Book 44 – THE CRIMSON KING
Graham McNeill

Book 45 – TALLARN
John French

Book 46 – RUINSTORM
David Annandale

Book 47 – OLD EARTH
Nick Kyme

Book 48 – THE BURDEN OF LOYALTY
edited by Laurie Goulding

Book 49 – WOLFSBANE
Guy Haley

Book 50 – BORN OF FLAME
Nick Kyme

Book 51 – SLAVES TO DARKNESS
John French

Book 52 – HERALDS OF THE SIEGE
edited by Nick Kyme and Laurie Goulding

Book 53 – TITANDEATH
Guy Haley

Book 54 – THE BURIED DAGGER
James Swallow

THE HORUS HERESY®
SIEGE OF TERRA

Book 1 – THE SOLAR WAR
John French

Book 2 – THE LOST AND THE DAMNED
Guy Haley

Book 3 – THE FIRST WALL
Gav Thorpe

Book 4 – SATURNINE
Dan Abnett

Book 5 – MORTIS
John French

Book 6 – WARHAWK
Chris Wraight

Book 7 – ECHOES OF ETERNITY
Aaron Dembski-Bowden

Book 8 – THE END AND THE DEATH:
VOLUME I
VOLUME II
VOLUME III
Dan Abnett

ERA OF RUIN (Anthology)
Dan Abnett, Aaron Dembski-Bowden,
John French, Guy Haley, Nick Kyme,
Gav Thorpe and Chris Wraight

GARRO: KNIGHT OF GREY (Novella)
James Swallow

THE HORUS HERESY®
SIEGE OF TERRA

THE SHATTERED AND THE SOULLESS

Graham McNeill

BLACK LIBRARY

A BLACK LIBRARY PUBLICATION

Sons of the Selenar and *Fury of Magnus* first published in 2020.
This edition published in 2026 by
Black Library, Games Workshop Ltd.,
Willow Road, Nottingham, NG7 2WS, UK.

Represented by: Games Workshop Limited – Irish branch,
Unit 3, Lower Liffey Street, Dublin 1,
D01 K199, Ireland.

10 9 8 7 6 5 4 3 2 1

Produced by Games Workshop in Nottingham.
Cover illustration by Neil Roberts.

A CIP record for this book is available from the British Library.

ISBN 13: 978-1-83609-019-9

Printed and bound in the UK.

THE HORUS HERESY®

SIEGE OF TERRA

It is a time of legend.

The galaxy is in flames. The Emperor's glorious vision for humanity is in ruins. His favoured son, Horus, has turned from his father's light and embraced Chaos.

His armies, the mighty and redoubtable Space Marines, are locked in a brutal civil war. Once, these ultimate warriors fought side by side as brothers, protecting the galaxy and bringing mankind back into the Emperor's light. Now they are divided.

Some remain loyal to the Emperor, whilst others have sided with the Warmaster. Pre-eminent amongst them, the leaders of their thousands-strong Legions, are the primarchs. Magnificent, superhuman beings, they are the crowning achievement of the Emperor's genetic science. Thrust into battle against one another, victory is uncertain for either side.

Worlds are burning. At Isstvan V, Horus dealt a vicious blow and three loyal Legions were all but destroyed. War was begun, a conflict that will engulf all mankind in fire. Treachery and betrayal have usurped honour and nobility. Assassins lurk in every shadow. Armies are gathering. All must choose a side or die.

Horus musters his armada, Terra itself the object of his wrath. Seated upon the Golden Throne, the Emperor waits for his wayward son to return. But his true enemy is Chaos, a primordial force that seeks to enslave mankind to its capricious whims.

The screams of the innocent, the pleas of the righteous resound to the cruel laughter of Dark Gods. Suffering and damnation await all should the Emperor fail and the war be lost.

The end is here. The skies darken, colossal armies gather. For the fate of the Throneworld, for the fate of mankind itself...
The Siege of Terra has begun.

CONTENTS

Sons of the Selenar 11

Fury of Magnus 181

SONS OF THE SELENAR

DRAMATIS PERSONAE

The Sisypheum

Ulrach Branthan	Captain, Iron Hands 65th Clan-Company
Cadmus Tyro	Acting captain of the *Sisypheum*
Frater Thamatica	Ironwrought, Avernii veteran
Ignatius Numen	Battle-brother
Sabik Wayland	Iron Father
Garuda	Eagle construct of Ulrach Branthan
Nykona Sharrowkyn	Raven Guard 66th Company
Atesh Tarsa	Apothecary, Salamanders 24th Company

The Selenar

Heliosa-54	High Matriarch of Luna's Selenar cults
Ta'lab Vita-37	Gene-witch of the Selenar

The Sons of Horus

Trastevere	Justaerin, captain of the Eye's Watch
Vornak	Justaerin Terminator
Urgave	Justaerin Terminator

'I, for one, know of no sweeter sight for a man's eyes than his own country…'

– Omerus, the Blind Bard of Ionia

'A leader is ultimately responsible for everything.'

– The Primarch Guilliman

'Loyalist, traitor…? The distinction is irrelevant. They are all sons of the Selenar.'

– Ta'lab Vita-37

PROLOGUE

Do not swear by the moon,
for she changes constantly.

The surface of Terra was burning.

Its atmosphere glowed with the fires of Unity.

Storms of global war raged beneath toxic skies, like the banked embers of a hearth.

They bathed the Lunar surface in red.

Warfare had riven humanity's birthrock for as long as the Selenar could remember, the conflicts growing in scale with every passing epoch and each unchecked evolution of technology.

'War has recast the world in its image,' said Heliosa-54, the ruddy light of Terra's unification reflecting from the moulded surfaces of her chromium mask.

'It has always been thus, revered matriarch,' spat Ta'lab Vita-37, her multi-armed form hunched over the data-light of the command console. 'It is mankind's nature to destroy.'

The matriarch of the Selenar turned to her most trusted gene-maiden, hearing the stress placed on the *man* of mankind.

'That is likely true,' agreed Heliosa-54, 'but we too are a branch of that shared root. Yes, we distil the essences of singular genetic paths in search of the perfect aspects of our species, but follow the strands of history far enough back, and we are not so different.'

She felt Ta'lab Vita-37's urge to challenge that assertion, her consciously evolved nature as a contrarian and questioner warring with her respect for Heliosa-54's vaunted archetype.

'You disagree?'

'I would not presume to, revered matriarch. Not now.'

'Of course you would, it is the archetype you iterate upon with every evolution. Speak freely.'

'Very well, revered matriarch,' said Ta'lab Vita-37, pausing to gesture towards the grim situation unfolding in front of them. 'The Emperor's transhuman warriors are bred to wreak bloody ruin and nothing else. They are *capable* of nothing else. But we of the Selenar cults, by iterating upon the twin mysteries of the helix, perform acts of *devotion and creation*. The gene-wrights of the Emperor pursue only the science of death, and it is too late for them to change their course.'

'And our sciences? Do we not also craft killing engines of steel and flesh?'

'For the defence of our fiefdoms, yes,' Ta'lab Vita-37 conceded. 'But the Dianic rites bring us closer to the true potential of humanity. Ultimately they will move us *further* from the urge to destroy.'

'I hope that will one day prove to be the case,' said Heliosa-54. 'But do not be so quick to condemn our Terran brothers. In times past, there were moments when the better angels of human nature sought to turn our species from the bloody altars of war. To embrace peace.'

'Such times were few and far between,' pointed out Ta'lab Vita-37. 'And they never lasted.'

As if to reinforce her point, the curve-walled chamber at the heart of the moon shook with the impact of nearby detonations. Grey dust spilled from cracks in the ceiling. It danced in the suspensor fields surrounding Heliosa-54's floating, cursive-spined form. Fractal patterns of dust glittered in the actinic light thrown out by the gently spinning gene-looms woven into the stone walls.

The pneuma-tubes along Heliosa-54's neck pulsed in time with her frosted breath, crafting a twisting helix at her throat.

'Why does the Emperor seek to destroy us?' asked Ta'lab Vita-37.

'The Emperor does not seek to destroy us.'

Ta'lab Vita-37 extended a curved, talon-like fingertip, hooking a disc of noospheric light from the gloss-black of the command console and lifting it up between them.

A rapidly shrinking noose of red light converged on their location, a silver icon of the crescent moon. Previously muted vox-channels surged with screams of the doomed and dying. The unmistakable bangs of bolter fire and shrieking plasma explosions formed a deafening cacophony of slaughter.

'All available data suggests otherwise,' she said. 'Warriors of the Seventh and Sixteenth Legions are slaughtering everything in their path. Our cults are dying as we speak.'

The howls of their attackers were a screeching din that scraped the spine, feral war-shouts of men born in the dark and raised on murder. Such men would accept nothing less than the complete destruction of whoever dared stand before them.

'The Emperor does not seek to destroy us,' repeated Heliosa-54. 'He seeks to yoke us to His great work. Not without some justification, He hopes we fear annihilation more than servitude. His hubris requires our science, our looms and our mysteries. He knows much, but He does not know everything.'

'Is that why you brought me here?' asked Ta'lab Vita-37. 'Is that why you still remain?'

'Yes. If the Emperor's killers do not find me here, they will tear Luna apart until they do. They will break me and I will be forced to give them the Magna Mater.'

Ta'lab Vita-37 flinched at the thought, and said, 'What is it you require of me?'

Heliosa-54 extended a dextrous, needle-like hand, one whose fingertips had crafted gene-sequences of such dizzying complexity that it seemed inconceivable they did not belong to some ancient creator goddess.

'To forsake me,' said Heliosa-54.

'I do not understand,' said Ta'lab Vita-37.

Data flowed between them, coiling spirals of light bearing gene sequences, marker codes and swathes of information so complex it made Ta'lab Vita-37 gasp at the density of inload.

'Go below to the Ergodic Vault. Sever your connections to the Luna Manifold, take the Magna Mater and vanish. I cannot divulge what I do not know. Too few of the high priestesses remain alive to destroy the Magna Mater, so you must keep it from the Emperor, you understand?'

'I understand,' said Ta'lab Vita-37.

Heliosa-54 saw Ta'lab Vita-37's shoulders slump, the gene-maiden already burdened by the terrible duty she had placed upon her.

'And if they should eventually find me?'

'Then pray that he who takes the Magna Mater is a wiser soul and has greater vision than Terra's new master.'

Ta'lab Vita-37 bowed, clasping her hands across her chest.

'It shall be as you say, revered matriarch,' she said. 'I will not fail you.'

Heliosa-54 did not watch her go, already beginning a mnemonic purge. Sadness touched her as precious memories burned away in the fires of synaptic erasure. She had loved Ta'lab Vita-37 as a daughter, but could not allow any trace of the gene-maiden to be found within her neural network.

She turned back to the console.

Barely six hours had passed since the sudden, shocking assault of the brute-crafted gene-warriors from Terra.

Every war front on Luna told the same story of defeat.

Her heart heavy with fear for the future, the High Matriarch of Luna opened a broad-spectrum vox-channel.

She knew the Emperor would hear her.

She hoped His warriors would.

'Call off your wolves,' she begged.

BOOK 1

MAIDEN

She is a wild, tangled forest with temples and treasures concealed within.

I

A Captain Remade
Skeleton Crew
Carnager

How best should a warrior die?

He had given much thought to this over the years.

As a neophyte, he imagined his end would come in a terrible war against some hideous xenoform, fighting side by side with his brothers for a noble and heroic cause. His last moments would come in a battle spoken of in awe by the warriors of ages yet to pass.

In the following millennia, lessons learned from his end would be taught in every academy of war – required reading for the youth of this new age.

Libraries of books would be written of that bloody time.

But war cares nothing for the arrogant imaginings of young men.

Its teachings are bloody and indifferent.

Yes, heroes are forged in the crucible of combat, and the legacies of a handful live on in the memories of those who endure. But for every hero whose deeds transcend their death, tens of thousands more are forgotten or never known at all.

Their courage goes unrecorded.

Their stories are never told.

Nykona Sharrowkyn was no longer a neophyte, and ever since Sabik Wayland had dragged his ruined body from the betrayal on Isstvan V, he'd long known he would die in the dark, alone and unremembered.

A fitting end for a warrior of the Raven Guard.

How best should a warrior die?

In a little over two minutes, he'd likely find out.

Spots of light flickered like auspex glitches on the ochre orb of Jupiter, which filled the *Sisypheum*'s viewscreen. But they weren't glitches, they were burning weapons platforms struck from their orbital anchors and now dragged to destruction by the vast planet's gravity. In the foreground, pyrochemical lightning and ash storms distorted the gunmetal ellipse of Ganymede as its vast hydro-stacks burned in the fury of traitor bombardments.

The Solar War was raging, hot and bright, but drawing inexorably closer to Terra from the outer-system planets. The Warmaster was tightening his noose, but every minute the loyalists kept the traitors from the Throneworld's glory was a victory.

Dying ships blazed in Jupiter's high orbit, skeletons of blackened metal alight from within. Atomic storms raged in their wakes as millions of megatons of ship-killing ordnance detonated like distant supernovas.

Not as distant as Nykona Sharrowkyn would have liked.

Swarms of torpedoes flew hot in the void. Macro shells lit up space in blinding explosions. Banks of lasers blinked in collimated lines of actinic brightness.

Something detonated off the ventral axis. Sharrowkyn had no idea what it might have been. A torpedo warhead? A ship exploding? A hunter-killer mine?

Three hundred and sixty-seven ships manoeuvred aggressively within the Jovian engagement volume. Escorts and destroyers mostly. At least seventy vessels of capital displacement also.

Sharrowkyn had little skill in coordinating void fights or the operation of a starship, but after the disastrous mission to Lerna Two-Twelve and the decimation of the *Sisypheum*'s crew, he'd had to learn something of the craft.

A twisting shape emerged from the screeching static and waves of interference rippled through the holographic representation of the void brawl.

Huge, and coming right at them.

Range markers and ident-tags flickered to life.

'Tumbling Lunar-class dead ahead!' shouted Sharrowkyn.

'I see it,' replied Sabik Wayland, spliced into the *Sisypheum*'s multiple helm controls via neuro-proxy devices crafted by Frater Thamatica. 'Manoeuvring now.'

Wayland sounded matter-of-fact, but Sharrowkyn had fought beside the warrior of the Iron Hands long enough to hear the strain beneath his outward calm.

The bridge deck tilted violently as the Iron Father threw the *Sisypheum* into a hard, rolling turn. The heavily modified strike cruiser shuddered. Its hull plates buckled and up-armoured bulkheads groaned in protest as the kilometres-long keel flexed.

Gravity shifted with the violence of the manoeuvre and proximity alarms brayed. The clashing, discordant shriek of intersecting void shields filled the bridge. Hardwired servitors maintaining shield integrity spasmed as electrical feedback burned them alive from within. Sharrowkyn gagged at the smell of scorched machine oil and flesh.

The unimaginable scale of the gutted Lunar-class vessel filled the viewscreen. Sharrowkyn felt himself ducking as its burning superstructure passed over them. So vast it felt like it would never end. So close he felt he could reach the other ship's bridge in one powered leap.

'Didn't even come close,' said Wayland, pulling out of the turn and leaving the doomed ship in their wake as he angled them back to the battle.

'That warning was too damn late, Sharrowkyn!' bellowed Ulrach Branthan, the newly resurrected captain of the *Sisypheum*. His voice was a hideous amalgam of ruined human vocal cords and ad hoc augmetics. 'You're supposed to be tracking the flow of this battle.'

'Do I *look* like the master of surveyors?' snapped Sharrowkyn.

'Then step aside and find someone who can read a damn auspex!' said Branthan, his towering form stepping down from the command podium with a booming thud of asymmetrical, splay-clawed feet.

The captain's body was a nightmarish fusion of flesh and machine, but it bore only a passing resemblance to the honourable chassis of the Dreadnought from which its parts had been cannibalised. Rather, he was now a thing of biomechanical horror wrought by Atesh Tarsa in a moment of madness and desperation. The ancient relic known as the Heart of Iron was enmeshed in Branthan's exposed ribs and musculature like a chromium spider, beating with a loathsomeness Sharrowkyn could barely stomach.

The spoiled-meat stink of Branthan's body and the noxious chemicals keeping his rotten flesh alive reminded Sharrowkyn of his youth – of when he would find milky, bloated bodies afloat in the deep salt pools of Lycaeus.

A psyber-eagle wrought from pale steel and brass perched at his shoulder. The Iron Hands had named it Garuda, after an ancient Medusan myth, and, like the crew of the *Sisypheum*, it had suffered great hurts, but yet endured. On Iydris, it had taken a bolt-round from the swordsman Lucius, but Thamatica and Wayland had restored its mechanical life.

The surveyor station was awash with flickering ghost-images of the absurdly close-range battle. Wayland rolled them around the shuddering wreck of the *Glory Hound*, a Mars-class warship burning from bow to stern.

Booming clangs echoed through the ship's superstructure. Repurposed maintenance servitors at damage control blurted screeds of binaric gibberish.

'What was that?' demanded Branthan.

'I don't know,' said Sharrowkyn. 'Suicidal bombers or fighter craft with no carrier to return to? Maybe drifting wreckage too small for the auspex to pick up.'

'Not good enough, Raven Guard!'

Sharrowkyn bit back an angry retort as the display flared with signal bloom. Threat warnings blazed to life across the glowing surface of the slate.

'Capital vessel coming about on our rearward quarter,' he called. 'Oberon-class, I think.'

'The *Covenant of Truth*. Seventeenth Legion predator-ship,' replied Wayland sharply. 'But it's not coming for us.'

Dozens of threat runes blinked to life on the viewscreen.

'How can you be sure?' barked Branthan.

'The Kryptos,' said Wayland, pulling the *Sisypheum* away from the larger vessel's void-wake. 'It's feeding me the *Covenant*'s encrypted vox. Its captain is communicating with two other ships. They're moving to bracket the *Europa's Wrath*.'

Sharrowkyn tried to sort the conflicting auspex returns and match what he was seeing to what Wayland was telling him.

'Are you certain?' he asked. 'Looks to me like the *Covenant* is manoeuvring for a raking barrage across our drive.'

'I don't like ships on my rear!' said Branthan. Garuda spread its wings and squawked angrily.

'It's *not* coming for us,' insisted Wayland.

'It has a perfect firing position,' said Sharrowkyn.

'Holding course,' said Wayland.

'Throne damn you, Sabik Wayland!' cried Branthan, pounding across the deck towards the Iron Father. For an instant, Sharrowkyn thought he was going to rip Wayland from helm control.

The range counters slowed and extended.

Sharrowkyn let out a breath. 'It's pulling away.'

'I told you, the *Covenant* is hungry to kill the *Europa's Wrath*.'

The viewscreen erupted with light as the *Covenant of Truth* launched staggered broadsides into its victim. Boxed in by the barrages of two other traitor warships, the Imperial vessel was forced to endure the punishing fire flaying its shields.

Torpedo boats and bomber wings flew in close to the *Europa's Wrath*, and wave upon wave of ordnance punched into the titanic warship's hull. Secondary boosters thrust warheads farther into the larger ship before delayed-action fuses detonated them deep in its vitals.

A rippling wave travelled the length of the vessel as explosions raced through its internal compartments, tearing it apart from the inside. Swirling conflagrations erupted from the *Wrath*'s many wounds, burning white-hot with pure oxygen and the chemical fire of its blood. Sharrowkyn felt his heart clamped by an icy fist as he watched the majestic ship die. Like the last of a species finally brought to extinction, it fought to the end, but its doom was assured. The rad-wash of its murder fouled every sensor return, but Sharrowkyn saw rampant cascades of high-band atomics flaring deep in its enginarium.

That could only mean one thing.

'She's going critical,' shouted Sharrowkyn, 'Get us clear, Wayland.'

'Belay that!' ordered Branthan. 'Get us closer!'

'What?' shouted Sharrowkyn. 'No! You'll kill us all!'

He took a half-step towards Branthan.

'Remain at your post!' barked the monstrous captain of the Iron Hands.

'Wayland, no!' shouted Sharrowkyn. 'It's suicide to be anywhere near that ship.'

'Bring us around,' said Branthan. 'The *Covenant of Truth*'s shields are down. Vector a course directly towards its bridge. Sharrowkyn, get me a firing solution right now!'

'Wayland, get us out of here,' pleaded Sharrowkyn. 'He'll kill us all for the sake of vengeance.'

Branthan spun around, murderously swift for something so hulking. A powerful fist, ripped from the chassis of the fallen Brother Bombastus, slammed into Sharrowkyn's chest.

He flew backwards, twisting in the air to land in a crouched skid across the deck. Muscle memory made his hand fly to his hip, where his black-bladed gladius was sheathed.

He looked up to see Garuda perched on the edge of the auspex table, its head cocked to the side as it regarded him with its unblinking eyes.

Was it just his imagination or did the bird shake its head?

Sharrowkyn let out a breath as Garuda took flight and returned to Branthan's shoulder. The deck shuddered as the *Sisypheum* fired its prow bombardment cannon at point-blank range. The *Covenant of Truth*'s close-in defence systems had no time to react, and the city-levelling ordnance impacted on its command deck with devastating effect.

An Oberon-class battleship was a monstrously powerful ship of the line, heavily armoured and bristling with weapons systems, but without shields it was vulnerable. The *Sisypheum*'s shells punched deep into the nexus of its command centre, gouging mortal wounds into its brain. Plumes of fire and blossoming clouds of molten steel vented into space.

The *Sisypheum* flew through the expanding clouds of superheated vapour and cascades of wreckage, chased by a storm of hastily aimed las-fire and burst shells from anti-torpedo frag-launchers.

Branthan turned from Sharrowkyn, Garuda once again at his shoulder.

'Hard turn, bring us back around,' said Branthan. 'I want to finish this bastard off.'

'It's already out of the fight,' said Sharrowkyn.

'I don't want it *out of the fight*,' snapped Branthan. 'I want it *dead*!'

The *Sisypheum* shuddered as Wayland put the ship into a tight corkscrewing turn to starboard. He angled the prow down to obscure their course in the blazing plasma wake of the wounded battleship.

'Thamatica!' barked Wayland over the vox. 'I'm going to need those reactors burning hotter.'

The vox crackled with a blurt of angry binaric code before Thamatica answered from the enginarium.

'I assure you, Iron Father, it is taking everything I have simply to keep the reactors from overloading and killing us all. I can do only so much with barely a handful of menial servitors assisting me.'

'Do what you can, Ironwrought,' said Wayland, snapping off the vox. 'Nykona?'

Sharrowkyn didn't answer, his gaze fixed on Ulrach Branthan's back. He released the breath he'd been holding, feeling a sharp pain in his ribs. He relaxed his white-knuckled grip on his gladius, understanding that he had been on the verge of unleashing lethal violence on a fellow legionary.

An insane fellow legionary, yes, but one whose loyalty was still given to the Emperor.

'Nykona,' said Wayland, his voice calm but authoritative. 'I need eyes in this fight. Return to your station, brother.'

Sharrowkyn nodded slowly and sheathed his blade.

The void was burning with innumerable atomic flare-storms,

pulsing tsunamis of e-mag surges and the detonation echoes of the *Covenant*'s magazine stores.

Situational awareness was next to impossible to determine. Even an auspex-savant or an officer with decades of experience would likely divine nothing from this sensory anarchy.

'Coming about,' said Wayland matter-of-factly, as if announcing mundane orbital manoeuvres. 'Gun deck, how long till the bombardment cannon is back online?'

The pained voice of Atesh Tarsa, the Salamanders Apothecary, echoed through the bridge.

'Numen's working on it, but it will be at least seven minutes before the weapon is ready to fire. Every part of the reload process has to be done manually.'

Wayland cut the link and said, 'Broadsides it is then.'

A discordant wailing cut over the vox-bands, and Sharrowkyn winced at the torment he heard in the nightmarish howls.

Part binaric code, part daemonic cant.

In its purest form, the Mechanicum called it scrapcode.

It was the Kryptos, screaming from its below-decks cell.

Not a warning, a shriek of terror…

'Brace, brace, brace!' yelled Wayland.

Sharrowkyn saw it a second later.

A tapered prow knifing through the void, vectoring in at the perfect kill angle, murder-torpedoes already loose, stabbing lasers stripping away the last of the *Sisypheum*'s shields.

The ship screamed over the vox, tearing through the *Sisypheum*'s security protocols with the visceral trauma of its name.

Carnager! Carnager! Carnager!

White-hot beams of light seared through the strike cruiser's many decks, the relative movement of the two vessels causing them to whipsaw through its reinforced superstructure. Hundreds of metres of hull plate peeled away, like meat pared from the bone by a butcher's knife.

The force of entire sections venting explosively into hard vacuum heeled the ship over like a pugilist rocked back on their heels.

The auspex screamed with incoming ordnance.

The blood-red light of a mortal wound filled the bridge. It painted Branthan in a daemonic glow.

'You've killed us all,' hissed Sharrowkyn.

Then the world turned inside out.

And red light turned to white.

2

The Way is Open
Echoes of the Past
Back from the Dead

A frozen moment of time.

It stretched, soundless and serene.

Sharrowkyn's first thought was that if this was death, then everything the old-timers on Lycaeus had told him as a rebel youth was wrong.

They'd spoken of death as a fire that consumed you.

It would be painful, they said.

Death was *always* painful in the old-timers' tales, and it was never easy. A good death would be sudden and, if you were lucky, one you wouldn't see coming.

But *this* moment? This eternal moment was peaceful.

Which told Sharrowkyn it wasn't death.

This was something else.

Cold and weightless, Sharrowkyn's gut swelled with nausea, like the worst translation sickness imaginable. His eyes burned, as if microscopic needles were slowly pushing into his pupils.

He saw nothing but blinding, searing light.

His senses swam in and out of coherence.

Screaming voices, cries of horror, unbridled joy.

These were not voices he knew, for there were men, women and children who screamed names he'd never heard.

A thousand voices, *tens* of thousands.

He recognised languages of Terra, as well as dialects that had only taken root in the centuries since humanity first set sail from its birthworld. Woven within them were words never meant to be given voice, daemonic chatterings of razor teeth and loathsome appetites.

Sharrowkyn's mouth tasted metal, and his skull bloated with a raging storm of emotions, only a few of which were his.

Fear, guilt, hoped-for redemption, and overwhelming horror that was only kept from turning into a raging storm of self-destruction by iron discipline.

Too much. Too fast.

He felt the synapses within his mind coming untethered, the torrent of emotions eroding them like a surge tide that rips away the supports of a bridge.

The empty white of his vision cleared, and once again he saw the cold steel of buttressed gantries and the riveted steel plates of the ship's bridge.

The *Sisypheum* spun like a leaf on the wind, and an awful sense of vertigo permeated every fibre of Sharrowkyn's being. From his marrow to his psyche, he felt as though he were folding inside out – as if every dimension of his existence were now revealed to be a flimsy construct.

No sirens blared, and only the warning hiss of static filled the bridge, like the droning of carrion flies swarming the meat of the battle-fallen. Light flickered at the corner of his vision, and he rolled onto his side, closing his eyes as a fresh stab of nausea ripped up through his stomach. The sensation was so unnatural to his transhuman physiology that he almost didn't recognise it.

The feeling passed, and Sharrowkyn gripped the edge of the nearest console to pull himself upright, feeling as weak as a newborn. He blinked away the last of the burning pain in his vision, seeing the rest of the bridge crew recovering from whatever had just happened.

'Wayland, what in Medusa's name was that?' demanded Branthan, his mechanised body drooling coolant fluids and crackling with what looked like warp corposant. Garuda lay on the ground, its legs twitching and its eyes flickering with machine light.

Sabik didn't answer, his eyes wide and his lips moving soundlessly, like a servitor in the midst of a mindwipe. Strapped to his command throne, Sabik hadn't fallen like the rest of them, but integrated with the rest of the *Sisypheum*'s systems, he'd felt everything the ship had suffered.

'What was that?' repeated Branthan.

Sharrowkyn wanted to check his friend, but knew he had to deal with the most pressing demand before moving to the next.

Prioritise and execute.

The surveyor array was a flaring mess of static and distortions, a jumble of signals, datum points and navigational beacons that bore no resemblance to those in Jupiter's vicinity.

'I don't know,' said Sharrowkyn. 'None of the readings on the auspex make any sense.'

'*Make* them make sense,' ordered Branthan, as if the reality of their surroundings could be made clearer simply by force of will. 'The *Carnager* could be ready to finish us off!'

Sharrowkyn shook his head. 'No,' he said. 'I'm not picking up any ship signatures or engine flares in the void. We're alone out here.'

'And where exactly is *here*? We can't fight effectively if we don't know where we are.'

'If the few datum points I'm picking up are correct, then it looks like…'

'Like what?' said Branthan when Sharrowkyn didn't continue.

'Like we made a warp jump,' he said, trying to make sense of what little information he could confirm. 'Everything I'm seeing suggests we're no longer in the Jovian battlespace. We're somewhere above the solar disc, in the outer reaches of the trans-Martian void. Roughly a third of an AU from Terra…'

'That's impossible,' snapped Branthan. 'A warp jump this close to the sun would have torn us apart.'

'I don't know how else to explain it,' said Sharrowkyn, his words growing more confident as fresh information confirmed his hypothesis.

'He's right, captain,' said Wayland, his words slurred with system-shock. 'I felt a huge spike in warp spectra right after the *Carnager* hit us. I don't know exactly what it was, but it was somewhere in the vicinity of the Comet Shrine. Similar to what I'd expect to see when a war fleet translates, but many orders of magnitude larger.'

'A warp rift? This deep in the Solar System? How?' said Branthan, and every one of them knew there could be only one architect of such a traumatic wound in reality.

'Horus Lupercal,' said Sharrowkyn.

'That's how he's going to do it, how he was *always* going to do it,' said Wayland, unable to conceal a fleeting admiration for the sheer audacity of so bold a plan's execution. 'The fighting around the Kthonic and Elysian Gates was just to spread out our defences along the solar perimeter. We assumed the gates were the only way Horus could bring his fleets through, but if the scale of these readings is even vaguely accurate, then the traitors could sail a hundred fleets through that rift. Practically into Terra's orbit…'

'So we have a new target,' said Branthan.

'A new target?' said Sharrowkyn, struggling to contain his anger. 'We're dead in the void. The *Carnager*'s lasers all but disembowelled us. Every deck below the waterline is compromised. Our drive is offline, and one of the reactors is venting radiation into space like a damn signal flare.'

'Then we find somewhere to repair,' said Branthan.

'Where?' said Sharrowkyn. 'There's nothing out here.'

'An old way station, an abandoned graving yard, a lost research post, *something*,' said Branthan. 'There must be relics of the first push from Terra drifting out here.'

'I'm telling you, there's nothing,' repeated Sharrowkyn.

Wayland twisted in his grav-couch and fixed Sharrowkyn with a piercing stare.

'Nykona,' he said, holding Sharrowkyn's gaze. 'If there is one man I would trust to find something lost in the darkness, it is you. Find us somewhere to heal the hurts done to the *Sisypheum* and we will live to fight on. What is it your brothers say? *From the darkness we strike, fast and lethal. And by the time our foes can react...*'

Sharrowkyn grinned. '...*Darkness there, and nothing more.*'

It took Sharrowkyn twenty-five hours to locate somewhere viable for the *Sisypheum* to effect repairs. Anchored in the void and all but invisible, it was a nameless, hollow cavern of iron with only rudimentary docking facilities and fractional life support.

In the earliest days of warships traversing the oceans of Old Earth, such places were known as coaling stations, ports that allowed the navies of the great powers to extend the range and influence of their fleets.

This structure had been designed to allow the first monitor ships to remain on station for extended patrol circuits of the inner-system gulfs. With Old Earth isolated for millennia, and many of the outer reaches of the Solar System in the hands of xenos, the thin line keeping Terra safe while the Emperor assembled His forces was only maintained by the bravery of its frontier fleets and refuelling stations such as this.

The search for a safe haven had also revealed more about the traumatic warp event that had ripped the fabric of the Solar System asunder. With every passing moment, the scale of the armada passing through the rift opened close to Terra became horrifyingly apparent.

Fleets of such size as had not been seen since the earliest days of the Imperium were translating into real space in an unending flood. Prodigal sons now returned to the system of their birth with blades bared for the sole purpose of murdering their sire.

Bombs would already be falling on Terra, but the *Sisypheum* could do nothing to help.

With the Iron Hands and their monotasked servitors engaged in the repair efforts to the *Sisypheum*, Sharrowkyn had taken to spending his days roaming the cavernous halls of the nameless coaling station. Centuries had passed since ships had last docked here, but the titanic fuelling silos still reeked of congealed promethium and the scabbed residue of volatile engine plasma.

The darkness within was home to Sharrowkyn.

The interior of the *Sisypheum* was a gloomy place, for transhuman warriors had little need of light, and it had no serfs remaining who required illumination. Beyond the handful of Space Marines, only servitors prowled its lonely halls, and they cared nothing for their surroundings.

But this blackness was absolute, a place where light went to die – so all-encompassing, it took Sharrowkyn back to his training with the Shadowmasters, where he had lived for two years without light or vision. Terrifying to a youth, even one blooded in the darkness of Lycaeus, then bearable, before finally becoming bonded so intimately to him that he became part of it.

Sharrowkyn embraced the darkness as a reminder of simpler times.

The echoes of the warships that had docked here at the dawn of the Imperium, perhaps similarly wounded, were all around him. The names of proud vessels were etched into the walls, names that sounded absurdly quaint to Sharrowkyn: *Black Joke, Divine Lip, Dextrous Gladiator* and *Bittersweet Reunion*.

The crews of these ships had left their mark too, so many names etched over each other that they had become unreadable. Tens of thousands of them, more. Sharrowkyn understood that this was no mere utilitarian relic of a bygone age.

It was a memorial to the dead, a vast record of those who had conquered the Solar System.

Sharrowkyn wasn't vain enough to imagine that anyone would leave such a memorial for him or the millions who had died in the fires of the Warmaster's betrayal. No, he would die in the dark, forgotten and beyond anyone's wit to recall.

Assuming the Emperor's armies could defeat the traitors, this would be a war the Imperium would wish consigned to the shadows, for it would only serve as a reminder of when humanity's will had failed. Only if Terra fell to the traitors would it be celebrated: as the beginning of a new age, the dawning of Lupercal Imperator's reign.

He paused to run his fingers over the carvings, picturing a crewman in a bulky vac-suit, likely dying of radiation poisoning, as he cut into the metal with the tip of a drill bit to secure his little piece of immortality.

Centuries separated Sharrowkyn from this long-dead crewman.

But at that moment, alone at the edge of the dark, he felt a powerful connection pass down through the ages.

Sharrowkyn set off once more, pausing every now and then when he saw a name legible enough to read. No one save he would ever read them, but it felt important that at least one person in all the galaxy remember that these men and women had existed at all.

He wished he knew the name of this place, to truly mark their passing.

The vox chirruped in Sharrowkyn's ear.

'Nykona?' said the unmistakably gruff voice of ash and smoke that belonged to Atesh Tarsa. The Apothecary of the Salamanders Legion had kept them alive over the years on the bleeding edges of this conflict, and everyone aboard the *Sisypheum* owed him their life.

But Sharrowkyn wished Tarsa had let one of their number die.

'Where are you?' asked the Apothecary.

'In the darkness. What do you want, Atesh?'

'It's Cadmus Tyro.'

'What about him?'

'He's awake, and he wants to speak to you.'

The apothecarion of the *Sisypheum* had once been as much a place of death as the nameless coaling station. Since the massacre on the black sands of Isstvan V, Ulrach Branthan had lain entombed in ice, his body a wretched conglomeration of torn meat and bone held together by sinew and pure will.

Only the Heart of Iron had kept the captain alive as he writhed in stasis, its Dark Age technologies simultaneously reweaving his flesh and blood even as his mind annealed into the singular blade of vengeance.

And there he would have remained until death had it not been for the damn bird.

For reasons known only to its inscrutable machine consciousness, Garuda had chosen to irreparably disable the stasis controls of Branthan's cryo-chamber, leaving Tarsa no option but to resort to desperate measures to save the life of his patient.

'You should have let him die,' Sharrowkyn had told the Apothecary in the wake of the captain's rebirth. 'His thirst for vengeance will kill us all.'

'If I had let him die, I would have broken my Apothecary's Oath,' Tarsa had replied. 'I would have been finishing the work of the traitors.'

Sharrowkyn had wanted to dispute the point, but this galaxy had seen far too much faithlessness for him to wish one more broken oath on the cosmos.

He passed through the pressurised vestibule and its fog of counterseptic decontaminants.

The airlock hissed closed behind him, sealing him within the sterile environment of the apothecarion. He found Tarsa hunched over a spinning centrifuge. Blood samples whirred in glass tubes and the hum of medicae machinery filled the space. The air tasted of tin, and the lumens flickered overhead, fizzing with poor connectivity to the ship's main grid.

'I see the power is still intermittent,' said Sharrowkyn.

Tarsa looked up, his ebon-black face the opposite of the Raven Guard's pallid features. Dull red eyes were set in a craggy, hairless skull, and Sharrowkyn saw a lifetime's sorrow in their depths. He saw Sharrowkyn and smiled weakly.

'Nykona,' he said, offering his hand. 'Welcome back to the light.'

Sharrowkyn took his fellow warrior's wrist. 'I apologise, brother. I have been a stranger of late.'

Tarsa nodded, and said, 'The sons of the Raven Lord understand the value of solitude. It is a trait I admire. Some of our more... *boisterous* Legion brothers prefer raucous gatherings and overt displays of brotherhood, but, like you, I find such displays tiresome.'

Sharrowkyn smiled. 'There's virtue in both. I'm no hermit, but after Eirene Septimus I needed to take some time to clear my head. I needed to re-evaluate my perceptions.'

'You weren't to blame for what happened,' said Tarsa.

'I *knew*,' said Sharrowkyn. 'I knew and I still went along with *Meduson's* plan.'

'Alpharius fooled us all, brother,' said Tarsa. 'And you were not in command.'

'You... should... listen to him,' said a voice from behind a surgical curtain.

Tarsa parted the curtain, and beckoned Sharrowkyn through.

Cadmus Tyro lay upon a steel gurney, surrounded by banks of throbbing machinery: blood pumps, autoimmune boosters and a dozen different monitoring devices plugged directly into the weeping interfaces cut into his flesh.

His wounds had been horrific, near mortal – shattered bones, unchecked internal bleeding, mass-reactive trauma and the complete destruction of numerous organs. That he still drew breath at all was a miracle; few could face a primarch and live.

Tarsa had employed every one of the Apothecary's arts to keep him alive, but the *Sisypheum*'s former captain had fallen into a deathly slumber from which no one had expected him to rise.

Yet, here he was, awake and clear-eyed. Sharrowkyn's eyes roved the captain's synth-wrapped body. The wounds in his chest cavity had been packed and bound, and new flesh was filling the void. Bone splices had stimulated fresh growth, though much of the ossification of his ribs was yet to occur. Bloodstained steel rods scaffolded his legs and left arm, but even now, they were being withdrawn by a pair of drifting servo-skulls.

The agony of the procedure was etched into Tyro's face. Like all Iron Hands, he bore pain stoically. Anything else was weakness, and Sharrowkyn's admiration for Cadmus Tyro rose another notch.

'The blame for what happened on Eirene Septimus is mine to bear,' said Tyro. 'For I *was* in command.'

'I could have stopped you.'

Tyro shook his head, the motion causing a visible stab of pain to spasm through him. The skulls chirruped like irritated insects at his movement.

'All this time on a Tenth Legion ship, and you still don't understand us.'

Sharrowkyn bowed, conceding the point.

'You're looking well for a man Tarsa said would die,' said Sharrowkyn.

'No, I said it was highly *likely* he would die,' clarified Tarsa.

'I look like I sparred with a Titan and lost,' said Tyro. 'And feel worse.'

'You fought a primarch,' said Sharrowkyn. 'That's a whole lot better than I'd expect.'

Tyro nodded, glancing down as another steel rod as thick as his finger was eased out of his flesh. Droplets of blood fell to the brushed-steel floor before the wound sealed behind it.

'Tarsa tells me we are returned to the Solar System?'

'Yes. What else did he tell you?'

'Not much beyond the fact that we are all but dead in the void, and that you found a place for us to repair.'

'Anything else?'

'Ulrach Branthan,' said Tyro. 'He is back in command now, yes?'

'He is,' said Sharrowkyn.

'And how... how is he?'

Sharrowkyn glanced at Tarsa. The Apothecary had clearly skirted the issue of Branthan's madness. Sharrowkyn had little time for diplomacy. Tyro would demand directness, but how would he react to the truth about his superior?

'Branthan is insane,' he said.

It took another nine days before the *Sisypheum* was able to sail again.

The graving dock was a titanic, zero-gravity volume of heavy machinery that had taken the combined genius of Thamatica and Wayland to return to functionality. Grinding lifter-cranes hauled vast sheets of battered steel into place for constructor engines to weld in showers of blue sparks. Cable-slaved proxy drones of ancient, bulky aspect crawled across the vessel's battle-scarred hull, closing tears with web-sealant and anchoring torn plating back to its superstructure.

The servitors and Iron Hands were working wonders to repair it enough to be void-worthy.

The *Sisypheum* would fly again, but its first serious engagement would likely tear the ship apart.

Sharrowkyn found Thamatica, Numen and Wayland arguing in the shadow of the vessel's up-armoured prow. He watched them from the shadows wreathing the gantry above the platform hung upon its battlements.

'Prow cannons. It's the only answer that makes sense,' said Numen, his booming voice crackling over the vox. 'We need our hardest fist ready to strike.'

'It'll certainly hit the hardest,' agreed Thamatica. 'But the link from its firing mechanism to weapons control on the bridge is woefully degraded. It will be next to impossible to guarantee a hit unless we're at point-blank range. I assure you, Ignatius, the batteries will work best for us. A better spread of munitions, that's the way.'

'Port-side batteries are smashed, and the starboard capacitors are non-functional,' grunted Numen. 'We'll get one broadside, maybe, then they'll not shoot again. I'm telling you, the prow cannon is the weapon we need.'

Wayland looked up and said, 'What do you think, Nykona?'

Sharrowkyn looped over the gantry and pushed down to the iron decking. He landed lightly and engaged the mag-clamps in his boots. He hadn't truly been trying to hide, and Sabik knew him well enough to know when he was lurking.

'Forget weapons,' he said. 'We don't need them any more. Put their energy to better use.'

'Typical Raven Guard,' said Numen, too loudly. The gruff veteran had lost almost all his hearing in battle against the Emperor's Children and had chosen to endure that injury until the war was over. 'What kind of warship goes into battle unarmed?'

Sharrowkyn swept his gaze along the strike cruiser's hull. Its entire length was torn and battered, a ship desperately in need of peace. It bore its many scars proudly, like a prize fighter training for one last bout he couldn't possibly win.

Much like us all.

'The *Sisypheum*'s fight is done,' said Sharrowkyn. 'One hard turn will break her in two.'

'Then we take as many of those traitorous bastards with us as we can,' said Numen. 'One last thrust into the Warmaster's heart.'

'That's Branthan talking,' said Sharrowkyn.

'*Captain* Branthan,' said Numen. 'You will show him respect, Raven Guard.'

'No disrespect to his rank was intended,' Sharrowkyn assured him. 'And you all know me enough to know that I do not fear death in battle. But we have not fought our way back from Isstvan V just to throw our lives away within sight of Terra.'

'We can still fight,' said Thamatica. 'There is damage we can yet do.'

Sharrowkyn shook his head. 'That's arrogance talking,' he said. 'You all saw the scale of the fleet that came through the rift at the Comet Shrine. Even the grandest destruction we might possibly wreak would be like spitting in the wind.'

'So what are you suggesting?' snorted Numen, his words dripping with contempt. 'That we *hide*? Wait until this war is decided then limp back into the light?'

Sharrowkyn ignored the barb and said, 'We have fought as brothers for years, but it is over. It is time for us to return to our Legions.'

'Captain Branthan will never allow that,' said Wayland.

'Captain Tyro believes it is the right answer,' replied Sharrowkyn.

His words were unexpected and hit them hard in the flank, just as he'd intended.

'The captain has risen from his coma?' said Thamatica.

Sharrowkyn pointed to the *Sisypheum*. 'He has, and this has been his ship longer than Branthan's.'

The implications of Sharrowkyn's words were so unexpectedly direct that it took the three Iron Hands a full second to realise what he was suggesting.

'You dare suggest mutiny against my captain?' raged Numen, his hand on his bolter.

'Branthan is a madman,' said Sharrowkyn. 'He will see us all dead for the sake of his madness. You all know it.'

'You go too far, Sharrowkyn,' said Thamatica, stepping between them. 'You are not Iron Hands – you do not see things as we see them.'

'You are correct, Frater,' said Sharrowkyn. 'Just as I saw them differently when Alpharius walked among us with Shadrak Meduson's face. You should have listened to me then, and you need to listen to me now. Ulrach Branthan is not fighting for any cause beyond his own vengeance. The pain has broken him, and he will damn us all in the fires of his madness.'

Numen wrenched his bolter free, but Wayland had seen the fury building in him and held his arm down. The veteran made a quarter-turn to Wayland in furious disbelief.

'You would defend these words, Sabik?' he demanded.

'I think we should at least hear him out.'

'I have heard enough,' snapped Numen. 'This is mutiny.'

'Tyro agrees with me,' said Sharrowkyn. 'As does Tarsa. And so do you, Sabik.'

'Is that true, Wayland?' asked Thamatica.

Thamatica was known for his mordant sense of humour, but Sharrowkyn heard the tension resonating within his tone like a taut cable on the verge of snapping.

Wayland heard it too and glanced up. Sharrowkyn felt his friend's disappointment that he had forced him into this corner, but what other choice was there?

Wayland released Numen's arm and took a step away.

'Throne help me, but I do,' he said, 'though it cuts against the grain of all I have been trained to believe. The chain of command is meant to be inviolable, but the forge teaches us that when a blade is tempered it becomes hard *and* brittle. To remove that brittleness, the smiter must use a careful heat before allowing his metal to cool over time. Captain Branthan's soul is fresh from the furnace of his resurrection, and if we participate in a plan of action we know to be flawed, then *we* are just as responsible for the consequences of its failure.'

Numen slowly mag-locked his bolter back to his armour and shook his head in disgust.

'That it should come to this,' said the veteran with real

remorse. 'We face the ruin of the Imperium, and still we find ways to turn on one another.'

'I am not turning on you, brother,' said Wayland.

'You talk of usurping the captain of this vessel!' snapped Numen. 'A warrior appointed by the Great Ferrus himself. How else can your words be interpreted?'

The veteran turned and marched away.

Thamatica sighed. 'He will go straight to Branthan.'

'We all should,' said Wayland.

3

Counsel of Traitors
Lunar Voices
Good Kill

Cadmus Tyro walked back onto the bridge of the *Sisypheum* to see Ulrach Branthan standing at the captain's lectern, two things he hadn't expected after the mission to Eirene Septimus. He buried his shock at Branthan's appearance in a grimace of pain, horrified at what had become of his brother warrior.

He'd caught a glimpse of him as Sharrowkyn and Wayland hauled his broken body from the belly of the Storm Eagle. In his pain-filled delirium, he'd thought Brother Bombastus had returned, before remembering his death on the eldar crone world.

The bridge smelled of hot metal and electricity. Servitors worked to return the various bridge stations to functionality. Data screens fizzed with static, and a tattoo of hammers on metal echoed strangely through the superstructure. Garuda flitted from the stanchions overhead, the clicking of its wings blending with the clatter of machines.

Atesh Tarsa walked behind Tyro. He had told the Apothecary to stay back, to not hover at his side. He couldn't be seen to return as an invalid. Ignatius Numen stood next to Branthan, with Frater Thamatica close by. Nykona Sharrowkyn, as always, lurked on the periphery, near the auspex station, with Sabik Wayland seated next to helm control.

The gulf between these warriors was clear.

The Iron Hands stood taller and prouder at the sight of him. Regardless of what threatened their unity, he was still a captain and deserving of their respect.

Tyro raised his fist and gently tapped it against his chest. He'd wanted to wear his armour, to show he was returned entirely, but Tarsa had point-blank refused to allow it. And for once, Tyro had acquiesced to a demand.

'Brothers,' he said. 'Rumours of my death have been greatly exaggerated.'

Wayland came forward and they clasped arms in the warrior's grip, wrist to wrist.

'Welcome back, Captain Tyro,' said Wayland.

Sharrowkyn gave him a nod of respect. Tyro stepped towards his Iron Hands brothers, reading the twin emotions of joy and wariness at his revival. Joy, for he was their captain and had led them in battle against traitors and primarchs; wariness, because his return might be the unwitting cause of a schism within their ranks.

Thamatica bowed deeply and said, 'It pleases me to see you back among the living.'

'Not as much as it pleases me,' Tyro assured him, now facing Numen. 'You've healed well, brother,' he said.

The veteran had suffered grievous wounds at the hands of Gaskon Malthace, one of Alpharius' killers, but it took more than an Alpha Legionnaire to put down one of the Avernii.

'The Salamander knows his craft,' said Numen, managing to sound grateful and begrudging at the same time.

Tyro finally turned to Ulrach Branthan.

Tarsa and Sharrowkyn had warned him of the hideous transformation wrought upon Branthan, but it was still a shock to see how profoundly the captain had changed. What had not changed was the intensity of the zeal burning behind his eyes. The monstrous captain had always been one of the Legion's most fervent adherents to the Iron Creed, but Tyro saw immediately that Sharrowkyn had been right.

There was little left of Ulrach Branthan in his brother's gaze, only a depth of madness and pain too awful to contemplate.

'I am so sorry, brother,' said Tyro. 'To see you like this...'

'Spare me your pity,' said Branthan. 'I am thankful for this new chance to serve the Emperor. Pain is my blood now – it sustains me. It empowers me.'

Tyro nodded, not knowing how to answer something that sounded like a sentiment their foes might express.

'The *Sisypheum*'s seen a hard fight,' he said. 'She has fought proudly, has she not?'

'You make it sound like her war is over,' said Branthan.

Tyro frowned. 'Isn't it? Iron Father Wayland apprised me of her condition. Even half the damage she has sustained would condemn her in the eyes of a shipwright assayer.'

'You underestimate this ship,' said Branthan, stepping down from the command rostrum and moving from station to station with thudding, iron footfalls. 'She fought her way clear of the massacre on Isstvan V, and sustained us through years of guerilla warfare. She broke a traitor blockade and flew through cursed space to a lost world of the eldar. And lastly, under my command, she took on the *Iron Heart*, a ship many times her size.'

Branthan returned to the command lectern and stood behind it.

The blatant symbolism was not lost on Tyro.

This is no longer your ship...

'While the *Sisypheum* yet has fight left in her we will continue to bring death to the traitors. Do you take issue with that, or my resumption of command?'

'I take issue with neither, my captain,' said Tyro. 'But the *Sisypheum* cannot fight like this. *We* cannot fight like this. Look around you – six legionaries and a handful of servitors to crew a strike cruiser? It cannot be done.'

'It *has* been done,' said Branthan. 'In the Jovian engagement we slew the *Covenant of Truth*, an Oberon-class predator-ship.'

'I studied the battle-vectors of that fight,' said Tyro, following Branthan's example and pacing from station to station. 'It was a good kill, an *excellent* kill. Boldly made, but you were lucky beyond belief. Had the *Covenant*'s captain not been so obsessed with his own kill, we would all be dead.'

Branthan stepped down to meet him. 'This is war for the survival of the Imperium, Cadmus,' he said. 'Without boldness we will not win. Horus will take Terra, and all we have fought and bled for will have been for nothing.'

The tension thickened, everyone on the bridge save for the servitors keeping utterly silent and motionless. Veils of light sparked into life, cascades of sensor data drifting like fireflies. Garbled voices scratched the air in blurts of static.

Squalls of ghost binaric code faded in and out of audibility.

Garuda flew down from above and landed at the edge of the console between the two captains, as though ready to arbitrate some dispute. It looked from captain to captain.

'Honour has been satisfied, Ulrach,' said Tyro, keeping his voice low and even. 'Look around you. Look at our ship. Look at how few of us remain. No one could say we did not do battle with all our hearts, but the time of the Shattered Legions is over. Our war in the shadows is done, and we must rejoin our brethren to look our enemies in the face. To do otherwise is to gainsay the word of Rogal Dorn.'

'You speak for the lord of the Seventh?'

'I presume no such thing,' said Tyro, 'but all the Emperor's loyal sons have heard the call to return to defend the Throneworld. It is time for us to heed that call, Ulrach. It is time for us to come in from the cold.'

Branthan listened to Tyro's impassioned plea, but it was impossible to read his ravaged features. The captain remained silent for long moments, eventually turning to face Sabik Wayland.

'How long before we can be underway?'

'The *Sisypheum* can fly, but there are critical systems not yet fully functional. Long-range auspex, full weapons control and vox are all still offline.'

'How long?'

Wayland glanced at Tyro. Branthan saw it, and said, 'Cadmus Tyro is not the commander of this vessel, *I* am! Answer me.'

'The reactors are still hot,' said Wayland. 'We can be underway as soon as the word is given.'

'The word is given,' said Branthan.

'Ulrach–' began Tyro.

'Enough!' snapped Branthan, towering over him. 'I am captain of this vessel and we fight until we are dead. There is no turning away, no retreat to Terra. You think a handful of us skulking behind a wall will make more of a difference than we can with a starship? To turn and run for the imagined safety of Terra is not an honourable laying down of our burden, it is *cowardice*! I will not allow it. Not on my ship.'

A flurry of sparks erupted from the comms-station behind Sabik Wayland, as if in response to Branthan's outburst. A screaming wail of howling binaric erupted from the vox-horns mounted on buckled stanchions.

'Shut that off!' said Branthan, striding over to the station and pushing the hapless servitor out of his path. The console was smashed, almost every panel removed to reveal its guts of wires and glass valves.

He turned to face Wayland with a groan of hydraulics and a crackle of uninsulated cabling.

'I thought you said the vox was inactive?'

'It is,' said Wayland, rushing to Branthan's side. 'The antenna array is smashed.'

'Then explain what we're hearing.'

Wayland sorted through a handful of cables, found the ones he wanted and slotted them home into jacks built into the underside of his gauntlet. Thamatica hurried over to the console and followed suit. The two Iron Fathers stood riveted to the spot, a pale nimbus of light surrounding their hands. The sounds of the message hissed all around them, as if carried on the air.

'It's not coming through the ship's vox,' said Wayland.

'Then where is it coming from?' said Tyro.

'It's coming from the Kryptos,' said Thamatica. 'The creature is routing it to this console.'

'The Kryptos?' said Tyro. 'Is it picking up some stray Mechanicum transmissions?'

'That's not Martian code,' said Wayland, adjusting the dials and gain levers on the smashed console. 'That's the code of Luna.'

'What are you talking about?' said Tyro. 'Luna has fallen.'

'It's coming from a native of Luna,' insisted Wayland. 'Only they can send in this form.'

'We trained on Mars,' said Thamatica. 'We know Mechanicum code, and that's not it.'

'Then it's traitor communication,' said Branthan. 'The Sons of Horus have their Terran bridgehead there. They must have compromised the Selenar's systems.'

Wayland's face was bathed silver in the light of a helical waveform flickering on the last, cracked display slate.

'Wait, is that...?' said Wayland.

'Throne! Yes... I think it is. But how...?'

'What is it, Frater?' asked Branthan.

Thamatica disconnected from the console and said, 'If we're right, and I suspect we are, then this is not a Mechanicum or Imperial transmission. Nor is it from the traitors.'

'Then who is it from?' asked Tyro.

'This is a long-dead channel,' said Wayland. 'It's a Selenar cult signal.'

'But what is it saying?' asked Branthan.

'We don't know yet,' said Wayland. 'But a gene-witch is screaming into the void.'

Atesh Tarsa remembered the first time he had set eyes on the Kryptos when Sharrowkyn and Sabik Wayland had brought it aboard the *Sisypheum*. Its hideous appearance had sickened him. He had hated it, but as the years passed, he began to pity what had been done to it – living in agony, forever bound to a singular purpose for cruel masters who cared nothing for its suffering.

That was no life, but were he and the crew of the *Sisypheum* any better?

The Kryptos had not left this cell of bare iron, as much a slave to their purpose as it had been to its former masters. It sat bound to an iron throne, surrounded by banks of humming machinery and linked to chattering cogitators by snaking lengths of heavily insulated cables.

That such a thing could exist at all flew in the face of all he had learned in the apothecarion. Its head slumped to the side, and its pale flesh, stinking and greasy, was pasted over the sunken bones of its skull like wet parchment. The lower half of its face was a grotesquerie of moving parts, augmitters, vox-implants and sound-creating anatomies that chattered with strange clicks, whistles and ticks. Its skull had been taken apart and remade: a mix of brass, bone and glass, like a vat for the preservation of a hideous medical anomaly. The fluid within was cloudy and stagnant, and the visible portions of its hybridised brain pressed against the glass, the bleached white of something long dead.

Nor was it wholly human – portions of its mandibular structure were clearly xenos in origin, though sourced from no alien Tarsa had ever fought. It wore a blindfold, for no one could look into its pain-filled eyes and not be horrified at its suffering.

Garuda shuffled from clawed foot to clawed foot atop the throne. Tarsa thought it looked like some scavenger bird, waiting for a hanged man to die so it could peck his eyes out.

A wet, organic-sounding binaric issued from its throat. Yellowish fluid dribbled from its jaws as it formed the un-words over and over again. A lectern bolted to the deck before it flickered with light, burbling a stream of nonsensical data in an endless loop.

'What is this abomination saying?' asked Ulrach Branthan, leaning down so that his mutilated features were an inch from those of the Kryptos.

The irony of Branthan calling the Kryptos an abomination was not lost on Tarsa.

'The cogitators are trying to figure it out,' said Wayland, feeding brass-edged punch cards into the logic engine. 'This is a dead vox-band. No one's used these channels for centuries. Whoever is transmitting must be desperate indeed to hope their message will be picked up by anyone with the capabilities to translate it. The Selenar were said to use an organic form of *genobinary*, a lingua-technis utilising a rotating cypher based upon the sender's unique genome sequence. Which made it almost impossible to decode.'

'So we can't know what it's saying?' said Branthan.

'Ah, I didn't say that,' said Thamatica, wagging an admonishing finger.

'Can you break the code? And spare me a historia lecture. Yes or no?'

'I rather suspect the Selenar did not envisage the existence of the Kryptos when they developed this form of communication,' said Thamatica. 'Which surprises me, as some of the bioengineered chimeras they wrought in their vaults were not entirely dissimilar, and–'

'I said yes or no, Frater.'

'Yes!' said Wayland, as the cogitator spat out glowing lines of text.

'You have it?' said Thamatica.

'I have it,' said Wayland. 'You were right – I had to run the genome sample back multiple iterations until the Kryptos was able to break it.'

'What does it say?' said Tarsa, before the two Iron Fathers could go deep into the technicalities of their cryptography.

Wayland nodded and said, 'It says: "These are the words of Ta'lab Vita-37. My iteration is my name. My sequence speaks to the veracity of my words. The Wolves are loosed, and Luna falls again. My truth is this, I have failed. For centuries I kept the Magna Mater safe, but the First Son of Horus calls 'Aebathan' to his master. Any who hear this, I beg you to destroy Lunar Dome Herodotus Omega. Wipe it clean of life before he breaks the seventh seal."'

A shiver ran down Tarsa's spine.

'The Magna Mater...?' he said.

'Do those words mean something to you, Apothecary?' asked Branthan.

'Yes. It means we must reach Luna with all haste,' said Tarsa.

Before Branthan could ask anything else, the Kryptos shrieked in paroxysms of agony.

Its back arched and it thrashed in the throes of a violent seizure as the shrieks of something infernal tore through its open mind.

'Carnager! Carnager! Carnager!'

'Get us out of here!' barked Tyro, getting behind the command lectern.

Sharrowkyn tried to make sense of what he was seeing on the auspex station. The display screamed with the lunatic ravings of the incoming vessel. Its ululating howl was a mindless exultation, insane agony given voice.

'We're still anchored to the graving dock,' said Sharrowkyn.

'Then cast us off!'

'Working on it!'

The *Sisypheum* shuddered as enemy munitions detonated on its rear quarter.

'Work faster,' ordered Tyro.

A deep bass rumble echoed through the *Sisypheum*'s superstructure. The booming clangs of docking clamps disengaging sent shuddering vibrations through the deck plates.

'Releasing,' said Sharrowkyn.

'Now find that ship.'

The deck tilted underfoot as Tyro pushed power to the drives. Local gravity skewed strangely as the *Sisypheum* powered away from the mass of the coaling station. More juddering tremors raced the length of the ship, its steel skeleton deforming under the torsion and shearing forces of battle.

A powerful explosion rocked the ship. Gravity weakened, then strengthened. Recently repaired systems blew out again. The servitors chattered to one another in squeals of simplified binaric.

'Where is it, Sharrowkyn?'

'Below us, I think.'

'Show me.'

Sharrowkyn threw the display onto the viewscreen. Cascades of crackling photons fell in a waterfall of light. Patterns of distortion swam in the illumination, peaks and troughs representing energy signatures, radiation spikes and patches of heat.

Sharrowkyn could make little of what he was seeing, but Tyro was a master of void war and immediately saw opportunity in the riot of atomic flares and laser discharges.

'He's damaged and too eager,' said Tyro. 'His auspex couldn't clearly distinguish us from the coaling station so he fired too soon.'

The vox-horns blared. *'Carnager! Carnager! Carnager!'*

'He's pushing in on our ventral axis,' said Tyro. 'Trying to disembowel us.'

'And you know how to prevent that?'

'I fought us clear of Isstvan V, didn't I?'

'Then this should be easy.'

More hits struck the ship's underside, raking fire designed to strip a vessel's shields. The *Sisypheum*'s voids had yet to ignite, and every hit was a penetrating wound. Fire bloomed alongside jets of freezing oxygen. Their ship was bleeding into the vacuum of space.

'Please tell me Thamatica chose to rearm the prow cannon,' said Tyro.

'I don't know, captain.'

'Get me a firing solution anyway.'

'A firing solution? How? Weapons control is smashed.'

'Then give it your best guess. Hold on.'

Sharrowkyn stumbled over to weapons control as Tyro cut the *Sisypheum*'s drive and fired every one of its manoeuvring thrusters against their direction of travel.

The ship groaned in protest at so drastic a deceleration, compressional forces stressing the keel from stern to bow.

Sharrowkyn slammed into the console. Freshly welded armour plates tore loose and hydraulic lines blew out all along the strike cruiser's length.

Deafening squalls of interference echoed through the vaults of the bridge as close-in deflectors ruptured and the *Carnager*'s course angled it upwards in front of the *Sisypheum*.

Proximity alarms blared as the two city-sized ships practically grazed one another.

'We're going to collide,' said Sharrowkyn.

He had witnessed two capital ships crashing once before, in low orbit over Kiavahr. Until the massacre at Isstvan V, it had been one of the worst things he'd ever seen. Ancient works of the shipwright's art torn apart by unimaginable forces. Ten thousand dead in the first instant, flash-frozen by the hard vacuum of space as their hulls ripped open. A hundred thousand more burned in oxygen-rich fires sprinting through the wreckage and vaporising everything in their path.

The auspex swelled with e-mag bloom. The *Carnager* was everything. It blotted out all else with its murder-bulk.

'Carnager! Carnager! Carnager!'

The signature was so vast it filled the auspex. Sharrowkyn switched back to the ordinary view through the oculus bay. The jagged, blood-daubed hull of the *Carnager* filled the viewscreen.

'Fire!' yelled Tyro.

Sharrowkyn sent the order, hoping against hope that Numen's argument had won out.

The bombardment cannon's shell travelled the distance to its target in a fraction of a second, and its armour-piercing cone bored through the plating of its command deck half a second later.

The *Carnager* spasmed with the force of the blast, the cone of the explosion's plasma jet cutting down like a power sword through the spine of an outflanked foe. The traitor vessel's keel was sliced clean through, and the two halves of the ship buckled inward as though folding at a hinge point.

Plumes of fire filled the screen, a blazing inferno devouring every scrap of oxygen within the *Carnager*. Its hull bulged and blew out as secondary explosions ripped along its length in a cascade of obliteration.

The *Sisypheum* powered through the explosion, the light of the *Carnager*'s destruction filling the bridge with the hellish fire of a void-death. Warning lights and damage icons lit up across every station, but it didn't matter.

The *Carnager* was dead.

'Good kill,' said Tyro.

BOOK 2

MOTHER

She has become everything and everyone.
To recognise this is to live in wonder.

4

Aebathan
Magna Mater
The Ocean of Storms

The descent through the solar disc took another seven days. Branthan demanded greater speed, but the *Sisypheum* was slowly dying. Critical systems were failing faster than the Iron Hands could repair them, and if Branthan pushed too hard, he would strand them in the endless dark.

Snapshots of the war came to them through intermittent vox signals – impossible reports of exploding moons, of Rogal Dorn's flagship besieged, and fleet engagements beyond anything anyone had seen in living memory. So many lurid tales of the void afire and planets shattered that they blurred together in an unending stream of horror, death and atrocity.

The Warmaster had come in overwhelming force, leaving nothing to chance and wrong-footing the defenders of Terra at every turn.

The Solar System was burning.

After Tyro and Sharrowkyn's destruction of the *Carnager*, an uneasy comity had been restored to the *Sisypheum*. In part, due to the revelations brought to them by Atesh Tarsa via the Kryptos, but also Branthan's acceptance that Tyro was his equal.

The silver disc of Luna filled the viewscreen, the first light of Old Earth's night.

Wayland brought them in slowly, as far as possible from the vast traitor fleets anchored in high orbit and awaiting their tasking orders for Terra. Despite every horror the warriors aboard the *Sisypheum* had faced and overcome, nothing could have prepared them for the sight of their former brothers massing over the Throneworld.

World Eaters, Sons of Horus, Death Guard, Emperor's Children, Thousand Sons…

Names that were once bywords for courage, honour and nobility.

Now they could no longer be said without suffering a blade of grief to the heart.

'So many…' said Thamatica. 'How can Terra possibly hold?'

'Lord Dorn has had years to prepare for this day,' said Cadmus Tyro. 'If anyone can hold Terra, it will be him. Hold to that, brothers.'

Tyro's words were spoken confidently, and though the Praetorian of Terra's reputation was well deserved, everyone on the *Sisypheum* understood that even the greatest master of siege defence would blanch at facing this numberless host.

The dark side was lousy with the burning wrecks of defence platforms whose orbits were steadily declining as they shed plates of armour like bladed rain to the Lunar surface. Wayland fought to keep the *Sisypheum*'s plasma signatures low, relying on the manoeuvring jets to fractionally alter course to avoid drifting, city-sized chunks of debris hurled into orbit by the force of the traitor bombardments.

In truth there was virtually no need for stealth: the wounded emissions of their ship's reactor core blended with the atomic firestorms painting the black curve of the horizon with a borealis of blood.

'The Selenar cults fought hard,' said Tyro. 'The traitors paid a heavy price.'

'As did the Imperium at its dawn,' pointed out Wayland.

Explosions still flared over the glowing curve of the Lunar surface, and blinking streams of laser light flashed between the last remaining defenders and the enemy's murder ships.

'Are we sure the fight is over?' asked Numen.

'It's over,' said Tarsa.

'How do you know, Salamander?' said Branthan.

Tarsa drew a finger across his neck.

'*Aebathan*,' he said.

In the wake of the *Carnager*'s destruction they had gathered in the armoury to debate the significance of the message received by the Kryptos. Surrounded by their meagre supply of weapons and ammunition, Atesh Tarsa told them what he knew.

'You have heard the term Aebathan before?' asked Tyro.

Tarsa nodded. 'I have. My Legion fought alongside the Luna Wolves, back when they still held to that name. Back when we still counted them as brothers. During those years, I heard the word Aebathan more than any other.'

'What does it mean?' said Sharrowkyn, seated on an empty ammo crate.

'It is a Cthonian term for the cutting of a rival gang leader's throat all the way back to the spine,' explained Tarsa. 'The term was adopted by the Legion to mean the successful conclusion of a campaign.'

Tyro shook his head. 'So it signals the traitors have taken Luna? We already knew that. It changes nothing. We should still make for Terra.'

'No,' insisted Tarsa. 'We *have* to reach Luna.'

'Why?' said Branthan. 'Because of this Magna Mater? What is it?'

Tarsa hesitated before speaking. Eventually he took a breath and said, 'I am a proud son of Nocturne, born and raised in the shadow of Mount Deathfire. My first breath was ashes and smoke, my first sight a sky filled with flame, and my first grip was upon a smiting hammer. My word is my bond, and every oath I have sworn remains unbroken.'

'None gathered here doubt you, Brother Tarsa,' said Wayland. 'Why do you tell us this?'

'Because just as every tech-priest is inducted into the mysteries of the sacred machine on the red planet, so too are Apothecaries made privy to secret knowledge birthed deep in Luna's vaults. To reveal the moon's secrets, even to my battle-sworn brothers, would be to break a gravely sworn oath.'

'Understood, Apothecary,' said Branthan. 'But if this is information your commander requires, you are duty-bound to reveal it. I give you leave to break your oath.'

'With respect, Captain Branthan, you are not of the Eighteenth, and even if you were, that leave is not yours to give,' said Tarsa. 'In this moment, I *choose* to break this oath. The burden of that will be mine to bear until my death.'

Nykona Sharrowkyn came forward and placed a hand on Tarsa's shoulder guard.

'I have known you since the betrayal at Isstvan,' said the Raven Guard. 'In that time we have shed our own blood and that of the traitors. You call a different world home, and name another primarch as your liege lord, but we are brothers, you and I. We are bonded in a way that few beyond our grim confraternity will ever know. All of us here understand what holding true to an oath means, what it *really* means. We would not be fighting our brothers if we did not. We fight against a foe that broke their sacred oaths, so I understand why you hesitate. But we are nearing the end of this war, and even a fractional misstep may cost us dearly. I know it is wrong of us to expect this of you, but if breaking your oath shares information that will help us fight the traitors, then it is a burden I willingly share.'

'As do I,' said Sabik Wayland.

'And I,' said Thamatica.

Ignatius Numen said, 'I'd sooner die than break an oath, but if you must, then I'll gladly share the burden of yours if it means we stick a pneuma-wrench in the Warmaster's plans.'

'Thank you, brothers,' said Tarsa.

'So tell us,' said Branthan. 'What is the Magna Mater?'

'Understand this first, Captain Branthan,' said Tarsa. 'The Selenar's rites are shrouded in metaphor and symbolism. Even after years learning from them, it was difficult to be certain of anything, especially when the Legion warriors were viewed as little better than spies. My understanding of the Lunar faith is incomplete, for the Selenar do not easily share the truth of a belief system that almost saw them destroyed in the earliest days of the First Solar War. I want you all to understand that before I go on.'

'We understand,' said Tyro. 'Go on.'

Tarsa nodded. 'Broadly speaking, their cults believe each individual life is but the sum total of genetic archetypes that have endured throughout human history. Like most faiths, they are heavily factionalised, and each cult venerates the helical mysteries of our species in different ways.'

Numen growled and shook his head. 'We've wiped out cultures for less.'

'Indeed we have,' said Tarsa, more sharply than he intended. 'But the Selenar had two things the Emperor needed – a knowledge of gene-craft that outstripped His own, and industrial-scale facilities to match the scope of His ambition. Thus they were spared obliteration. The Emperor yoked Luna's cults and tasked them with building armies mighty enough to conquer a galaxy.'

'And the Magna Mater? It was linked to this *faith* of theirs?' asked Tyro.

'I never heard any of the gene-witches speak of the Magna Mater directly, but oblique references to it lie at the heart of every one of their most secret mysteries,' said Tarsa, struggling to find words to express a mystery even he did not fully understand. 'Its literal meaning is "Great Mother", an ancient Romanii name for Cybele.'

'The Anatolian goddess of fertility and creation?' said Thamatica.

'Yes. During my time on Luna, it was little more than a myth, said to be the fabled fountainhead of the earliest and most powerful Space Marine genetics. I never believed it ever truly existed, more that it was likely an allegorical representation of their vast knowledge. But what if it *does* exist? What if it is something tangible? What if it is the very *source code* of the Space Marines? Imagine that power in the hands of the traitors. *That* is why we must set course to Luna and not Terra.'

'And this Ta'lab Vita-37...? Her words carry weight?' asked Ulrach Branthan.

Tarsa nodded. 'Given the numerals following her designation, Ta'lab Vita-37 must be a senior member of the Selenar cults. So, yes, her words carry weight.'

'Then do we do as she asks?' said Numen. 'Do we destroy the Lunar dome?'

'Let us not be hasty,' said Thamatica. 'If the Magna Mater is *literally* the root of the most powerful Space Marine genetics, surely we cannot simply destroy it out of hand?'

'If a gene-witch of Ta'lab Vita-37's rank says it must be done, then she has good reason,' said Tarsa. 'The Luna Wolves must be close to taking it.'

'How would we even destroy a mountain?' asked Tyro. 'That's what she's ultimately asking for, is it not? A Lunar dome is a dead volcano, yes?'

'It is,' said Tarsa.

'Then how do you imagine we could do that?' said Numen. 'The *Sisypheum* no longer has the capability to destroy much of anything, let alone an entire volcano.'

'You can destroy *any* location if you can get inside it,' said Sharrowkyn.

'Wayland, your support here would be appreciated,' said Thamatica. 'You cannot seriously think this is the right course of action? No Iron Father would sanction the destruction of knowledge.'

'In that you are correct,' said Wayland. 'But if the Magna Mater truly is what Apothecary Tarsa suspects it may be, then the threat of the traitors getting it off Luna is too great to risk. Regrettably, I believe we have no choice but to destroy the Lunar dome.'

In desperation, Thamatica turned his focus to Cadmus Tyro and Ulrach Branthan.

'Captains, this knowledge is what allowed the Emperor Himself to build the Legiones Astartes. None of us would be here without it. It is our *heritage*, our genetic link to the past. To allow it to be consumed by fire will deny the hope for a future.'

Thamatica paused to collect his thoughts before speaking again, taking great effort to contain his mounting frustration and disbelief at what he was hearing.

'Brothers, this war against Horus has taken a grievous toll on our ranks, and who knows how many of us will be left alive when finally the guns fall silent? The Emperor will *need* this knowledge if He is to rebuild the Imperium back from the ashes. It is our sacred duty to save it for the Space Marines yet to be, the warriors who will come after us and stand on the walls in the ages yet to come.'

Cadmus Tyro folded his arms and said, 'I agree with you, but the risks are too great. Captain Branthan, what are your thoughts?'

'The risks are great,' agreed Ulrach Branthan. 'But nothing of worth was ever achieved without some risk. I will offer you this course of action, Frater Thamatica. We will go to Luna, and we will make every attempt to secure the Magna Mater. But if there is even the slightest chance of it falling into the hands of the traitors, we destroy it. Agreed?'

It was the best Thamatica was going to get, and he knew it.

'Agreed,' he said.

The *Sisypheum* drifted through the debris field of Luna's great Ring. The destroyed belt of defensive platforms had once formed an unbreakable circuit around the moon's circumference, a lethal cordon of lance batteries, torpedo launchers and macro-cannon arrays.

Wreckage from the devastated Ring still tumbled in the upper reaches of Lunar space, burning like comets in the void. Layered banks of debris wreathed the surface in shadow as clouds of ablated fragments and pulverised metal fell in ever-declining orbits to the surface.

To see something so monolithic brought low was almost beyond comprehension. Its defences had been designed to repel a sustained campaign of invasion, but it had been obliterated in an instant.

The darkness over Luna was a stark reminder that *nothing* was unbreakable.

Even with the distortions and interference fouling the Lunar atmosphere, the descent of a vessel of the *Sisypheum*'s displacement would not go unnoticed, so Wayland had brought them close to the surface within a vast, hollowed-out cylinder of falling wreckage. In addition to enabling them to reach the surface undetected, it served the secondary purpose of shielding them from the falling debris.

It had once been a facility for mass-warhead launches on the Ring's coreward defensive array, and its smouldering descent was currently arcing a solder-bright line over the Oceanus Procellarum. Its rate of tumble was low, and thus Wayland had moored the *Sisypheum* within its latticed structure in a feat of bravura piloting skills.

Mag-locks and sinew-taut tethers kept the ship in place, immobile and silent.

In around fifteen hours, the falling structure would slam down somewhere over the southern polar regions

The *Sisypheum*'s mission would be over then.

Sharrowkyn peered over Wayland's shoulder through the patched and cracked canopy of the Storm Eagle as the endless grey expanse of Terra's moon drifted below. The battered gunship hung inverted from an open embarkation deck, ready to drop to the surface at Wayland's command. Even though they were shielded from the worst of the debris rain falling from orbit, a rattling, clanging of impacts transferring through the gunship's hull sounded unnervingly like taking small-arms fire.

Lunar Dome Herodotus Omega was a solitary shield volcano to the south of a pair of impact craters in the midst of the Oceanus Procellarum. One, a high-albedo crater known as Aristarchus, was empty and desolate, but the other was filled with the arc lights of a port facility. The rim of this crater was ringed with lifter arrays, hanging limp over fire-dusted platforms, surrounded by materiel hangars and transit hubs that wound out over the surface.

Stationed five hundred metres above the largest platform was the bladed form of a starship.

'Sons of Horus destroyer,' said Wayland, reading the vessel's mass and displacement by its outline. 'Hunter-class. Onboard registry lists it as the *Cthonian Scion*.'

'Just a gunboat,' said Sharrowkyn.

'Still orders of magnitude too powerful for us,' said Wayland. 'We've enough rounds for *maybe* one dogfight. After that, we'll be shooting mass-reactives from the hatches.'

Wayland opened a vox-channel to the troop compartment.

'There's an enemy vessel stationed on target,' he said.

The vox crackled with a strange double echo as Branthan replied. *'Has it seen us?'*

'No,' said Wayland. 'We'd already be dead if it had.'

'Then we proceed as planned,' ordered Branthan.

'Understood, captain,' he said.

Sharrowkyn had never thought to be this close to Luna, one of the great, mythic locations of the Solar System. Its rugged surface was strewn with blackened battle wreckage from the destroyed Ring, and shards of metal hung in glittering veils like layered bands of sediment in a dark ocean. Despite all that, Luna was something of a disappointment.

'Not much to look at, is it?' said Wayland, as if reading his thoughts.

'It's not what I expected,' admitted Sharrowkyn.

'What did you expect?'

'Something like a forge world, I suppose. Temples, towers and domes. That sort of thing.'

'Ah, then you should see Mars sometime,' said Wayland fondly. 'The seat of the Martian priesthood is studded with ancient structures, its volcanoes crowned with glittering forge-temples and titanic monuments to man's union with machinery. The planet's metal skin is threaded with thrumming power conduits like veins through red flesh, and to watch the rise of the Mechanicum Borealis as it crowns Olympus Mons is to know beauty.'

'That's certainly not Luna,' said Sharrowkyn, staring at the ocean of silver dust and ancient impact craters.

'No,' agreed Wayland. 'Mars has always been brash in its displays of power, but the Selenar keep their secrets well hidden.'

'The best way to keep a secret is to not let anyone know you *have* a secret in the first place,' said Sharrowkyn.

'The ability to create life is the greatest power of all,' said Wayland. 'It's hard to keep something like that secret.'

'It surprises me to hear an Iron Hand say that,' said Sharrowkyn.

'Why? Because we know that flesh is ultimately weaker than iron? Or because you think we despise flesh?'

'I'm not sure. Both? Your creed is still a mystery to me.'

'You are not Medusan, and your gene-sire was not murdered before your very eyes – how could you possibly understand my Legion?' said Wayland. 'I do not say that as any kind of insult, my friend. It is simply a fact. You would not expect me to understand the soul of your Legion after so short a time, would you?'

'No.'

'The Tenth know that flesh is weak, but the mystery of its *creation*? That is miraculous – not even the greatest minds of Mars could achieve that.'

'Don't let Thamatica hear you say that or he'll take it as a challenge.'

Wayland grinned and pointed farther south as the flat, oblate form of Herodotus Omega slid into view upon the inverted horizon. A waypoint alert chimed on the avionics panel.

Wayland toggled the vox.

'Drop in ten,' he said, then, to Sharrowkyn, 'You should get back to the troop compartment. This cockpit isn't really designed for a co-pilot.'

'This isn't going to be a high-G launch, is it?'

'No, just a detachment and a glide.'

'Then I'll stay,' said Sharrowkyn, his gaze fixed on the unremarkable form of the volcano, wondering what secrets it held. 'Do you believe the Magna Mater is real?'

Wayland nodded to the looming shadow of the destroyer holding station over the landing platforms. A repulsor haze blurred the ground beneath it, and clashing vortices of gravitational force surrounded it in a spinning cloud of dust and razored fragments.

'The Sons of Horus believe it,' he said. 'That is enough for me.'

Sharrowkyn nodded.

'Detachment in three... two... one... Release.'

There was no thunder of launch rails or shuddering scream of ramjets. No boom of disengaging docking clamps, just the distant tremor of tethers retracting into the Storm Eagle's hull. Gravity shifted a heartbeat to the left, and the gunship drifted into the Lunar void, carried clear by a gentle viff of manoeuvring jets and the rotation of the torpedo launch facility. Borne outwards and down by a combination of weak gravity and thrust, the Storm Eagle rotated on its long axis and tilted its nose upward.

Sharrowkyn's breath caught in his throat as sunlight flared on the canopy, and an armoured grey orb hove into view. Its surface was mottled brown and steel-dust grey, with volatile patches of sulphurous yellow drifting in the upper atmosphere. Swirls of storms were already developing over the northern hemisphere, and spots of light – traitor war fleets taking up bombardment positions – glittered like fireflies in high orbit.

'Terra,' breathed Sharrowkyn.

The Throneworld: humanity's birthrock and cardinal world of the Imperium.

World of legend, where his species had first crawled from the ocean so many millions of years ago. Where life had first looked up at the starry night.

First with wonder, then intrepidity, before, finally, ambition.

'Even at bay, it's beautiful,' said Wayland.

'I saw a painting by Serena d'Angelus once,' said Sharrowkyn. 'I mean, it was a pict render of it, but her colours were like nothing I had ever seen. I know little of beauty beyond the play of shadows in darkness, but even to my eyes it was beautiful. It was called *Terra Gaia* and was said to be what the Throneworld looked like back when it was known as Earth. *A blue-green orb, radiant with life and wonder…*'

'*…before the choking breath of its endless forges brought life to the edge of extinction,*' finished Wayland. 'Yes, I know the piece.'

'I wish I had known Terra when it had colour like that,' said Sharrowkyn as the contested planet slid out of view. 'It must have been wondrous.'

5

Landing
The Sibylline Oracle
Moon-blooded

Herodotus Omega filled the horizon, its trench-like caldera frozen and its magma heart long since extinct. Many of the Lunar volcanos had been brought back to life by the core-drills of Martian geoformers, but Herodotus Omega had, for unknown reasons, remained cold and dead.

Little could be gleaned of what they might expect to find within from the meagre records available. With the *Cthonian Scion* so close, Wayland didn't dare risk an active surveyor sweep or attempt a penetration of whatever remained of the Luna noospheric network. The *Sisypheum*'s cogitators listed Herodotus Omega only as an abandoned research site, but those records were over two centuries old and likely out of date, so were next to valueless.

Passive surveyors detected scores of vessels charting leisurely circuits far overhead, and numerous, seemingly random surveyor pulses. None of them were directed at the surface.

The only threat that truly mattered was the *Cthonian Scion*.

Wayland kept his attention split between the threat board and the view beyond the canopy.

The traitor destroyer wasn't actively surveying the local area, but all it would take was one glitch of the Storm Eagle's damaged systems, or one lousy interaction with the endless drift of tumbling debris fouling an engine to alert the machine-spirits of the enemy auspex.

If that happened, this mission was over.

Destruction would follow detection, as sure as day followed night.

The Storm Eagle was now a glider, descending on a gently curving arc towards the looming form of Herodotus Omega. Wayland had kept the *Sisypheum* concealed in the launch facility's wreckage long enough that the Storm Eagle was likely below any local survey nets, or the watchful eyes of any Lunar auspex sites that hadn't already been destroyed.

Sharrowkyn flinched as the avionics panel chimed with faint warnings.

A rotating sine wave jumped on the brass-rimmed slate as low-grade emissions washed over the gunship. Burbling static hissed from the panel, followed by a squall of binaric pops and screeches.

'Don't worry,' said Wayland, sensing his reaction. 'They're just auspex ghosts. Trapped echoes bouncing from the crater walls.'

Sharrowkyn craned his neck to scan the horizon, searching for any sign that another ship had them locked in its sights and was even now preparing to blast them from the sky.

He saw nothing, but wasn't that always the way of it?

The old-timers always said it was the strike you never saw coming that killed you.

'Are you sure?' he asked.

'No, but given the density of the orbital traffic around Luna, it seems likely.'

Sharrowkyn now understood enough about auspex-craft to know Wayland was probably right, but the crackling hisses issuing from the panel felt like more than just echoes. There was something oddly *predatory* to them, like the malicious purring of a felid toying with its prey before delivering the crippling blow. But the sound faded and the jumping sine wave on the slate returned to its safe, rippling line.

He let out a breath and said, 'Where do you plan to set down?'

'At the end of the valley,' said Wayland, pointing to the north-eastern flank of Herodotus Omega, where the sharply defined shadow of a deep chasm approached the lower haunches of the volcano. 'From the orbital picts I took, it looks like there's an unfinished geothermal venting station built into the dome's flank.'

'Unfinished?'

'So it appears,' said Wayland. 'If I had to hazard a guess, I'd say the Mechanicum originally planned to reignite the volcano, but the work was never completed.'

'Why not?'

'Who can say?' replied Wayland.

A Storm Eagle was a heavy assault gunship that could transport up to twenty Space Marines into the heart of a battle. Its armour was rugged and durable, and its weapons normally packed a punch far beyond its relatively small size.

Tyro scanned the numerous empty seats around him with a deep sense of melancholy.

He remembered this ship filled with warriors, the midnight black and burnished silver of their battleplate gleaming and bedecked with oaths of moment.

How proud they had been. How noble.

He remembered gut-churning drops through volatile

atmospheres, thundering runs through enemy flak, steel and fire as hulls ripped open and seeing a sky filled with explosions. Given the wounds he had suffered at the hands of Alpharius on Eirene Septimus, he ought to be confined to the apothecarion, but this was a moment where every one of them had to dig deep into what made them sons of Ferrus Manus.

Wayland and Thamatica had helped him don his armour, a time-consuming and painful process, but it felt good to be clad in iron once more. The war-plate compensated for the worst of his wounds, but Tyro knew he was entering this fight with his body nigh broken.

Appropriate, he thought.

Some among the guerrilla forces fighting in the hidden spaces between the major engagements of the war against Horus had taken to calling themselves warriors of the Shattered Legions. Tyro had not liked the term upon first hearing it, believing it diminished their capabilities and cohesion. That warriors of the Iron Tenth could ever be described as *shattered* sat poorly with him, but as time had gone on, he had come to see it for what it truly meant.

You may break and burn us, but still we rise.

Tyro's eyes slid over his fellow warriors, as ragged and ill-tempered a group of survivors as any commander had known. He rose from his armoured grav-seat and moved down the compartment, pausing beside Ignatius Numen to rap the knuckles of his gauntlet upon the warrior's dented and offset shoulder guard.

'I should upbraid you for the poor condition of your armour.'

Numen looked up, uncertain, deaf to what Tyro had just said.

Tyro moved on, lifting Tarsa's bolter from his hands and turning it over with a judgemental eye. The eagle-stamped magazine was chipped and dented, the trigger guard snapped off. He handed it back to the Salamander and said, 'I would assign you punishment duty for the unrepaired damage to your weapon.'

Stopping in front of Thamatica, Tyro examined the configuration of his grenades and ammunition. 'And as for you, Iron Father… What battlefield role is your load out designed for?'

'For whatever awaits us on the surface,' said Thamatica. 'We have little left with which to fight in any formally prescribed manner.'

Tyro nodded and turned to face his Legion brothers, marking each of them in turn. As a captain, he had led the warriors of the Iron Tenth for over a century, fighting from the fringes of the Solar System all the way to Isstvan V. He had seen courage beyond anything the most fanciful retelling of a remembrancer could invent.

Yet that paled in comparison to the courage of the men arrayed before him in this moment.

'On any normal day, I would censure every one of you,' he began. 'But this is not a normal day. Since Isstvan V, we have known no normal days. Since that black day of betrayal, we have come far, risked much and lost more. We have travelled into the realm of monsters to face our greatest foes, and we have *hurt* them. Like Taliansa of ancient Medusa, we lanced the belly of the great dragon and left a trail of its blood for others to follow, slowing it and weakening it in readiness for the death blow. It has been a long, dark and bloody road, brothers. We have seen comrades fall, one by one, but we have never faltered.'

Tyro paused before continuing, seeing Ulrach Branthan at the far end of the troop compartment, watching him with pain-filled eyes.

'This will be our last mission together,' said Tyro, 'and no matter what happens, know that I am prouder than I have ever been to have known you and fought alongside you.'

The assembled warriors nodded solemnly. They were grateful

for the truth of his sentiment, but no one gave a rousing response or hammered a fist to the chest at his words.

Too much blood had been spilled and too many friends lost along the way for that.

Tyro marched between them to take a seat close to Branthan. The grav-seats were too small for the transformed captain's armoured bulk. He simply stood, hunched over at the end of the compartment, like the statue of some grotesque god at the nave of a heathen fane. Garuda sat over his head in the stowage rack, its head folded under one wing as though it were asleep.

'Fine words, Captain Tyro,' said Branthan. 'Though they were laden with a sense of finality. Do you think we will fail?'

'These men have triumphed against impossible odds time and time again,' said Tyro.

'That's not an answer,' said Branthan, reading the undertow in Tyro's words.

'I know,' said Tyro. 'But win or die, this *will* be our last fight.'

The Lunar landscape rose to meet them, but Sharrowkyn found it hard to gauge just how high they were. The rugged grey landscape was without defining characteristics to give it scale, and what few features there were offered no clue to their true size.

They could have been a thousand metres above the ground or a hundred.

The threat display continued to pop and whistle with a strange doggerel of electronic noise.

The gentle bulge of Herodotus Omega filled the canopy, its distance likewise impossible to accurately measure by sight alone. Its flanks were smooth silver, its peak ridged with glittering lights that might be structures or marker beacons. Distortion from the *Cthonian Scion*'s grav-wash rippled the top of the extinct volcano, and billowing clouds of Lunar dust haloed the summit like mountain mist.

'Bringing her down,' said Wayland, easing the Storm Eagle into a curving turn to starboard. The movement was sluggish and heavy. Without thrusters, the gunship was simply a mass of metal falling gracefully through a low-G environment.

'How are you planning to land this thing without thrusters?' said Sharrowkyn.

'Once we're in the canyon, I'll risk some low-level bursts,' said Wayland. 'Enough to set us down in one piece, though it will still be an... *interesting* landing.'

Sharrowkyn had experienced enough hostile landings, under-fire evacs and burning intercepts Wayland had defined simply as *interesting* to know that this would be only fractionally better than going down in flames.

'I'll brace for impact then,' he said, turning to head back to the troop compartment.

'That might be wise,' agreed Wayland.

Before Sharrowkyn moved, a furious wail erupted from the vox. The sine wave he'd seen earlier on the emissions slate suddenly burst into life. Then, it had been jumpy, its strength varying wildly, but now it was a constant blare of energy coming straight at them.

'Something knows we're here,' he said.

Wayland didn't respond, but drove the control column forward, pushing them into a steep, almost vertical dive. Sharrowkyn gripped the sides of his pilot's compartment, hating the lack of control he always felt when his fate was in the hands of others.

'What is it?' said Sharrowkyn.

'Hunters,' replied Wayland.

'From where?'

'I don't know yet. Let me process.'

'Process faster,' said Sharrowkyn, watching the ground rushing up to meet them. He hoped Wayland had a better idea of their altitude. The jumping sine wave flattened, becoming a single, shrieking howl that surely meant that whatever auspex was hunting them had now found them.

'It's trying to fix our position,' said Wayland.

'What is? The *Cthonian Scion*?'

'I don't think so. I don't recognise the frequency type.'

The ground rolled. Silver and black inverted as the ground became the sky.

Sharrowkyn caught a glimpse of something to their port rear quarter as Wayland jinked the gunship in a plunging dive. Too fast to see clearly, a thing of brass and silver. Spider-like and with too many hooked limbs.

A machine of some sort, a predator-drone or hybrid fighter craft, perhaps.

Wayland pushed power to the engines, thoughts of stealth forgotten as the ground closed in. Sharrowkyn lost sight of their pursuer as the force of Wayland's dive threw him against the fuselage. He felt the punch of high-G in his gut and his vision greyed for an instant. The Storm Eagle shuddered, and the sound of groaning metal ran its length.

The Iron Hands had maintained the gunship over the years as best they could, but with the limited resources available to them, the repairs of battle damage had been ad hoc at best. Welded seams split with the violence of the manoeuvre. Sparks spilled from a ruptured conduit, and warning bells echoed from the troop compartment behind them.

Sharrowkyn felt the juddering tear of something coming loose from the hull.

The darkness of the shallow canyon enfolded them, the shadows stark and inviting.

Wayland jinked the Storm Eagle to the side, ramming power back into the engines as the signal strength from the hunter-killer machine shrieked.

The altimeter spun crazily as Wayland pushed them closer to the dirt. Jagged outcroppings and tank-sized boulders flashed past the canopy, insanely close.

Suddenly, Sharrowkyn knew *exactly* how close to the ground they were.

The avionics panel sputtered, and a crackling voice spat from the vox.

'Come to heading zero three seven,' it said, croaking as if formed by a throat parched from a lifetime in the desert. *'Then cut your thrust and drop ten metres on my mark if you want to live.'*

'What the…?' began Sharrowkyn.

Wayland didn't argue, but simply nudged the control column as instructed.

The Storm Eagle banked sharply into a branch canyon, much narrower than before, and Sharrowkyn wanted to squeeze himself smaller. No warrior of the Raven Guard was claustrophobic, but this was threading the eye of a needle with a seventy-ton aircraft at high speed.

The sine wave bottomed out, a low, flat line of a constant signal.

'It's locked on,' said Sharrowkyn.

Wayland grunted as he fought to manoeuvre, but the canyon walls were too narrow, the ground too close.

'I have nowhere to go,' he said.

Sharrowkyn peered through the canopy, eyes narrowing as he picked out something ahead.

Something that shouldn't be there.

A lone figure standing on a raised bluff of rock. Wreathed in shadows so deep even he couldn't pick out any details beyond a chromium helmet that gleamed silver like a crescent moon. Something long and slender snapped into position at its shoulder.

'Now,' scratched the voice. *'Drop.'*

Again, Wayland didn't argue, nudging the stick forward and

cutting the engines. No sooner had the prow dipped than the device at the figure's shoulder bloomed with pale smoke and cherry-red fire.

Sharrowkyn ducked involuntarily as a dart-shaped missile flashed over the Storm Eagle, its blue-hot jet wash blistering the gunship's canopy as it passed within two metres. Sharrowkyn expected to see a reflected flash of detonation or feel the pressure wave of an explosion, but nothing came.

'Everyone brace!' yelled Wayland as the Storm Eagle made an *interesting* landing on the Lunar surface.

The gunship's prow was crumpled, its spine buckled and the fuselage split open all along its length. An outcropping of rock had gouged a tear in one wing and spun the craft around, leaving it listing like a beached whale in a pale cloud of dust. The right engine cowling leaked fumes and coolant, while the left hung by threads of cabling and a seam of blackened metal.

The warriors of the *Sisypheum* staggered from the hole torn in the hull where the rear assault ramp used to be, their dark armour paled by hanging Lunar particles.

Cadmus Tyro was first from the wreckage, moving with pained steps and his bolter at the ready as he scanned the deep furrow of their descent in search of attackers. The darkness overhead was streaked with light, and explosions of dust billowed on the upper walls of the canyon as falling debris impacted. Luckily, the angle of its descent and the depth of the canyon kept the worst of it from impacting around them.

Ignatius Numen followed an instant later, his volkite cannon held out before him, the barrel crackling with barely contained energies. Frater Thamatica and Atesh Tarsa flanked him, and Ulrach Branthan came next, bending back part of the torn metal to emerge into the hostile Lunar atmosphere. Garuda perched on his shoulder, its head jerking from side to side as though irritated at having been woken.

'What brought us down?' asked Branthan.

'I don't know,' said Tyro. 'Wayland's warning came only a second before we hit.'

Branthan looked to the horizon. 'We need to move. The crash will draw the enemy's eye.'

Tyro nodded, and turned to issue orders to his fellow warriors. 'Frater, head to the top of the dune ridge. Keep watch on our surroundings, passive auspex only. Numen, gather up the ammunition still in the gunship. Tarsa, go forward and check on Sharrowkyn and Wayland.'

The Salamander nodded and headed around to the buried prow of the gunship.

Numen didn't move, his gaze fixed on the tops of the canyon walls.

'Numen, do as he says,' said Branthan.

The veteran nodded curtly and lumbered back inside the gunship. Anger touched Tyro at Numen's flagrant deferment to Branthan, but now wasn't the time for a contest of wills between captains.

Tyro's eyes narrowed as he saw a patina of frost crawling across Branthan's grey skin.

Exposed to the full force of the sun's radiation, a Lunar day could reach temperatures of up to two hundred degrees. At night, or in the shadow of a canyon as they were now, it was registering at one hundred and ninety-five degrees below zero. Insulated and reflective suits had kept the earliest Lunar pioneers safe, but Ulrach Branthan's flesh was exposed to the lethal cold.

'How are you enduring this temperature?' asked Tyro. 'The flesh should be freezing solid on your bones.'

Branthan shrugged, the movement unnatural.

'Ulrach,' pressed Tyro. 'Answer me.'

At first, he thought Branthan was going to ignore him, but then the captain spoke in a voice that was unlike his normal default-aggressive tone. If anything, Branthan sounded *vulnerable*, a trait never normally associated with a captain of the Iron Hands.

'Atesh Tarsa told me the Heart of Iron had... *changed* me,' said Branthan. 'My physiology, the functioning of my organs.'

'Should I be concerned?'

'About what?'

'About what else it might have changed,' said Tyro.

'What are you suggesting?' snapped Branthan, any sense of vulnerability evaporating in the face of Tyro's words.

'Since leaving stasis, your mental state could be described as... *erratic*.'

'Are you questioning my loyalty, Cadmus?'

'No, never that,' said Tyro. 'But none of us know the true nature of the Heart of Iron. We don't know who made it or what changes its creators intended for it to work. That should concern us both.'

'Dedicate your efforts to killing traitors and you will have no concerns, Captain Tyro.'

Thamatica's voice hissed over the vox.

'Movement,' said the Iron Father. *'One figure, coming in low along the furrow of our landing.'*

'Can you identify?'

'Not yet.'

'You have it covered?'

'Of course.'

The Lunar dust hung thick in the low gravity, masking movement. Tyro squinted, his auto-senses crackling with static as they tried to sort true images from ghost-images.

A figure stepped into view.

Its hunched shoulders were draped in a voluminous russet

cloak, ragged like a burned wing, and a long-barrelled weapon of weathered bronze was mounted at its shoulder, rotated back on its mount to the safe position.

The figure wore a gleaming silver helmet, and a wire-wound staff of cables and jangling charms held in its left hand looked like something a tribal shaman might carry. Its body was insulated within a series of heavy thermal bandages, looped around its body and upper limbs – two at each shoulder, two at the waist – in a repeating angular pattern, like an ancient, mummified queen of Gyptus.

Queen, because what body plan was visible of the figure was unmistakably female.

'Is that a gene-witch?' said Tyro, pulling his bolter in tight to his shoulder.

'I don't know,' answered Branthan. 'I have never seen one before.'

The arm that had once belonged to Brother Bombastus came up, and the flex-steel ammo belt of the storm bolter clattered as it fed oversized shells into the weapon.

One of the figure's hands clutched a disturbingly organic collection of biomechanical, tentacle-like limbs, which were in turn attached to the body of a ridged and segmented *thing* she was dragging behind her like a hunter returning with a prize kill. To Tyro, it looked like the bastard offspring of a spider and a squid.

Garuda pushed off Branthan's shoulder, its beak opening and closing, screeching in silent hostility.

'That's far enough,' said Branthan. The figure looked up, as though only now aware of their presence. 'Identify yourself!'

A grating wheeze, like rusty spars of metal being dragged across an iron deck, issued from beneath the figure's helmet.

'You come to *my* world and demand to know who *I* am?'

She kept coming, hauling the machine carcass behind her.

'This demersal-splicer almost latched on to your craft,' she said. 'Lucky for you I still had a low-yield e-mag, eh? It's one of our uglier creations, this. Would've slaved your avionics system to its control and flown you into a cliff. That'd be a wreck you wouldn't be walking out of, I can tell you!'

Crackling traceries of violet light flickered across the segmented surfaces of the splicer.

Haywire, thought Tyro. The downed machine wasn't dead, just paralysed.

Thamatica moved parallel to her, his aim never wavering from the beacon of her silver skull. If she so much as twitched in a hostile manner, the Iron Father would put a mass-reactive through her brain.

'Identify yourself!' ordered Branthan again, as the figure kept coming.

The gene-witch lifted her staff, and every weapon snapped to her.

'Kill me, and I'll make this machine scream loud enough the Sons of Horus will hear it with their own flesh ears,' she said.

'Who are you?' demanded Tyro.

'I know who it is,' said Sabik Wayland, coming around the flanks of the downed gunship.

Nykona Sharrowkyn and Atesh Tarsa had to hold him upright, as the lower portion of the Iron Father's right leg was missing below the middle of his thigh. Tattered shreds of meat and metal hung from the crude seal of a synth-skin dressing.

'Bad landing,' said the gene-witch.

'I've had better,' agreed Wayland. 'But I can get it to fly again.'

'Doubt it,' said the figure. 'Came down hard.'

'No thanks to you.'

'What's going on, Wayland?' said Branthan, without taking his aim from the silver-helmed figure. 'Who is that?'

'Put your guns away,' said Wayland. 'That is Ta'lab Vita-37, and she just saved our lives.'

6

The Paths Below
Not Meant to Be
Change of Plans

The gene-witch tilted her head back to scan the light-streaked sky.

'What are you looking for?' asked Tyro.

'Your fleet,' said Ta'lab Vita-37. 'Squadrons of attack ships in formation. A lone warship with city-levelling ordnance. Something that tells me you heard my message and took it seriously.'

'We heard it,' said Tyro, 'but the only things like that in orbit are traitor ships.'

'So it's just you?'

'It's just us.'

'Then how do you intend to destroy Herodotus Omega? My message was specific, yes? *Wipe it clean of life.*'

'We are Space Marines,' said Branthan. 'We can destroy anything, and we do not need starships to do it.'

'So sure of yourself,' said Ta'lab Vita-37. 'That always was your kind's flaw. Those who embrace certainty and reject doubt are the ones we should have feared. We should have seen it back then. Should have seen it and refused to comply... That's the truth of it.'

Ta'lab Vita-37 shrugged and spun her staff around, then sheathed it over her shoulder.

She dropped the coiled tentacle-cables of the demersal-splicer and said, 'Never liked these bio-constructs. Vicious things with delusions of grandeur and a sadistic streak. Didn't do a damn thing but slow Lupercal's curs by a minute or less anyway.'

The gene-witch unsettled Tyro in a way he could not articulate, and it took a measure of self-restraint he hadn't known he possessed to let her approach unharmed.

He tried to rationalise it as just his war-posture in the face of an unknown entity, but part of him knew there was more to it than that. The gene-witches were an ancient, potent force, and rumours of their existence went back to a time when the secret knowledge they had possessed was thought to be magic.

'You are Ta'lab Vita-37?' asked Branthan.

She stopped and looked at him curiously.

'I am Ta'lab Vita-37. Daughter of the Moon. Child of Luna. Who are you?'

'Ulrach Branthan, captain of the Tenth Legion.'

Ta'lab Vita-37 looked him up and down. 'And *what* are you? Something worse than even we made. And we made *nightmares*...'

She didn't wait for an answer and turned to Tyro. 'And you? Who are you?'

'Cadmus Tyro.'

'Iron Hands,' said Ta'lab Vita-37, turning to scan the rest of the warriors and seeing Atesh Tarsa and Nykona Sharrowkyn. 'But not all of you.'

'Not all of us,' agreed Tyro. 'The infamy at Isstvan V brought brothers of many Legions together, and the fighting since then has forged our brotherhood in iron.'

Ta'lab Vita-37 nodded and reached up to snap a frozen droplet of blood from his armour. She held it to the reflective surface of her helmet, and Tyro's visor detected radiant heat emanating from its surface. As the blood began to melt she smeared it over where her mouth would have been if she'd had any features to discern. Cursive forms of light played under the helmet's surface, crescents and loops of helical spirals.

'Tenth Legion. Third generation. Medusan-born,' said Ta'lab Vita-37. 'Blood type AXR positive theta. Part of the Omnia-Schiaparelli stratum. High concentrations of the Stallix genotype, a modification of the *garjana* generation-pairings. Too high, really. Can lead to a predisposition for pain-induced psycho-trauma. But I expect you already know that.'

'What are you talking about? What does any of that mean?'

'It means we bred you all to be resilient,' said Ta'lab Vita-37, 'but you exhibit levels I haven't seen in a long time. Put a bolt through *your* skull and I think you might still get up, eh?'

'We are the Iron Tenth,' said Branthan. 'We endure pain. It is what we do.'

'There's truth in that,' agreed Ta'lab Vita-37, 'but your Legion's gene-code is concentrated beyond what we advised. Your sire always did like to push things farther than He ought.'

'Our sire? You mean Ferrus Manus?' said Branthan.

'No,' said Ta'lab Vita-37, turning to face the Iron Father. 'Your other sire. The one who sent His wolves to first yoke us to His terrible ambition.'

Tyro's anger simmered just below the surface, and he saw it mirrored in the tension of his battle-brothers.

'To speak such words while the Throneworld is besieged is a sure and certain way to find death,' said Branthan.

Ta'lab Vita-37 regarded him quizzically, and shook her head.

'So fragile,' she said with a throaty wheeze that might have been a chuckle. 'Another side effect of hyper-aggressive masculine traits. Time is against us, and you *still* look to find fault in warm air passing over my lips.'

Tyro felt Branthan's fury ratchet up a notch, and fought to quell his own.

After all, she was right. Time was the enemy now.

'The Magna Mater, where is it?'

Ta'lab Vita-37 shook her head, somehow managing to look contrite and dejected without so much as a single facial feature.

'I bore its burden for so long, alone and hidden from my sisters. I could not take my ease with them or find succour at any of the wellsprings, for Heliosa-54 made sure every scrap of me was erased for fear I would be revealed and taken. My sisters forgot me. The moon herself forgot me. But I kept it safe, bound to Luna, but passing unseen in the cracks of existence and perception.'

She sank to her knees, and Tyro saw the immense depths of sadness within her.

'I kept it with me for two centuries and more,' she continued. 'Until my flesh and mind could bear the toll of solitude no longer. Heliosa-54 had tasked me, you see? Tasked me with keeping it safe. Close, but far from those who would misuse it. I could not do that if my body failed. I needed to rest, to regenerate in the healing light of the wellsprings, but I could not take the Magna Mater with me for fear its power would reveal it. So I reopened the secret vaults within the gene-labs of Herodotus Omega, vaults that were rightly condemned and long ago sealed. I hid the Magna Mater deep and wove unbreakable seals about them while I slumbered.'

'Let me guess,' said Tyro. 'Those seals weren't as unbreakable as you thought.'

'Even on Luna, it seems the rot of treachery runs deep,' said Ta'lab Vita-37 sadly. 'As I regenerated, building the strength to continue my duty, enemy hunters learned of my lone vigil and tracked me to my refuge. Corrupted cybernetics almost took me, but they underestimated the power of a gene-maiden, even an old and frail one. I unmade them, and fled into the silver oceans, using the old ways to send a message of desperation into the void.'

'And we have answered your call, so what would you have us do?' said Branthan.

Ta'lab Vita-37 aimed her staff in the direction of the volcano.

'Time is short,' she said. 'Renegade Martian tech-priests are using a degenerative viral sentience to undo the gene-seals I placed upon the vaults within Herodotus Omega.'

'How long do we have before they break in?' asked Tyro.

'Five of the seals have already succumbed, the sixth is almost gone, and it is only a matter of time until the seventh seal is no more and the Sons of Horus will be within.'

'If the Sons of Horus hold the main entrance, how do we get inside?' asked Tyro.

'Main entrance?' cackled Ta'lab Vita-37. 'Your kind is always so literal.'

Leaving Wayland and Thamatica to try to get the Storm Eagle airborne, Ta'lab Vita-37 led the others deeper into the canyon. Sharrowkyn gripped Wayland's arm as he left. The Iron Father's face was pale, but he gave no sign of any pain from the leg he had lost in the crash. He had already bound a broken stanchion to the severed stump to act as a crutch, using cable and insulation material pulled from the torn fuselage.

'Be safe, brother,' said Wayland.

'You too, brother,' said Sharrowkyn, unable to shake a feeling of grim premonition.

'I'll have this flying before you get back, mark my words.'

Sharrowkyn had seen aircraft in worse states keep flying, but not for long, and few of them ever got back in the air once they were down.

'I don't doubt it,' he said.

That farewell had been two hours and fifteen kilometres ago.

Sharrowkyn scouted ahead of the others as they pushed along the canyon towards the unfinished venting station built into the haunches of the volcano. Dust fragments drifted down like ashen rain into the canyon, as well as larger pieces of fused metal smashed from orbit. Sharrowkyn had passed a number of bodies too, but hadn't stopped to examine them.

Occasional flashes of secondary detonations in orbit, or the streaks of burning debris carving a fiery line across the sky, briefly illuminated the canyon floor. Ten metres behind, Ignatius Numen swept the ground before him with his volkite. The veteran had fought with Sharrowkyn long enough to know the Raven Guard warrior was in no danger from any shots he might fire. Atesh Tarsa and Branthan flanked Ta'lab Vita-37, while Cadmus Tyro provided rear security. Garuda circled above him, keeping below the lip of the canyon. It irked Sharrowkyn that the bird was keeping pace with him, but the bird went where it wanted, and nothing anyone could do or say to it made any difference.

Sharrowkyn moved silently, his steps lighter than air, barely disturbing the dust and leaving no mark of his passing. Moving this way was instinctual to him.

The darkness in the canyon was deep and comforting, even if he didn't know this world's shadows. Their nuances were unknown to him, but they welcomed him nonetheless. To those not trained by the Shadowmasters, all such umbra were alike, but Sharrowkyn knew better.

He had been born to the shadows and they had raised him, nurtured him and taught him, like a child raised by beasts in a forest. He knew their ways, and they his.

Ta'lab Vita-37 had told him to look for a section of canyon wall with three teardrop-shaped impact craters in a pattern resembling an elongated spear tip aimed at the dead volcano. Sharrowkyn's eyes were in constant motion, but he had seen nothing resembling such a formation, and they were getting dangerously close to the enemy auspex net his passive auto-senses were detecting.

Three hundred metres later, he halted as a bloom of light from an explosion threw the eastern wall into sharp relief. And there they were – three impact craters, the result of meteors having struck the canyon wall at the precise angle to form a spear tip, the pattern entirely natural yet completely distinct.

Sharrowkyn stepped from the shadows, an act that would tell Numen they had reached their destination. He hunted for any sign of something man-made, but could see nothing special about this location. A sliver of the volcano's summit was just visible between the narrow walls and through the veil of drifting fragments.

Ta'lab Vita-37 and the others approached, and Sharrowkyn indicated the impact craters in the wall.

'You have good eyes.' Ta'lab Vita-37 said.

'You should know,' said Sharrowkyn. 'Your kind enhanced them.'

'That we did, Raven Guard, irreducible complexity be damned,' she replied.

'So why are we here? What do these marks signify?'

'That we have our way in,' said Ta'lab Vita-37.

'Where?' demanded Branthan. 'There is nothing here.'

'If there's a way in here, it's well hidden,' said Sharrowkyn.

'Your eyes are keen, but you don't see everything, Raven,' said Ta'lab Vita-37.

The gene-witch approached the dark rock of the canyon wall and set her staff of charms and cables against it. More lights flickered beneath the surface of her helm, and previously invisible seams opened in the rock, seams Sharrowkyn knew with absolute certainty that no Shadowmaster or high fabricatus of the Mechanicum would ever have found.

'Two hundred years I have travelled the moon, beyond sight and out of mind,' said Ta'lab Vita-37. 'Do you really think I don't know all her secret ways?'

The cavern within the canyon wall was rough-hewn, its walls curved and scored with napped patterns that made Sharrowkyn feel as if he stood within some giant sea creature's shell. He ran his finger along the inner walls, feeling repetition in the patterns, as if the rock had been dug by the rhythmic gestures of something desperate to claw its way out.

That impression was only reinforced by the sight of an exposed sheet of metal on the far wall of the cave, a portion of ductwork revealed by excavations into the rock. A ragged hole had been cut into the metal from within by what looked like a thermal lance, and the portion excised from the duct lay on the ground.

'What is this?' Sharrowkyn asked.

'A segment of venting ductwork that leads from inside and eventually comes out high on the flanks of the volcano,' said Ta'lab Vita-37.

'This our way in?'

'Yes.'

Sharrowkyn leaned cautiously into the duct, feeling the passage of warm, ionised air drifting from somewhere deep inside the mountain.

'This leads to the vaults?'

'It does,' confirmed Ta'lab Vita-37. 'To a sealed storage facility.'

'Wait,' said Atesh Tarsa, kneeling by the edge of the hole cut in the duct and consulting the readout on his narthecium. 'What are these pipes venting? What machinery is this ducting connected to?'

'This ductwork is part of the radiation filtration system,' said Ta'lab Vita-37.

'Radiation?' said Tyro. 'How bad is it, Tarsa?'

'The levels are below lethal, but still significant,' said Tarsa.

'A radiation filter?' said Tyro. 'Why do you need a radiation filtration system that requires ducting of this size? Didn't you say there were gene-labs in here?'

'This facility was built upon one of the original Koenig Alpha atomic waste sites.'

'*What?* Why would you build a gene-lab on an atomic waste site?'

'The containment systems were more than adequate to render the internal environment sterile,' said Ta'lab Vita-37. 'But the proximity to a waste site would convince anyone who thought to look this way that no work of any import could possibly be carried out here.'

'What work *was* being carried out here?' asked Tyro.

Ta'lab Vita-37 hesitated before answering. 'Highly secret research that was intended to become a new branch of Legion genetics, but which was abandoned when it only produced freaks and monsters. We destroyed them, and this place was shut down long ago.'

'And this is where you hid the Magna Mater?' asked Tyro.

'Yes. It is a place of forgotten echoes now.'

'Well that doesn't sound ominous at all,' said Sharrowkyn.

7

No More to Give
Infiltration
Too Late

Wayland leaned back in his pilot's seat and gritted his teeth against the pain.

It raced around his body in rivers of fire from his severed leg, suffusing every fibre of his being with almost paralysing agony. His armour had long since exhausted its supply of balms in the years since Isstvan V, but not all the pain he was feeling was his own.

Thick cables ran from his gauntlet into an exposed conduit of wires he'd unscrewed from the interior of the Storm Eagle's fuselage. He felt the agony of the machine-spirit at the heart of the gunship, its fury and its torment at being grounded.

It overwhelmed his pain, for it was the pain of desire broken on the wheel of reality.

Wayland whispered the binaric catechisms of repair and restoration to soothe its broken spirit. The machine's pain was hideous, and he felt its wounded soul on the verge of dissipating into the ether. He reached for it, but it turned at bay, screeds of binary lashing out at him.

The connection between the gunship and Wayland was abruptly severed with a screeching roar of fury from the vox, and Wayland's eyes snapped open, his skin lathered in icy sweat.

He disconnected from the avionics panel, his movements clumsy with pain and residual echoes of his conjoined consciousness. He pulled himself from the pilot's seat and limped back to the troop compartment.

Frater Thamatica knelt by the dormant form of the demersal-splicer Ta'lab Vita-37 had brought down. Its appearance bore few hallmarks of Imperial craft, and its grotesque, cephalopodic body possessed a more organic form than Wayland was used to seeing. Ever the tinkerer, Thamatica had the mechanised arms of his servo-harness prodding circuitry within an access panel he'd prised open.

The Iron Father usually preferred to work manually, but such was the scale of repairs needed to render the Storm Eagle flyable that he had been forced to dig a servo-harness from its stowage bay. The welder tips on its fusion torch arms still glowed red with heat.

'What are you doing with that?' asked Wayland.

'Investigating,' said Thamatica without looking up. 'I've never seen technology like this before. It would be a shame not to at least take a look at it. The MIU links are extraordinary, verging on the edge of true machine autonomy. Given free rein, this could fly a fleet of gunships on its own. If I can just disengage these inhibitors, I could link it with–'

'The Storm Eagle,' interrupted Wayland. 'Walk me through it.'

Now Thamatica looked up, and the multiple arms of the servo-harness folded into their collapsed forms on his back.

'The fuselage was split in so many places I lost count, and a great many of the control surfaces are so badly damaged that it will be almost impossible to manoeuvre effectively. The landing gear is shattered and the fuel tanks are all but empty.'

'What's your prognosis? Is it fit to fly?'

Thamatica said, 'I've sealed up all our wounds and realigned what I can, but without a Legion graving dock and a squadron of servitors, I fear this will be its final flight.'

Wayland nodded and lowered himself into one of the compartment's armoured bucket seats. Pain from his leg was burning through his endurance, but he forced it into a sealed box in his mind. He was an Iron Hand; pain was part of the journey.

Birth to death. Flesh to Iron.

Thamatica put a hand on Wayland's shoulder and nodded to the cockpit.

'But nothing I can do to get us up in the air will matter if the machine-spirit is broken.'

'I can't reach it, Frater,' said Wayland. 'The spirit recoils from my every entreaty like a wild animal in a snare, too consumed by rage and pain to understand I am trying to help.'

'No one has a way with the spirit of machines like you, Sabik,' said Thamatica. 'I know you can reach it. You just need to be patient with it. And all being well, we only need to be airborne long enough to return to the *Sisypheum*.'

'All being well?' snapped Wayland. 'How well have things gone for us since Isstvan V?'

'Not like you to be defeatist, Sabik.'

Wayland sighed. 'We all only have so much to give, Frater.'

Hot, irradiated fumes and radioactive dust blew along the ductwork, in levels high enough to be deadly to a mortal but harmless to the warriors of the Legions. Ta'lab Vita-37 led them through the twisting lengths of ducts, and it did not take long for them to reach the interior of the mountain.

They emerged in a storage chamber, a cold space of angle-cut stone, stacked high with construction materiel that would never be used, broken machinery and the accumulated detritus of abandoned spaces. A single trapezoidal archway led deeper into the mountain.

Sharrowkyn heard the distant sounds of shouting voices, mixed with the clang of metal on metal and the idling thrum of engines belonging to something heavy.

A transport of some kind, a trans-orbital at least.

One by one, they moved into the chamber. Cadmus Tyro and Ta'lab Vita-37 followed Sharrowkyn, then Tarsa. Ignatius Numen came next, and finally Ulrach Branthan ducked down as he entered. Garuda clung to the metal at his shoulders.

'The vault is ahead,' said Ta'lab Vita-37.

'Should we expect to meet resistance?' asked Tyro.

'No,' said Ta'lab Vita-37. 'At least, not until we reach the vault chamber itself.'

Despite the gene-witch's assurances, the Space Marines moved off in perfect cover formation, each warrior protecting the other as they moved deeper into the mountain.

The interior tunnels of the volcano were faced with pressed steel, and dust and silence hung heavy over them all. They moved from junction to junction, with Ta'lab Vita-37 leading them unerringly onwards. At the arched entrance to an opened chamber, they found barricades of collapsed gurneys and empty barrels stamped with biohazard markings. Las-burns, grenade shrapnel and bullet impacts had chewed up the walls.

'What's in there?' asked Sharrowkyn.

'The growth chambers,' said Ta'lab Vita-37. 'Where viable subjects were hothoused and matured in gene-pods.'

'The freaks and monsters?' Sharrowkyn asked. 'Is that all that's left here?'

'No,' said Ta'lab Vita-37. 'We purged all the monsters the Emperor couldn't use.'

They passed through the smashed barricade and entered a vast chamber of dripping echoes and cold darkness. Long-dead machinery gathered dust on the walls, rigging chains dangled from lifter cranes, and heavy-duty cabling lay inert on the floor amid shards of broken glass.

Lined up in their thousands, like warriors at a Legion muster, were row upon row of clear-fronted gene-pods. Most were empty, but those that were not were filled with stagnant, milky residue in which hulking forms could be glimpsed through the clouded glass. It was impossible to make out their exact nature, but Sharrowkyn saw figures with transhuman bulk – but these were monstrous ogres, taller and broader than even the largest Space Marine.

Sharrowkyn kept pace with Ta'lab Vita-37 and took a moment to study the gene-witch.

'What is it you want to know?' she asked, sensing his scrutiny.

'I'm not sure,' he said. 'It's not every day you get to meet one of your creators.'

'Is that how you think of me?'

Sharrowkyn shrugged. 'Until we came to the moon I had not thought of the Selenar much at all. You were a footnote to the early histories of the drive from Terra. So little is known of you and your sect.'

'Did you pause to wonder why that might be?'

'Not at all.'

Ta'lab Vita-37 turned to face him, but her featureless helm gave no clue to her emotions.

'The Selenar have always existed in the cracks between perception,' she said. 'We have gone by many names and used many guises through the ages to move through the world of men – the Eleusinians, Oesirica, the Damia, the Immacolata…

The list goes on, but every name and every guise had but one purpose. Do you know what that was?'

'No,' said Sharrowkyn.

'To keep our power of creation out of the hands of men.'

'Why?'

Ta'lab Vita-37 gave one of her wheezing laughs. 'Because we knew you would do what your kind always does with such a gift – you would seek to turn it into a weapon of conquest and dominance. And that's exactly what the Emperor did when He stole it from us all those years ago.'

'Stole? My understanding was that Luna and Terra fought, yes, but that when the Emperor laid out His vision for the Imperium, the Selenar willingly joined forces to see it done.'

Ta'lab Vita-37 shook her head, as though Sharrowkyn had disappointed her.

'*Of course* that is your understanding. To accept that everything for which you fight is built on lies, murder and theft does not fit the narrative you must craft in order to keep believing you are the heroes of this galaxy. Look at what has become of your Imperium and tell me we were not wise to keep such awesome power secret as long as we did?'

'There have been wars long before this one.'

'There have indeed, Raven Guard, but wars waged by mortals burn out in mortal spans – they do not set the galaxy ablaze,' said Ta'lab Vita-37, turning to rap her over-articulated knuckles on his eagle-stamped plastron. 'When gods make war, everyone burns in the fire with them.'

Before Sharrowkyn could reply, Ta'lab Vita-37 bent double with a cry of pain.

Sharrowkyn immediately grabbed her and pulled her into cover, scanning for threats. He hadn't heard or sensed anything. The others followed his lead, finding machinery and structural elements to shelter behind.

Ta'lab Vita-37 clutched her gut, sinking to her knees. But for her staff, she would have fallen to the floor. Her body spasmed, as though struck with a shock maul.

'What's happening?' asked Sharrowkyn. 'Are you hurt?'

Her chest hiked with rapid, staccato breaths.

Angry red spirals looped on the surface of her helmet.

'The seventh seal is broken,' said Ta'lab Vita-37. 'The traitors are in the vault.'

Thamatica had done as much as he could with the tools and materials he had to make the Storm Eagle flyable, but even then he wasn't sure it would be enough. So many elements of its structure were beyond battlefield repair, and the constant recycling and reuse of worn-out parts over the years had finally taken its inevitable toll.

He felt reasonably confident it was structurally *capable* of getting airborne, but without a willing machine-spirit, it likely wouldn't remain in the air for long. Without a machine-spirit, a gunship was just tons of scrap metal.

Thamatica glanced along the troop compartment towards the cockpit, where Wayland again sought to coax the gunship's spirit back from the brink. Cables ran from his arm to the avionics panel, and pulsing communications passed back and forth between man and machine. Thamatica had offered to help, but Wayland had shaken his head.

'No,' he'd said. 'I flew this gunship out of the fires of Isstvan V. I flew it against Fulgrim's warriors and against those of Alpharius. Its spirit knows me. It trusts me. But it is wary of you.'

Thamatica couldn't blame it. Not really. The machine-spirits of the *Sisypheum* gossiped with one another, passing secret machine knowledge in every binaric whisper. They knew Thamatica as an... *experimenter*. As one who sought to *change* them.

No, Wayland was right to decline his help.

But this splicer, that was a different story entirely.

It was a fascinating piece of technology.

He'd exposed the length of its interior, and its workings were a marvel. Its roots were old, its components built from scratch without recourse to anything Thamatica recognised as an STC pattern. Its circuitry looked handmade. Bespoke. The very thought of such a thing sent a thrill of excitement through him and had given him an idea of how they might employ it, though Wayland had already decried it as too dangerous.

Its control module was dizzyingly complex, an artificial neural web with heuristic capabilities that far outstripped what they'd seen inside Garuda when he and Wayland had stripped the bird down to repair it. Ta'lab Vita-37 had said it was designed to take control of enemy aircraft in order to crash them or take control of vital systems. An ingenious and efficient way to turn an enemy's strength against them.

'Damnation!' snapped Wayland from the cockpit.

'Still not responding?' asked Thamatica.

'No,' said Wayland, sounding exhausted. 'It's all but given up.'

The vault chamber had been carved deep into the southern haunches of the volcano, a rough circle a kilometre in diameter. It was filled with the actinic reek of burning metal and the molten heat of lascutters.

Like every chamber they'd passed through, it was littered with derelict machinery, broken loader servitors and emptied stowage bins. Sharrowkyn eased into cover behind a haphazardly stacked collection of metalled crates. Dust and fumes hung in the air in a thick fog, rendering the shapes moving through the space as blurred outlines.

The entire caldera at the volcano's summit was peeled back,

and the darkness of the void rippled through the energies of an integrity field. The light of stars beyond was indistinguishable from the winking lights of orbital detonations and falling debris. A bulky trans-orbital without markings squatted directly below the high entrance, its engines glowing with heat, spooling up in readiness for lift-off.

A cadre of lifter servitors hauled dozens of bulky powercells on repulsor pallets up the embarkation ramp lowered beneath its aft section. Behind them, a multi-limbed tech-priest supervised a group of glitching tech-thralls in oil-stained canvas vac-suits as they loaded steaming coolant cylinders into the trans-orbital's stowage bays.

At the centre of the cavernous space was a deep, circular shaft, putting Sharrowkyn in mind of the eldar crone world they'd followed Fulgrim and Perturabo to, and the depthless pit at its heart. Two dog-toothed silo doors, each five metres thick and thirty metres in length, were raised up on either side of the shaft. Noxious steam issued from below like clouds rising from some hideous underworld.

The floor around the vault opening was littered with the bodies of servitors and dark-robed lexmechanics. They were clearly dead, but their bodies jerked and twisted, purging vital fluids as the flesh rippled beneath the fabric of their robes like the surface of a restless ocean.

'What's happening to them?' asked Numen, rapping his fingers on the stock of his volkite.

'The fail-safes on my gene-locks are not kind to those who try to break them,' said Ta'lab Vita-37.

'What does that mean?'

Lights flickered across Ta'lab Vita-37's helm in a pattern Sharrowkyn had come to associate with grim amusement. 'Unsuccessful attempts to break my gene-codes transfers a hyper-aggressive mutagen into the attacker that instantaneously and randomly sends their genetic order into chaos. Death is assured, and it is not painless.'

Sharrowkyn grinned in admiration. He counted at least two hundred bodies, maybe more.

However many it was, it hadn't been enough.

'You underestimated the traitors' willingness to pay any price to breach your sanctum.'

'Underestimating the depth of cruelty men possess has always been our problem,' said Ta'lab Vita-37.

'We can't linger here,' said Atesh Tarsa, consulting his narthecium and gesturing to the towering red silos lining the circumference of the cavernous space. 'The rad-levels are so high that even our armour won't keep us safe for long.'

Each silo was banded with yellow and black hazard stripes and marked with the unmistakable radiation symbol. Sharrowkyn was acutely reminded that this place had continued to serve as a repository of atomic waste deposited here in the moon's distant past.

'I thought you said this place was sterile,' said Ulrach Branthan, crouched awkwardly in the shadow of a heavy, tracked lifter-rig.

'During this facility's years of operation it was,' said Ta'lab Vita-37. 'But the filtration system has long since failed to scrub the atmosphere in any meaningful way, and this internal volume is thick with a broth of heavy metals and lethal isotopes.'

'Then let's get this thing done,' said Tyro, his fingers tightening on his bolter's grip.

'Wait,' said Sharrowkyn as growing tremors shook the ground with a deep vibration. Orange hazard lights began flashing around the edge of the vault shaft as a heavy transit-elevator ground its way up from somewhere deep below.

The tech-priest and his thralls watched in reverence as *something* came into view, its form obscured by reeking clouds of misty condensate. As the ammoniac clouds dispersed into the cold of the cavern, Sharrowkyn's eyes grew wide at the sight of a monstrous servitor palanquin of flesh and metal. Wrought from the body of a hulking *migou,* its frame had been augmented with steel-jacketed limbs, chemical shunts and an MIU drive unit. Its back was artificially hunched, and brass steps had been implanted onto the meat and bone of its haunches.

A tall and willow-thin Martian adept in red and black, his true form impossible to classify but fringed with cabled limbs and surgical attachments, sat atop this grotesque palanquin on a chained harness. The migou's body was rapidly devolving into a mass of pulsing lesions and unnatural growths, splitting and reforming between laboured breaths.

The consequence of one of Ta'lab Vita-37's fail-safes?

The necrotic texture of the migou's waxen flesh rippled beneath its many augments, and its head swayed from side to side as it brayed in pain. Tortured beyond endurance by the genetic chaos at work within its body, the creature collapsed, and its riotous anatomy poured from its mouth in a frothed soup of liquefaction. Even as Sharrowkyn watched, devolved portions of its body sought to recombine, healing and degenerating once again in the blink of an eye.

'Throne,' hissed Tarsa at the sight of the creature's death.

The magos atop the afflicted beast slid from his harness and stepped down to the cavern floor without missing a beat. The tech-priest and his entourage of thralls dropped to their knees as he turned to retrieve something from the back of the shuddering corpse.

Ta'lab Vita-37's body language instantly changed as the magos lifted down a heavy-looking case of silver steel.

Sharrowkyn thought it an unremarkable object to contain the secrets of life itself.

'Magna Mater…' hissed the gene-witch.

BOOK 3

CRONE

Death may be the greatest
of all human blessings.

8

Into Them
Iron Endures
Active Glories

The magos boarded the trans-orbital, leaving his dead mount behind. The tempo of operations increased as the mindless thralls began the last preparations for launch. The aircraft's engines pulsed with an increase in power and the fog of dust and fumes burned off at its rear.

'We can't let that ship take off,' said Ta'lab Vita-37.

'Do you see any weapons capable of bringing a ship that size down?' asked Tyro.

'Then we need to get on board,' insisted the gene-witch.

'We can do that,' said Sharrowkyn. 'Then we fight our way to the cockpit.'

'How?' said Tyro. 'We don't exactly look as though we belong here.'

Sharrowkyn reached down and scooped a handful of pale dust from the floor and smeared it across his armour. He patted a disruptive pattern across the Legion symbol on his shoulder guard. It didn't obscure it, but it would be camouflage enough to get them close to the trans-orbital before their loyalist provenance became obvious.

'Captain Branthan, pick up a pallet crate,' said Sharrowkyn. 'Your scale might fool them into thinking you are a load-lifter or bulk-servitor. The dust should conceal our insignia until we reach the embarkation ramp. Then we fight our way to the command deck.'

'I'll not hide the hand of the Tenth,' said Numen, watching Sharrowkyn dusting his armour.

'If you have another plan, let's hear it,' said Sharrowkyn, 'but we need to move now.'

Numen looked at Branthan, who nodded, and, reluctantly, the veteran began patting his own armour down with dust. He made only a cursory attempt to obscure the mailed hand at his shoulder, and Sharrowkyn didn't ask him to deface his war-plate any further.

Branthan turned to lift a heavy crate while the Space Marines finished applying enough dust to obscure their identity.

Tyro nodded and said, 'Move out. Move confidently. They must think we belong here.'

Atesh Tarsa led them from cover. Patched with the pale dust, his green armour most resembled that of the sea green of the Sons of Horus, and, as poor a disguise as it was, it might buy them a few metres.

And a few metres could mean the difference between life and death.

Sharrowkyn and the Iron Hands kept moving behind Tarsa, and the Raven Guard felt every fibre of his body screaming at being so brazen. To move in the open, directly towards the enemy, was the antithesis of everything he had been taught, and went against every principle by which his Legion operated.

They moved quickly, pushing out around the edge of the

central shaft towards the trans-orbital. Its engines burned a hot shade of blue, the dust swirling in spiralling thermal vortices.

Sharrowkyn walked swiftly, keeping his upper body a quarter-turn away from the thralls positioned at the embarkation ramp. His hand rested on the grip of his bolter, out of sight.

He glanced behind him, seeing Tyro and Numen looking awkward in the open. So much of the fighting they had done since Isstvan had been on the fringes of the war, biting hard and falling back, moving so as not to be seen.

This approach bothered them as much as it did him.

Branthan lurched behind them, bearing a heavy crate in his outstretched arms. He kept his burden lifted high to better obscure his unnatural body. Sharrowkyn couldn't see Garuda, and just hoped the bird wasn't about to do something inexplicably stupid.

He saw the blurred outlines of the thralls turn to face them.

Their body language registered no threat. Why would it? Luna was now the dominion of their masters – they had no reason to expect any transhumans who were not Sons of Horus. One of the thralls voiced a blurt of harsh static, a binaric yell to be heard over the growing roar of the engines. The others turned as one, the movement eerily synchronistic.

The nearest thrall shouted again, this time with the augmitter implanted in its neck.

'We bring prize to you, masters!' it said. *'Much speed.'*

Sharrowkyn willed Tarsa not to answer.

Fifty metres yet separated them from the trans-orbital. To be revealed now would leave no time to get aboard before the ramp could be closed.

The thrall stepped forward, confused. Its stunted autonomy was slaved to the tech-priest already aboard the trans-orbital.

It could make no decision without its master's leave, and the proxy-collar it wore winked with light as it sought orders.

Forty metres.

A shape moved into view at the top of the ramp, a robed figure with glowing augmetic eyes. No amount of dust or fog would fool those optics. The tech-priest was sure to see through their primitive camouflage in an instant.

Thirty metres.

Sharrowkyn tightened his grip on the bolter.

His armour registered the passage of an energy wave, its machine-spirit's hackles raised by an interrogative sweep of an auspex. Immediately, the tech-priest stiffened, and the ventral lights on the trans-orbital began flashing as the embarkation ramp began to rise.

Sharrowkyn's muscles were already tensed, ready to explode him into action, when a blur of silver shot down through the fog and enveloped the tech-priest's head like a gleaming metal mask.

Thrashing mechanical wings, razor-edged with flensing blades, sliced flesh and steel with every beat. Garuda's talons were like curved punch-daggers, gouging and tearing at the knot of cables rising from the traitorous Martian's spine. An arcing spray of jet-black fluid squirted down the embarkation ramp as the psyber-eagle's beak ripped out the tech-priest's throat.

The thralls jerked in empathetic shock, their nervous systems intrinsically linked to the physiology of their master.

'Into them!' yelled Sharrowkyn.

Tarsa put a mass-reactive through the head of the nearest thrall, then switched his aim to the second. Sharrowkyn sped forward, bringing his bolter up to his shoulder and firing a pair of expertly aimed shots that detonated the skulls of the next two thralls.

In the face of certain death, the last four thralls threw off the shock-trauma of the tech-priest's pain and turned to run.

Two more bolter shots punched into the closest thralls and burst their unprotected bodies apart from the inside. Sharrowkyn ran for the rising embarkation ramp, his bolter now mag-locked to his thigh and a black-bladed gladius in each hand. He launched himself onto the ramp, rolling and slicing low to hack through the spine of the first thrall before spinning around to hurl his second blade.

It plunged into the back of the last thrall, buried to the hilt between its shoulder blades.

Garuda finished savaging the tech-priest's head, its beak and claws wet with black-red fluids that looked nothing like human blood.

The bird cawed and launched into the air, flying deeper into the trans-orbital.

'Where are you going?' he yelled after it, but the bird, as always, kept its counsel.

Garuda vanished, and Sharrowkyn bent to retrieve his thrown blade. He wiped it clean, looking for the mechanism to reverse the rise of the embarkation ramp as he felt a lurch in his equilibrium that told him the trans-orbital had begun to lift from the ground.

'Damn it, we're taking off.'

A screeching whine of protesting hydraulics made him look back, and he saw Ulrach Branthan holding the ramp in place as the others climbed up.

Tarsa, Numen and Tyro were already aboard, and Branthan grunted as he pulled the ramp down enough for him to step onto it. Surprisingly agile for something so large, he all but vaulted into the trans-orbital as it finally dusted off and the ramp locked into place.

'Move as one,' he said, shucking his arms back to load his underslung storm bolters. 'We take this ship. Fast.'

***

For so valuable a prize, the trans-orbital was sparsely crewed. The warriors of the *Sisypheum* moved through its bare companionways and transits almost without resistance. Thralls and servitors for the most part manned its stations.

The thralls they killed, the servitors they spared – not for mercy's sake, but so they could continue to fly the trans-orbital.

They found the magos assigned to the craft plugged into a console bank like the grand organ of some theatrica hall. He juddered with traceries of lightning coruscating around his body, as though in the grip of a system-wide seizure.

Branthan put him down with a bolt-round through his spinal cord, and the juddering stopped. Ta'lab Vita-37 stepped over the body and wrenched all the magos' mechadendrites and data-spikes from the machine. For good measure, she bent and extended a spike of her own from her wrist and rammed it through the fallen magos' temple.

'He was calling for help,' she said.

'Did he succeed?' asked Branthan.

Tyro swept his gaze over the numerous panels and data-slates embedded in the console.

'I can't say,' he replied. 'But we'll know soon enough if he did.'

The silver case the magos had carried out from the shaft lay next to him, and Ta'lab Vita-37 pulled it close to her, like a mother reunited with her child after a long separation. She slid her still-wet data-spike into a slot at its side, and her entire body language changed.

'It's safe,' she said. 'They got into the vault, but they didn't try to open the Magna Mater itself. They didn't dare.'

Tarsa knelt beside Ta'lab Vita-37, like a knight at the end of his journey before the object of his quest.

'Can… can I see it?' he said. 'We never… never thought it was real. It was a myth to us.'

'That is what we wanted you to think,' said Ta'lab Vita-37, pulling the case away from him in an unconscious act of protection. 'A power that you could never possess needed to be reduced to allegory so you would never seek it.'

'No, I...'

'What is to stop us taking it now?' said Branthan.

'It would do you no good,' said Ta'lab Vita-37. 'It will not open for you. Or me, for that matter. Only the High Matriarch can open it.'

'And the Sons of Horus likely have her,' said Branthan.

'All the more reason to get this away from Luna,' said Tarsa.

'All the more reason to *destroy* it,' said Tyro.

Further discussion was halted as the trans-orbital lurched to the side, and Sharrowkyn felt a ripple of atmospheric change as the lumbering aircraft passed through the integrity field, swiftly followed by the awful sound of steel grinding on rock.

'Something's wrong,' he said. 'We need to get to the bridge.'

Sharrowkyn set off at a run, following the stencilled markings on the wall that led to the bridge. A ship of war would never provide such markers, but this was a vessel designed simply to ferry cargo between a planet's surface and orbiting vessels. It wasn't designed for combat or to be held against a boarding action.

Another impact struck the craft, but Sharrowkyn easily compensated.

The approach to the bridge was a long, narrow passageway, a sole concession to possible defence. Sharrowkyn and Tyro took up positions on either side.

'In all likelihood, the pilots will just be hardwired monotasks,' said Ta'lab Vita-37.

'We can't take that chance,' said Sharrowkyn. 'For all we know, there might be another magos in there, or, worse, a Sons of Horus legionary.'

'Or better, you mean,' said Tyro.

Sharrowkyn grinned. 'Or better.'

'On two,' said Tyro.

'One,' said Sharrowkyn.

'Two,' finished Tyro, and they broke from cover, moving fast, bolters locked on the entrance to the bridge. Branthan filled the corridor behind them, his storm bolters aimed over their heads. The armoured door slid open, and Sharrowkyn's finger tensed on the trigger.

Nothing came out, no storm of solid rounds or flurry of las-fire.

They reached the blast door and swept inside, weapons tracking left and right.

Warning lights flashed and proximity alarms blared angrily.

Jagged bursts of binaric cant spat from a vox-horn dangling from the avionics panel.

'Clear,' said Sharrowkyn, and Tyro echoed that confirmation.

'Throne,' said Tarsa, entering the wide bridge space and seeing what lay within.

As Ta'lab Vita-37 had predicted, the trans-orbital was crewed by a complement of hardwired monotask servitors, hybrids of men and machine who never left their seats and only ever fulfilled one function: piloting the ship up and down, over and over in an endless loop of repetition.

A ship this size had a bridge crew of six, and all of them were dead.

The canopy and instrument panels were crimson and wet with blood spray.

Each pilot's skull had been caved in, the lid of bone peeled back like a ration can in a mess pack and the organ within pulped and pierced. The tops of their heads were sopping red craters, and every lurching shift of the trans-orbital's movement spilled tears of pinkish brain matter down their expressionless faces.

Garuda perched on the back of the lead pilot's grav-seat,

grooming itself. Its wings, beak and claws were wet with blood. Almost no trace of the silver beneath could be seen.

'Throne,' said Tyro. 'What did you do?'

'No time for that now,' said Sharrowkyn urgently.

'What is it?' said Tyro.

'Two things,' said Sharrowkyn. 'One, with the pilots dead, we're going to crash. Two…'

He pointed through the blood-spattered canopy and said, 'Look.'

The *Cthonian Scion* was turning, its black-and-gold prow angling towards the volcano, like a sword being drawn from its scabbard. A bloom of light, tiny at this distance, detached from its launch bay and streaked across the darkness of the Lunar sky.

'Thunderhawk,' said Tyro. 'Sons of Horus.'

'The magos got his warning off,' said Sharrowkyn.

Wayland felt the body of the wounded gunship surround him.

Its pain was his pain, and it burned through his veins. It bled fire along the fibre-bundle cables that connected them, wracking his body with its many hurts. Part of him wished his body was more augmetic, so as to diminish the agony of the experience, but the greater part of him knew that not sharing the machine's suffering would dishonour its sacrifice.

The message from Sharrowkyn had been brief and to the point.

Need immediate extraction. Sons of Horus inbound.

He'd watched the trans-orbital rise from the volcano's caldera, then almost immediately sink back down into the volcano. Something was wrong, and no one was responding over the vox. Wayland had plugged straight back into the Storm Eagle's cogitators.

'I know you are hurting, and I know I ask too much, but I

need you to fly, more than ever. Our brothers are in harm's way and they need us in the air.'

He felt the machine's desire, felt the last of its power push back into the steel of its bones.

'Yes, *yes*! Flesh may fail, but iron endures. The *machine* endures,' he said, knowing the spirit would hear him, if not in words at least in sentiment. 'Where one exists, so too does the other. Where one endures, the other may renew. You are a predator of the iron skies, a hunter of the weak. Your wings are broken, your claws dulled, but you can yet hunt, you can yet kill your enemies.'

His words fanned the fire of the Storm Eagle's soul, a burning coal deep in its heart, but still he wondered whether it would be enough.

Thamatica had worked wonders on the gunship's frame to render it airworthy, but its spirit was all but broken, leaking into the ether with every passing second. Wayland knew machine-spirits, had bonded with them and earned their trust. In the ruins of Eskalor, he had nurtured the fading embers of a wrecked Land Raider, its spirit wounded nigh unto death, and driven it straight through the heart of the enemy lines to ultimate victory.

That spirit had endured, and it had spoken of Wayland as a friend to machines.

'What say you, brother?' asked Wayland. 'One last hunt.'

He felt the Storm Eagle respond, pulsing flows of energy and machine vitality rippling to life around him. Ruptured connections surged with renewed power.

The avionics panel flickered, the gem-lights blinking in sequence.

He eased power through the Storm Eagle's veins, careful not to push too hard, and smiled as the craft lifted from the furrow it had ploughed in the dust. Clouds billowed around it as Wayland teased the gunship back into the air, lifting the nose and pushing power to the engines.

'That's it, brother. One final flight together.'

When it came, the impact was ferocious.

Locked in the death throes of its slain pilots, the trans-orbital fell fifteen hundred metres back down into the volcano, a slow-moving wrecking ball with a mass of over a thousand tons. Dragged down by the internal gravity of the caldera's habitable interior, it rolled with ponderous majesty and slammed against the inside face of the hollowed-out mountain.

Its hull buckled, and thousands of litres of fuel-grade promethium gushed out in viscous sheets that fell like iridescent rainbows. Silver-skinned freight containers spilled from its ruptured cargo bays in their hundreds, tumbling like a rain of coins from a dead man's hand.

The trans-orbital rolled onto its side, its drive unit still firing as it ploughed into the towering silos of ancient atomic waste. Irradiated slag from lethally unsafe power plants and dangerous fissile reactions mushroomed into the air and hung suspended between the competing forces of internal gravity and external weightlessness.

Blazing wreckage peeled from the falling trans-orbital as it tore down through the silos to smash back onto the landing platform. The vessel struck hard, its keel splitting with the force of the impact. Its internal spaces folded inwards like crumpled foil as its enormous mass buckled structural stanchions and drove it into the ground.

The heat from its drive ignited the aerosolised fuel-air mix filling the volcano's interior and transformed its volume into a roiling inferno of atomic flame.

A plume of white-hot fire raced up the throat of the volcano and burst from the caldera.

As though Herodotus Omega were reclaiming the active glories of its past.

9

The Mountain Wakes
Ur-Drakes
They Will Survive

All Sharrowkyn could see was fire.

Orange flames filled the cracked lenses of his helm, and he could feel their heat through rents in his armour. His visor hazed red, crazed with distortion. The internal auspex was sending him a continuous stream of warning clicks, but with the right lens splintered, he couldn't read what it was telling him.

Sharrowkyn pushed himself upright, blinking back the pain from numerous crushed vertebrae and a piercing wound in his side. Blood loss was minimal – his enhanced physiology had seen to that – but his armour could do nothing to keep the pain at bay.

He pushed off, trying to find his bearings.

The vox screeched static. No one was answering.

Red-hued smoke filled the wreckage, and he saw a slumped form crushed against a cogitator panel. Smoke and heat made it impossible to tell who it was. Structural elements strong enough to survive breaking atmosphere and re-entry were bent like stalks of corn by the force of the crash. He lurched over to the body, pushing through ropes of hanging cables and sheets of metal flapping like cloth.

Cadmus Tyro. It was Cadmus Tyro.

Sharrowkyn tried to see exactly how the captain was pinned. To move something wrongly could cause a catastrophic movement of the steelwork and kill Tyro. He was no Techmarine, and found it impossible to tell how the interconnected elements of structure were supported.

Sharrowkyn knew he didn't have time to be careful.

He took his best guess and pushed.

Nothing.

'Out of the way, Sharrowkyn,' said Ulrach Branthan, stepping through the smoke.

Branthan bent his mechanised bulk to the nearest stanchion and braced his shoulder against the metal. Grunting with effort, Branthan pushed, spliced fibre-bundle muscles of a Dreadnought and pure will against the crushing weight pinning Tyro.

The column of steel groaned as it bent upwards.

Only fractionally, but it was enough.

Sharrowkyn dragged Tyro clear, and as soon as the pressure on the captain's chest was eased, Tyro drew in a huge, sucking breath. He got his feet under him and stood, taking Sharrowkyn's outstretched hand.

'Is everyone accounted for?' he asked, his voice little more than a wheeze.

'No,' said Sharrowkyn. 'I haven't seen anyone else.'

The wreckage around them groaned, heavy beams of structural steel twisting like a wet cloth being wrung out. A billowing wall of flame erupted from somewhere below. A booming string of explosions shook the ruins of the trans-orbital.

'We have to get out of here, or we'll be buried alive,' said Sharrowkyn.

A cascade of debris fell all around them as if in confirmation, steel, pipework, cables and burning insulation material.

'The Magna Mater?' asked Tyro.

'Who knows? If someone didn't get it out, then it's gone.'

Branthan led the way, with Sharrowkyn and Tyro following in his wake. They weaved a zigzagging path through the wreckage. Passages that ought to have led to evacuation points were choked with debris or fire, forcing them to double back or push through torn bulkheads in search of a way out.

The insistent clicking in Sharrowkyn's ear kept getting louder, but he couldn't disable it.

Deafening roars of flame and splitting metal filled the crashed trans-orbital, but Sharrowkyn's senses picked out something rhythmic, something *deliberate* that didn't fit the chaotic narrative of the ship's death screams.

'Wait,' he said, halting their progress along a flame-filled companionway.

'Whatever it is, Sharrowkyn, we don't have time to stop,' said Branthan.

Sharrowkyn set off along a buckled transit, the ceiling dripping with globules of ignited fuel like sizzling pearls.

'Come on!' yelled Sharrowkyn as the walls bulged inwards with pressure from above.

The Iron Hands followed him immediately, trusting his survival instincts to find a way out. Now that he knew what he was listening for, Sharrowkyn could easily pick out the hammering sound.

He pushed into a wide gallery that should have been deep in the dorsal section of the ship, but which was now almost open to the outside. Whole decks had been torn away, and Ignatius Numen was busy punching his way through a buckled portion of what was now effectively the outer hull.

His helmet had been smashed and lay in splintered pieces at

his feet, and even had he not been rendered all but deaf, the roar of flames would have covered their approach. Sharrowkyn approached from the side, letting Numen know he was there with plenty of distance. The veteran looked up, startled. He nodded, checking who was with Sharrowkyn.

'Tarsa? The gene-witch?' he asked.

'Unknown,' said Branthan, pushing through the wreckage to add his own fists to Numen's work. Between them, they soon tore the metal hide of the trans-orbital apart, and a wave of furnace heat surged inside. Flames from the wrecked vessel's fuel cells reached hundreds of metres into the air, and billowing clouds of tar-black smoke gathered and seethed like an endless storm.

'Go!' said Branthan, and Numen pushed his way through. Sharrowkyn followed him, then Tyro, and finally Branthan.

Visibility was near zero thanks to the heat and smoke, and even Sharrowkyn struggled to get his bearings. He crouched as low to the ground as he could, scanning for points of reference. Lakes of burning fuel pooled in craters, and a waterfall of flaming promethium spilled into the chasm at the chamber's heart.

The heat in the chamber was becoming intolerable, a bone-deep, searing pain against which his armour was offering no protection. He could feel his normally ashen skin reacting to the temperature. Oily sweat oozed from his pores, to protect him as much as cool him.

Sharrowkyn saw the crates and packing materials they had sheltered behind. Miraculously, they remained unscathed, and behind them, he saw the way back through the mountain to where the Storm Eagle had gone down. Wayland was savvy enough to know that would need to serve as their extraction point, having surely seen the trans-orbital crash.

'There,' he said, springing to his feet. 'That's our way out.'

'What about the Magna Mater?' said Numen. 'Do we have it?'

'Perhaps Ta'lab Vita-37 has it, perhaps not. But if it's still on the ship, it won't last much longer,' said Tyro. '*We* may not have it, but at least the traitors won't either. I call that a win for us.'

'But the others...?' Numen said. 'We can't leave our brother behind.'

'If we go back in there looking for Tarsa, then we all die,' said Sharrowkyn.

'No, there must be a way,' protested Numen.

'Ignatius,' said Tyro, firmly but not unkindly. 'He's gone.'

Ever the pragmatist, Numen nodded, and Sharrowkyn led them through the destruction.

Explosions detonated all around them, and rubble fell from above as weakened structures and rock crashed down. Each breath caught in Sharrowkyn's chest, searing and agonising to take. He felt wet movement in his throat, and knew his lungs and oesophagus were adapting to better filter each inhalation.

But it didn't seem to be helping. He felt his skin burning beneath his armour, and a deadly, caustic lethargy settled within his marrow.

He stumbled, but Tyro caught him. Together they pushed onwards.

Sharrowkyn's vision was swimming, and grey, vein-shot clouds seeped into his eyes. He saw movement ahead, a flash of silver, but couldn't be sure it wasn't some trick of the heat or whatever was affecting his vision.

Tyro dropped to one knee, his chest heaving with effort. Even Branthan struggled in the smoke and heat, the Heart of Iron pulsing in his chest as though in distress.

'What's happening?' said Sharrowkyn, the words slurred and hard to form. 'Fire alone should not affect us this way.'

'It's not just the heat,' said Tyro, hauling him to his feet.

They pressed on, and again, Sharrowkyn saw the gleam of silver ahead. A mummified figure, bandage-wrapped and with her cloak on fire. The gene-witch tore the cloak from her shoulders and beckoned them onwards.

Limping, battered and weary beyond endurance, the four Space Marines slumped into the cover of the materiel crates. The intolerable heat dropped fractionally, and smoke peeled from the crates. This cover wouldn't last for long.

'Do you have it?' asked Ta'lab Vita-37. They all knew what she meant.

Sharrowkyn shook his head. 'No.'

Ta'lab Vita-37's head sank to her chest.

'I failed you, my matriarch,' she said, talking to someone likely already dead.

'Maybe it is better that it burns,' said Sharrowkyn. 'You said yourself the Magna Mater was too dangerous to fall into the wrong hands.'

'Dangerous or not,' she said, 'it was the legacy of the Selenar, and I swore an oath to keep it safe.'

'Better it burns than falls into the hands of traitors,' said Tyro.

'Better it burns than *any* of you claim it,' spat Ta'lab Vita-37. 'Loyalist? Traitor...? Fo was right, you are *all* misbegotten monsters.'

'Throne!' said Ulrach Branthan, pointing back the way they had come.

Sharrowkyn turned, and now understood the source of the insistent, clicking warnings in his ear.

The heat he was feeling wasn't simply from the flames.

All but one of the giant silos of ancient radioactive waste were catastrophically ruptured. Cascades of irradiated dust, disintegrated ferrocrete and spent fuel rods were spilling into the chamber and filling the air with enormous quantities of lethally toxic particles and fumes.

But it wasn't the ruptured silos to which Branthan was pointing.

A lone figure emerged from the flames of the trans-orbital's wreckage.

He waded through the very worst of the radioactive waste, the once jade green of his armour blackened, the metal and ceramite bubbling as it melted.

He swayed with every faltering step, dragging the silver case of the Magna Mater.

His helmet was gone, and even through the haze of fire, his agony was unmistakable.

'Tarsa!' cried Numen.

The pain was unimaginable. It seared down through his armour, past his flesh and into his very spirit. He could see nothing but flames, but fire held no fear for Atesh Tarsa.

He was Nocturne born. A Promethean son, raised in the shadow of Mount Deathfire and forged on its basalt slopes. Every step sent shooting spikes of pain up through his pelvis and into his spine. Tarsa could barely remember why he was here, his mind filled with broken glass and the flesh burning off his bones.

His skin crisped and roasted in the heat, flaking from the thinnest portions of his skull.

One step, then another. Keep going. Head down into the flames.

Fire roared across the red earth, scorching the surface of the mountain. He looked up, seeing the slopes of Mount Deathfire belching smoke and flame. Through all the agony wracking his body, Tarsa smiled. He had long given up any hope of seeing Nocturne again, yet here it was, welcoming him home as a true son of Vulkan.

A burning sun glared down, and Tarsa gasped as he saw the

silhouette of an eagle sweep across it. Its wings were golden in the firelight.

Tarsa had never seen anything quite as beautiful.

A silver case, heavy beyond what its appearance would suggest, dragged behind him, but he no longer knew what it was. All he knew was that it had been entrusted to him, and that he must bear it to safety. But it was too heavy a burden.

Too much for any warrior to bear. Who could ask such a thing of him?

But the duty of every Salamander was to bear the burdens others could not.

To stand where others fell, to march into the fire when others turned their backs.

All sense of the world around him was consumed in fire and smoke.

The darkness of his skin peeled back, flesh flying in the hellstorm surrounding him like cinders stamped from a hearth.

Yet still he marched. Nothing would stop him. Nothing could.

He staggered, a vortex of superheated air threatening to drive him to his knees.

He wouldn't let it.

Another step through the fire that was killing him with every poisoned breath.

Onwards into the flames and searing atomic haze he walked.

The eagle flew with him every step of the way as the sky burned and the ground ran molten. His every step across the mountain's haunches was a homecoming, and he welcomed it, wishing he could have gazed upon the face of his primarch one last time.

His foot slipped, and Tarsa dropped to one knee.

He tried to rise, but the strength had fled his body.

How easy it would be to simply lie down and die.

But that was not the way of the Salamanders. They lived for the fire, relished the challenge of facing it every day. To be burned was to know you were alive.

He heard the eagle's cry, and with a roar of defiance, Tarsa rose to his feet, his body all but flayed alive by the atomic fury raging around him. He took another step.

Two more. He slipped again, and this time there would be no getting up.

But he did not fall.

A giant in burning armour was there to catch him.

'I've got you, brother,' he said.

Tarsa looked up into a face as midnight black as his own, the face of a Salamander.

But no ordinary Salamander. This was the face of a demigod. Haloed by fire and the black slopes of the mountain that forged him, with a smiting hammer in one hand, a blade in the other.

'My lord...' said Tarsa. 'You... *live*!'

'Aye, Tarsa, I live,' said Primarch Vulkan.

'I... saw you,' gasped Tarsa, desperate to pass on these last words. 'On Terra... dead, but I held true. I knew. *Vulkan lives!* I knew you would... never... leave your sons.'

'I leave no one behind,' said Vulkan.

Tarsa nodded and tried to turn, to pass his burden on, but he had no more strength to give.

Vulkan reached over him and hefted the silver case as though it weighed nothing at all.

He was a primarch, after all, one of the Emperor's favoured sons.

'I... tried... my lord,' said Tarsa, the last embers of his soul dimming. 'I tried to prove worthy of you.'

Vulkan nodded and said, 'You asked me once if I trusted you. Do you remember?'

Tarsa could not, but he nodded. Anything for his gene-sire.

'I said, "You come from a land of fire. You lived in the light of burning mountains. Aye, you I trust." Do you remember that?'

A memory surfaced, a brutish giant knee-deep in corpses. But it meant nothing to him now.

He heard the roar of a Firedrake somewhere nearby. A big one, by the sound of it.

'I trust you, Atesh Tarsa,' said Vulkan.

The crimson of Tarsa's eyes dulled like the last light of a cooling forge.

He heard the roaring once more, a swelling chorus of Nocturne's beasts.

And the ur-drakes dwelling in Nocturne's molten heart rose up to bring him home.

Wayland kept the power low, flying a figure-of-eight pattern around the southern flanks of Herodotus Omega. The gunship shook with the violence of the volcano's eruption. The initial firespout had been enormous, a concentrated blast of superheated gas and flame.

He'd pulled the craft away from its slopes, instinctively fearing a devastating pyroclastic rain of debris and rock, but the concentration of the flame and lack of debris told him this was no normal volcanic event.

This fire had all the hallmarks of a cataclysmic crash on a landing platform.

He'd seen the trans-orbital going down, but had hoped whoever was at the helm had skill enough to bring it down safely. The eruption of fire from the caldera had put that hope to the sword and set a cold hand around his heart.

Wayland concentrated on keeping the gunship aloft, while Thamatica scanned the vox-channels in search of transmissions from their brothers.

'Anything?' he asked.

Thamatica shook his head. They could both imagine the devastation that must be filling the volcano. Legion warriors could withstand much, *but this…*?

'They will survive,' said Wayland, as though the power of his words could force the universe to bend to his need. 'They *will* survive.'

'Aye, Sabik,' said Thamatica. 'They will.'

IO

Time to Die
On the Run
Freaks and Monsters

Pride and awe filled Cadmus Tyro as he watched Ignatius Numen carry Atesh Tarsa and the Magna Mater from the atomic firestorm engulfing the trans-orbital. They'd watched the Salamanders warrior fall, and to see their prize within sight but beyond reach was a knife in the heart.

That Tarsa had made it as far as he had was nothing short of a miracle, but Tyro saw that not even Garuda's cawing encouragement would help him reach them.

Ignatius Numen had immediately stepped towards the doomed warrior, throwing off Tyro's grip with an angry growl that was somewhere between grief and anger.

'I have to get him. He is our brother.'

'You'll die,' said Tyro.

Numen shrugged. 'Did any of us think we would live this long anyway?'

Tyro had no answer, and was humbled to witness one of the most selfless acts he had ever seen. He saw Tarsa fall, only to be caught by the Iron Hand. He saw Numen hold Tarsa as he died, honouring his sacrifice with words none of them would know.

And now Ignatius Numen completed the Salamander's journey.

The veteran staggered back out of the growing firestorm, his head seared to the bone by the radioactive fire. He fell to his knees alongside Tyro and Sharrowkyn, finally allowing Tarsa's body to slip from his shoulder and allowing Ta'lab Vita-37 to take the Magna Mater from him. They lowered the veteran to the ground, and Tyro winced to see his wounds. Numen's chest was a ruin of molten metal and blackened flesh, bone and organs gleaming wetly from within.

Garuda swooped down from the storm, its wings trailing smoke and dust.

Its head was bowed. It too knew this was the end.

'Is it safe?' asked Numen.

'Don't speak,' said Tyro. 'Save your strength for the march out of here.'

'Is it safe?' Numen asked again, looking past Tyro to Ta'lab Vita-37.

She looked up from a readout on the front of the silver case and nodded. 'It's safe.'

'Good,' said Numen. 'I think I'll die now.'

Tyro took Numen's arm in the warrior's grip. He wanted to say something meaningful to mark this warrior's heroic sacrifice, to voice his boundless pride and admiration for the veteran's service.

But Ignatius Numen was dead.

'We have to go, Captain Tyro,' said Ta'lab Vita-37. 'The radiation levels are rising.'

Tyro ignored her, holding Numen's fist against the eagle of his plastron.

'I never knew a warrior as strong and fearless as you,' he

said. 'Your trust was not given lightly, but when it was, it was unbreakable. You were a true Iron Ha–'

'Come on!' snapped Ta'lab Vita-37. 'We have not time for dreary sentimentality.'

Anger filled Tyro, and he turned that fury on Ta'lab Vita-37. He surged upright, and his gauntlet closed around the gene-witch's throat. He pulled her around and forced her to her knees beside the burned bodies of Tarsa and Numen. With a fractional increase in pressure, he could crush her neck, and for the briefest instant he *wanted* to.

'These men were heroes,' he roared. 'Look at them!'

Tyro felt a gentle touch on his arm, and turned to see Sharrowkyn.

The Raven Guard shook his head. 'Ease back, captain,' he said.

Tyro's rage was abruptly replaced with a hollow emptiness in his gut he knew all too well. The pain of losing men under his command that never, *ever* got easier.

Tyro released Ta'lab Vita-37 and said, 'These warriors died for what is in that container. They did their duty, and you will honour their memory or I *will* kill you right now.'

Ta'lab Vita-37 nodded, and rose to her feet, rubbing the bruises blossoming on her neck.

'Make no mistake, Cadmus Tyro, I despise your kind and the purpose for which you were created,' she said, 'but I swear I will honour their names. Now we have to go, and we have to go *now*.'

'She's right,' said Ulrach Branthan, looking up into the fire and smoke boiling out through the volcano's summit. A ululating howl echoed from the interior of the caldera, and a blazing jet wash pummelled the ground with a concussive blast of superheated air.

A Thunderhawk gunship plunged through the smoke, executing a textbook assault drop.

The fire had burned its colours down to the bare metal, but the carved wolf's-head panel on the sloped glacis was unmistakable.

'The Sons of Horus,' cried Ta'lab Vita-37. 'They're here.'

The assault doors slammed back on its fuselage, and six hulking figures dropped from the gunship's interior. Armoured entirely in black, and too titanically bulky to be legionaries in Mark IV plate, they landed with the booming slam of metal on metal.

There was only one class of warrior that would dare assault into the heart of an expanding atomic hellstorm.

Terminators.

'Run!' yelled Tyro.

They ran.

There could be no standing against six warriors in Terminator armour.

Each was a walking tank, impregnable to anything except the heaviest weapons and all but unkillable. Three grievously wounded legionaries and a half-mad gene-witch would have no chance at all.

Portions of Tyro's spine had been crushed by the debris in the trans-orbital, and both his lungs had been ruptured. His multi-lung was damaged too, and it was only a matter of time until it collapsed. A looseness in his chest told him the bone shield protecting his internal organs had been shattered. Every breath and footfall sent bolts of fire shooting through his body, and he felt blood pooling within the cavities of his armour.

The darkness of the tunnels carved through the volcano was stark after the searing brightness of the caldera. Grey-walled passages split in a Y, leading back through the abandoned laboratories and deserted research temples.

'Come on,' said Ta'lab Vita-37, taking the leftmost tunnel. 'Back the way we came.'

Sharrowkyn turned as the smoke twitched behind them. Hideous shadows twisted over the bare rock floor, and Sharrowkyn detected an awful, sour-milk taste he had come to recognise as warpcraft.

'Down!' he cried as a hosing blast of storm bolter fire chewed up the rockcrete. The hard bangs of mass-reactives filled the passageway. A devastating impact spun Tyro from his feet, and the heat and fragments of the detonation shredded his cheek and pulped his left eye.

Branthan lifted the gene-witch and dragged her behind him. A pair of mass-reactives punched into his back. Chunks of flesh and bone fragments exploded from Branthan's ribs like shrapnel and sliced Ta'lab Vita-37's arms and legs.

She screamed in pain, and the case containing the Magna Mater fell to the ground.

Sharrowkyn dived to retrieve it as Branthan sank to his knees, two fist-sized craters gouged in his back, exit wounds twice that.

'Ulrach!' cried Tyro, his vision filled with blood as he rolled into the cover of the passageway. Branthan didn't answer, just shook his head and grunted as he pushed himself upright. Again, he dragged the gene-witch behind him, copious volumes of blood pouring from his wounds, too severe for even transhuman physiology to repair. The Heart of Iron emitted a pulsing, emerald glow, pushed to the limits of its Dark Age power in keeping Branthan alive.

'Lead us,' he said to Sharrowkyn between gritted teeth.

The Raven Guard nodded and headed deeper into the mountain.

There was no more gunfire, only the sounds of inhuman laughter following in their wake.

Tyro knew their enemies were toying with them. Terminators were awesomely powerful, and though they were not fast, they were utterly relentless. They knew there was no way their quarry could escape them. Running them down was just a matter of *when*, not *if*.

'You're hurt,' said Branthan, noting Tyro's bloodied face.

'So are you,' replied Tyro. 'More so.'

Sharrowkyn led them into the vast chamber of lined-up gene-pods. The lifter chains rattled from their mounts on the cavern roof and the rumble of ancient, buried machinery gave the air a greasy, electrical tang. The explosion in the caldera had shaken hundreds of the pods from their mounts to shatter on the cavern floor.

Pools of milky, viscous fluids drained through iron grates, and the crackling energies of long-dormant machinery coming to life filled the chamber with traceries of light.

'What's happening here?' said Tyro, struggling to draw breath.

Ta'lab Vita-37 rapped her staff on the ground, and red lights flickered behind her smooth-faced helm. She too was nearing the end of her endurance. Her left arm hung limp at her side, and her right leg was drenched in red from the hip down.

A portion of the floor in the centre of the cavern groaned as shuttered portions began to roll back. Warning lights blinked as a wide platform of dark metal rose from below. Ten gloss-black gene-pods were spaced in a circle around a central cogitator panel. Unlike the others, these offered no window onto what lay within, their surfaces frosted and opaque.

Dragging her bloodied leg behind her, Ta'lab Vita-37 made her way towards the centre of the raised platform and the panel.

'What are these?' said Sharrowkyn.

'I told you that this place produced freaks and monsters, yes?' said Ta'lab Vita-37, extruding a forked data cable from the back of her wrist. One connected to the panel, the other slotted home into her staff. Lights flickered up and down its length.

'You did,' replied Sharrowkyn. 'You also told us you destroyed them all.'

'I lied,' said Ta'lab Vita-37.

Trastevere pushed deeper into the mountain, his storm bolter extended before him. He and his squad of Justaerin could take a city without effort, could storm a fortress and render it rubble in a day. To bring this many warriors to hunt down a few upstart legionaries who had somehow found their way to Luna's surface was overkill of such preposterous scale that he had almost questioned the First Captain's order.

But one look into Ezekyle Abaddon's eyes told him any such question would be the last mistake he ever made. Whatever was at stake here was clearly enough to divert the elite troops of the Sons of Horus.

Their quarry was wounded and at bay. Spilled blood traced a path directly towards them, and – cumbersome as Terminator armour rendered its wearer – there could be no escaping their pursuit. The mountain tremored with the beat of buried machinery, as though it were slowly coming to life after centuries of dormancy.

Trastevere was reminded of his youth in the murder caves of Cthonia. His life then was one of darkness and hearing the ever-present drum beat of mining machinery. Death lurked around every outcropping, and life was held cheaper than a cupped hand of water.

But he was no longer the callow youth who clutched punch-daggers of flinted razor shards and fought with teeth and fury to survive. Now *he* was the stalking death.

'Life signs ahead,' said Vornak, looking up from his auspex.

'Combat spread,' ordered Trastevere, rapping his storm bolter against his chest.

'Seriously?' said Urgave. 'There's only four of them, and they're badly hurt.'

'They're legionaries,' cautioned Trastevere.

'They're rabble,' said Urgave. 'I saw the armour tags. They're scraps from Isstvan V.'

Anger touched Trastevere. 'Then the fact they've survived this long should be a warning not to underestimate them.'

He heard his own words and suddenly believed them.

Perhaps the First Captain had been right to send them in such numbers. Any loyalists that had fought their way from the massacre on the black sands were clearly warriors whose prowess demanded respect.

'Hold,' said Vornak.

'What is it?'

'The life readings.'

'What about them?' demanded Trastevere.

'I'm... not sure,' said Vornak. 'For a second it looked like...'

'Like what?'

'Like there were new signals,' finished Vornak.

'New? There's only four of them,' hissed Urgave. 'We're wasting time. Let's get in there and be done with this. You think Lupercal will wait for us before the assault on Terra begins? Damned if I won't be in the spear tip to the surface of the Throneworld.'

Trastevere pulled the feed from Vornak's auspex onto his visor.

The imagery was confusing, a blurring of swelling signals of disproportionate potency.

He could make no sense of it, but his orders were clear.

Kill the intruders and secure the prize beneath Herodotus Omega.

'We are within a sanctum of the Selenar,' he said. 'It is only to be expected that we will encounter anomalous life signs.'

The matter decided, Trastevere led them onwards, following the traces of their prey: blood, sweat and fear-stink. The darkness beneath the mountain was lit with flickering lumens. Had their prey smashed them, hoping it would slow their pursuers?

The passage opened into an echoing chamber that stank of spilled amniotic fluids and spoiled meat. Upright pods stood in ordered ranks, like sus-an tanks in an apothecarion. Ghostly forms drifted within, strangely shaped and dead.

The ceiling of the chamber was hundreds of metres high, and heavy lifter-rigs on deep rails spanned the space from wall to wall. Hooked chains hung from above, bearing heavy cargo containers that swayed overhead.

His auto-senses detected a rancid smell familiar to every warrior.

Rotten meat, and organs spoiled with decomposition.

Trastevere scanned left and right, his senses alert for movement. Instincts honed over centuries of war told him something was amiss, but he could not make out any distinct signals from their prey.

A low moaning drifted through the chamber. Settling metal or something hostile?

'What was that?' said Vornak.

'Silence,' snapped Trastevere.

They reached the centre of the chamber, where a platform bore ten of the same sus-an tanks standing in ranked-up formation. A cloaked figure lay slumped in a spreading pool of blood, her body resting against a raised cogitator panel. A slow dance of fading light slithered across the blood-spattered face of a gleaming silver helmet.

A gene-witch.

The figure looked up as the Justaerin approached.

'You're too late,' said the gene-witch. 'They're already gone.'

'You're lying,' said Trastevere. 'I can smell them.'

She tried to speak, but her chest hacked a lungful of bilious fluid into her helmet. She reached up and removed it, dropping it to the platform with a heavy clang of metal.

Her revealed face was narrow, angular and androgynous, with skin as pale as the moon itself, her skull shaven and scarred. Her eyes were a shockingly vivid indigo, but Trastevere could see the life fading from them with every slowing heartbeat.

'You have only moments left to you,' said Trastevere.

'I have lived long enough,' she said. 'Long enough to see my sons born and grow.'

Trastevere aimed his weapon at her chest and said, 'What sons? What is in those pods?'

'Nothing,' said the gene-witch with her last breath. 'At least, not any more.'

A screaming howl burst from the left, and Trastevere turned in time to see his rearguard barrelled from his feet by something as hulking as he was. Wet and stinking, its flesh was bloated and ghoul-pallid from long immersion in unknown fluids. It trailed drooling cables from unfinished plug ports in its spine.

It howled in fury, the nightmarish creation of a mad anatomist, a freak of nature that had somehow not spontaneously aborted itself. Even the stuttering light of the chamber and the speed with which it moved couldn't conceal its hideous form.

Swollen, twisted musculature and plastic limbs now fused with vestigial organs and bone-horns growing beyond its flesh. Distended nubs of bone and flopping sheets of unused skin. Gristle and meat formed from aberrant genomes never intended for human flesh-smithing.

And teeth, so many teeth.

It lifted fists like forge hammers and slammed them down

in a two-handed blow that crushed the warrior's helmet and skull to shards.

Mass-reactives punched through its unnatural body, blasting wet chunks of deathly meat from its back and side. Shredded, the thing dropped to its knees, roaring in mindless fury. Trastevere put a bolt through its skull and it fell with a grunt of pain. Still it struggled to rise, and he fired another two shots to make sure.

'Kill it with fire,' he said, and Urgave turned the black-copper nozzles of his heavy flame-unit upon it.

A jet of sun-bright promethium blazed over the thing's body.

The firelight glittered on the predatory eyes of more of the monsters.

They burst from concealment in the tanks around the Justaerin, a pack of ravening beasts with horrifically mutated bodies. All gristle and exposed ribs, the meat of their bodies was punctured with blistered bone-horns and patched with coarse hair like wire. Their multiple eyes were lit with the madness and animal fury of eternal pain. Storm bolters roared and scores of mass-reactives detonated within their attackers' bodies.

The stink of boiled blood and voided intestines filled Trastevere's senses.

'What *are* they?' said Vornak.

Abominations. That was the word that sprang to mind, but Trastevere saw something hideously familiar in their gene-bulked scale and the hints of a hardened carapace beneath the slabs of overgrown muscle and bone, as though one of his kind had been unnaturally packed with growth-enhancers then recklessly stirred in the primordial soup with a random assortment of genetic material.

Typical Selenar.

'They are monsters,' he said, blazing at targets. 'Selenar by-blows.'

Mass-reactives would kill most things thrice over with a single impact, but it took entire magazines of shells to kill these.

Another of the Justaerin was dragged down, his armour torn apart like paper by the immense strength of the Selenar's monsters. Vornak howled in anger as a creature with six brutally strong arms ripped his storm bolter and then his arm from him. He took a quarter-step back and pistoned his remaining fist through the creature's face.

It didn't stop, for it had other faces – one half-submerged in a fold of flesh that was frilled like a lizard's, one with a fang-toothed orifice that served as its mouth.

Another creature had what looked like steel cabling for sinews and the multifaceted eyes of an arachnid. And yet another was so strangely and ethereally beautiful that it reminded Trastevere of the time he had seen the Phoenician fighting on the field of Isstvan.

Vornak fell beneath the pounding fists of the bestial mob. They tore his throat out, and as one lifted its head with a mouthful of bloody meat in its jaws, Trastevere saw an echo that was so dreadfully familiar to him that he actually paused in shock.

Alone among their attackers, it had a face that was entirely human, or, more accurately, entirely transhuman. It had the same wide, gene-bulked cheekbones and high forehead common to most legionaries, but this *thing* echoed the sardonic, hawkish features of Horus Lupercal himself.

Trastevere's anger threatened to overwhelm him, but he was Justaerin and did not succumb to emotion. He detached from the primal urge to strike out in blind fury. He compartmentalised his rage, ready to unleash it upon the loyalist legionaries.

Five of his men were down, the others bloodied but still fighting with rigid discipline.

That was the difference here. *That* would decide this fight.

The monsters had no honed skill, and no discipline.

They did not fight as a unified whole, but as individual monsters. The shock of their assault had been brutal, but only seconds had passed since its beginning.

'Close ranks,' ordered Trastevere.

And now the discipline and training of the Justaerin took its toll on their attackers.

The last of the gunfire died away, and Sharrowkyn knew Ta'lab Vita-37's monsters were all dead. She had promised her ur-legionaries would buy them some time, but Sharrowkyn had seen the Justaerin in action and knew it wouldn't be much.

They'd survived longer than he had expected, but it still wouldn't be enough.

He, Tyro and Branthan were badly wounded, their bodies all but broken and losing lethal volumes of blood inside their war-plate. They were leaving sticky tracks even a blind man could follow. Garuda flew alongside them, its flight erratic thanks to its buckled wings and crash-dented body.

Branthan staggered with every step, one hand pressed to the wall to support him as he moved. The Heart of Iron was keeping him alive through some ancient miracle of technology he didn't understand, but surely even it could not support his existence much longer.

Tyro ran hunched over, the grinding pressure of his broken back doubling him up as his spine tore itself to splinters within its muscled sheath. If he reached beyond the mountain it would be a tale worthy of Medusa's finest, a legend to inspire future generations of Iron Hands, were there going to be any.

His own wounds were minor by comparison, though the pain racing around his body did not match that objective assessment. The crushed vertebrae in his back screamed agony with every running footfall, and the wound in his side kept tearing open. A sensation of emptiness in his chest told him his primary heart had been ruptured and the secondary organ was taking the strain. A legionary's reserve heart was only intended to sustain a wounded warrior for short bursts of time until he could reach the Apothecaries.

It hadn't been designed for extended stresses like this.

He wondered how much longer it could last.

'Did you hear that?' gasped Tyro, falling to his knees with a grunt of pain. 'They'll be coming now.'

'Then get up, damn you,' said Branthan, hauling Tyro to his feet. 'You are an Iron Hand. We don't kneel in the presence of the enemy.'

Tyro bit back a cry of pain and drew a sucking breath.

'Apologies, captain,' he grunted, his fists bunched against the pain. 'Won't happen again.'

'The entrance to the ductway isn't far,' Sharrowkyn told him. Tyro nodded, but said nothing, his every scrap of will focused on simply putting one foot in front of the other.

A booming voice echoed through the underground passageways, full of indignant anger and a hunger for vengeance.

'You cannot run forever,' it said. 'We will catch you, and your deaths will not be as quick as your gene-witch's monsters'. I, Trastevere of the Justaerin, captain of the Eye's Watch, promise you this.'

They pushed onwards, every metre gained a victory, every step that brought them closer to the outside a gift. They could hear the crashing footsteps of the Justaerin behind them, ponderous and inevitable as a coming storm.

Trastevere's taunts followed them, each word promising bloody retribution and pain.

Sharrowkyn believed every word of it.

His spirits soared as he saw the single trapezoidal archway that led to the storage chamber. Irradiated fumes swirled just below the ceiling, the venting system no longer functional nor drawing any of the toxins from within.

'We're here,' said Sharrowkyn, threading the stacks of piled-high construction materiel and broken machinery towards the entrance of the venting network. 'Come on.'

He paused at the entrance to the ductway when he saw that Tyro and Branthan were not following him. One look at how the two captains had positioned themselves told Sharrowkyn what they were planning.

'If you fight they'll kill you,' he said.

Tyro worked the action of his bolter, checking what load he had left. The underslung loaders on Branthan's arms clattered with the last of his shells shucking into the flexmag.

'We cannot outrun them,' said Branthan, staring through the arch. 'So we will *fight* them.'

Sharrowkyn's instinct to strike back at the traitors warred with his urge to escape the mountain. He had no love for Branthan, but counted Tyro as a loyal comrade in arms. They were not friends, but they had shed blood together. Their own and that of traitors.

Branthan read the turbulent struggle of emotions within him.

'We cannot outpace the Sons of Horus, but *you* can,' he said, turning away. 'Go, Raven Guard, get the Magna Mater out of here. Consider this my last command.'

Sharrowkyn hesitated, torn between obeying the order and fighting alongside his brothers.

'Nykona,' said Tyro. 'The mission comes first. It always does. It can be no other way.'

Sharrowkyn snapped the magazine from his bolter. He handed the shells to Tyro.

'Make every shell count, Cadmus,' he said.

II

A Glorious Death
Breaking Free
Alone in the Dark

A curious calm settled over Cadmus Tyro as he thumbed the last of the shells into the magazine of his bolter. He wished he'd had better words to see the Raven Guard warrior on his way, some way to convey the honour it had been to fight alongside him.

Now only he and Branthan remained.

Even Garuda was gone. The bird had perched on Branthan's shoulder and leaned down as if whispering silently in his ear. Branthan had nodded, and the bird had flown off into the ductwork without a backward glance.

'Where is it going?' asked Tyro.

'Wherever it wills,' replied Branthan. 'Enough of Garuda. Look to your weapon.'

Tyro had. Even with Sharrowkyn's ammo, the magazine wasn't full.

'A few bursts and we'll be hand to hand,' he said.

'Against Terminators,' said Branthan.

Tyro looked up, and with a slow nod said, 'Almost seems unfair to them.'

'We will give them a glorious death by which to remember us.'

Tyro said, 'Since the fire and fury of Isstvan V, I have been ready to meet this day. Our escape from the world of the black sands only delayed this death.'

'I died there,' said Branthan. 'Or as near as makes no difference. Every time you brought me back from my frozen stasis, I assumed it would be for the last time. I always knew I would be forced to pay back the debt of life incurred on that day. Now that debt is due.'

'I always expected to die far from Terra's light, on some nameless battlefield at the limits of known space,' said Tyro. 'I would be centuries older, grizzled and with a long history of service to the Imperium. I would have lived a life of honour and few regrets.'

'Before the galaxy went mad, I never considered my own death,' replied Branthan. 'Not even in theoretical dialogues with the Thirteenth. The Apothecaries told me that we were basically immortal, and the remembrancers claimed we were gods. That should have been warning enough, for what story of gods does not end with them cast down and destroyed?'

Tyro didn't answer. He saw the shadows of the approaching Justaerin.

He said, 'Captain Branthan, it has been an honour.'

Three hulking shapes moved into the span of the archway, Terminators in armour of deepest black. Their appearance shocked Tyro, for they were torn up and looked as though they had fought their way from one end of a starship to another. Seldom did any foe give company veterans such a beating.

Branthan seemed to shrug, and his underslung guns chugged out heavy bolt-rounds at subsonic velocities. They struck the lead Terminator, and sparks blazed where they met war-plate. Metal tore and ceramite chips flew like shrapnel.

The warrior staggered and took a step back, but didn't fall. He swung his weapon to bear.

Tyro leaned out from his cover, aimed, and squeezed the trigger. A pair of mass-reactives struck the Terminator's magazine, and the warrior's fist vanished in a blazing shower of secondary detonations. The second Terminator swung his assault cannon towards Tyro, its long rotary barrels already spun up to firing speed.

A blitzing storm of high-velocity shells ripped through the crates and materiel. Tyro dived to the side, shooting as he went. The grinding of shattered bone in his back filled his body with pain, and a grey haze dropped across his eyes. He rolled to his feet in agony and aimed for the cannon's ammo hopper at the weapon's rear. He fired, but his aim was skewed and the shell only creased the box. It ricocheted away, and Tyro gritted his teeth against the pain that bathed his body in fire.

A shell struck him in the chest and exploded against the face of his plastron. It didn't penetrate, but impact trauma drove him back. He staggered and returned fire. Another shell struck him at the junction of thigh and hip, and this one did penetrate.

The explosion blew out the left side of his pelvis, shards of his femur and metal driving up into his gut and groin. Blood filled Tyro's mouth, and he felt entire portions of his internal anatomy come undone. The damage to his organs was catastrophic and utterly non-survivable. Ferocious pain engulfed him, and he fell backwards against a stack of crates, like a king reclining on his throne.

The grey haze over his vision bled into red, and he saw Branthan moving as though in a pict-capture running at half speed, the slides of his bolters racked back empty. His fellow captain's chest was a shattered, chewed-up mess of bloody tunnels carved through his body.

Only the Heart of Iron remained untouched, its silver body pulsing fit to burst.

Branthan ripped the assault cannon from one of the Justaerin and swung it like a club. The heavy breech section caved in the skull of the weapon's bearer. Vast quantities of blood, bone fragments and sopping brain matter sprayed from the ruins of the warrior's helm.

He turned to swing it at the third Terminator, but a shell from a storm bolter ploughed a furrow through the top of his skull. It didn't detonate, but carved a canyon through his forehead. Branthan swayed, but remained upright, his body locked in place.

For the briefest moment, Tyro dared hope he might fight on, as he had many times before.

But one look into Branthan's blood-filled eyes told him he was dead. The Heart of Iron was finally stilled, and a hero of the Iron Hands had passed from this life. Though his body of flesh and blood was no more, the rigid chassis that had once been the sarcophagus of Brother Bombastus still held him upright.

Even in death, Ulrach Branthan did not kneel in the presence of the enemy.

The Sons of Horus turned on Tyro.

He raised his bolter and pulled the trigger one last time.

The weapon clicked empty. Like him, it had nothing left to give.

The Justaerin who had killed Branthan towered over him, a warrior bearing the rank insignia of a captain as well as other markings Tyro didn't recognise, but from which he instinctively recoiled. The Justaerin captain held the assault cannon, his fallen brother's blood and brains still wet on its metal. Surely this was Trastevere.

'Only one more remains,' said the traitor.

Tyro summoned his last breath to spit defiance.

'Only one, yes, but he is Raven Guard,' said Tyro with the last of his strength. 'He has a four-minute head start, which is more than he needs. Sharrowkyn was trained by the Shadow-masters of Lycaeus and knows every secret path from here to the Mare Tranquillitatis. Throne, he knows Luna's craters better than the Selenar! With any luck, he's already halfway to Terra.'

Trastevere laughed, a rank, bitter sound, and said, 'Iron Hands make terrible liars.'

Tyro shook his head. 'And Sons of Horus make terrible legionaries.'

Trastevere raised the assault cannon. 'You have a valediction?'

'I have lived a life of honour and few regrets,' said Tyro. 'Can you say the same?'

The assault cannon roared, and the debt incurred on Isstvan V was finally paid in full.

Sharrowkyn emerged from the volcano to the vox in his helmet screeching with static and Wayland's frantic voice.

'...kyn...spond... If you can...give...posi...'

'Wayland, I'm out,' he said, breathless and in pain. 'I have the Magna Mater and require immediate extraction. Emphasis on the *immediate* part.'

No response, just the hiss of more static. He scanned the inky blackness above him, searching for any sign of the Storm Eagle, but could see nothing. He turned as he heard a clatter of metal, reaching for his bolter before he remembered he had given the last of his ammo to Cadmus Tyro.

Garuda flew out, its dented wings spread. Its flight was erratic. It too was hurt. At first he was pleased to see the bird, but his heart sank at the realisation that its appearance could only mean that Tyro and Branthan were dead.

Sharrowkyn tamped down the grief that threatened to swamp him.

'Wayland? Are you there?'

Still no answer. Were they still at the crash site? Had the damage been too devastating for Wayland and Thamatica to repair? No, he wouldn't believe that. If there had been even the slightest chance of coaxing the gunship into the air, the Iron Fathers would have taken it.

'Throne, Sharrowkyn,' said Wayland. *'We feared the worst. I have you in sight. Coming in behind you.'*

Sharrowkyn turned to see the form of the Storm Eagle coming towards him, little more than a metre of clearance between its wings and the canyon walls. The gunship passed overhead, Wayland keeping its speed low for fear it might break apart. Its engines were screaming and stuttering, and Sharrowkyn saw the full extent of the damage it had suffered in the crash.

'Throne, I can't believe you got it flying again,' he said as the gunship descended and the rear assault ramp lowered. Wayland kept it a metre from the ground, as was standard for a combat extraction, but Sharrowkyn saw he couldn't have landed it safely anyway – the landing skids were smashed.

As soon as the ramp was lowered enough, Sharrowkyn swung the Magna Mater into the hold and climbed aboard himself. Garuda flew into the gunship after him and all but fell to the perforated deck.

Every part of Sharrowkyn's body and soul was hurting, but he pushed himself upright and hammered his palm against the closing mechanism for the ramp.

'I'm in,' he said. 'Get us out of here!'

'What about the others?'

'It's just me,' he said, struggling to contain his emotions.

* * *

Trastevere and Urgave reached the Lunar surface in time to see a Storm Eagle gunship that had no right to be airborne lifting on damaged engines that flared and stuttered with blue fire. Its hull was buckled and torn, but the glittering silver hand on its flank was undimmed.

He saw a warrior in dusty black armour through the assault ramp as it juddered closed.

Trastevere grunted in amusement.

'Halfway to Terra indeed.'

He lifted the assault cannon and squeezed the trigger.

Sharrowkyn felt the shells tear through his chest and back like searing rods of fire.

The force of the impacts spun him around, and he collapsed to the deck of the gunship, vast quantities of blood pouring from his ruptured body. Fiery heat spread from the wounds as his overtaxed physiology struggled to contain the damage.

The Magna Mater's container fell beside him, its surface splashed red.

'Sharrowkyn,' called Wayland from the pilot's compartment. 'What was that?'

He slid down the battered fuselage, struggling to speak as pain coursed around his body.

He tried to detach, to assess the damage and what he could do about it.

Two smoking gouges had shattered his right shoulder, an exit wound like a bowl of blood yawned in the knot of cables at his belly, and there was precious little he could do about either.

'If I had to guess,' he said between sucking gulps of red breath, 'I'd say an assault cannon.'

***

Wayland lifted clear of the canyon walls and rotated the gunship on its axis, aiming it towards the steadily falling debris containing the *Sisypheum*. More impacts struck the hull. Assault cannon fire, if Sharrowkyn was correct. Normally that wouldn't trouble a Storm Eagle, but the hull was compromised in ways too numerous to count.

He pushed the engines out as far as he dared, and the impacts died away.

'We're clear,' he said.

The time for stealth was over, and a journey to the surface that had taken them several hours would take a little over three minutes in reverse. But those three minutes would see them exposed and vulnerable.

All they could do was run.

The gunship raced, low to the ground, over the pale surface of the Oceanus Procellarum, kicking up lingering veils of dust in its wake. Ahead, and closer to the Lunar surface than he'd have liked, Wayland saw the glinting form of the wrecked launch facility in which they'd hidden the *Sisypheum*.

Perhaps two thousand metres and thirty minutes from impacting on the surface.

He angled a correction in their course, risking a little altitude as he struggled to hold the gunship steady. Its damaged control surfaces made flying in anything resembling a straight line difficult.

A screeching wail sounded from the threat panel.

'Missile in the air!' he yelled, wrenching the control column to the side. The gunship rolled on its central axis, and Wayland felt the airframe shudder in protest. Still linked to its wounded machine-spirit, he felt freshly welded seams split along the length of the fuselage.

Thamatica had done as much as he could to get them airborne, but evasive manoeuvres were another thing entirely.

Wayland saw the burning tail of the missile slam into the surface, the slow-moving after-effects of its detonation muffled by the dense Lunar regolith.

'Just one?' hissed Wayland. 'How little you think of us.'

He rolled and banked as much as he dared, trying to get a fix on their attacker.

There! A Thunderhawk gunship, hull scorched and burned from its combat drop into the volcano's fiery caldera. It rolled around, moving into a perfect attack position, above and behind, and Wayland saw long tongues of muzzle flare erupt from its prow cannons.

He pulled up. Too late to avoid the streams of shells.

The Storm Eagle shuddered and lurched sideways with hammering impacts. Wayland grimaced with repercussive pain. He felt the fuselage tear open on the port side.

More stitching blasts of cannon fire punched through the Storm Eagle's dorsal armour, tearing forward as the Thunderhawk strafed them from above. The pilot's canopy shattered and the threat panel exploded as high-calibre shells ripped through it.

Blood of man and machine sprayed the interior of the cockpit.

Wayland gasped in sudden and shocking pain.

'Thamatica!' he yelled. 'Now might be the right time to try that dangerous idea of yours!'

Thamatica barely heard Wayland.

He'd seen Sharrowkyn fall to the deck of the gunship, but had been powerless to help.

His body was locked rigid in a grav-seat, connected via a score of subcutaneous jacks to the interior of the demersal-splicer. Its alien interior was awash with violet light, and the machine-spirits within were not the feral things at the heart of most Imperial machinery: these were systems of cold, calculating malevolence.

He'd linked with it in the hopes of bolstering the machine-spirit of the Storm Eagle, but the spirit in the gunship's soul had rallied at Wayland's imprecations. It had not needed the touch of this pitiless machine of Luna.

But now its unique powers of machine-to-machine communication were in desperate need.

Thamatica could see in realms beyond his normal sight.

As if he were standing within a hyper-detailed noospheric volume, Thamatica saw drifting screeds of light all around him, sig-idents and datableed from a million Selenar machines all across and beneath Luna. He could see them all as bright traceries moving in an exquisite ballet.

'We never knew...' he breathed. 'How different you are...'

He was not welcome within this space, a purveyor of antithetical Martian teachings, a destroyer and enslaver of machines. He felt the tech of Luna grating at his consciousness, looking to eject him from its network, as flesh seeks to expel a foreign body.

No, more like white blood cells looking to overwhelm and destroy an infection.

The only reason he could access this space was because the demersal-splicer had been damaged. Ta'lab Vita-37's staff had broken its ability to defend itself, and that had given Thamatica his way in. The Canticles of Devotion, perfected by the Iron Fathers of Medusa, had it yoked for now, but like a wild grox, it sought to buck him and trample his bones.

It hated him, and he knew it would turn on him the first chance it got.

He felt the gunship scream, and angled spears of light blinked into being as strafing fire punched through the hull.

Thamatica felt the gunship start to pull itself apart as Wayland threw it into ever more desperate manoeuvres to keep them in the air and out of the line of fire. It wouldn't work.

The patched-up Storm Eagle was no match for a fully functional Thunderhawk.

Only a matter of seconds remained to them.

Thamatica drove deep into the mindspace of the splicer, casting his net wide across the local area. It took him barely a fraction of a second to find the bellicose spirit of the Thunderhawk, an interloper just like them.

In the noospheric volume, it was an angry red dart, a bloody knife aimed at their heart.

'You see it?' he said, his words echoing within their shared mindspace.

The splicer growled, a predator on a fraying leash.

It growled in a strange machine cant. Its words were unknown, but the meaning was clear.

First this, then you.

Thamatica turned the splicer loose.

He watched its consciousness unwind like a twisting double helix of data, beautiful in a way the noospheric renditions of Martian code never were. It closed the virtual distance to the Thunderhawk in the blink of an eye and immediately enmeshed itself in the brutal consciousness of its machine-spirit.

Thamatica felt a momentary pang of regret as he watched the icy claws of the splicer tear into the Thunderhawk's spirit, tendrils of its cold consciousness burrowing into every facet of the gunship's being and co-opting them one by one.

The red dart of the Sons of Horus craft wobbled in the air as its pilot fought the rebellion fomenting deep in its systems. Seeing the total devastation being wrought within, Thamatica knew the enemy pilot had no chance whatsoever.

The Thunderhawk abruptly nosed over, rolling and diving straight into the ground.

Thamatica saw the dissolution of its machine-spirit and offered a prayer to the Omnissiah to forgive him for its murder.

The splicer arced away from its kill, and even though he knew it was hopeless, Thamatica fought to disengage himself from the shared mindspace.

It raced towards him, the predator unleashed.

Now you.

Wayland guided the Storm Eagle into the *Sisypheum*'s forward embarkation deck and quickly spooled the engines down. The full weight of the gunship strained its broken frame, and Wayland gritted his teeth as the strike cruiser's gravity pulled it apart.

He tried to rise from the pilot's seat, but his legs wouldn't work.

Only now did Wayland dare to look down.

The strafing shots that had blown out the canopy and smashed the threat board had punched through his lower back and shattered the base of his spinal column. He'd felt the pain, but so mingled were his and the gunship's sensations that he had not been able to differentiate between the two.

He felt a presence at his shoulder, but couldn't turn in the seat.

'Thamatica?'

'No,' wheezed Sharrowkyn through a sucking chest wound. 'He's gone.'

'Gone? How?'

'I don't know,' said Sharrowkyn. 'The machine he's linked to did something to him. Neural feedback or psycho-shock. Whatever it did, he didn't survive it.'

Wayland nodded and said, 'Help me up, my lower half isn't working too well now.'

Though he could barely stand, Sharrowkyn bent to lift him from the pilot's seat. Wayland's body was a dead weight, and he kept his arm wrapped around his friend's shoulders. Together, they struggled back into the troop compartment, where Garuda sat on Thamatica's shoulder. The Iron Father sat rigid in his grav-seat, a pale winter's light seething just below his skin and pulsing beneath his sightless eyes.

Wayland knew instantly what had happened.

'He saved us. He loosed the splicer to bring down the Thunderhawk, knowing it would turn on him.'

Sharrowkyn said nothing, but nodded in respect to the fallen Iron Father as they staggered from the gunship's interior.

'Get me to the bridge and plug me into the command module,' said Wayland. 'We have a little under fifteen minutes before the *Sisypheum* smashes into the surface.'

'And then what?'

'Then we get out of here,' said Wayland. 'And we find somewhere to hide.'

'Where? Amid all this, where?'

Wayland smiled through the pain and said, 'Somewhere lost in the darkness.'

It took them another twelve minutes to reach the bridge in a series of stumbling falls. Garuda flew alongside them, clattering against the ship's internal structure as it flew an irregular, weaving path ahead of them.

At a lateral transit, they requisitioned a maintenance servitor to help carry Wayland, and Sharrowkyn was able to concentrate on not passing out. Both warriors were at the end of their endurance, and by the time Sharrowkyn and the servitor hoisted Wayland into the pilot's command throne, he was breathless with exertion and blood loss.

Under Wayland's instructions, he plugged the Iron Father into the navigation cogitator and fired up the preset launch protocols. Knowing their escape might need to be executed at a moment's notice, Wayland had left the reactor ticking over and slaved the drive activations to an embedded macro he could control without the need of a bridge crew.

Within moments, the *Sisypheum* had cast off its tethers and mag-clamps and was under thrust. Sharrowkyn watched through the viewing bay as the remains of the launch facility tumbled away. His eyelids were getting heavy, and when he looked up again, it had slammed down into the pale dust at the edge of the Mare Cognitum.

How long had he been unconscious?

Gradually, the curve of the moon fell away, and the spectral glow of its surface was replaced with the inky blackness of space. Far above, mighty warships flew in diamond shoals, each a gleaming cathedral that could destroy them with ease.

Sharrowkyn's breathing slowed, and he rested his palm on the surface of the Magna Mater's case. His blood was still sticky, and he hoped that whatever lay within was worth the lives that had been lost to secure it. He felt his grip on consciousness fading.

Beside him, Garuda cawed as it stretched out one of its wings. As Sharrowkyn watched, the metal seemed to unfold and undo a measure of its damage, as though the bird were somehow repairing itself.

'You couldn't teach me the trick of that, could you?' he asked.

The bird cocked its head to the side as if deciding whether or not to answer.

Sharrowkyn put thoughts of the bird from his mind and looked back at Wayland. For a moment, he thought his friend was dead, but then saw the darting movements beneath his eyelids. He was one with the ship, conjoined with its soul and linked to its every system. The *Sisypheum*'s wounds were great, and where before Wayland had borne and healed its hurts, now it carried his.

Sharrowkyn blinked as a sound intruded on his fugue state.

Proximity alarms.

A fresh pane had opened in the viewing bay, and Sharrowkyn saw a knife-blade vessel of black and gold lifting from below like a deep-ocean predator rising to feed.

'The *Cthonian Scion*,' he said, turning to Wayland, but if the Iron Father heard him, he gave no sign. The Sons of Horus destroyer flew on a direct vector towards them, clearly aware of exactly where they were.

Downing a pursuing Thunderhawk was one thing, but a Space Marine destroyer...?

Blossoms of fire winked to life at the vessel's prow.

'Torpedoes in the void,' said Wayland tonelessly. 'Impact in eighty-five seconds.'

Sharrowkyn watched the approaching ship-killers, knowing there was absolutely nothing they could do to evade them. The *Sisypheum* was too badly damaged for evasive manoeuvres, and even with Wayland's control macros in place, it simply wasn't possible to fight a void engagement without a crew.

'Sixty seconds,' said Wayland, his voice sounding distant and lost. A chrono-timer spiralled downwards in the corner of the viewing bay, marking the last moments of their lives.

The proximity alarms were shrieking louder than before, as if warning them they were about to slam into a mountain.

Sharrowkyn pushed himself upright with a grunt of pain. The effort was almost too much for him, but he was damned if he would meet his death on his backside.

'Forty seconds.'

A shadow fell across the viewing bay and, for a brief moment, Sharrowkyn wondered if this was some reaction of the *Sisypheum* to its imminent destruction, dimming its sight to spare them witnessing their death.

Then he saw it was no act of mercy on behalf of the strike

cruiser, and nor were the proximity alarms in response to the approach of the *Cthonian Scion*.

The shadow became the ornamented ventral plates of a titanic warship, its gilded surface and vast sheets of armour clearly visible in exquisite detail. Its hull was golden and cerulean, with towering vanes jutting from its kilometres-long length. Its gravity wake shook the *Sisypheum* with its nearness, and every time Sharrowkyn thought the vessel was soon to finish passing over them, yet more crenellated elements of structure were revealed, each enamelled and patterned with swirling geometric patterns and heraldry of arcane symbolism.

'That's no ship of the line,' said Wayland, his eyes fluttering open in awe. 'That's a Gloriana...'

Yet more of the ship hove into view, and Sharrowkyn saw markings emblazoned on the forest of silver towers that trailed strange etheric energies. At the centre of the argent spines at its rear sat a vast crystalline pyramid, a sanctum and command bridge all in one.

'That's the *Photep*,' said Wayland. 'That's the flagship of the Crimson King.'

Its size was impossible to comprehend, so huge it defied the idea that it had been wrought by mortal hands and not willed into being by some inhuman deity. Sharrowkyn felt cold fire settle in his belly at the sight of the vast capital ship.

A memory surfaced. Wounded and alone on Eirene Septimus, facing Alpharius himself. The primarch of the Alpha Legion could have killed him without breaking sweat, but he had spared him. He had addressed Sharrowkyn by name, as if they were old friends instead of mortal enemies.

Sharrowkyn remembered the words that had passed between them as if they were carved into the forefront of his brain.

'You're not going to fight me?'

'As much as I want to, I'm not going to kill you, Nykona. At least, not today,' said Alpharius. 'Magnus asked me not to.'

When Cadmus Tyro had asked what that meant, Sharrowkyn had dismissed the primarch's words as manipulation and lies, but now here was the flagship of Magnus the Cyclops interposing itself between the *Sisypheum* and a killing barrage of torpedoes.

The countdown on the viewscreen blinked at zero.

But for the Crimson King sailing his vessel between the *Sisypheum* and the torpedoes, they would already be dead.

'Why?' he demanded of the glittering pyramid at the heart of the *Photep*. '*Why?*'

No answer was forthcoming, and a strange lethargy drew itself about Sharrowkyn as his body's healing mechanisms dragged him down into darkness.

He dreamed of glittering caves, a great golden light and an army of newborn giants who marched from that light into a war that never ended.

Sharrowkyn woke with Wayland's hand upon his shoulder. A moment of weightlessness filled him as he drifted up from his dreams of light and shadow. A fleeting moment before the bone-deep agonies of his wounds returned.

He groaned in pain and remembrance.

'We're here,' said Wayland. 'It's time to go.'

Pain and disorientation slowed Sharrowkyn's thought processes as he rose from the embrace of the sus-an membrane. He swallowed away a dryness in his throat and wiped the back of his red-stained hand across his eyes.

'Go? Go where? How long was I out?'

'Ten days,' said Wayland. 'The return journey took a little longer than our descent.'

Confusion was making it hard for Sharrowkyn to understand Wayland's words.

'Journey? Wayland, where are we?'

'I don't think it has a name,' said Wayland, and Sharrowkyn looked over at the viewing bay, seeing the black, slab-like form of the coaling station where they had repaired the *Sisypheum* prior to making their descent to Luna.

'You have to go,' said Wayland, and Sharrowkyn nodded, still not fully understanding the context of his friend's words.

'I don't think I can carry you,' said Sharrowkyn.

'That's all right, my friend,' said Wayland. 'You don't have to.'

'What do you mean?'

'I mean that you have to go on without me. This is the end of our path together.'

'No, I'll get that servitor,' protested Sharrowkyn, but he could see it was hopeless.

Wayland's body was past the point where any Apothecary could restore him or tech-priest rebuild him. His gaunt and ravaged features told a story of the internal anatomical cannibalism that had been required just to keep him alive this long.

'You need to take the Magna Mater off the *Sisypheum*,' said Wayland. 'The duty of Ta'lab Vita-37 now falls to you.'

'I can't,' said Sharrowkyn.

'You *must*,' said Wayland, and the desperation in his voice was taking the last of his strength to impart. 'Despite the intervention of the *Photep*, we did not leave the Solar System without hunters on our heels. I have evaded them for now, but they are almost upon us, and they must not find you and the Magna Mater aboard.'

'Where will you go?'

The Iron Father smiled, and a flash of the old Wayland was restored.

'The *Sisypheum* and I will lead them a merry dance way out beyond the Halo Stars, into the trans-galactic wastes,' said

Wayland with a hoarse chuckle. 'By the time they catch us, I'll be long dead and they will never find you.'

Sharrowkyn shook his head. 'No, let me carry you. Set the ship on its course and be done with it.'

'She won't make it far enough without a pilot at the helm,' said Wayland. 'It has to be this way. Now go, my friend.'

Sharrowkyn saw the determination in his friend's face, and knew he would not be dissuaded from this course. Besides, he was right.

With a heavy heart, Sharrowkyn lifted the Magna Mater and backed away from the command console.

'It was an honour to know you, Sabik Wayland,' he said.

'The honour was mine,' replied Wayland.

The nameless coaling station was just as dark as Sharrowkyn remembered it.

The *Sisypheum* and Wayland were long gone, sailing into the darkness between the stars.

Sharrowkyn was used to working in solitude, had *embraced* it, actively rejecting the company of others, but now, alone at the edge of wilderness space, he suddenly craved the company of his brothers.

He wasn't entirely alone. Garuda accompanied him, flying overhead in the wide open spaces of the coaling station. The bird looked new, like the first time Sharrowkyn had seen it, its wings resplendent and its feathers as crisply wrought as if fresh from the artisan's bench.

His transhuman physiology could sustain him in a form of hibernation for centuries, but he suspected whatever span he might reach here would be much reduced. The scabbed floors and scraps of atmosphere that clung to the walls of the cavernous chambers still reeked of unrefined promethium.

The black welcomed Sharrowkyn. It folded around him like an old friend welcoming a fellow traveller in darkness.

Sharrowkyn knew exactly where he would wait out the ages to come.

He and Garuda followed a path he had walked many times while the Iron Hands repaired the *Sisypheum*. It led unerringly to a chamber near the heart of the coaling station, its walls engraved with the names of beloved vessels and fallen shipmates.

He saw now that he had underestimated the sheer number of etchings.

Hundreds of thousands of names and deeds.

Men and women whose names had been forgotten, heroes all.

Their courage had gone unrecorded, save for these walls.

Their stories had never been told.

Sharrowkyn slumped with his back to the wall, his breathing slowing and his heart rate dropping as the mechanisms of the sus-an membrane tugged at his consciousness again.

No. Not yet. He still had work to do before then.

How best should a warrior die?

Sharrowkyn had given much thought to this over the years.

His neophyte thoughts of war-torn battlefields and glory were the dreams of folly.

This was as fitting a resting place for a warrior of the Raven Guard as he could imagine.

He drew his gladius and swept his fingertips over the wall, feeling the roughness where knives and chisels had scored it.

Finally he found a place to make his mark.

Sharrowkyn cut with swift, economical strokes, carving the names of the warriors who had crewed the *Sisypheum* next to the long-dead pioneers of the Imperium.

He cut his own name last, and with his task complete, set down his blade.

His body was ruined, unable to heal while he still drew waking breath.

Centuries might pass before he woke, if he woke at all, and the thought did not trouble him overmuch. He hoped some stranger in a far-distant age might find their names and wonder who they were, what kind of men they had been, and through that connection be joined to the deeds of those who had gone before.

Sharrowkyn rested his hand on the Magna Mater as Garuda flew down to settle upon his shoulder. He barely felt its weight. Its claws dug into the ceramite of his armour, and he doubted he could prise it loose even if he wanted to.

The bird lifted its head and spread its wings wide.

It froze in place, a silent watcher and sentinel all in one.

His eyes drifted downwards, and Sharrowkyn wished he knew the name of this place. It felt wrong to let the darkness claim him without knowing where he lay.

As if in answer to that thought, his drifting gaze found a carving made in the lee of the archway leading into the chamber. Half obscured by striated oil patterns and creeping rust, but still legible.

A nameplate, perhaps from a lost starship or a forgotten battle.

Sharrowkyn supposed it didn't matter.

It would serve.

Sangprimus Portum.

FURY OF MAGNUS

DRAMATIS PERSONAE

The XV Legion 'Thousand Sons'

Magnus the Red	'The Crimson King', Primarch of the XV Legion
Ahzek Ahriman	Chief Librarian
Amon	Equerry to the Primarch
Menkaura	Adept of the Corvidae
Atrahasis	Equerry to Ahriman

The VI Legion 'Space Wolves'

Bödvar Bjarki	Rune Priest of Tra
Svafnir Rackwulf	Woe-maker of Tra
Olgyr Widdowsyn	Shield Bearer

The XVIII Legion 'Salamanders'

Vulkan	'The Lord of Drakes', Primarch of the XVIII Legion
Atok Abidemi	Draaksward
Barek Zytos	Draaksward
Igen Gargo	Draaksward

The IV Legion 'Iron Warriors'

Perturabo	'The Lord of Iron', Primarch of the IV Legion

Imperial Personae

Malcador the Sigillite	Regent of the Imperium
Alivia Sureka	Perpetual
Promeus	Wyrd-wraith

'War is father and king of all. It proves some to be gods, and others merely human.'

– The Weeping Philosopher

'Cannon crashes eastward: magnificent, terrible thunder. Bright flash, night bordered, a surging mass explodes in storms of iron. Pageants of fire again, again. In savage awe, we celebrate the festival of death.'

– Pyotr Nash (First Lieutenant, 77th Europa Max)

'History is trying to tell the truth through the most acceptable lie.'

– Hari Harr, Imperial interrogator

BOOK ONE

SANCTUM IMPERIALIS

ONE

Time of Trial

The day was dark with the smoke of a burning world.

His armour's chrono indicated it was morning, but all divisions of time were virtually meaningless now. Day, night, morning, evening… they all blended into one span of flickering, hellish light that painted everything in the colours of a banked hearth-forge.

The distant glow of molten rock backlit misbegotten giants lumbering on the horizon, and plumes of fire from ruptured bedrock flickered low to the ground as boiling clouds of searing ash drifted over shattered ruins.

The Time of Trial was an extinction-level event on Nocturne, a time of fire and endings during which its Promethean moon would pass so close it would all but tear the planet apart. Clashing gravitational forces reached deeps into Nocturne's bedrock to wake the world-serpents coiled around its molten heart. Stirred from their deep slumbers, the ur-drakes roared and raged, shaking the world above with the fury of their fractured dreams.

Their terrible heat surged forth in the lava of a thousand volcanic eruptions that blotted out the sun. The movement of their titanic limbs shook the world with cataclysmic earthquakes that reshaped Nocturne's continents, and their breath sent boiling tsunamis to smash its coasts. And in the aftermath of their ferocious waking, a terrible winter fell upon the land as they returned to their slumbers and their searing fury subsided.

In such times, life beyond the protected walls of Nocturne's Sanctuary Cities became all but impossible. The plains camps, mountain holdfasts and coastal settlements emptied as Nocturne's people sought their fragile safety. Their gates would be flung open, and any who requested shelter would be offered a place within.

Atok Abidemi had seen only one Time of Trial before he had been chosen to join the ranks of the XVIII Legion, the Salamanders. He had been a boy, no more than four Terran-standard, but vividly remembered the sky afire with lightning as it raged with the warring of gods and the wrath of the world-serpents. Even as a child, he had seen meaning in the play of flames in the sky, fated significance in each peal of thunder and crash of volcanic fury.

Fleeing the approaching pyro-storms, his parents had abandoned their nomadic life on the T'harken Delta and sought refuge within the walls of Skarokk, the city of the Dragonspine. All Abidemi had known was a life on the plains, hunting the leo'nid with his father and grandfather, so when the gates of the Sanctuary City closed behind him, Abidemi felt the terrible claustrophobia of being trapped in a place from which there could be no escape.

That same sensation held his heart in a cold grip again.

Yet this was not the Dragonspine and he was not on Nocturne.

This was Terra.

But it *was* a Time of Trial.

'Stand to!'

The cry went up along the wall, all but drowned out by Indomitor's blaring klaxons.

Another alert, but it wasn't for them, not yet.

Abidemi flexed his fingers on the grip of *Draukoros*. Longer than a standard chainblade, the weapon was toothed with the ebon fangs of the great drake of Nocturne whose name it now bore. Once, it had belonged to Artellus Numeon, but with his disappearance upon Mount Deathfire, the honour of its use passed to Abidemi.

The shadow cast by its former bearer was long, and both Abidemi and the blade understood he was only its custodian. The blade would *always* be Numeon's, and it was Abidemi's fervent hope that one day he would return it to their fiery home world.

That hope was fading with every passing day, and as the discordant clamour of war pulled him back to the present, the tragedy engulfing Terra swelled around him.

White ash fell like snow. The sky burned with fiery colours, and the relentless drumbeat of war buckled the air with a continual rumble of explosions and big guns that would never tire.

He and his two Salamanders brothers were stationed on the Indomitor Wall, the towering north-eastern bulwark of the Sanctum Imperialis, the very heartland of the Emperor's Palace. It resembled nothing so much as a vast cliff carved into the bones of the mountains, twelve hundred metres tall, with an inner mustering ground behind the shielded and reinforced ramparts of its outer wall, which stepped down to layered outworks before diminishing to the ruined edges of the western Katabatic Plain.

Its outer faces were reinforced with steel and stone, its once glorious bas-reliefs peeled away at Lord Dorn's decree.

Its functionality was brutally simple, the newly raised drum towers, turrets and enfilading gun-boxes turning the fifteen kilometre strip of smouldering ruins beyond into a killing ground of almost perfect proportions.

In any conventional engagement, it would be a nigh-impregnable barrier, but the war the traitors had brought to Terra was anything but conventional.

Braying war-horns and screams issued from the host currently attacking the wall. Six times they had come at its defenders in the last two days, and six times they had been thrown back. Their thwarted howls were those of beasts, and to Abidemi's ears they sounded like a barbarian horde from an earlier epoch.

Smoke and a seething orange glow limned Indomitor's broken-toothed defences on this seventh attack, where fifty thousand soldiers fought the blood-maddened host. Explosions and plumes of blue-green fire rippled up from the base of the wall far below. Percussive blasts rocked the walls, chewing the rockcrete in fiery bites with every impact.

Shell blasts swept the parapet in storms of shrapnel, gunfire plucked troops from the firing step in droves, and the screams of the wounded were drowned out by the hammer blows of heavy artillery. Frag shells burst overhead, shredding flesh and stone, splintering the walls. The air was thick and toxic with a mixture of fyceline, propellant and promethium fumes.

Blasts from the autocannon turrets and the artillery mounted on the battered slopes of the Hegemon behind them answered the roar from beyond the wall.

But it would make little difference, the enemy host was seemingly without number.

This portion of the wall was designated Indomitor Three.

As much a name for us as it is the wall, thought Abidemi. *Perhaps if–*

A blackened smiter's gauntlet clapped him on the shoulder guard and a voice with the sharp accent of a Sanctuary City-dweller said, 'Focus, brother.'

Abidemi nodded, lifting his head from his contemplation to regard his battle-brother.

Barek Zytos was a solid mountain of dark skin and battered warplate that had somehow retained its dark green lustre, even amid the constant ash falls and tarry smoke banks drifting from the burning ruins of the Anterior Barbican and the smashed Brahmaputra Wall.

Abidemi and Zytos stood with Indomitor Three's reserve force, ten thousand soldiers and twelve ad hoc squadrons from a score of different regiments. This deep into the fighting, hundreds of Terra's regiments had been effectively wiped out and their scattered survivors quickly organised into scratch battalions with no names save any they gave themselves.

In honour of the Salamanders in their midst, these soldiers had named themselves *Vulkan's Own*. Normally such presumption on the part of mortals would have angered Abidemi, but in this place, at this time, he understood the honour these brave men and women did them. Once, their uniforms had been different in design and colour, but weeks of fighting in the mud and gore of Terra had rendered them all the same grey-brown and painted their exhausted faces with ash and grief.

They watched the fighting at the ramparts with a mixture of anger and horror, fearful of the slaughter being unleashed, yet eager to advance and push the enemy from the walls.

Abidemi understood that feeling all too well.

It railed against his warrior soul to stand and watch brother soldiers of the Imperium dying, but he and his brothers' strength was best spent when it would have the greatest impact.

Sensing his dark mood, Zytos nodded to the bloodshed on the wall.

'This is a bad one,' he said. 'Yes, a bad one indeed.'

Abidemi grunted. 'Has there ever been a *good* assault?'

'You know what I mean,' said Zytos, interlacing his fingers on the drake-skull pommel of his mighty thunder hammer. The weapon's killing head sat between his feet, engraved with scenes from the forge, its haft a length of unbending adamantium. 'The man who always looks to the sky does not see the drake at his feet.'

'And the man who looks to the ground does not see the winged dactyl,' finished Abidemi.

'Brother, are you here?' asked Barek. '*Really* here? Since Vulkan passed into the Palace your mind has wandered too often of late.'

'Apologies, brother,' said Abidemi, shaking his head. 'We sacrificed so much to bring the primarch to Terra… I feel lost without his presence.'

'He *is* here,' said Zytos. 'Doing his duty to the Emperor. As we must.'

'You're right,' said Abidemi. 'But this war saps my soul as much as it tests my body.'

Zytos rapped his knuckles on the pommel of his hammer and said, 'Concerns of the spirit must be put aside until after the fighting's done.'

'You're wrong,' said Abidemi. 'We must win both together or else we lose everything.'

'I'll put my faith in this,' said Zytos, swinging the hammer up from the ground and hefting its immense weight as easily as a mortal man might swing a walking cane.

Barek Zytos had ever been the most direct of his brothers, as was only to be expected of a man born to the city of warrior kings. The drakes cut into the onyx skin of his skull were markers of the beasts he had hunted on the Arridian Plain, and his words provided a much needed anchor for Abidemi.

'And though he's young, I put faith in *him*,' continued Zytos, nodding to where Igen Gargo stood scanning the ramparts atop the turret of a rust-brown Shadowsword. Above him, the unending barrage of shells and lasers flared and burst against the aegis shield: relentless impacts from orbit and plunging fire from distant batteries. The swirling patterns rippled like the violent borealis of the Time of Trial.

The colours reminded Abidemi of looking deep into the fires of a forge ready to receive metal. It was said a master smiter could look into a furnace and know the exact moment to thrust the iron into its heat, when to turn, and when to withdraw it just by listening to its song.

Zytos had led them back to Terra, but of the three of them, Igen Gargo was the master of reading the fire's song.

Gargo scanned the fighting, ready to call out any weakness or predict a rout. The burnished metal of his augmetic arms reflected the light of explosions, and fire danced in the red lenses of his battle helm.

Abidemi followed his gaze, but it was impossible to guess where one part of the line would bend or break. Lightning-shot smoke all but obscured the fighting, and the sounds of clashing metal and gunfire was much the same at one point as it was at another. Vast shapes reared up, bloated silhouettes and angular snapshots of unnatural creatures the enemy had pressed into its ranks.

Zytos lifted his helm and snapped it into place with a hiss of pressurised air.

'Here,' said Zytos, turning to retrieve a pair of battered breacher shields from the ground behind him and handing one to Abidemi. 'It's not Promethean craft, but it'll do.'

Abidemi nodded, scabbarding *Draukoros* and clamping the shield tight to his arm.

The yellow-gold metal was thick and dented, the ebon fist at its centre chipped and silvered by a hundred or more impacts. It felt unnatural to bear wargear marked with the heraldry of a Legion not his own, but these were desperate times and the shields had not failed them yet.

'It'll be soon,' said Zytos, looking back towards Gargo.

Abidemi snapped his own helmet on and engaged the gorget seals. Even insulated from the atmosphere, the air tasted of ash and burnt iron. His visor lit up with targeting information, damage assessments and energy-depletion warnings.

'How can you tell?' he answered.

'I can't read the fire as well as Gargo, but I can read him,' said Zytos.

'Stand to!' yelled Gargo.

'Told you,' said Zytos as the vehicles around them roared to life, reactors powering up and drive mechanisms shrieking like the magma vents of the Pyre Desert. Blue fumes belched from exhaust grilles, and commanders unfurled pennants of dead regiments upon their antennae.

'Watch the right,' ordered Gargo, pointing a silvered arm towards the wall.

Abidemi scanned the fighting.

'What does he see?'

'I don't–'

A thunderclap of shield failure was swiftly followed by a titanic blast that shook the staging area with the force of an orbital strike. Colossal blocks of stone lofted skyward as something exploded just below the level of the rampart Gargo had indicated. Abidemi couldn't see what had caused it, but a hundred-metre portion of the wall simply vanished in a blinding sheet of fire. The ringing echoes of its detonation were deafening, even within his helmet, and his auto-senses dimmed to shield his eyes against the incandescent brightness of the explosion.

It seemed the battle paused for breath, as though death were admiring its handiwork.

Gargo leapt from the Shadowsword's turret as a ululating roar swept up the molten remains of the wall. He too hefted a breacher shield and ran to join his brothers at the centre of the line.

'Into the breach?' asked Gargo.

'Once more,' agreed Zytos.

He lifted his hammer high and raised his voice beyond the tumult.

'Indomitor! *Into them!*'

With Abidemi, Gargo and Zytos forming the tip of a charging wedge, the reserves of *Vulkan's Own* advanced into the fire and smoke. Abidemi saw the half-molten shape of a siege belfry, monstrous shapes surging from its buckled assault gates: *migou* giants in heavy suits of heat-resistant plate and iron helms beaten into the forms of daemons. Each was a hulking abhuman carrying a belt-fed chain gun and with a drum-like ammo hopper bolted to its spine. Roaring with idiot hatred, they braced themselves and unleashed the full fury of their weapons.

Two-metre tongues of fire blazed from their flared muzzles. Hundreds of men went down in the first volley of scything, high-calibre shells. Indomitor's advance faltered, but pushed on into the storm of fire and steel.

'Into the fires of battle!' yelled Gargo.

'Unto the anvil of war!' answered Abidemi and Zytos.

Abidemi felt dozens of bludgeoning impacts on his shield, each one striking with the force of a forge-servitor swinging a sledgehammer. He gritted his teeth, locking his arm at ninety degrees as he slotted his bolter into the shield's firing notch.

More of the migou gunners were mounting the walls, unleashing fresh torrents of fire into the flanks of the defenders.

Clawed ladders and piston-driven grapnels bit stone. A tide

of degenerates swarmed behind them, scrambling for a foothold on the walls. Little more than a howling mob wielding crudely stamped weapons and mass-produced guns, but there were so many. So very many.

Prioritise. *Execute.*

'Take out those gunners!' Abidemi shouted.

Hammering impacts buckled the curved plates of his shield, the power of the shells making Abidemi feel like he was advancing into the teeth of a pyro-storm. He lined up a shot and fired his bolter, the hard bang swallowed in the thunder of gunfire. One of the abhuman gunners fell back, its chest blown open. He fired again, and another dropped to its knees with half its torso ripped away. A third migou vanished in a pyre of streaking rounds as a mass-reactive detonated inside its ammo hopper.

Abidemi's visor pinged each of the migou in turn. Pull the trigger: an enemy dead.

Single shots only. Not enough ammunition for any wasted shells!

Another target lit up, limned by his visor. Another round, another dead.

Then he was in amongst them. He clamped his bolter to his thigh and swept *Draukoros* from its sheath.

'Numeon!' he roared, hammering the foe with his shield and reaping a bloody harvest with every butcher's cleave of his sword.

His weapon was an extension of his arm, and he tore apart heavy plate and pallid flesh with every strike. The blade's shrieking teeth chewed through the armoured migou with all the hunger of a Nocturnean drake, devouring steel and flesh and bone with every ripping roar.

The enemy matched his bulk. Abidemi couldn't just smash them aside with his own mass. He kept moving, giving the migou no time to bracket him nor give his mortal enemies a chance to pin him in place with their numbers.

His shield was a bludgeon, pistoned forward to make space.

Breathe and swing. *Hack and cut.*

Each migou was a powerful foe, but they were *slow*. He slammed the hard edge of the shield into their faces. Ram the sword up and under their plates, twist, withdraw. Turn and move, do it again.

The slaughter was machine-like.

Repetition made it instinctual and unthinking.

Abidemi felt the presence of his brothers. Their grunts and oaths over the vox were wordless, but he understood every one. Zytos swung his hammer with a forging cadence as Gargo spun and lunged with his spear, scything and impaling men like wriggling fish.

The men and women of *Vulkan's Own* fought with rifle, pistol and bayonet; with iron bars or whatever else came to hand. The fighters were woven together so densely it was all but impossible to tell friend from foe. Men clawed at their enemies, bloodied fingers tearing off masks and thumbs gouging eyes.

This was not the war the remembrancers had spoken of in the earliest days of the crusade.

War, when it had come at all back then, had been filled with glory and heroics fit for song. Not this frenzied brawling in the mud of the Throneworld, scraping for a rusted blade to open a throat, or a chunk of fused masonry to bash in a skull. *This* was the true face of war: a desperate fight for survival; a scrambling, maddened horror in which only the insane survived.

All else was but a soldier's lie.

Abidemi slammed three men from the walls, their broken-limbed bodies spinning over the rampart to fall two hundred metres to the ruins below.

He let out a shuddering breath.

Remember to breathe! Take in oxygen. Turn and fight!

He'd fought to the very crest of the breach, where the vast

detonation had broken the rampart. The full horror of the broken landscape before Indomitor was revealed, and the shocking sight of the enemy was like plunging into an ice bath after a hard march over the Pyre Desert.

Abidemi had heard the estimates of the enemy's order of battle, the impossible numbers thrown around by Lord Dorn's strategos. He'd seen the vast shadows cast by the drop-ships blotting out the sky over Lion's Gate space port, and had fought this war long enough to know just how many of his fellow Imperials had cast off their oaths of loyalty.

But each time he saw the unending horde ranged against them, it broke his heart anew.

The force attacking Indomitor spread like an undulant sea beneath a choking layer of petrochemical smog. To Abidemi's eyes, it was like a host of pack predators swarming a leviathan at bay. Larger, battle-bred creatures moved among them: hideous by-blows of the fallen Mechanicum that walked on stilt-legs and loosed violent squalls of corrupt binharic hate, and things that might once have been living, but were now armoured, chimeric monsters transformed by warp-spawned rituals.

Far to the south, the air rippled around the immense form of Titans as they strode from the Anterior Barbican to pummel the strongholds protecting the Eternity Gate. Heedless of the life-and-death struggles at their feet, the god-machines howled their fury from war-horns at their shoulders, but even those sounds were overwhelmed by the rolling thunder of explosions and shellfire.

A series of seismic detonations smashed into the slope below, pulling him back to the present as a killing rain of debris hammered down. More of the mortals swarmed the breach below him. They fired their weapons into the air, hooting like maddened beasts. Huge stalk-tanks bristling with spikes and heavy ordnance stomped among them. Through the twitching smoke, Abidemi thought he saw the red-and-gold heraldry of swift-striding leviathans.

Too small to be Titans, even predatory Warhounds. Knights...?

He knew he was exposed here, backlit by the smoke and flames swirling around him, but didn't care. He *wanted* them to see him, to know the Emperor's warriors were not afraid of them, that the traitors would pay dearly for every step inwards they took.

This was an enemy driven by a hate Abidemi simply could not fathom.

A rippling string of ignitions bloomed in the smoke below, and the red-gold shapes strode from the fog banks in their wake. Low to the ground they came, heedless of the mortals they crushed beneath their splay-clawed feet: three giant bipedal forms with vast glaives and weapons mounted beneath wide pauldrons of bloody crimson and gold.

'Morbidia,' hissed Abidemi, recognising the spiked-helm sigil on the fire-blackened banner rising over the lead Knight's skull-faced cockpit.

A crackling voice blared a warning in his helmet vox. *Gargo.*

'Incoming!'

Abidemi looked up in time to see a salvo of Ironstorm missiles flashing downwards.

He closed his eyes.

'The man who looks to the ground does not see the winged dactyl...'

TWO

Survivors

The Field of Winged Victory.

That was what they called this place, a vast marshalling ground older than Bhab, a place that had been here in the days before Unification, before even the Palace itself.

Alivia Sureka remembered watching the first starships to leave Terra from terrain now occupied by the nearby towers of the Clanium Library, back when the marshalling ground's name had seemed fitting.

It had been a name to inspire greatness, to dream beyond humanity's birthrock and seize the manifest destiny of the species.

Now it felt like a grotesque joke.

Back then, a hundred thousand soldiers left Terra every day from here. Close to ten times that number now filled the open esplanade, but they weren't going anywhere: a living ocean of human misery. Numb with fear and daily atrocities, they huddled in makeshift refugee camps and shanties wedged between the Indomitor Wall and the canyon-precincts of the Hegemon. And this was but one of scores of such places jammed in wherever non-combatants could be accommodated.

High above the grand domes of Imperial bureaucracy, the sky bled its horror in purple bruises of light on the shield overhead. The air buckled with shock pulses from the constant ordnance barrages bursting against it.

Some of the plaza's earliest occupants had considered themselves the privileged few for having been granted access to the inner precincts of the Palace, but the inexorable pressure of the Outer Palace's systematic destruction had forced Terra's grandees to admit everyone.

Who was it that gave the order to open the gates?

Alivia doubted it had been Dorn.

Nor, she suspected, would it have been Valdor: the First of the Ten Thousand would have baulked at the notion of so many unknown souls this close to the Emperor.

The Sigillite then? The Master of Mankind had His gaze fixed on loftier outcomes than the survival of Terra's populace, but the Regent of Terra's voice bore the Emperor's authority.

So, yes, it would likely have been Malcador, which only went to prove that you could know someone for an eternity and still be surprised.

Alivia scanned the sea of faces around her, exhausted families aged by grief and coated in a fine layer of ash that fell like snow. No matter the money, position or power they had in the time before the Warmaster had invested Terra, they were all alike in fear. These were the survivors of Lion's Gate, the ruination of Angevin, or the Dusk Wall's breach, the razing of Magnifican. They had fled burning camps on the Gangetic Way, the Palatine's collapse or the loss of Dhwalagiri. Filthy, frightened and stained with mud, they watched and prayed for the fighting to end, but most could care little for whoever stood triumphant at its end.

The sound of prayers, despair and tears was a constant refrain.

This is the sound of the end of the world: men weeping as their doom approaches.

Alivia tried to keep her own anguish at bay, but she had heard enough horror stories to last all her many lifetimes: dead loved ones, grievously wounded partners, sons and daughters fighting on the walls, and – worst of all – tales of parents whose grip had slipped, and who now frantically scoured the camps in search of their lost children.

Alivia remembered the sense of relief that had filled her at their arrival on Terra. The journey from Molech had been long and hard, but when she'd breathed the ferrous air of the home world, it felt like she'd managed to outpace the war at their heels.

A fantasy, of course. It was inevitable Horus Lupercal would eventually lay siege to his father's Palace, but the sight of what Rogal Dorn had wrought gave her hope it would be enough to stop the arch-traitor in his tracks. She'd believed they would be safe in Lion's Gate space port, the Starspear's incomprehensible bulk dwarfing the mountains from which the Palace had been carved. Its towering immensity was awash with weapons, plated from surface to space in fortifications, and manned by the gilded host of Lord Dorn himself.

Surely such an invincible fortress could never fall?

But fall it had. The enemy had driven a wedge into its heart and split it from its uppermost platforms to its deepest underways. The bridges linking its gantries to the Eternity Wall were still burning, its spires aflame beyond thick black clouds.

She'd heard tales of red-spined *things* hunting across those bridges, of people dragged down into impossible shadows. Alivia had seen a man and woman running for the safety of the bridge gates plucked from the ground by invisible hands and torn limb from limb, the aerosolising mist of their blood limning the frenzied outlines of claw-armed monsters.

Laughter had chased them from Lion's Gate, malicious gales of throaty amusement that weren't loud enough to overcome the deafening crescendo of battle, but somehow resonated within the vault of every mortal skull.

When she closed her eyes she could still hear that laughter, buzzing like a furious insect trapped in a glass. It had been days since she'd slept, but the bone-deep tiredness was better than the alternative. Her dreams were plagued with dark visions: nightmares of snakes, a lightless cavern far beneath the world and a doorway to somewhere endless and terrible.

The horrors of war broke many a soldier, even those who came through the fighting with their limbs and bodies intact. The psychic wounds of battle and the anguish of seeing fellow soldiers die or suffer horrific injuries was enough to sunder even the strongest mind beyond the power of any medicae to heal.

Alivia saw those self-same wounds on the faces of everyone she passed.

No matter who claimed the throne of Terra, they would inherit a populace as traumatised as any of the soldiers who had fought for it.

Alivia passed a group of kneeling men and women, grimy with mud and dust. Heads bowed, they prayed, mouthing words with hymnal cadence. A man with weeping chem-blisters covering his face and neck spoke words handwritten on a twine-bound sheaf of papers. He looked up at her passing and she winced to see that one of his eyes was a ruined, empty socket set in a molten mass of blackened tissue. The whiteness of bone gleamed through his cheek.

'Pray with us, sister,' he said, the words mangled by his wounds.

'No,' she said, turning away. 'I won't.'

'Please, the Emperor needs all our love and devotion to defeat this foe.'

Alivia snorted. 'If He needs *my* love then we're in even more trouble than I thought.'

She pressed on, easing through the crowds of terror-numbed people, heading towards the muster column at the centre of the plaza as the man called after her.

'There is only the Emperor, and He is our shield and protector!'

Alivia shook her head. Since setting foot on Terra she had felt nothing of the Emperor's presence. Even she had to acknowledge how strange that was. Even on Molech, there'd been a sliver of His presence, a ghost of His power borne on that damn light of His, but here in the heart of His domain… nothing.

Did that mean anything? Probably not, but still…

'Alivia!' called Jeph, and she looked up to see him and the girls exactly where she'd left them at the base of the column with their meagre possessions. She was struck again at how *thin* he'd become. Working at Molech's starport had kept Jeph fit and given him some decent upper body strength, but the months of privation aboard *Molech's Enlightenment* had taken its toll, and the thin food-pastes spooned out in the feeding tents were almost valueless in terms of nourishment.

'What was that about?' he asked, looking back over her shoulder.

'Nothing,' she said. 'Just another of those damn prayer groups.'

'Lectitio Divinitatus?'

'Don't call it that,' she said. 'It's just desperate people looking for answers where they won't get any. It's just blind faith.'

'Maybe so, Liv, but could be that's better than hopelessness.'

She wanted to rebuke him for so naive a belief, but she suspected he was right. Besides, no one seemed to care any more about such theistic beliefs, so long as they weren't too overt.

Alivia supposed that, amid all this suffering, where any lifeline – no matter how flawed she believed it to be – could be the difference between survival or giving up, faith would have to be enough. She just hoped it would wither on the vine after this was all over.

Alivia leaned in to give him a kiss and bent down to her girls.

Miska was asleep, curled up on a thin blanket and sucking her thumb like she'd done when she was a baby. Tiredness and hunger had hardened her once cherub-like features, and her shaven head only emphasised how gaunt she'd become. With every step deeper into the Palace they'd taken, Miska had spoken less and less. Day by day, Alivia's mischief maker was fading away, and she felt tears threaten to spill down her cheeks.

She rubbed the heels of her palms against her eyes then ran her hands over the stubbled skin of her own head. She missed her hair, but the itching had been too irritating. A plague of lice had spread through the refugee camps, and so she'd taken a razor to her hair and that of her family. Jeph hadn't minded so much, he was thinning on top anyway, but the girls had protested loudly until Alivia had shown them the wriggling eggs on each other's scalp.

Vivyen looked up from the chapbook that never left her side and gave her a wan smile.

Like her sister, she too was suffering, her features raw with a fever that left her sweating in the cold nights and freezing during the days, no matter how they tried to warm her.

'Did you get them?' she asked.

'I'm so sorry, my love,' said Alivia. 'I couldn't. There's none to be had.'

The fever had struck on the retreat from Lion's Gate, and the thin air of the mountains, the cold and the lack of food was exacting a fearsome toll on her daughter.

Alivia had tried to get counterbiotics from a twitch-faced man who sold pilfered medicae supplies, a man she suspected had stripped his uniform to hide in the civilian populace. He hadn't wanted to part with his pills for what she had to offer, and no amount of psychic effort had convinced him to lower his price.

John had always been the best at reaching into another's mind and bending them to his will, but she wasn't without some skill in that arena. Since arriving on Terra, though, she'd found her ability to *push* a person to her way of thinking had all but vanished.

'Don't worry, I'll be okay,' Vivyen said, turning back to the book.

Dust had all but obscured the image on its cover, and Alivia remembered how vivid it had been on the day she'd slipped into the Odense Domkirke to steal it. The stories it contained were fairy tales, but that term was misleading. Each was a parable that spoke to the heart, stories that depicted the vast and complex tapestries of humanity in all their glorious and terrible forms. And like all stories, they had power.

A power Alivia didn't fully understand, but which had saved her life and her daughter's more than once. Those stories had kept Vivyen alive as a prisoner of a warp cult aboard *Molech's Enlightenment*, and they had offered up direction when Alivia had needed it most.

In that respect, was it so different from the *Lectitio Divinitatus*?

'What story are you reading?' she asked.

'The Nightingale.'

Alivia bit her lip. 'That's a good one.'

Vivyen coughed and said, 'I wish *our* Emperor had a nightingale.'

'Maybe He does,' said Alivia as she saw a man in a dress-black uniform and damask cloak coming towards her through the crowds of refugees. She recognised him immediately.

He came to attention before her, ramrod straight and with his hands laced behind his back.

'Khalid Hassan,' she said. 'I should have known you'd be back.'

'Did you ever doubt it?' he asked, his voice as tired as hers.

Malcador's man had summoned her to his master's side even before she'd stepped from *Molech's Enlightenment*'s embarkation ramp, but had left without her. Even as she rebuffed the Sigillite's summons, Alivia had known he would come again.

'You're looking tired,' said Alivia.

'This war taxes us all,' he replied.

'Hey,' said Jeph. 'She told you to get lost already. She's not going with you.'

Hassan ignored him and said, 'It's time to come in from the cold, Mistress Sureka.'

Alivia looked down at her girls, tired and hungry, thin and fevered.

She nodded slowly and said, 'They come with me. *All* of them.'

'Of course. The Sigillite offers you and your family sanctuary within the Bhab Bastion.'

'Then, okay,' said Alivia. 'It's time for this nightingale to come home.'

Pyroclastic clouds of fire stretched from horizon to horizon.

The taste of ash and iron filled his throat.

The pain was like stabbing obsidian blades paring the flesh from his bones, like magma straight from the heart of Nocturne filling his marrow. It troubled him not, for he was a Son of Vulkan; he was born to endure pain.

Abidemi beheld the end of days wrought in volcanic eruptions and seismic fury. Nocturne was tearing itself apart in wracking spasms of catastrophic eruptions. Fire filled his vision and steam scoured his lungs to mulch as distant oceans boiled to vapour.

Even the towering permanence of Mount Deathfire split apart in this final apocalypse, its flanks rupturing as something deep within surged and raged in deathless fury.

Abidemi stood alone as his world came undone, its imperishable bedrock crumbling to ash and its molten heart exploding as the ur-drakes rose to destroy the realm of man. Searing sheets of lava spurted skyward from yawning fissures that pulled wider with every breath. Boiling clouds of superheated smoke rolled across the heavens, where forks of lightning powerful enough to obliterate warships clashed.

He felt no fear, for the Salamanders had no eschatological mythology, but rather a belief in the eternal circle of fire that spoke of life arising from even the most terrible catastrophes. To the tribes of Nocturne every worthy act of creation was born of destruction – from the creation of the stars themselves to the crafting of a mighty blade.

The basalt cliffs of Mount Deathfire finally came apart, exploding in a cataclysmic avalanche of rock and magma as two colossal shapes were birthed from its fiery annihilation. Twisting shadows of draconic fury moved within the molten rock, inhumanly vast and monstrous. Abidemi gasped as red-lit veils of lava fell in a burning rain that turned the earth to liquid fire.

Two ur-drakes roared as they fought, titanic beasts beyond any human comprehension of scale, so vast that Abidemi's gaze could not encompass the entirety of their cosmic nature.

One was scaled all in deepest green and onyx, with claws of fire and eyes like burning red coals. The other glowed with the dull light of cooling magma and Abidemi saw that one of its eyes was naught but an empty socket, like a crater gouged in the surface of a moon.

They tore at one another with jaws that could sunder continents, and raked armoured flesh with talons to shatter mountains. Their blood was the coursing power of the planet, and with each ferocious blow, the beating heart at the centre of the world slowed and cooled, even as the world above burned.

The crimson ur-drake snapped its jaws shut on the throat of its drakescale-green opponent, tearing away armoured hide and furnace blood. The wounded ur-drake drove its claws of fire into the belly of its rival, scoring deep gouges in its flesh. Horns gored and tails lashed as the mighty serpents of legend fought, but already Abidemi could see that the green serpent was losing.

Its gaze was fixed on the far horizon, and in a contest between such beings, even the tiniest moment of inattention was fatal. The crimson ur-drake bore the green-and-black drake to the ground, and the planet shook with the force of their impact.

Abidemi fell to his knees and wept as the crimson drake snapped and tore at the other.

He despaired to see the green drake laid low, knowing with every fibre of his being that it was vital it not die, that he owed everything to it. He reached for *Draukoros* and as he drew the blade of Artellus Numeon, two burning figures appeared at his side. One bore a golden spear of caged lightning, the other a hammer of thunder, and he knew them as his brothers.

Abidemi lifted *Draukoros* high, the fires of battle reflecting from its ebon teeth.

'Father!' he cried. 'Your Promethean sons are with you!'

He charged towards the duelling world-serpents.

And his brothers in fire followed.

Then light, blinding and stabbing into his eyes like bright needles.

His vision of Nocturne's ending faded as the terrible reality of Terra's plight pressed in again. He felt the weight of his transhuman body compacted within the unyielding grasp of his warplate. Making sense of what he was seeing was proving difficult: both of his helm's eye-lenses were cracked, and fizzing static overlaid his sight with ghost images he couldn't quite make out.

Blood filled his mouth. His skin was sticky with it.

'Barek!' shouted a gruff voice he knew he should recognise. 'I have him. He's alive!'

Abidemi spat a mouthful of dust and ash, blinking to clear his eyes.

He saw Igen Gargo silhouetted against a shifting pattern of colours. It took Abidemi a moment to realise he was looking up through several tonnes of smashed debris pressing down on him, and that the borealis above his brother was the underside of the aegis shield.

The pressure on him shifted as Gargo dug him from the rubble, the power of his augmetic arms hauling broken slabs of rockcrete and steel from his pinned body as though he were tearing flakboard from a wall.

'Get me out of here,' said Abidemi, flexing his shoulders. The rock groaned around him.

'Hold still, Atok,' warned Gargo. 'That rocket strike brought half the damn breach down on you.'

'I… I thought I was dead,' he replied.

Barek Zytos appeared next to Gargo, his onyx skin pale with ash.

'It'll take more than half of Indomitor coming down to kill Atok Abidemi,' he declared.

'Not *much* more,' muttered Gargo.

Abidemi's arm came loose, and with both his brothers working to free him, enough of the rubble was removed for him to pull himself clear. The green of his armour was grey with rock dust, the metal and ceramite buckled and torn, yet mostly intact.

He climbed to his feet, and blinked in the pale light. Thick fog freighted with a strangely familiar taste shrouded the blasted edge of Indomitor. It obscured the dolorous sound of the enemy camps beyond the walls, muffling the chants of the lost and the damned and making the war seem far away.

'Morbidia?' said Abidemi. 'I saw Knights...'

'Shadowswords and *Vulkan's Own* saw them off,' said Gargo.

'Them and a Knight Castellan from House Cadmus,' added Zytos.

Abidemi nodded, taking a deep breath and finally recognising the familiar taste of the surrounding fog. It was faintly sulphurous and bore the earthy aroma of deep rock and raw metal.

...like the breath of a wounded drake with scale-green hide...

Abidemi felt a fist clench in his gut.

A terrible fear that the enemy beyond Indomitor was not the one they ought to be facing.

'Brothers,' he said, 'Vulkan needs us.'

THREE

Small Perturbations

It wasn't supposed to be this way...

Magnus paced the interior of his pavilion, a high-ceilinged war tent floored in overlapping rugs, the patterns of which formed an interlocking series of spirals and geometric designs. The pavilion's silken fabric pulsed in time with the primarch's furious heartbeat, and with every rustle of fabric, tendrils of low-lying fumes and the distant crump of explosions crept in.

A crazed looking glass set in a frame of plain gallowswood stood in a far corner of the pavilion. Restored from broken pieces like diamond daggers, it threw out jagged reflections of the three warriors gathered around the primarch's expansive map table.

All were Corvidae: Ahriman; Menkaura; Amon. Crimson armour gleamed and their cloaks of stars were untroubled by the mud and ash of this world.

Loyal warriors all, and each a traitor too in his own way.

They felt the anger radiating from Magnus in palpable waves.

They fear my retribution, that I blame them for the failure at Colossi.

The pavilion's walls were hung with brass-framed images of manuscripts Magnus had recreated from memory after the destruction of Tizca's libraries: Shakespire's greatest soliloquies; the last, stubbornly resistant page of the Voynich Manuscript; and his favourite couplets taken from the works of Khut-Nah, Laban and Eltdown.

Every item within the pavilion was vibrating at a pitch just below its shattering point.

'Colossi should have fallen,' stated Ahriman, wary of his gene-sire's fury.

'Yes,' sighed Magnus. ***'It should have.'***

'The Corvidae *saw* it,' added Amon, rallying to his Fellowship brother's aid. 'We all saw the wall aflame and the great gateway reduced to molten slag. Ignis himself declared the numbers auspicious and the result a virtual certainty.'

Little affection remained between Magnus' equerry and his Chief Librarian, so Amon coming to Ahriman's aid was testament to how unexpected was this moment in time. Since Ahriman's return with Magnus' scattered soul-shards, his star had risen among the Legion, something of which Amon had whispered darkly in the prophetic scriptures he kept secret from his brothers.

'The fault is not yours alone,' said Magnus, struggling to leash his anger. ***'I too walked the future echo of Colossi's doom. I too watched the Pale King's warriors of dusk pour inside. I believed we had achieved what was necessary. And yet it* held. *The Khan and Valdor fought us to a bloody standstill!'***

The primarch jabbed a red finger onto the unrolled sheet of wax paper spread upon the circular map table. A vast swathe of the Himalazia region was rendered in exquisite beauty and vivid colours. At its centre was the hand-drawn outline of the Emperor's Palace: a vast agglomeration of enormous man-made structures that formed an urbanised continent spread across the mighty peaks of this ancient land. Squirming formulae of incalculable complexity were etched on the chart, distilled to their deepest truths by the Legion's magi.

Magnus tapped a detailed representation of the smashed Colossi Gate, its towers toppled and its walls broken. Red-gold flames of fresh ink seemed to shimmer on the paper.

Contrary to the broken icon and against all predictions, Colossi had *held*.

Neither Perturabo nor Mortarion were aware of Magnus' designs, but even the newly elevated Plague Lord sensed that success at the Colossi Gate had held greater significance to his brother beyond the obvious tactical value.

How had it held?

Magnus had no satisfactory answer to that.

'Colossi's fall was to herald the crack in the telaethesic ward of the Sanctum Imperialis,' said Magnus. ***'The Red Angel rages at its edge and Mortarion curses that he cannot cross its threshold. While it remains intact, the warp-taken can go no farther.'***

'And you, my lord?' said Ahriman. 'Is the threshold barred to you also?'

'I am a numinous being of light,' said Magnus. ***'My subtle body is a weaving of broken flesh and splintered soul, but it is not yet fully given over to immaterial powers. If Colossi had fallen, yes, I could have stormed the heart of the Palace, but while it stands...'***

'It should have fallen,' said Amon.

'It was *seen*,' said Ahriman.

'It was seen,' agreed Menkaura.

Alone of the three Corvidae warriors, he kept his eyeless face obscured, enclosed within a featureless silver helm of an archaic armour mark. His aura spoke of hidden things, but

Magnus cared nothing for whatever petty betrayals or schemes he had worked since Prospero's fall.

The primarch swept his finger into the Palace as the image of Colossi restored itself on the map, its towers rebuilding and its gate reforming from molten shards to once again become a hardened strongpoint. He spiralled his finger anticlockwise, moving gradually inwards.

'Khat Mandau Precinct, the Bhab Bastion, the Hall of Leng…'

Here, he lingered a beat, before moving on.

'…the Investiary, the Dome of Illumination, the Hegemon, the Clanium Library.'

His finger finally stopped.

'The Throne Room,' said Magnus. ***'The Warmaster's final objective.'***

They all heard the emphasis he placed on *Warmaster*.

'But never ours,' said Ahriman.

'But never ours,' confirmed Magnus. ***'Of all the prizes to be taken on Terra, of supreme importance to me is the subterranean arcology where lies the last shard of my soul.'***

A coiling red light lifted from the paper, like a splintered sliver of glass shorn from a larger whole. Magnus was reminded of his earliest explorations of Prospero, and the tall statue of a great bird left on a clifftop path above a long-dead city.

Its fall and shattering into multicoloured fragments of glass had revealed to him the secret workings of the Primordial Creator and taught him the mechanics of what would later become the Fellowships of the Thousand Sons.

'All broken things will break to their own form and purpose,' said Magnus. ***'My soul, the Imperium, even this war of Horus Lupercal's. So, understand this, my sons, what my father holds captive beneath His Palace is not simply*** **part** ***of me, it is the*** **best** ***of me.'***

'We will not fail you again,' stated Amon, beating a hand to his breast.

Magnus nodded, clenching his fist as he felt a tremor begin at the tips of his fingers.

He turned away from his sons and said, *'Amon, Menkaura, return to your warriors and form mandala circles around the pavilion. Ahriman, remain with me. We will fly the Great Ocean, you and I.'*

'Sire, is that wise?' asked Ahriman. 'The tides of the Great Ocean are turbulent beyond anything we have known. The Neverborn surge and rage at the veil. Let slip, they care not if what they kill is friend or foe.'

'We must,' said Magnus. *'Guilliman and the Lion draw closer every day, and still the Palace stands. If there is a way inside to be found, only* I *can find it, no matter what Perturabo thinks. Now do as I command.'*

Amon and Menkaura saluted and left the pavilion, and with their departure Magnus let out a shuddering breath that was not breath and felt the quickening of a heart that was not a heart.

He clutched the edge of the map table as a spasm of pain passed through him.

'Sire, what is it?' asked Ahriman.

Magnus held up a hand and said, *'My father wrought this body with ancient science, forgotten alchemies and a pact even He could not entirely fathom, but I am no longer sure what I became after the Wolf King shattered my soul.'*

'You are Magnus the Red, the Crimson King,' said Ahriman.

'Once perhaps, but without the last part of my soul I am something more... and also something less.'

Magnus turned from the map table and stood before the broken looking glass.

'Ten million shards of glass and tears...' said Magnus.

'Sire?'

'I smashed this on Prospero when I destroyed my chambers

in a fit of rage. You remember? Just after I soared to Terra on warp-spawned wings, thinking to warn my father of the Warmaster's betrayal.'

'I remember,' said Ahriman. 'It was the beginning of the end for us.'

Magnus shook his head. *'No, our ending began long before that,'* he said sadly.

He reached out and ran a red finger along the cracks in the glass.

'I always used to mock Angron for his loss of control, his bestial rages. I believed him to be weak, but when I saw what I had done, I knew I was no better than him. I thought so much of myself, that I was infallible, that I knew better than everyone else.'

'Then why do you keep it, my lord?' asked Ahriman.

'I like to think that each shard displays a facet of my inner self,' he said. *'Some I know all too well, while others are reflections of unfamiliar faces. Some are noble, some are wondrous, others miraculous. And, forgive me, but many are dark and terrible.'*

His trailing finger reached the centre of the looking glass, where a single, teardrop-shaped shard of glass was missing from the frame.

'But always at the heart of the image is this... **emptiness.'**

Magnus stared at the looking glass, and his splintered reflection stared back at him.

Tall he was, even among his brother primarchs, red-fleshed and corded with muscle.

Red hair billowed around his face like a lion's mane, held in place by a gold-and-ivory circlet helm. His armour was bronze with a horned breastplate, rippling with a promethium sheen of colours as if freshly forged. Long pteruges of the finest boiled leather hung to his knees, their length set with golden studs and carved with esoteric scripture.

His solitary eye was a shimmer of endlessly varied colours

without name and set in skin the colour of molten copper. Magnus reached up to touch the crumpled skin covering where his other eye ought to be.

'With the merest thought, I can reshape my appearance, becoming godlike or mundane, beauteous or monstrous but **this...** ***this I will not change.'***

He lifted his hand from his face and opened his fingers.

The tremoring was getting worse.

If Ahriman saw it, he said nothing.

'Join me, my son,' said Magnus, moving to the centre of the pavilion and sitting cross-legged on the rugs at the confluence of their interlocking spirals. Ahriman took position opposite him, and already Magnus could feel the power of his sons flowing towards them as they formed mandala circles.

'You're right, Ahzek, it **is** ***supremely dangerous to fly the Great Ocean just now,'*** said Magnus. ***'But I am running out of time.'***

He looked skyward as power flowed into him.

'We all are.'

Magnus lifted from his physical self with an ease denied his sons.

His flesh was already transforming from material to immaterial. Unlike Ahriman, he needed no enumerations to pick the lock on the chains that fettered spirit to flesh. The sense of liberation was intoxicating, like bearing an invisible burden on a mountain climb and then casting it off at the summit to take flight.

The earth fell away from him as his subtle body soared free. Ahriman's followed behind him, a spiralling comet of ivory fire. Freed from his flesh, Magnus was a being of pure energy, a being of divine origin unbound by the limitations of flesh. Neither hunger nor thirst troubled him, nor did the boundaries of space and time constrain him overmuch.

To a being such as Magnus, all time and space were his to explore.

They will be…

Magnus knew well the whispers of the warp, but even he could not say for sure whether that was some Neverborn temptation or his own vaunting ambition.

He rose up, borne by thundering updraughts of psychic energy.

Normally, flight through the Great Ocean was made in stillness and tranquillity, but the war beneath them was bleeding violent storms of emotions into the aether. Psychic hurricanes were raging all across the globe, amplified by the madness, anger and horror this war had unleashed. Infernal tempests of furious psychic energy made the aether of Terra like flying a Stormbird straight into the Eye of Terror.

Most mortals knew nothing of this, but every living soul on Terra felt it in the darkness.

The constant terror and pain of the fighting was horrific, but the visions assailing them when they closed their eyes were far worse.

Beyond the psychic canopy protecting the inner precincts of the Palace, Magnus saw a swirling morass of ghostly forms: the Neverborn circling like carrion crows anticipating the slaughter to come.

Horns, and claws…

Too many eyes and too-wide jaws…

Unquenchable appetites…

Ahriman flew beside him, his body of light a pure and perfect being.

'We burn too brightly, my lord,' he said, pointing to where trails of warp-spawned monsters rose towards them like plasmic storms lifting from a star's corona: lone predators, swarms of pack hunters, and gibbering hosts of raw fury.

Magnus grinned and said, *'I dim my brilliance for no one, not for any man and certainly not for daemons.'*

And with a thought, he was armed with his heqa staff and a khopesh with a bronze blade wreathed in fire. Ahriman followed his father's example, and moments later, he too was clad in armour and armed with his ebon-black heqa staff.

The swarming host rose up to them in a boiling tide of insensate hunger.

'Into them,' said Magnus.

Together, father and son fought as one, burning with fire and fury. The light of Magnus' khopesh cut the Neverborn apart, dispersing their essences like mist before a hurricane. Mightier than even the most terrible of the daemons, he spun and dived between them. He felt their claws upon him like talons of ice even as he burned them away with searing lightning from his eye and coruscating fire from his staff.

Magnus wove a web of destruction through the Neverborn, his staff and blade and power not simply killing them but *unmaking* them. Their screams were piteous, but Magnus had no care for their dissolution, no thought beyond his own desire to reach out and *destroy*.

Ahriman matched his fury, a cathartic release for both of them after the failure at Colossi.

In the end, they were triumphant, blazing warriors resplendent amid tumbling scraps of sickly light that faded as they fell. Far below, the waking dreams and nightmares of mortals were filled with visions of fiery angels destroying the daemons, and depending on which side of the wall they fought, were either uplifted or plunged into despair.

'As above, so below,' said Magnus.

'That felt good,' admitted Ahriman.

Power surging between them, master and student looked down upon the surface of Terra.

As magnificent as Magnus' map of the Palace was, nothing could do justice to the vista spread out before him. Only the bombed-out mega-hives of SudMerica came close to the scale of the Palace, and even they were mere shanties in comparison. Neither could the subterranean arcologies of Marianas or the sprawling predator cities of ancient Kievan-Rus hope to match its scale.

'It is magnificent,' said Ahriman, his form still bleeding off streamers of his battle fury.

'It is indeed,' said Magnus. ***'In an earlier age, before the coming of the great hives of Europa, these mountains were the tallest peaks in the world and mantled in snow. Self-styled adventurers sought to conquer their lofty heights, and seekers of esoteric wisdom plumbed the secrets hidden in the darkness beneath them.'***

'I remember Lemuel Gaumon telling me he had travelled here in search of a cure for his wife's malady,' said Ahriman.

'A pity he did not find what he sought, but that path eventually led him to us, so perhaps it was not entirely a fool's errand.'

'I wonder if Bödvar Bjarki killed him on Nikaea,' said Ahriman.

'More than likely. Menkaura bound a fragment of my soul to his flesh. I imagine a zealot like Bjarki would cut him down as **maleficarum** ***as soon as we departed.'***

Ahriman didn't answer, but the ripples of colour running through his aura told Magnus that the notion of the remembrancer's death troubled him, and he put concerns for long-dead mortals aside as he surveyed the ground below.

The mountains of the Himalazia were no longer capped with snow, but scoured black and grey, their hearts gouged by industry and their flanks clad in silvered steel to prepare the ground for the building of the Palace. They were still wondrous, but now that wonder was brutalist and all the more melancholic for the lost beauty they had once possessed.

The Palace traversed ancient boundaries of nations, filled entire valleys, occupied planed shelves of rock where mountains had once stood, and squatted on the surface of Terra like an ever-growing parasite. In rough form, the outer circuit of the Eternity Wall resembled the infinity symbol, a geometry Magnus could not believe was accidental. Intentional or not, the symbolism of that perfect form had been brutally disrupted by the attackers tearing it down, stone by stone.

So much hate and destruction… What will be left when it is done?

'Rogal Dorn has worked miracles on the defences,' said Ahriman.

'I expected no less of my brother.'

'True, but I had hoped for more from the Warmaster and Perturabo,' said Ahriman.

'In what way?' said Magnus. He already knew the answer, but wanted to see if Ahriman had grasped the reality of Horus Lupercal's war.

'Our entire strategy seems to be built around the idea of simply battering our way in with brute force and attrition,' said Ahriman. 'I see no finesse nor flanking stratagems, nor any ruses to sway those within to betrayal. It has already cost so much to even reach the surface of Terra… how much more will the Warmaster be willing to pay?'

'You grasp the truth of it, Ahzek. The true enemy is not the walls of the Palace, nor even my brothers and their warriors within,' said Magnus. ***'No, for all of us, the enemy is time. Legions still loyal to the Emperor are even now traversing the void to return to their master's side. If they reach Terra before the Emperor falls, then the day is lost. Horus knows this, and so the Palace must be smashed open with all speed. And if the cost of that is the blood of his brother Legions and his mortal followers, then so be it.'***

'By following such a strategy, the vanquished will be obliterated, and the victor little better,' said Ahriman. 'Whoever wins this war will be punch-drunk and reeling, their forces reduced to ghosts.'

'This war has bled us, Ahzek, it has bled us **hard***,'* said Magnus, *'But we remain strong. Together with the warriors I sent away before Russ' dogs fell on Prospero, the Legion numbers just over nine thousand. A paltry number by most reckonings, but one warrior of the Fifteenth is worth ten or more of any other legionary. Unlike Horus, I have been careful in husbanding the blood of my Legion for just such a moment.'*

'Wait, are you suggesting what I think you are suggesting?'

'What do you believe I suggest?'

Ahriman's eyes widened as the implications of Magnus' unsaid words sank in.

'That you mean to topple whoever finally claims Terra's throne and take it for yourself...'

'Who among my brothers is as remotely suited as I for such a position?' demanded Magnus. *'Horus is already so rank with stolen powers that he burns from the inside out and sees it not. Perturabo might once have had the imagination to make such a leap, but it has been ground out of him. Angron or Mortarion are lords only of corpses and maggots, and as for Konrad and Fulgrim, they are not fit to rule* **themselves**, *let alone a galaxy.'*

He could see his son was still astounded by the idea, but that was only to be expected.

'Is this why we fly together?' asked Ahriman.

'I know it sounds fantastical, **treasonous** *even,'* said Magnus. *'But consider this – we have all become so blinded by the idea that Horus Lupercal would see this war to its conclusion, that no other solution or outcome has even been considered.'*

'I admit I had not contemplated it.'

'That is why it will work, Ahzek. No one will see the blow coming.'

'There is no other who could rule Terra like you,' said Ahriman.

Magnus nodded, pleased his greatest student had seen the truth of it.

'It will be glorious,' said Magnus. ***'Now, come, let us return to the world of flesh and blood, there is much we need to set in motion.'***

They flew back towards the ground, passing through turbulent psychic squalls until the individual peaks of towers and strongholds were visible, their gilded domes and buttressed redoubts lit by the strobing glow of impacts against the shields.

Magnus was on the verge of allowing the weight of his physical form to draw his spirit back within, when Ahriman's voice halted him.

'Sire!'

He followed Ahriman's pointing finger to a segment of the wall on the south-eastern corner of the Sanctum Imperialis, a section near the confluence of the Adamant Wall and the Western Hemispheric.

At first he wasn't sure what he was seeing, a twisting line of golden light.

Faint and almost invisible, yet stark against the spectral resolution of the Palace.

It flickered in and out of existence, like an image of a lightning bolt caught on a picter.

'What is it?' asked Ahriman.

Magnus narrowed his vision as he tried to fix it in place, but it twisted and danced before him, refusing to be pinned down. He reached out with his aetheric senses and recoiled as he sensed the awesome power behind the light and realised what he was seeing.

'Father…' breathed Magnus, not daring to believe that it was real. ***'You sit upon your throne, hidden behind your wards and shields. I should be blind to your presence – I* have *been blind to your power since you retreated within your sanctum – but now I see what I was looking for…* I see you…*'***

'My lord, is that…?'

'That light is a whisper of the Emperor's power, a breath of His presence leaking from within the Palace.'

Ahriman's aura blossomed as he understood the significance of that.

'The crack we wrought in the telaethesic ward,' said Magnus. ***'Our way in.'***

FOUR

Wheels within Wheels

Encased in his grand lifter-throne strategium, the Lord of Iron was haloed by the flickering glow of his pict slates. His grim features were sheened with the pallid glow of the screens, his scalp pierced with cabling and studded with implants. Hooded eyes, always in motion, took in the vast quantities of data, processing and coordinating with every blink. Not even the greatest adept of the Martian priesthood could match Perturabo's speed of cognitive processing in matters of war.

Every screen flickered with brutal imagery, passing too swiftly for the unaugmented eye to follow: thousands of updates from ten thousand separate engagements across this war front and hundreds more across the globe. Only a handful of beings throughout the entire history of the species could coordinate battle over so many complex theatres of war.

Perturabo's fingers – *artist's fingers*, thought Magnus – danced across invisible haptic keyboards, and with every stroke he sent scores of orders, altered multiple avenues of advance, or adjusted a hundred or more creeping barrages in real time.

To watch him was to witness a master craftsman at work.

More than any of his artificer brothers, Perturabo had been an artist and a creator. Yes, Vulkan had his forge-craft, and Ferrus Manus his proficiency with technology, but Perturabo had been an architect of beauty, a dreamer of things unimaginable to others.

Magnus remembered Perturabo's private repository, the walls of its many rooms hung with plans for grand theatres, awe-inspiring palaces wrought in steel and glass, and cities of such grandeur that they approached Tizca in their ambition.

That so very few had ever been realised was an affront to his genius.

That his mastery was now employed simply to destroy was a waste of potential that still sat ill with Magnus, even as it now served his purpose.

On the heels of that thought, his eyes shifted to *Forgebreaker*, the mighty warhammer wrought by Fulgrim in the great Terrawatt forge of Mount Narodnya. Gifted to Ferrus Manus, it had been presented to the Warmaster upon his death, and subsequently passed to Perturabo.

The Lord of Iron had heavily modified the hammer, much to the Phoenician's chagrin.

Towering battle-automata cranked to face Magnus as he approached, Perturabo's Iron Circle. Their burnished metal skins were soot-blackened and pocked by recent shell impacts and las-burns after a desperate sortie of Imperial Thunderbolts had somehow managed to fight through the defences of the Citadel of Iron. The fighters had launched a desperate attack, and though every one of them had been blasted from the air, two had managed to strafe his position before ploughing their burning wrecks into his vantage point.

The upper observation deck was gone, sheared away by the wing of a tumbling aircraft, and thus this penultimate level was now open to the sky. Bruised flarelight and booming shock pulses spread over the flickering remnants of the aegis shields as petrochemical conflagrations burned the sky in striated veils. Twisting firestacks danced like *ifrit* in the gutted remains of the Imperial Fleet College and made sport in the ruins of Aurum Bar. Radial processionals of gilded glory that had once hosted grand triumphs were rivers of brilliant gold, and their molten ruins were like the earliest days of a newborn world.

Plumes of smoke without number gave the air a gritty, acidic flavour, and the constant crackling of detonations drew the eye with phosphor-bright blossoms in every direction.

Before Magnus could speak, Perturabo said, 'I'm busy, brother.'

Brusqueness was nothing new to the Lord of Iron, and Magnus was not offended. After the failures of Saturnine and Colossi, the pressure bearing down on Perturabo from the Warmaster was immense and only increasing.

'I do not doubt it, but I would beg a moment of your time.'

'I would deny any of our other brothers,' said Perturabo, stepping down from his throne, 'but for you I will spare that moment.'

Magnus turned back to the vista of destruction spread before them.

'Soaring on the aether winds of the Great Ocean, it is possible to view the siegeworks as something abstract,' he said. ***'As though it is a sculpted board in an exhibit meant to convey the scale of long-ago events to future historians. Untold millions are at war on Terra, slogging through mud, dust and bones to claw each other to death. Individually, their deaths are irrelevant. Even added together they are meaningless, just as each drop of water in a mountain river is meaningless. And yet still it cleaves the mountain.'***

'This is how you would spend my time? In metaphor?' said Perturabo. 'Learn to curb your tendency to overspeak, brother. I have fifteen major assaults commencing in moments.'

Fifteen, auspicious.

'I only meant to say that the war looks different at every level,' said Magnus. ***'Saturnine taught me that.'***

'You mean Dorn taught us that,' snapped Perturabo.

Magnus needed no special sensitivity to see how deep the failure of Saturnine had cut the Lord of Iron. The long war for supremacy fought between Perturabo and Rogal had come down to this battle, this moment, and Dorn – that most singularly unimaginative of warriors – had somehow managed to outfox them all.

'We all underestimated him,' said Magnus. ***'We forgot that his talent would soar in response to your genius.'***

'Spare me the salve to my ego, Magnus. Rogal saw the weakness in his defence in time, and knowing I must have already seen it, baited us into a trap. It was breathtakingly daring. Had I not seen it with my own eyes, I would have thought my brother incapable of so astonishingly risky a ploy. And letting the Eternity Wall go...'

'You believe he sacrificed the starport and everyone within it willingly?'

'Of course,' said Perturabo, looking at him as if he were a fool for not understanding the audacity of their brother's ploy. 'It would have been the only way he could convince me he hadn't seen the weakness at Saturnine. If I didn't hate him so much, I would congratulate him on such ruthless triage.'

'If even stolid Dorn can surprise us,' said Magnus, ***'then these truly are the end times.'***

Perturabo shrugged, the plates of his armour rasping against the cabling of his skull. 'We were outmanoeuvred, it happens. But all our brother won was a brief respite. I *will* break open the Palace, that outcome is certain. The only question is how long it will take.'

'An important question given the unknown whereabouts of Roboute and the Lion,' pointed out Magnus.

'I am well aware that the clock is ticking. So unless you have some new information or the power to slow time, let me get back to work.'

Magnus gestured towards Perturabo's lifter-throne and said, *'The new attacks you plan, will one of them be against Western Hemispheric?'*

'Yes,' said Perturabo. 'A pinning assault. I will throw troops against it and so Dorn must defend it. While they are engaged at Western Hemispheric and a dozen other fronts, the real blows will fall elsewhere. And don't ask me where, I won't tell you.'

'You don't trust me?'

The Lord of Iron's eyes narrowed, as though trying to decide if the question were serious.

'You always have your schemes, Magnus,' he said. 'You brought your Legion to Terra with an objective not aligned with that of the Warmaster. I won't pretend to understand what secret game you are playing, but I know you have held your warriors back from all major engagements, probing the walls like a caged animal testing the limits of its confinement.'

'You're right,' admitted Magnus, circling the lifter-throne and its flickering pict slates. *'But in this moment, your goals, mine, and Horus' are in perfect synchrony.'*

'So what is it you want of me? And speak plainly for once.'

'What if you could convince Dorn or his advisors that the attack on Western Hemispheric was something more, say, by placing the Thousand Sons in the order of battle as the Phoenician and the Third were at the Saturnine Wall?'

Perturabo climbed back onto his lifter-throne, and the pict slates resumed their ultra-rapid cycling of war fronts. 'What would be the point? The aim is to convince the defenders that any one attack could be the iron fist. To overemphasise one over another defeats that aim.'

'Unless they believe the attack on Western Hemispheric is the main one and divert additional strength to its defence. If Dorn must send reinforcements everywhere, he will everywhere be weak.'

Perturabo shook his head. 'You don't know what you're asking. Our forces are committed now – deployed, supplied, and already in motion. You more than most should understand that small imbalances on one front will have a correspondingly greater effect on another. But if you wish to commit your forces to the assault on Western Hemispheric, I will allow it. Submit your order of battle and I will factor it into my calculations, but I'll not indulge your emotions or need for reparations.'

'Is that why you think I ask?'

'Isn't it?'

Magnus grinned. ***'Maybe a little.'***

Two days after coming for her in the refugee camps, Hassan brought Alivia to an old candlelit gallery within a drum tower high on the outskirts of the Hegemon, where the thunder of war and booms of ongoing engagements were subdued.

An isolated place, it had the look of a chapel, deep with memory and old prayers. Alivia felt cold, as if something terrible had once happened here, and its echo had seeped into the rough, bas-relief carved walls, never to be forgotten. A long wooden table, unevenly stained with lacquer, ran the length of the gallery, carved from a single, massive slab of dark wood.

'Please sit,' said Hassan, pulling a chair out for her.

Alivia took a seat and rested her palms flat on the table. The wood was smooth, the sweep of the grain comfortingly natural.

Hassan left through the door by which they had entered, and was it just her imagination or did she see a look of pity in his eyes?

A dozen seats surrounded the table, but only half were occupied.

Three beings of mortal scale, three of transhuman proportions.

Malcador sat at the head of the table, looking as frail as any of the hollow-cheeked venerables wheezing out their last breaths in the camps. His robe of office hung loose on his frame of bones, and the fingers that held his eagle-topped staff reminded Alivia of ancient images of a deathly reaper clutching his scythe in a fleshless grip.

'Hello, Alivia,' he said, the strength of his voice giving the lie to his appearance. But that was Malcador in a nutshell, lies wrapped in untruths and cloaked in falsehoods. 'I trust your family are well situated now?'

She nodded, but didn't answer. Instead, she studied the others around the table.

The three Astartes were clearly VI Legion, execution killers with ice-weathered skin, iron-braided beards and winter-blue warplate. They looked at her as a pack, wordlessly sharing how best to tear her apart.

Of all the loyalist Space Marines Alivia had met, she liked Space Wolves the least.

Malcador's two companions were unknown to her.

The first was a bronze-armoured woman... or at least Alivia assumed so. It was hard to be sure. Her armoured hands tapped restlessly on the table, and whether it was a trick of the candlelight or the play of shadows around her masked face, Alivia couldn't bring her features into focus, as though her eyes refused to linger and kept sliding clear.

One of the Soulless Sisterhood...

Alivia signed a question, her fingers slow as she struggled to remember the silent speech.

The woman seemed taken aback to have been addressed, but she soon overcame her surprise to sign an answer.

Vigil Sister Challis Vedia.

Across from Vedia was an unremarkable man garbed in the traditional flowing robes of Afrique. His skin was dark but ashen, and his eyes spoke of suffering and guilt still simmering within: dangerous emotions that could easily tip to vengeance. His left arm was a prosthetic, high-end augmetic work with a glossy black sheen.

'And you? Who are you?' she asked.

The man's eyes darted to Malcador, who gave a soft nod of assent.

'My name is Promeus.'

Alivia's eyes narrowed. 'But that's not the one your mother gave you, is it? Let's not start out on a lie, shall we?'

He met her gaze and said, 'My given name was Lemuel Gaumon. I took this name to honour a fallen warrior of the Emperor.'

She saw the bristling of the Space Marines at *that* remark.

'Why are they here?' she asked him. 'The vox-casters tell us the warriors of Fenris are racing to reach Terra. Are they already here?'

'This is the watch pack of Bödvar Bjarki,' said Promeus.

'I can speak for myself, *wyrd-wraith*,' said the warrior who was obviously their leader, a giant with a tattooed face and fetish-hung armour. Even through his beard, Alivia could see candlelight gleaming on the edges of his fangs.

This one has power.

'I am Bödvar Bjarki of the Rout, Rune Priest of Tra,' said the bearded warrior.

He slapped a meaty palm on the shoulder of the warrior to his right, a long-limbed brute whose skull was a nightmare of plated bronze and burn scars. One eye was a blue-glowing augmetic, the other milky and off-centre, as if it had melted back across his face.

'This is Svafnir Rackwulf, Woe-maker of Tra,' said Bjarki.

'Greatest harpoon-caster of the Varangai,' said Rackwulf, his words slurred and wet sounding, 'and slayer of traitors.'

Alivia didn't like the emphasis he placed on *traitors*, or the way his grip tightened on the long spear he held. Half its length was toothed in bone barbs, and despite the ruination of his eye, Alivia didn't doubt he was as accurate with it as he had ever been. Its black haft seemed to soak up the light, and Alivia felt an instinctive dislike of it.

A null-weapon then…

'And this,' said Bjarki with a bark of amusement, 'is Olgyr Widdowsyn of Balt. He is our shield bearer and nursemaid when we are sick.'

'Ach,' said Widdowsyn, a hulking warrior with the face of a brawler encased in armour that seemed altogether too small for his Astartes bulk. 'I set one broken bone and suddenly I am Apothecary.'

Alivia ignored their banter, knowing it was simply an act, a way to get her to lower her expectations of their cunning, to underestimate them. She had met Wolves before, and would never make that mistake again.

'He called you a watch pack,' said Alivia. 'So what do you watch for?'

'*Maleficarum*,' spat Bjarki. 'We watch for treachery at the highest level. Our packs stood as loyal bodyguards to the All-father's sons, and if it was their wyrd to become oath-breakers we were also to serve as their executioners.'

Alivia laughed. 'Really? I can imagine how well *that* went down with the primarchs.'

'You can imagine how little the Rout cares about that.'

Alivia looked back at the door and said, 'I don't know if

you've noticed the fighting outside, but it doesn't look like your packs did a very good job.'

Fangs were bared and Alivia felt the air in the room thicken with a hot, animal stink. Both Vedia and Promeus recoiled from it, but Alivia had stared into the murderous eyes of the primarch Horus, so their predator musk held no fear for her.

'And you?' said Bjarki, leaning in and resting his elbows on the table, addressing the question to Malcador as much as her. 'Who are *you*?'

'Me? I'm Alivia Sureka. I'm nobody, and I have no idea why I'm here.'

Bjarki laughed again and wagged an admonishing finger.

'*Fenrys hjolda!* A woman whose wyrd is woven with more threads than the ropes binding the great sails of the Allfather's dragonship says she is nobody! Now who is lying? Your thread is so long it stretches back into darkness like an anchor into the deepest ocean chasm, but know this, Mistress Sureka, I fear it nears its end.'

'If you only knew how many times I've wished that were true,' she said, turning back to Malcador. The old man was a shadow of his former self, but Alivia knew better than to take anything he presented to the world at face value. The Sigillite was the very epitome of the first warmaster's words.

When you are strong, appear weak.

But even as the thought came to her, something told her that perhaps here, at the end, *this* was the real face of Malcador. For all his glamour, deceits and stratagems, this was who he truly was: an old man with nothing left to give.

'What say you, Sigillite?' said Bjarki. 'We brought you Promeus and his knowledge of the Crimson King's quest. The time of the watch packs is done. Release us from our oaths and give us leave to join our brothers on the walls.'

'Not yet,' said Malcador.

Bjarki stabbed an accusing finger vaguely in the direction of Vedia and said, 'Then tell me why we meet in this place of secrets with one who blinds me to the wyrd?'

Malcador nodded and said, 'I have one last task I require of you.'

Alivia rapped her knuckles on the table and shook her head. 'And there it is. There's always *just one more task*. It never ends until you turn your back on him and walk away.'

'Yet here you are, Alivia,' said Malcador. 'Every step you took on the road away from Terra has led you back here. This is where you were meant to be. You know *He* needs you, but I need you most of all.'

'Why?'

'Because I need you to save the Emperor.'

Alivia wanted to laugh, but saw Malcador was deadly serious.

'I know it's been a while since I've set foot on Terra, so maybe things have changed some, but… isn't that the job of the Custodians?' said Alivia.

'They would never agree to what I am about to ask of you,' said Malcador. 'Hence the presence of Mistress Vedia. Constantin and his Custodians cannot know what is planned or they would execute us all, even me.'

The Silent Sister's fingers moved in a blur of frustration.

Secrets and lies are what brought us to this moment.

Malcador at least had the decency to look ashamed.

'We all must bear our burdens, Sister, but know that His is the greatest of all,' said Malcador. 'And the words I will speak come directly from Him.'

'How are we few to save the Allfather?' said Bjarki.

Malcador traced an ever-shrinking figure of eight on the tabletop.

'You have all seen beyond the walls and know the host we face,' he said. 'Deep down, you all acknowledge the inescapable truth that we cannot win this fight. Horus has a virtually endless supply of troops and war machines he can throw at us, where our resources deplete every day. The numbers do not lie – we cannot hold with the forces we have left. It may take weeks or even months, but Terra *will* fall.'

Such a defeatist pronouncement, so baldly made, shocked them all, even the Astartes.

'Guilliman and the Lion will be here any day,' managed Promeus. 'That's what the vox-clarions keep telling us. Is that a... *lie*? Are we alone...?'

'We believe they are fighting to reach us, yes, but they will not arrive in time to save us. If things continue as they are, any relief force will reach Terra only to find Horus the master of our ashes and bones.'

Malcador paused and drew a reluctant breath. 'But the fates have seen fit to offer one chance, the merest sliver of one to be sure, but a chance nonetheless.'

'A chance for what?' asked Alivia, fearful of the answer.

'To deprive the enemy of one of their most potent weapons.'

'And how will we do that?' asked Alivia.

'With redemption,' said Malcador. 'And forgiveness.'

Before Alivia could ask any more, Promeus let out a gasp of pain, leaning over the table and clutching his chest as if he were having a heart attack. His already pallid features turned ashen, his eyes saucer-wide with fear.

'He's here,' said Promeus. 'I can feel him...'

'Who's here?' said Alivia.

'*Him!*' cried Promeus. 'Oh, Throne, I feel the scars of his fury inside me still!'

Blood filled Promeus' left eye, and red tears spilled out to run down his cheek.

'*Who?*' demanded Alivia.

'The Crimson King!' screamed Promeus. 'He's here!'

BOOK TWO

WESTERN HEMISPHERIC

FIVE

Opportunities Multiply

The assault on Western Hemispheric began with a bombardment.

In previous epochs, it would have been recorded by historians as something monumental: the largest deployment of heavy siege guns in history; the most explosive force brought to bear in one battle; the most concentrated area of shelling ever seen.

In truth, it was one of the smaller artillery duels of the day.

The heaviest guns, mounted on fixed rails and crewed by gibbering, glass-eyed giants, hurled penetrator warheads from smoke-filled revetments as mobile howitzer batteries advanced down zigzagging trenches the size of deep-ocean canyons. Hundreds of multi-launchers streaked a thousand missiles into the sky every second.

Vast bombards advanced behind crawling behemoths fitted with angled glacis, lobbing titanic spheres laden with volatile fuel-air explosives. Phosphex missiles and napthek shells seared the ground to glass and set the Imperial outworks aflame. Withering streams of gunfire flared, lashing the ramparts and outer bulwarks in streams of high-velocity steel and las.

Smoke and fumes thickened the air, the thunder of detonations and launches almost impossible to separate. The screams of the dying went unheard as the earth shook with the violence of its pummelling.

The Imperial counter-battery fire was no less ferocious.

With their guns ranged, kill-zones marked and the artillerymen drilled to the highest level, return fire punished the traitors for every metre they advanced. Mine launchers seeded the ground with melta charges before the advancing mantlet screens, and deadly accurate plunging fire turned the canyon trenches into charnel houses of burning fuel and seared flesh.

Secondary detonations split the trenches open and laid them bare to enfilading fire. Mangled bodies choked their width, and shredded walls of flesh offered literal meat shields to cover later marching detachments.

Rogal Dorn's masterful placement of outflung redoubts, ravelins and hornworks gave no place for the attackers to advance in cover. Merciless grazing fire sawed through the ranks of traitors massing behind the towering barriers protecting the artillery. Advances faltered as the front lines spasmed with casualties, then pushed onward as whip-masters and braying war-horns drove the host towards the walls.

Masked soldiers bearing profane banners were scythed down by airbursting shells that flensed their ranks with white-hot steel. Entire regiments were obliterated in the blink of an eye, wholesale slaughters ignored as following troops marched over the smashed bones and torn meat of their fellows.

Cohorts of screeching Knights strode through the host, bounding between ruins and unleashing torrents of fire with each step. Behind them, smoke-shrouded Reavers of Magna, and a rogue Warlord of Tempestus, stalked like apex predators awaiting the soft underbelly of the enemy to be exposed before striking.

Pain-maddened abhumans charged the outermost redoubts, scrambling through mined ditches, and up near-vertical walls. They were bestial things with branded fur and curling horns sheathed in brass. Murderous gunfire flayed them from every side, and only a handful survived to reach the ramparts, but that was often enough to rip through its defenders.

As each redoubt was abandoned or taken by storm, its open rear gave no succour to the enemy. Overwatching gunners in revetted bunkers and gun-boxes flayed the beasts with bracketed fire, and when they were dead, fresh Imperial detachments pushed out to take their position on the blood-slick walls.

Squadrons of traitor armour attempted to push forward through the smoking ruins, but were quickly bogged down in the mud. The vehicles' crews fought to free them as hounding fire blazed from sponsons and screaming turrets as yet more artillery was brought to bear. Little by little, the space between the two opposing forces shrank, a death zone where nothing could lift its head without being cut down.

The carnage was inhuman, thousands of lives spent with no thought for the price of blood being paid every second. Besieging a heavily defended emplacement was the most brutal and uncaring of war's many incarnations, and this was its most extreme manifestation. The bloody arithmetic of combat was unflinching, and every advantage a defender might muster was being brought to bear to deny, delay and destroy the enemy approach.

But it wouldn't be enough, it could *never* be enough.

Rogal Dorn's initial calculations had been made with estimated projections of enemy numbers that were woefully conservative, and assumed breaking points of courage. But every variable in these equations was rendered null and void by a zealous fury no Imperial planner could have foreseen, a level of insanity beyond comprehension.

It drove the attackers into the teeth of the Imperial guns without thought for their survival.

It showed they were more afraid of their masters than the enemy.

But even had the Praetorian of Terra accepted the most outlandish estimates of the enemy soldiers' capability and resolve in the face of almost certain death, there was one variable neither he nor his command staff could possibly have accounted for.

The warlocks of the Thousand Sons.

It felt like their wars of old.

Fellowships working together, their powers alloyed to one purpose. Ahriman's Scarab elite followed in the wake of rainbow-hued monsters with matted fur and forking horns that sparked with corposant. Pyrae cultists ignited the hanging veils of fyceline-laced air, and adepts of the Raptora swept it forwards in blazing curtains of dancing fire.

Athanaeans reached into the aether to twist the perceptions of the men and women on the wall who beheld this sight, rendering the flames into howling maws that screamed horrors unique to every mind.

Such was the volume of destruction, the most colossally heavy transports were forced to lead the way. Leviathans and profaned Capitol Imperialis flattened what weeks of artillery bombardment had not, crushing the titanic remains of shell-smashed ruins for smaller transports to follow.

Keeping low to the ground, Ahriman led his fellowship through the three-metre-deep trenches of crushed rock carved by the grinding tracks of *Khasisatra*, a Monolith-class Capitol Imperialis, as it ground its way towards the Palace walls.

Battle cannons blazed from its topside and every twenty-seven minutes its axial-mounted macro cannon would fire. When it did, every mortal warrior within five hundred metres needed to turn away, cover their ears and open their mouth to keep the shock pulse of its firing from collapsing their lungs and pulping their internal organs.

Las-fire zipped overhead, as dust and rock fragments drizzled into the trench.

Strobing shadows stretched and swelled, retreated and danced around the fires overhead. The greasy taste of rancid fat and the scratching pressure on his aetheric senses told Ahriman that not all such shadows were natural.

The crackling golden light he and Magnus had seen when flying the Great Ocean was still there, so very faint, and so very fragile. Ahriman didn't dare linger on it, for fear that acknowledging it in this realm of the mundane would alert the defenders to its presence.

It felt like an itch he couldn't scratch, a presence that was only perceptible by *not* seeking it out. But it was there and could yet be prised open.

The endless tide of Neverborn can sense it too...

Samus, Oholoxene, Vhargal, Cor'bax, Ur-nephre, and unnumbered more.

So many names, so many secrets to pull from their immortal minds.

He could feel them scratching at the walls of reality, frenzied and maddened by the bloodshed engulfing the Throneworld. The veil was pierced in thousands of places, allowing the daemons to vomit onto the surface of the world in unthinking murder-packs of claw and fang. But here, this close to the telaethesic shield, they were yet barred from the inner precincts of the Palace.

Nothing truly daemonic could manifest within that psychic umbra.

But the pressure was building, and soon the Emperor's shield would shatter.

'You know what this reminds me of?' said Ahriman, turning to look over his shoulder at the flattened ground behind the advancing leviathans. A hundred legionaries followed him down the gouged trench, together with five thousand mortal soldiers in ochre and black bearing scale-hooks and rotor-ladders.

Every one of the scores of giant vehicles boasted similar entourages.

'I don't,' replied Atrahasis, his new equerry. 'I'm not Athanaean.'

Atrahasis was an adept of the Raptora with all the blunt directness of that Fellowship.

The pearlescent red and ivory of the warrior's armour gleamed, not a single mote of dust or smoke besmirching its burnished plate. The perfection of its form put Ahriman in mind of Hathor Maat, and his former brother's face flashed before his eyes.

He pushed the memory of the fallen Pavoni adept from his mind.

No, not fallen. Sacrificed. By my hand.

'So what does it remind you of?' said Atrahasis when Ahriman did not continue.

'Ullanor,' said Ahriman at last. 'When the geoformer fleets levelled an entire continent for one man's vanity. We were told it was to honour us, but really it was for Him, a narcissistic salve to His ego, to know that so many were His to command.'

'That was when He stepped away from the crusade,' pointed out Atrahasis. 'He passed command of His hosts to the Warmaster.'

'Because the work of the crusade had become tedious to Him,' said Ahriman. 'The glory days of its early decades were long passed, all that remained was the final grind to the end. *That* was why He stepped away. Horus' elevation was symbolic, nothing more. The Emperor was done with us, and sought only to return to His latest endeavour.'

A thunder of sirens blared from *Khasisatra*'s topside and a rising pressure of internal fury built deep within its armoured hull. The enormous war engine's void shields crackled as its projector vanes retracted, and the blast shutters descended.

Bracing pinions slammed down by its towering wheels as the macro cannon powered up.

+Kneel,+ ordered Ahriman, sending his command psychically. +And brace.+

He went to the ground as the smoke and fog wreathing the upper reaches of Western Hemispheric parted for an instant, revealing saw-toothed ramparts flickering with muzzle flare and detonations. Streaking arcs of petrary shells exploded above them, most detonating against the aegis or blasted from the air by the wall's close-in defence turrets. Some struck home and liquefied the parapet with flame, sending cascades of rubble and bodies down its cliff-high slopes.

Ahriman watched the play of light, beautiful in its own way, seeing patterns and meaning in its interactions. The breath quickened in his throat, his heart pounded, as the vision stuttering together in his mind was one he knew he was not seeing with his eyes.

This was the blessing and curse of the Corvidae – to see portents in everything, to hear the echoes of the future and feel the emotion of their passing before their time. An aetheric knife to the heart made him look up in sudden apprehension as he heard a sound like a whipcrack of lightning.

He tasted the volcanic heat of an open blast furnace, the scream of tortured metal, the thunder of an earthquake. An overwhelming pressure on his senses, like an oncoming storm.

+Up!+ he cried. +Everyone out the trench! Go!+

The Thousand Sons following him obeyed instantly, powering up the rocky slopes of the trench or punching through its ruined sections where the cratered ground overlapped its length. The mortal soldiers behind them watched in confusion, not understanding what was happening.

Ahriman climbed the trench wall and vaulted over its lip. He rolled to his knees and ran through the razed ruins of the Palace, glancing over his shoulder just before he heard the distinct hard crack of wall-mounted defence lasers.

Like molten rods of glass blinking into existence for a trillionth of a second, the concentrated fire of three defence lasers punched through the frontal armour of *Khasisatra.* Its shuttered magazine bays were open, its main gun was primed, and the Capitol Imperialis was as devastatingly vulnerable as it was possible to be.

The seams of its heavy armour plates blazed with phosphor-bright illumination. Spears of white-hot fire lanced through its vents, vision blocks and the joints of its weapon ports.

For the briefest moment, the Capitol Imperialis seemed to swell as if inflating.

And then it froze.

Ahriman skidded behind a fragmentary nub of stonework, the remains of a fluted column, its Doric base miraculously untouched by the shelling. The sound of artillery dropped away, the sudden silence shocking after living with the endless cacophony of battle for so long.

He knew what he was seeing was impossible.

A detonation frozen in time.

He felt the certainty of his prescient vision unravel within him, the heat and fire and light of the inevitable explosion he'd seen and felt like a ghost in his mind.

+Look!+ cried Atrahasis, the blunt force of his communication making Ahriman wince.

He followed his equerry's warning and looked up to see the tar-black clouds above *Khasisatra* writhing as though stirred by an unseen hand. Constant lightning burst from the epicentre of the dark maelstrom, reaching down with forking hands to envelop the Capitol Imperialis in a web of crackling lines of power.

Icy blue light burned through the heart of the storm, a pinprick at first then bursting open the clouds like a wound in the sky. A figure emerged from the light, golden and crimson, beatific and terrible. Too raw and beautiful to look upon directly.

+Sire…+ breathed Ahriman.

Magnus descended from the heart of the swirling light and smoke, his skin burning with the magnitude of his powers, his eye filled with warp light. One hand was aimed at the Palace wall, the other ablaze with the source of the lightning.

He clenched his lightning-wreathed fist and lifted his arm.

And *Khasisatra* lifted with it.

Rock and mud and dust spilled from its tracks as all sixty-seven thousand tonnes of its mass lifted into the air. Howls and cheers rose from the ruins as the titanic vehicle rose higher. Blinding veins of light traced eager paths over Magnus' flesh as he rose skyward, dragging the seething bulk of the *Khasisatra* with him. Motes of ash peeled from him.

A storm of light from the Palace reached out to Magnus, the Imperial gunners understanding that a target of incalculable worth had just presented itself. Laser and shell bursts exploded around the primarch, but the lightning surrounding him was proof against all attacks.

With a roar, Magnus wrenched his fist around, and the enormous vehicle swung up through the air as though launched from a trebuchet. Ahriman watched in disbelief as the doomed *Khasisatra* flew towards the Palace, still wreathed in a web of lightning at the frozen nanosecond of its destruction. Defensive gunfire flashed, but none of the weapons that could react fast enough could stop something of such inconceivably colossal mass.

It arced down to the wall in agonisingly slow motion, and

the instant it struck the upper reaches of Western Hemispheric, Magnus released his hold on the flow of time surrounding its immensity.

Ahriman turned away as the Capitol Imperialis detonated with the power of an exploding star.

Its reactor and all the city-levelling ordnance it carried was equal to the force of a dozen battlefield atomics, and the searing flash of its detonation momentarily dispelled the constant twilight of the siege. A fraction of a second later, the building rumble of the explosion raced out from the walls, a roar that was deafening, even over the already apocalyptic battle.

Ahriman's auto-senses shut him off from the outside world, but the sound within his helm was still like a Dreadnought's siege hammer pounding on his skull. Moments later, the force of the blast wave rocked him sprawling.

Scalding smoke billowed around the Thousand Sons in a lethal, superheated fog, and Ahriman felt it even through the ceramite of his warplate. The earth shook as though trying to dislodge the puny mortals crawling upon its surface, as the overpressure rolled outwards in dynamic storms of hurricane-force winds that hurled debris and loose stone back to the traitor camps.

Warning sigils flashed onto his visor: lethal spikes of ionising radiation, e-mag pulses and deadly heat. Seconds later the secondary flash of the explosion lit up the sky and threw out long, stark shadows in a world turned a brilliant, bleached white by the blast.

As the eye-burning light faded, Ahriman rolled onto his front to see a towering mushroom cloud of roiling, superheated smoke climbing and spreading from the section of Western Hemispheric directly before him.

Or, rather, what remained of it.

An entire section of the wall and its defensive outworks

had simply vanished, vaporised in the nuclear fire of the initial blast or flattened by the force of the shock wave. As if a vast beast had reached down from the sky to bite a V-shaped segment from the wall, an immense, sloping breach had just opened up in the Palace defences.

Finally daring to open up his aetheric senses, Ahriman rose through his psychic mantras to the ninth enumeration. The chattering of Neverborn hunger rose to an unending, bestial howl and shimmering auras lifted off every living being around him. Fierce blues, golds and greens from the Thousand Sons, bleeding reds and oranges from the burned and blinded mortals staggering in mute agony behind him.

There!

The frozen golden light of the Emperor's presence was bright and golden in his mind. It felt brighter than before, as if an all-but-invisible crack had been forced fractionally wider.

+Up!+ pulsed Ahriman. +Forward!+

Abidemi sat above the right sponson of the Sicaran Venator battle tank as it roared past the Dome of Illumination at speed. The Venator was among the fastest tanks in the Imperial inventory, and Zytos had brooked no argument from its bewildered crew when he had commandeered it. The Sanctum Imperialis was roughly eight hundred kilometres in diameter, and Abidemi knew they must make that crossing with all possible speed. Gargo was pushing it hard, and if the vehicle lasted long enough to reach Western Hemispheric, it would likely never move again under its own power.

Zytos sat across from him above the opposite gun, while Igen Gargo looked out of the driver's hatch, scanning the ground ahead. The air around the Venator tasted like tin, the actinic reek of its overworked plasma ioniser drive core causing Abidemi's visor to glitch and fizz with static bleed.

He tilted his head to the side and hammered the palm of his gauntlet against his helmet. The static eventually cleared and he looked over with great sadness into the vast space encompassed by the Dome of Illumination.

Dark deeds had transpired here; traitors had set foot beneath its hallowed canopy, and brother legionaries had died. The kilometre-wide dome was askew now, and the water that once poured from its upper reaches had been diverted from the basin below to hardened cisterns deep beneath the Palace's bedrock. The three squatting colossi supporting the dome's vast weight were blackened by fire, their limbs gouged by rogue shell impacts and air-bursting shrapnel that had ricocheted in beneath the aegis. The light coming through the wide eye at its centre and holes punched by shell impacts swam with motes of dust and ash trapped beneath by vortices of tortured air.

'Good craft in those statues,' said Zytos, following Abidemi's gaze to study the dome's smoke-stained underside. 'Even scarred and off balance, they still perform their duty.'

'As do we all,' said Gargo, and Zytos gave a wry nod.

Abidemi saw the symbolism too, and drew strength from it as he turned to look back the way they had come. Mottled clouds of purple and red hung over Indomitor, some five hundred kilometres behind them to the east. The fighting still raged at their old station, as it did all around the circuit of the Eternity Wall.

Zytos had tasked the soldiers of *Vulkan's Own* with the defence of the wall, and its ad hoc command staff had sworn solemn oaths to give their lives in its defence when it became clear they could no longer fight alongside the Salamanders. These were men and women without regiments, without banners, but they had come together in the face of the enemy, and would do honour to their adopted name.

The paths around the dome were broken, demolished by explosives by the looks of the burn-scars and shrapnel wounds in the surrounding rock, so Gargo took a looping route past the grand, high-walled estates of the Viridarium Nobiles.

The precincts of the Sanctum Imperialis were thronged with refugees: tens of thousands of dusty, tired and exhausted people. They spilled from the overcrowded camps filling its wide thoroughfares and processional boulevards, taking shelter from the gently falling ash and caustic rain beneath awnings of canvas and tarpaulin. The dispossessed of Terra huddled against the walls of palaces of governance and grand temples to bureaucracy like drifts of snow. They looked up as the smoking battle tank passed, moving from its path in fear.

Fighting vehicles meant danger, no matter which banner flew from their vox-masts.

The roads here were not designed to bear the weight of tanks, and Abidemi's heart was heavy as they rode roughshod over the Palace's gilded streets. The hand-carved cobbles, each bearing a master's mark, were ripped up by the passage of the armoured tracks and scattered in their wake like clinker from a forge.

Zytos saw Abidemi's concern and said, 'I wonder if this was how Lord Dorn felt as he peeled back the beauty of his father's Palace and sheathed it in ugly plates of armour.'

'His warriors claim he has promised to rebuild the Palace, to restore every wall, tower and gate to its former glory,' said Gargo.

'He can try,' said Zytos, shaking his head, 'but any craftsman worthy of the name knows that once you break something of beauty it's never the same.'

'Sometimes it can be better,' said Abidemi. 'The artisans of Clymene hold to the aesthetic that beauty is sometimes derived from the imperfect, the impermanent and the incomplete.'

'I know of it,' said Zytos. 'I spent two years sweating in the forge of Master Koren and arguing against his ideas of "nothing lasts, nothing is finished, and nothing is perfect" but it seems as apt a fit as any philosophy these days.'

'Perhaps,' said Abidemi, and they rounded the perimeter of the dome and connected with the Via Martial that led to the House of Weapons. Two hundred kilometres to the south-west, it was possible to see the rearing cliff that was the noble bulwark of Adamant and Western Hemispheric. A bombardment was underway, the horizon afire with impacts and aegis flare.

'This is a bad one,' said Zytos. 'Yes, a bad one indeed.'

'One section of wall under assault looks much like another from this distance,' said Gargo to Abidemi. 'Are you sure this is where your vision leads us?'

Abidemi was about to reply when the sky lit with the fury of an atomic explosion.

This far from the detonation, the blast was a groaning rumble of deep movement within the earth, but it soon swelled to the throaty roar of a drake in heat. A mushrooming storm cloud of pyroclastic fire reared up from the wall, and Abidemi remembered the ash column of Mount Deathfire on the day the primarch had been returned to them.

'I am sure,' he said.

SIX

The Breach

All was fire and smoke and dust.

The ground before Western Hemispheric was a smoking nightmare of utter destruction. Superheated ash clouds twisted like living things over the molten rock and burning ruins, hungry to devour whatever combustible material hadn't already been consumed by *Khasisatra*'s detonation.

Ahriman's armour glowed with heat, and he felt his skin crisping through the layered ceramite with every ponderous step he took. The ground underfoot would burn with radiation for thousands of years, and skeletal figures crumbled beneath his tread. His body felt as though it were being slowly cooked within his plate, like the rivers of sweat running from his flesh were runnels of fat coming off sizzling meat.

He bent low to push through the violent thermals surging in random vortices. He lost track of time. Every step felt like a lifetime, his advance slow and purposeful and grimly inevitable.

Shrieking voices called from rad-squalls that danced in the firestorms raging throughout the blast zone. Some of them had faces and half-formed arms, creatures beyond the veil pushing into the material world.

Ahriman's warplate struggled to make sense of the myriad inputs it was receiving. The e-mag pulse of the detonation sent crazed spikes of static through his visor, and heat bloom made thermal layers useless. He could see nothing but ghosts moving through the red-lit landscape – as sure a vision of hell as had ever been conjured in verse or dreamed of by madmen and artists.

His mundane senses were all but blind, so he relied on his other gifts.

A glimmering figure of fire approached through the smoke.

Its aura told him it was Atrahasis, his equerry staggering through the storm of ash and rock. Debris parted before him, shunted from his path by a kine layer of pure force.

The vox crackled, but whatever had been said was lost in the howl of e-mag interference.

+Speak with your mind,+ sent Ahriman.

Atrahasis nodded. +One hundred and seventy-one of us remain in this thrust. The thousands of mortals who began this march with us are already dead or will be dying in agony within a matter of hours. Only legionaries remain.+

+Good,+ said Ahriman.

+Good?+

+No mortal soldiers will be left alive on the wall. We strike hard for the breach. This is Astartes war now.+

Atrahasis nodded. +As it was always meant to be.+

Ahriman focused his senses and sent out a pulse of psychic energy.

+Fifteenth Legion! Rise to the second enumeration. Pavoni, dampen the radiation, Raptora, push a kine barrier before us.+

Ahriman turned on the spot as shimmering slicks of light resolved into focus around him, gods of battle wreathed in golden radiance. Two hundred warriors of the Thousand Sons had followed him into the fire, and he felt the presence of hundreds more.

Amon's warriors to the left, Menkaura's to the right, but so powerful was the telaethesic ward that he could barely sense them at all.

Have we changed so much that it blunts our aetheric powers as well as the daemonic?

The only constant in the firestorm of lethal ash, strobing flashes of secondary detonations and choking smoke was the Crimson King. The primarch burned like a bloated red sun in its last moments, bathing the shattered ruins of Terra in a hellish, bloodstained light.

+Follow the primarch,+ he said. +He is our lodestar. He leads us to victory!+

Ahriman turned and pushed onward into the teeth of the storm like every infantryman who had ever marched through mud, snow or heat to cross the last hundred metres to close with the enemy and destroy them. Their pace was glacial, but it hardly mattered any more.

No one remained on the wall to oppose them.

The psychic barrier of the Raptora ploughed the air, pushing the ash and smoke around them to reveal the vitrified ruin of the landscape. The outworks before Western Hemispheric had been utterly flattened by the blast wave, only the stubs of foundations and waving tangles of rebar indicating where they had once stood.

A pack of hulking Castellax battle cybernetics lumbered through the smoke, but so burned were their outer carapaces that Ahriman could not tell to which side they belonged, nor how they had come to be so far out from the walls. He felt the pain of their tortured psyches hardwired to their biomechanical cortexes, enslaved souls screaming in pain-filled madness.

Whatever surveyor gear was left to them screeched as it detected them, and the machines lashed out with insensate fury. Their gunfire was wild and inaccurate, and kine shields deflected any shots that came too close, but the hyper-aggressive machine-spirits within them now had purpose, and thus were dangerous.

+Yoke their souls,+ ordered Ahriman. +And bring them.+

Threads of witchfire reached out to the robots as the Athanaeans stabbed their power into the broken minds of the cybernetics. Some were too lost to madness, and those pitiful few were destroyed by their fellows in a merciless display of decimation.

The gunfire ceased, and the robots fell in with the Thousand Sons' advance.

Like all simple-minded things, they *craved* the comfort of obedience.

They're not Castellax-Achea, but they'll do.

Ahriman saw the wreckage of armoured vehicles amid the flames, some Imperial, some from Perturabo's host. Mostly Army, some Legion, and others that were the strange hybrid things of the Mechanicum forces loyal to the Warmaster. Fires burned in their hollowed-out guts, and cinder-black bodies hung from broken hatches as stalk-limbed machines twitched in their death throes.

Trapped machine-spirits begged for release or whispered dark promises in return for the loan of their wrath. Ahriman knew better than to trust such damaged things, and he left them to burn in the fires. A few lone vehicles had survived the initial blast and ridden out the shock wave. These now prowled the wreckage, but they were few and far between and wandered the ruins like blind men.

The smoke was thinning now. The fires at the site of the explosion were being drawn upwards and spreading in a wide umbra like a fresh layer of tar painting the sky. It was testament to Dorn's skill that much of the soaring wall and its many guntowers remained standing, though its cladding of adamantium, steel and stone had been pared away. Only the bare rock of the original wall remained, and a portion of that was a vitrified gap, like a missing tooth in a gum line.

Smoking debris and rubble formed a ready-made ramp to the crest of the breach. The sheer scale of the wall's height and its clifflike nature still rendered it a formidable barrier, but without its flanking outworks and enfilading ravelins, the wall was – for now – wide open.

+Send in the automata first,+ ordered Ahriman, and immediately the lumbering Castellax began climbing the slope, iron limbs and servo-assisted muscles driving them up faster than any mortal.

Maybe this will work better than we dared hope.

+Raptora!+ sent Ahriman. +Discs!+

In the wake of the detonation, Imperial Fists under Captain Iacono redeployed to Hemispheric Nine, two thousand gold-clad warriors held in reserve to blunt any breakthrough. They disembarked from Rhinos, Tauroxes and heavy-duty cargo flatbeds, quickly forming up by squads and rushing to the walls.

The muster points behind the walls were charnel houses of burned bodies, rubble and screams. Irradiated lumps of rockcrete were strewn around, the adamantium rebar still glowing orange and as flexible as wire. Shielded pioneer crews were already on-site, spraying the wreckage with retardant foam to dampen the rad-levels, though extended exposure to the radiation soaking Hemispheric Nine's rock would be lethal to unaugmented humans for at least three years.

Scattered bands of Blood Angels commanded by Captain Tamaya added their weight to the Imperial Fists' attempt to seal the breach, some three hundred of Baal's finest.

After Saturnine, Lord Dorn had reappraised every aspect of his defence plan, declared no detail, however slight, sacrosanct and directed his chief aides to find fault with his preparations. Little was uncovered the Praetorian had not already conceived, but no one had attributed any especial strategic significance to Hemispheric Nine beyond the obvious.

Now word that one of the Emperor's fallen sons had revealed his presence in the attack had changed that, especially given that primarch was said to be Magnus the Cyclops. His intellect was prodigious, his mind working on levels beyond the understanding of mere mortals. If Magnus was taking part in this attack, then clearly Hemispheric Nine held significance beyond what any Imperial planner had seen.

Thousands more Space Marines were being drawn from positions all along the Eternity Wall to reinforce Hemispheric Nine. The speed of the Imperial response was dazzling. Moving soldiers from pre-prepared defensive positions and redeploying them was no small task, requiring hundreds of orders, confirmations, logistical support and coordination, as well as the one thing in shortest supply at such pivotal moments.

Time.

It took seventy-six minutes for the first Imperial Fists to arrive at Hemispheric Nine, eighty-one for the Blood Angels. Thankfully, the ferocity of the explosion had delayed the traitors from exploiting the breach as quickly as they might otherwise have done, and the first warriors of the Legiones Astartes to arrive were not of the Legion of Magnus.

Nor were they Imperial Fists or Blood Angels.

They were Salamanders.

The Time of Trial.

Abidemi stood in the breach, looking out over a vision of Terra that more closely resembled Nocturne in its violent seasonal seizure. The surface of the Throneworld ran with living fire and raging pyro-storms devoured anything combustible as far as the eye could see.

Gales of radiation-laced wind howled over the walls as though Terra itself were screaming. Bent against their burning force, Gargo and Zytos heaped rubble into a makeshift barrier of interlocking debris and shattered rockcrete.

It wasn't the Barbican of Themis, but it would do for now.

'Hurry,' said Abidemi, spying a brilliant figure drifting in the storms raging over the battlefield, a demigod haloed by the light of a dying sun. 'The crimson drake nears.'

Numeon had spoken of how Magnus had appeared before him in the warp during their journey to bring Vulkan back to Nocturne. His lost brother had spoken of a primarch, mighty in his own way and deserving of respect, but also somehow… *diminished*.

Abidemi saw none of that here.

Magnus burned like a frozen explosion, a numinous being of radiant energy, his hair billowing around him like a bloody starburst, his armour dazzling in its brilliance. And his eye, *his eye*, burning with the light of impossible stars.

An angel in red and gold, to look upon him was like staring into the sun itself. His armour was brazen, his bearing majestic, and how Abidemi dearly wished things had been different, still feeling that unconscious, unbidden desire to drop to his knees before a primarch.

Magnus was wondrous, yes, but they all felt it: incredulity that a being who could trace his lineage from the Emperor Himself had now set himself to bloody purpose against them.

'Angron and Fulgrim are monsters,' said Abidemi, 'and their corruption is plain for all to see, but Magnus… He could yet fight by his father's side and not look out of place.'

'When was the moment?' Barek Zytos asked the distant

figure of Magnus as he swung the enormous hammer to his shoulder. 'When did you first step from the light?'

'He'd likely not know himself,' said Abidemi, 'for nothing ever begins – there is never just *one* root cause for anything, no singular deed or moment from which an act springs.'

'Why do you say that?' asked Gargo.

'The seeds of any outcome can always be traced back to some earlier moment, and to all those that preceded it. The further back we trace the path, the hazier the connections will become until the tiniest action might be said to have been the origin of any great event.'

'It doesn't matter how it happened,' said Zytos. 'Right now we have enemies to our front and no allies yet at our back.'

'The Blood Angels and the Imperial Fists are en route,' said Abidemi. 'We only have to hold a short time.'

'A short time feels like an eternity when awaiting reinforcements,' said Zytos.

'We are Salamanders,' replied Abidemi as a ragged cohort of limping automata emerged from the fire and smoke of the breach. 'Eternity is our watchword.'

At the sight of the Salamanders, the battle-automata howled with static-laced rage from skewed augmitters, their lolling, half-severed machine skulls flaring with target-locks.

'Down,' said Gargo as heavy shells chugged from smoking rotor cannons and corkscrewing rockets streaked from buckled launchers in fiery trails. The impacts felt like a series of pounding hammer blows on the ground, but the shoulder-high wall Gargo and Zytos had constructed possessed a strength that belied its hasty construction. Its structure was layered and formed from the interlinked stones of Terra that took strength from their neighbour.

A rolling wall of flames billowed over its angled summit, but fire held no fear for Salamanders. They were born of fire and felt its burning kiss every day of their lives. Heavy shells chipped away at the stone, but the shots were wild and inaccurate.

'The radiation is fouling their auspex,' shouted Zytos over the barrage.

More rockets exploded overhead and scything fragments of red-hot steel rained down. The sound within Abidemi's armour was like a bucket of smiter's nails tipped onto a steel plate.

'Give the word,' he said to Gargo.

Gargo placed his hand flat on the ground, and the lenses of his helm dimmed as he read the currents of the earth. Even dulled through the millions of tonnes of metal and stone, he could sense Terra's enemies approaching. Heavy footfalls rang out over rockcrete, and Abidemi's grip tightened on *Draukoros*.

'They're right on top of us,' he shouted.

'Not yet,' promised Gargo.

A grazing blast of solid slugs scythed the air above the wall as a trio of heavy blasts rocked Hemispheric Nine. Chips of stone lashed their armour and sizzling chunks of shrapnel pinged from the rocks in corkscrewing trails.

'Now!' shouted Gargo, and the three Salamanders rose from cover.

The battle-automata were right on top of them, eight within striking distance of their wall. Their armour was bare metal or black; impossible to tell from which maniple they had come. Behind them, the air shimmered with strangely lit fogs, through which flitting shapes darted between firespouts and the crump of secondary and tertiary detonations.

Zytos stepped up onto the chewed-up barrier of rocks and vaulted towards the nearest battle-automaton, a fire-blackened Castellan equipped with a heavy siege-fist and a rotor-barrelled autocannon.

'In Vulkan's name!' he cried, swinging his hammer in a slaughterman's arc.

The killing weight smashed the automaton's already buckled cranial section to ruin. Its limbs folded and flames jetted from its split gorget as it crashed to the ground.

Zytos landed, keeping the hammer in motion and smashing the legs of the machine next to him. The cybernetic's kneecap exploded into shattered fragments, tipping it back down the breach. Gunfire blazed from its weapons, tearing through the lighter backplate of a third automaton and shredding its internal mechanisms.

Gargo dived aside as a siege hammer slammed down on the wall, shattering their barricade to broken pieces. He rolled to his feet before the cybernetic and thrust his spear like a harpoon, driving it deep through a shattered access plate into its guts. He cranked the haft in a circle, drawing a machine shriek of pain from its augmitters before it dropped to its knees, locked in position like a supplicant in a fane.

Abidemi made a quarter-turn to the right and pulled *Draukoros* back as a cybernetic fired a chimeric bolter-assault cannon variant. Heavy shells thundered from the weapon, but its sights were misaligned and the mass-reactives blasted a half-metre gouge through the crest of the breach beside him.

He sprang forward, swaying aside as the machine brought its other arm down, one equipped with a colossal shot-cannon that drooled smoking oil-mix. *Draukoros* chopped through the barrels and the weapon exploded as shells thundered through it. The force of the explosion rocked the machine back on its heels and Abidemi thundered his boot into its chest.

It toppled backwards, the internal mechanisms that had kept it upright scrambled by the blast and the impact. Igen Gargo emptied his bolter into the split carapace of another Castellan.

Mass-reactives detonated in shuddering blasts within, and blue fire erupted from its vent-plates. Zytos slammed his hammer down on the chest of a kneeling robot, and sent it skidding back down the breach.

A burst of shells exploded next to Abidemi, and he threw himself to the side as a whipping coil of energy tore up the stone of the sundered wall. He rolled. The crackling lightning followed him and he grunted as it carved a blistering path across the chestplate of his armour. He felt the heat searing against the carapace beneath. An iron fist plucked him from the ground, and he grunted in pain as burning plates of ceramite were crushed against his chest.

The Castellan hauled him upright and he saw its head section had been split open, revealing a hideous mix of bio-organic machinery. Its torso was leaking flames and smoke, and a hideous screeching machine howl of pain blurted from a dangling augmitter.

The robot rocked back as flames washed over its carapace.

Knowing it was dying, the machine sought to exact its last revenge.

Abidemi felt his bones grind as its fist began to crush his chest.

He hacked *Draukoros* against the automaton's shoulder, but his pain and the angle of the blow robbed it of strength.

He heard the voices of his brothers, shouts of anger and warning.

Hard bangs of bolter fire, and flaming blasts of explosions bursting nearby. A series of thumping detonations erupted farther down the slope of the breach, sending up fiery plumes of irradiated rock and toxic dust.

Even as the flames blurred in his vision, a piercing cold enveloped him, the sensation as sudden as if he had fallen through the ice of a frozen lake.

Dimly he recognised the distinctive double thump of Imperial artillery fire patterns, a strange, ululating howl. Gunship engines?

No, those are the howls of living beings.

The arm of the automaton glistened white, ice particles forming with ultra-rapidity. Abidemi brought *Draukoros* around in one final blow and hacked down on the machine's shoulder.

The metal shattered into frozen fragments and he fell to the crest of the breach, the ground now slick with frost and wet with pools of meltwater. A blizzard of icy needles swirled around him and ferocious winds doused the fires engulfing the remains of the ramparts.

Stalking shapes moved through the cold mist. Hunched and furred like hunters, they moved like feral beasts: hungry, and pitiless. They fell upon the wounded automaton in a flurry of blades, one gutting the machine with a wickedly toothed harpoon as another split it from gorget to belly with a looping axe blow.

A third warrior, armoured in ice grey and mantled in thick furs, slammed down his bone-coloured staff and the stone of the wall split apart as though an earthquake tore at the fortress walls. A wide trench ripped across the length of the breach, fully five metres deep and filled with razored spikes of hardened ice.

Satisfied with his work, he turned to Abidemi.

The warrior's bearded face was cracked and lined like old saddle leather, his beard braided with chips of glass and carved sigils. His eyes were hard flint, cold and sharp.

He had the face of a grinning killer, his teeth sharpened to razor fangs.

'I am Bjarki,' he said. 'This is Svafnir Rackwulf and Olgyr Widdowsyn. We kill sorcerers.'

'What?' said Abidemi. 'Sorcerers?'

'Them,' said Bjarki, pointing to shapes emerging from the glowing mist.

A host of red-armoured warriors of the Thousand Sons, mounted on shimmering discs of light, and led by a towering figure of fire and wrath.

'Magnus...' said Abidemi.

'Maleficarum,' growled Bjarki.

SEVEN

The Wolf and the Dragon

Seeing the red sorcerers sent a tremor of excitement along Bjarki's spine. It had been too long since he'd spilled the blood of his enemies. Though only three of the Rout stood before the Sons of Magnus, too many of his brothers had fallen to their malefic ways for him ever to fear them.

Not even the jagged memories of Nikaea or the newly inconstant path of his wyrd held any terror for him. Since Promeus had told him Magnus would return to the birthrock of humanity in search of his final soul-shard, the suspicion that Terra would be the place of his dying had grown with every passing day.

He'd hoped his thread would finally be cut on Fenris, in battle, knee-deep in icewater and with bloody axe in hand as the final song of the wild hunt echoed in his skull. That hope felt more and more distant every day, but to die in the shadow of the Allfather's Palace was as good a place to meet the end as any warrior might wish.

'They come to finish what they started on Nikaea!' he

shouted, with his fetish-hung staff raised high. 'They took our brothers, cut their threads before their time. Say their names!'

'Gierlothnir Helblind!' cried Svafnir Rackwulf.

'Harr Baelgyr!' shouted Olgyr Widdowsyn.

'Brothers to us all,' answered Bjarki, turning to the three sons of Vulkan. 'But the Allfather brings us new brothers. Tell me your names.'

'I am Atok Abidemi,' said the first of the Salamanders, a powerful warrior with a mighty fang-toothed blade held at his shoulder. 'And these are my fellow Draaksward.'

'Draaksward?' interrupted Bjarki.

'It means Sword Dragon in the old tongue of Nocturne.'

'Good name.'

'The hammer bearer is Barek Zytos,' continued Abidemi. 'The spearman, Igen Gargo.'

'Draaksward, eh? Well, today you are brothers to the Rout,' said Bjarki, slapping a heavy palm on Abidemi's shoulder guard. 'You are part of our watch pack! Six against the hundreds! They will sing songs of our glorious deaths!'

Before the Salamander could object, rippling traceries of light lifted from Bjarki's staff, cold blue and actinic bright. The light was echoed in his eyes as the blistering heat of the breach dropped sharply and fresh webs of frost patterned the molten rocks. Sharp cracks sounded as hardened stone split with the sudden drop in temperature, and the howling of an oncoming gale swept down from the borealis of shield impacts overhead.

The world around Bjarki faded, the outlines of the warriors around him becoming faint, almost ghostlike. Their flesh, that crude matter that bore their true forms, dimmed in his sight, but the souls within...

How bright we all burn. No wonder we were not made to last.

The mortal world was a blur of meaningless shadows. Instead, he now saw avatars of spirit at his side: his fellow sons of Fenris as blooms of cold fire, the Salamanders searing their forms into the air. Streamers of black flame and molten heat buckled the air around them, warrior souls birthed in the violent upheavals of their home world's core.

He heard the muffled barks of bolter fire and felt the bilious taste of warp magic: a mockery of the power infusing his flesh, a corruption of the link between man and the earth they trod. That compact was ancient and sacred, and the powers wielded by the sons of the Cyclops were a sick perversion of that singular bond.

Bjarki could see the enemy coming, too-bright flames against the grey mist of the physical realm, their spirits burning with such all-consuming light he wondered how they could not see that it was devouring them from within. Such a fire would burn away whatever humanity was left to them and leave them naught but ghosts.

Steel clashed with steel, gunfire whipped the smoke, and crumping detonations threw up fountains of rock and dust. None of it touched Bjarki, every shard and fragment whipped away by the whirlwind building around him.

The bleak sorcery of the Thousand Sons twisted reality and broke every natural law, but the icy winds of psychic force building around Bjarki kept the worst of it at bay. Searing fires bent and twisted in the face of his storm's fury. Shivering terrors torn from the blackest corners of a warrior's fear died in the teeth of its spectral ice. The howling unpredictability of the storm made a mockery of any attempt to scry its future path and the actions of the warriors who stood ready at its razored edges.

He saw a shimmering form of mercury brightness. A warrior leaping from the air towards him. Bjarki caught the traitor in an icy squall and slammed him to the ground, stepping in and driving the blazing tip of his staff down through the warrior's chest. Plumes of violet light sprayed from the wound as Bjarki worked the staff deeper. The sorcerer's magic withered in the face of his fraying thread, and Bjarki felt not a moment's pity for him.

The heavy, brutal clash of armour echoed dully within the mist and ice of the storm. This was the oldest form of war known to humanity: grunting men heaving at one another in a contest of strength of arms and legs, of will and determination. No matter how far technology advanced, no matter the sophistication of foes, or whatever arcane rules of combat were in place, it always came down to warriors at close quarters, looking one another in the eye as death hovered close.

An impact spun him around. Mass-reactive. It detonated a fraction of a second later, a tumbling fragment slicing the shaven skin just above his ear. Warm blood ran down his cheek and over his lips. He tasted the hard metal flavour of it and grinned, spreading the blood over his teeth and cheeks with his palm like the savage the Prosperines believed him to be.

Fire bloomed as a phosphor-bright warrior reared up before him. A thrusting staff rammed into his midriff, driving him down to one knee. His foe expected him to retreat, to regain his feet and breath, but Bjarki leaned in. He lunged forward and swung his own staff low, hooking the legs out from the warrior before him.

His fist closed over the helmet of the downed warrior and twin blades of ice stabbed from his palm and through the lenses of the sorcerer's faceplate. Unclean fire gouted from the warrior's mouth, a psychic death spasm that made Bjarki feel unclean to witness.

He shielded his eyes as a newborn sun flared to life overhead.

Looking up through splayed fingers, he saw a titanic form, red and winged, feathered and hard-edged in gold. A rippling vessel of divine flesh forged in a crucible of magic and science. It cycled through a thousand forms in an instant: a wandering sage, a winged avatar of temptation, a vast wheel of eyes that turned ten thousand times in an instant – wing upon wing, millions of seething protean forms that would never be born, and multitudes more that would be.

Bjarki felt a sliver of horror slide into his soul.

Magnus the Red.

They had fought avatars of the Crimson King's soul on Aghoru and Nikaea, but this was the primarch restored. Before, they'd possessed weapons to fight Magnus: a vessel to bind his soul, or a monster that was his equal. Now they had nothing but their own skill at arms and strength of heart.

How pitiful that was.

The thought lasted a fraction of a second only, but it was enough to stoke the fires of Bjarki's rage. They were the Sons of Russ, warriors of the Wolf King. No fight was unwinnable to them, no foe invincible. The Allfather had seen fit to bring him to this place, and for his own resolve to falter at the first sight of the enemy drove Bjarki into a towering fury.

He threw back his head and loosed a howl that would have frozen the blood of every prey creature on Fenris. It was the howl of the world wolf, the weaver of wyrd, and the heart-beat of the universe.

He felt the smouldering, soot-black presence of Nocturne's sons and grinned.

'What are you doing?' said Abidemi, sensing the imminence of his power.

'The icy heart of Fenris is far, and its song is little more than a whisper on the wind,' said Bjarki, his voice oddly textured, as though echoing from the heart of a cave. 'But the world spirit of Terra…? It is *old* and it is *deep*. The power that moves within its bedrock and flows in the seams between its skin of stone is the strongest I have ever felt.'

Bjarki extended his bloodied gauntlet.

'Take my hand, Atok Abidemi, and we will fly as dragons of fire and ice!'

The Draaksward gripped his arm in the old way, and Bjarki brought his staff down hard.

The rock beneath split with the otherworldly force of impact, as if the hand-carved wolfwood of the staff had bored down into the very heart of the world.

So much power. Truly, where else could the Allfather's dream take flight but here…?

A geyser of power poured into Bjarki and Abidemi, channelled by the grain and whorls of the staff's structure and given form by the legacies of honour carried by the two warriors.

Razored daggers of ice and ash swirled around him, and he spun his staff to drive the furious ambition of the power wrought between them to greater intensity. The icy winds surrounding Bjarki howled as though the fanged companions of the Wolf King himself attended him, even as the choking heat of the ash blistered his skin.

An eruption of light exploded above them, twin forms intertwining, serpentine and *alive*.

They coiled around one another as they rose higher into the air, screaming at this birth as though the mortal world were hostile to them. One was sheened in white, blinding in its feral radiance: a rearing wolf of dazzling brilliance, woven from raptures and the cold legends of Fenris. Its twin was its opposite in every way, a draconic titan of burning black smoke, shot through with blazing veins of molten orange.

Its eyes were smouldering coals, tempered in the heart of a forge and ready to burn, its teeth and claws were ebon hooks.

Their howls and roars shook the earth itself as they reared beyond Abidemi and Bjarki, twisting around one another until their opposing natures forced them apart.

The twin avatars fell upon the blazing light of Magnus on wings of ember and howls of vengeance. Claws of ice tore at the primarch as pyroclastic clouds billowed in the breath of the furnace serpent. It choked the vents and rebreathers of the traitors below with burning ash.

The storm of ash and fire scoured the ground before the breach, throwing up screeds of irradiated rubble and debris. Superheated steam vaporised unprotected flesh, and frozen limbs shattered at the slightest impact. Fused with the energies of Terra's world spirit, no sorcery could breach that barrier, or harm those behind it.

'It's beautiful...' whispered Abidemi, his voice carrying to Bjarki despite the storm.

'Do not look upon it,' replied Bjarki, his voice cracking with the strain of conjuring such awesome energies. 'Such powers do not suffer the sight of mortals.'

The forge dragon coiled around Magnus, and Bjarki could see flickering points of light borne up by its motion. The light of subtle bodies, dimming like drifting cinders blown from a dying fire. The lone wolf, never one for the leash, circled the primarch, its jaws snapping shut on Magnus' light even as it herded others into the fires of the dragon's wrath.

The wolf and the dragon basked in their freedom, revelling in the all-too-mortal urge to destroy without conscience, to wreak havoc without consequence. The light of Magnus dimmed, obscured by a blizzard of ice and seething clouds of volcanic smoke. A black rain, cold and caustic, fell in greasy sheets, and Bjarki tasted the hot metal and molten stone borne upwards from Terra's lightless depths.

He felt the presence of Magnus diminish. Not in death,

never that. No power conjured by mere mortals could achieve such a feat. Not in death, but in defeat. Bjarki felt the fury of the Red Cyclops, the arrogant rage of a victory snatched away. Magnus was strong, but his certainty of his own infallibility was his greatest weakness.

Bjarki sank to his knees, savouring the fury of the world wolf even as the connection to it devoured him from within. Abidemi went down with him, unable to release his grip, their arms locked together as surely as if they were conjoined from birth.

Explosions painted the air, hundreds of detonations marching down the breach. Hard echoes of mass-reactives burst around them in swelling volleys. He caught glimpses of transhuman figures in blood red and vivid gold.

Imperial banners whipped by the thermal vortices.

'So… powerful,' he said. 'Have you ever felt anything like it…?'

'Bjarki,' grunted Abidemi. 'It's… killing… us. Let it go!'

He felt Abidemi struggle to release his grip, the dragon's continued existence consuming the Salamander as surely as the wolf was Bjarki. But he tightened his hold, binding them together and ignoring his own warning to stare into the struggle above.

'Must hold… on,' he said through gritted, bloody teeth. 'Magnus must pay!'

'Release me!' demanded Abidemi, surging to his feet, but Bjarki could not follow. His limbs were powerless, drained of marrow and bone and meat and muscle, utterly without strength.

'You must let it go!' yelled Abidemi. 'The warriors of the Angel and Dorn are here!'

'No, brother…' he said. 'Not yet. Must… finish this…'

Bjarki's vision faded to grey, misty as the thread of his life unwound. He felt the brightness of unshakeable resolve fill his brother Astartes.

Was it time already? Surely not so soon…

He looked up and saw the flash of an ancient blade being raised.

Firelight glinted from ebon teeth that tore the air with a roar to match that of the dragon.

Bjarki had given all to bring the world wolf and forge dragon into being.

It was killing him, but he had driven the Crimson King back.

Bjarki was not about to give up power such as that.

And Atok Abidemi knew it.

'I am sorry, brother,' said Abidemi.

Draukoros swung down, severing Bjarki's arm just below the elbow.

Alivia did not know where she was.

Down in the darkness beneath the world that shouldn't have surprised her. The foundations of the Imperial Palace were ancient and deep, built and rebuilt a thousand times over the millennia. No cartographer could ever fully map its labyrinthine depths, and no technology had reliably plumbed its endlessly twisting passageways.

But no one knew these secret ways better than Malcador.

The passage he led Alivia down was uncomfortably narrow, wide enough only for her to follow in the Sigillite's footsteps. The walls were fashioned from glossy black tiles, repellently slick to the touch and suspiciously free of dust or cracks. Something in the oddly angled dimensions of the tunnel, together with the offset placement of the unique tiles and their ill-proportioned scale, sent a tremor of unease down Alivia's spine. No two tiles were alike, and Alivia's suspicion was that some fundamental difference existed between her human sensory perceptions and those of the passageway's builders.

With each branching twist downwards, she felt less and less sure that she could navigate back to the surface and the unremarkable door at the base of the drum tower through which they'd begun this journey.

With Promeus' pronouncement that Magnus was attacking the Western Hemispheric, the warriors of the Rout had rushed away. Just before slamming the door behind him, Bjarki had looked back at her and she'd thought for a single, ridiculous, moment he was expecting her to follow him.

Yes, Alivia had some skill at arms, and yes, she had killed more people than she cared to remember, but she wasn't a soldier. She hadn't stood in the ranks since the conquests of Boeotia and Euboea, and this was not a war where individual martial ability mattered, not in any meaningful way.

But Bjarki had only sent a warning glance at Malcador and said, 'Watch that one, and take care with your wyrd, Mistress Sureka,' before vanishing with his brothers.

Alivia kept her gaze fixed on Malcador's back, finding that looking too long at the oddly angled tiles made her feel mildly nauseous. It was cold down here, and she was thankful for the thermal bindings beneath her thick coat. Vivyen's chapbook nestled inside a pocket of the inner liner, her daughter insisting on the verge of tears that she take it with her before leaving for her meeting with Malcador in the drum tower. Alivia had gratefully accepted it, knowing she would have little time to read any of the many stories within.

To keep her head warm, she wore a thick *ushanka* with furred flaps that covered her ears and tied beneath her chin. Above her right eye, a brass pin badge depicted a pair of crossed lances over a silver skull. What regiment it represented was a mystery, and Alivia hoped there wasn't a soldier somewhere out on the walls with ears that were freezing off thanks to her petty theft.

Malcador, too, wore a heavy cloak of furs and a thick, turban-like head covering, though she suspected his concession to warmth was an affectation. Still, the fingers gripping the onyx black of his staff were pale and bloodless, so perhaps he *did* feel the cold.

'You still haven't told me where we're going,' she said.

Her voice echoed strangely, as if the gloss black walls weren't reflecting sound quite the way they should.

'And nor shall I,' said Malcador. 'To speak of a thing is to fix it in place, and the paths I must navigate through the Palace will only lead us astray if our destination is named.'

'Always with the riddles. It's one of the many, *many* things I hate about you.'

Malcador looked up and around, as though afraid of being overheard.

'I don't seek to deceive you, Alivia, but you know as well as I that some things cannot be spoken of simply.'

'These aren't normal tunnels, are they?'

'No, they are not,' admitted Malcador. 'Sometimes even I must move unseen through the warp and weft of its architect's grand design.'

'Does the Emperor know of these tunnels? The Custodians? I imagine Valdor would be *very* interested to know there are secret ways through the Palace even he doesn't know.'

'Constantin protects the Emperor in his way, I protect Him in mine.'

'And I'm guessing Valdor wouldn't approve of your way. Why is that?'

'The Custodians are loyal beyond imagining,' said Malcador. 'Beyond any understanding you or I could possibly comprehend. It is literally coded into their very genes and psyche, and while that iron devotion is necessary, it is sometimes too dogmatic to accept any option that might place their charge in danger.'

Alivia stopped, as shocked as if Malcador had slapped her. 'Is this, whatever *this* is, putting the Emperor in danger?'

'It might, yes, but it is by His own design and His own devising,' said Malcador.

'Why?'

'Redemption.'

'Redemption? Whose?'

'Perhaps all of us,' said Malcador, turning and walking away.

Alivia shook her head. Was nothing simple any more?

When had things ever *been simple?*

'Well, if you won't say where we're going, at least tell me why you need *me*,' said Alivia. 'What can I do, *only* me, that makes you willing to listen to John and ease my family's passage to Terra? And then grant them sanctuary within the inner walls of the Palace. Tell me that, and no riddles or I swear I'll strangle you right now.'

'I told you, I need you to save the Emperor.'

'I presumed that was grandstanding for Promeus and the Wolves. Tell me the real reason.'

'That *is* the real reason,' said Malcador, pausing to rest on his staff. 'I know you don't trust me, Alivia–'

She laughed bitterly. 'You've never given me a reason to trust you. All the long years I've known you, known Him, I can count on one hand the number of times you've given me a straight answer.'

'Civilisations are not won and held by men who give straight answers.'

'That's a depressing world view.'

Malcador sighed, as if tiring of her barbs.

'The war against Horus has many fronts,' he said. 'It is fought in grand strategic realms where the likes of Rogal Dorn and his brothers excel, and it is fought through the sights of a lowly las-trooper, such as the young man of the Sixteenth Arctic Hort whose ushanka you wear.'

Alivia took off her hat and squinted at the regimental crest.

'And it is waged by those who walk in shadow, who must shoulder the burden of decisions too terrible for others to bear, who must make dreadful choices no one should ever face.'

Here he paused to look back at Alivia. 'And it is waged by those who can suffer the many hurts such a long war entails.'

'Is that why John and I are here?' asked Alivia. 'What about the others? Oll? Prytanis? What about them? Are they here too?'

'Some, and they too will play their part. Some willingly, some less so.'

'Is John here? In the Palace, I mean?'

He hesitated before answering. 'Wherever John is, he is where he needs to be.'

Malcador led them to a tapered doorway, barely tall or wide enough for either of them to pass through. Alivia had the sense of a large space beyond and felt a cold wind caress the skin of her cheeks, bearing the taste of salt: like ocean spray at a wharf. It didn't taste like any air she'd breathed on Terra. It felt old and dead.

She ducked through and a moment of dizzying vertigo seized her as she moved from the claustrophobic passageway to a vast cavern whose ceiling rose to cloud-lapped heights, and which fell into a depthless chasm that echoed to the sound of waterfalls.

Alivia sank to one knee, pressing a palm flat on the ground to steady herself.

Malcador reached out to touch her shoulder. The strength of his grip was surprising for a man so thin-boned and tired looking.

She flinched in revulsion. He hadn't made contact with her skin, but her reaction was instinctual: a primate's reaction to being touched by things that squirm and crawl in darkness.

'Alivia?'

'Don't touch me again,' she said, taking a deep breath.

He nodded and turned back to their route.

'Then follow me. And stay close.'

She rose on unsteady legs and followed him onto an outflung walkway that arched out over the chasm to a distant column of red stone that looked wholly alien to Terra.

Square-cut steps corkscrewed down its length, descending into darkness.

'These are *definitely* not normal tunnels,' said Alivia.

'They were abandoned before the first stone of the first tower was laid on the mountains above,' said Malcador. 'The builders of Leng knew of these low roads, but eventually abandoned them. Some of the markers down here are theirs, but they had long departed this realm before the Emperor unlocked the gates sealing them.'

'How do you navigate down here?' asked Alivia. 'I get the sense there isn't a map. At least not in any normal sense.'

'There are maps of meaning if you know where to look and how to read them, but even I walk these paths with care. A way that was open one time may be closed another. Or ways that never were now beckon the unwary traveller.'

'Have you ever got lost down here?'

'Thankfully not,' said Malcador. 'But I have seen the bones of those who have.'

'Well, that's reassuring.'

'Come,' said Malcador. 'Stay close, and I will show you where gods have walked.'

'I've seen places like that,' said Alivia. 'They're filled with the blood and bodies of mortals.'

BOOK THREE

HALL OF LENG

EIGHT

Souls of Consequence

The scale of the devastation was almost impossible to process.

Viewed through the cracked and filmy armourglass of a circling Storm Eagle, Promeus guessed the entire nineteen-kilometre stretch of Western Hemispheric had borne the brunt of this latest assault.

Fires burned all along the length of the wall, and soot-black smoke shrouded the ramparts.

A pall of dust and aerosolised blood made every breath taste of metal.

The entirety of the wall was a scene of horror, but it was upon the breach where the atomic had detonated that Promeus focused his gaze.

'Radiation levels are too high for non-Astartes,' said the pilot over the vox.

His name was Kandallo, and he was a stoic warrior in the gold livery of an Imperial Fist. His right arm was missing, as was most of his left leg. Wire-bound lengths of neuro-activator cable clamped to his raw stumps allowed him to fly the Storm

Eagle one-handed until he could be fitted with augmetics that would allow him to return to the front lines.

The clicking of the gunship's rad counter had become so concentrated that it was now a continuous, droning backdrop that not even the deafening roar of the Storm Eagle's engines could entirely obscure.

'I've taken high-dose anti-rad meds,' said Promeus, 'and I don't intend to be here long.'

'Every minute you spend in these levels is one minute too many.'

'Then I'll be quick.'

'Be sure that you are.'

Promeus knew that coming this close to the aftermath of an atomic detonation was recklessly dangerous, but the nagging sensation of something terribly amiss was a hungry rat gnawing its way out of his belly. He didn't know *what* was wrong, only that something was off-kilter in a fundamental way.

Kandallo brought the gunship in low from the north-east, keeping as close to the shattered rooftops as possible. Airspace within the aegis was rigidly controlled, and anything airborne was considered a target unless proven otherwise. Their authorisation to fly within the Palace precincts came from the Sigillite himself – by virtue of Promeus' connection to Magnus – but even so, the dull, psychic awareness of the servitor-crewed guns on the walls tracking them was unmistakeable.

He tried and failed to process the scale of the fight that had taken place here; it was impossible to comprehend – as was almost every engagement in this siege. Corpses without number bedecked the walls and the slopes before them, the swathes of ruined flesh badly mangled and so thoroughly dismembered that it was impossible even to guess how many had died.

Thousands? Tens of thousands? Just another day, another *afternoon*, on Terra.

Hundreds of wounded stumbled away from the walls, covered in blood and lost to the shock-trauma of the assault. Many were missing limbs and didn't seem to notice, or carried them bundled in their uniform jackets. Flash-blinded wretches clung to the walls in darkness or were helped by their sobbing comrades. The death toll here would be abominable, but the roll call for the wounded would be many times larger.

'Even if we win, will we be able to bear the cost…?' he whispered.

His gaze lingered on a group of Blood Angels moving through the crowds of wounded, the red of their warplate scoured by the fire and fury of the attack. Something in their bearing struck Promeus as unusual, but a drifting bank of smoke obscured the ground, and when he looked again, he could no longer see them.

Human remains mingled with Astartes bodies and those of other creatures with matted fur, scaled hides and leathery flesh, for the attack had not simply ended with the arrival of the IX and VII Legions. It had taken the ferocity of the combined Blood Angels, Imperial Fists and Army reserves in sealed tanks to push the Thousand Sons and their bestial allies from the wall. The beasts had been scorched hairless by radiation, their wasted bodies blistering and sloughing flesh from their bones, but they had fought tooth and claw to cling to the walls.

Tamaya's Blood Angels held the flanks of the main breach, with an unbroken wall of Iacono's Imperial Fists holding and rebuilding the centre. A haze of furnace heat rippled the air over the wall as securement parties hosed the breach with rapid-setting lockcrete, pierced the ground with blast-shot rebar, and bolted refractor generators into place atop the surviving portions of the parapet.

'Given twelve hours, the Imperial Fists could make this wall viable again,' said Kandallo.

'Time is the one thing we don't have,' said Promeus, looking into the crackling smog banks beyond the walls, like tsunamis of elemental force ready to crash over the Palace and everyone within it. 'And no matter what they're able to do, it won't be enough.'

Shadows jerked and stuttered in the fog, fleeting impressions of horns and claws, teeth and unblinking eyes. Such malice was hidden within, potent and hate-filled.

So much had happened since the heady, innocent days when he and Kallista, Camille and Mahavastu had shared caffeine under an awning and debated why they had been assigned as remembrancers to the XV Legion. Back then, the galaxy made sense, and the idea that the Thousand Sons would follow the Warmaster down the road of treachery was absurd.

Treachery.

The very word tasted ashen in his mouth.

Even after all he had seen and done, he could still barely bring himself to speak it.

The Storm Eagle tilted on its axis and began a rapid downwards spiral, guided in by an Imperial Fist in armour so drenched in gore that Promeus first mistook him for one of the Angel's warriors.

Promeus unbuckled himself from the grav-seat as the crew door rolled back and hot air surged inside. Immediately, his skin felt the killing blush of radiation, and his heart rate spiked as he tasted the heavy metals, isotopic toxins and caustic fumes casting a pall over Western Hemispheric.

'Remember, do not linger here,' warned Kandallo.

Promeus nodded and stepped down from the gunship. He felt the heat through his boots, each step sticky as the thick rubber soles softened. Thousands of warriors moved through the space behind the wall, bulky transhumans in heavy warplate, masked Army and dozens of pioneer units working to shore up the damage.

'This is no place for mortals,' said the Imperial Fist who'd guided the gunship down.

'So I'm told,' replied Promeus.

'You should get back on that gunship and leave,' insisted the warrior.

Promeus shook his head. 'I'm looking for Bödvar Bjarki, a warrior of the Sixth Legion.'

The Imperial Fist jerked his thumb in the direction of a series of plastic-sided tents set up in the lee of the wall. A hastily assembled aid station.

Promeus started to thank him, but the warrior was already moving away, discarding any memory of his presence. He shrugged and hurried over to the aid station, clutching his musette bag tight as he heard loud cursing in *Futharc* from within. Lakes of murky water pooled around its perimeter, and acrid counterseptic fumes hung in the air.

He pushed through a rubber strip-curtain, tasting the bitter reek of lye and the warm, metallic flavour of the decontamination showers. The interior of the aid station was filled with Astartes warriors, the vulnerable joints and cabling of their armour being hosed clean of radioactive dust. Most were Blood Angels and Imperial Fists, so it wasn't hard to spot Svafnir Rackwulf and Olgyr Widdowsyn. They stood with their arms upraised as medicae personnel in hazmat suits hosed them down with chlorinated water and scrubbed their armour with hard-bristled brushes.

Both Astartes seemed to find the process wildly amusing, and laughed at the none-too-gentle attentions of the medicae staff. Patches of bare metal gleamed where their Legion colours had been scoured away by radiation and the decontamination process.

Rackwulf saw him coming and said, 'You come for a cooling shower too, wyrd-wraith?'

'These men with the brushes, they tickle,' added Widdowsyn.

'Where's Bjarki?' he said.

'There,' said Rackwulf, spitting a wad of phlegm to the rear of the aid station.

Promeus nodded and eased his way through the masked staff and armoured warriors to find Bjarki sitting on an empty ammo crate. A warrior in unfamiliar armour and with his back to Promeus was bent over the Space Wolf, working on something he couldn't see.

Two warriors in dripping, gleaming warplate stood over him, and such was the damage done to their armour, it took Promeus a second to realise they were XVIII Legion. Like Rackwulf and Widdowsyn, much of their colours had been burned and scoured away, leaving their armour a patchwork of jade green and raw ceramite.

'Salamanders?' he said, and the two warriors turned to face him.

Hostility bristled from them, and Promeus halted, his hands spread wide.

'Promeus?' said Bjarki without looking up. 'Even over the stink of decontaminants I can still smell you. Your sweat tastes of *hrosshvalus* blubber, but you shouldn't be here unless it's to take a shower. There's rad-fire all around. Very bad for mortals, they tell me. Bad for us too, but not so bad it'll kill us.'

'Did you see him?' asked Promeus.

'See who?'

'Magnus, who else? Did you… Wait, what happened to your arm?'

The Salamander with his back to Promeus had sat up straight, revealing the work he'd been doing to seal off the stump where Bjarki's left arm had once been. A crude clamp had been affixed to Bjarki's armour around his elbow, a beaten metal cap to cover the stump of his arm. Promeus' hand of flesh and blood went to the porcelain smoothness of his own augmetic as the memory of Kamiti Sona and the agonising fire that burned away his limb returned.

Bjarki saw the gesture and said, '*Ja*, I now know your pain, remembrancer.'

'What happened?'

Bjarki nodded to the towering Salamander and said, 'My new brother, Atok Abidemi, cut it off with that big bastard sword of his.'

Promeus glanced at the monstrous, jagged-toothed chain-sword at Abidemi's back, and didn't doubt for a second that it might have hewn Bjarki's arm.

'Why?'

'Because he would have killed us both if I had not,' said the warrior Bjarki had named Abidemi, his voice like blocks of igneous rock grinding together in the throat of a volcano.

'He's not wrong,' said Bjarki, as if the matter of his missing arm were of no consequence. 'The power of the world wolf is like too much *dzira*. Once it gets in your blood, it is hard to resist holding on to that feeling just a little longer, even as it kills you. I used my strength and that of Atok to draw forth the manifest power of our Legions – a mighty dragon of fire and ash from his, a winter wolf of endless ice from mine. Such a sight, Promeus, you would have written epics of their battle! They tore at the Red Cyclops, and by the Allfather's oath he shed blood. To see him hurting… ah, it was a fine thing, too fine. In my fury, I would have killed us both to see the monster bleed a little longer…'

'You hurt him? *You actually hurt Magnus the Red?*'

'Aye, we did!'

The warrior Bjarki had named Abidemi appraised him coolly.

'This is the one you spoke of?' he said, rising to his full height. 'The one who hosted the Crimson King's soul for a time?'

The words were edged in violence, as though Abidemi might reach for his hideous sword and split Promeus in two.

'That's him,' replied Bjarki, flexing what remained of his arm. 'He doesn't look like much, but there's strength to him. You have no cause to fret on his loyalty, fireborn. His wyrd and that of the Red Cyclops are no longer entwined, but they do remember each other. It was Promeus who warned us of the traitor's presence at Western Hemispheric.'

Abidemi tilted his head to the side, reappraising him. Promeus' heart thudded hard in his chest as the Salamander swept up his sword, but it was only to sheathe it over his shoulder.

The warrior took a step towards Promeus, his red eyes boring into him.

'Why are you here?' he asked. 'You must have been told this area was lethally dangerous to mortals, yet still you came. Why?'

Promeus resisted taking a backward step in the face of the Salamander's bulk. The man's ebon skin and burning eyes were utterly inhuman, but he saw something there he recognised.

'Because something's wrong. I don't know what, but nothing of this attack makes sense. For as long as the Warmaster's forces have been attacking the walls, we've seen nothing of Magnus beyond the attack on Gorgon Bar and Colossi. Why Western Hemispheric? Why now? Why use a weapon to breach the walls that prevents you using your overwhelming advantage in numbers? Why give up so easily after such an explosive breach?'

'You think the Sons gave up *easily*?' said one of the Salamanders behind him, a titan with a grotesquely oversized hammer held at his shoulders. Promeus hadn't noticed until now, but he was completely boxed in by the Salamanders.

Despite Bjarki's vouchsafe, they didn't trust him.

In their eyes he was tainted by the touch of the Crimson King.

'Tell me what happened with Magnus,' said Promeus. 'All of you. Leave nothing out.'

Abidemi began the tale, his account dry and factual, and Promeus let his psychic senses drift slowly outwards, drawing in the memory of what the Salamander had seen and felt. As Bjarki added his own account to the story, more details took shape in Promeus' mind.

In his original life, the one before his selection to the remembrancer order, before even the fruitless years he'd spent scouring the globe in search of a cure for his dying wife, he had used his psychic ability to read the auras of those with whom he did business, sifting truth from lies and following his preternatural intuition to become absurdly wealthy.

Now he built the memory of these warriors into a mental projection within his mind, seeing the desperate conflict on the ramparts. The smoke, the blood, the screaming and the thunderous blasts of artillery. He felt the heat of the dragon's birth and the bone-freezing cold of the wolf's breath.

As truly awesome as they were, his mortal heart quailed at the sight of them.

These were the unleashed souls of Bjarki and Abidemi's Legions, and only a madman wouldn't recoil in horror at the sight of such pure destructive force given form.

We yoked the power of monsters to our cause.

He stiffened as he saw the Legion avatars coil around the numinous figure of Magnus, clawing and biting, tearing and ripping the pristine gold of his armoured form. Promeus tasted the black rain, like the deluge that had drowned Prospero's last moments. He had not seen that rain, hadn't tasted its ashen, brackish flavour, but the shard of the Crimson King's soul had seen it and tasted it, so the memory was as strong as if he'd stood amid the fires of Tizca's doom and watched it burn.

He saw Magnus scream in pain, and understood Bjarki's reluctance to release the power that was hurting his most hated enemy. A flash of gold, a bloom of red in the tortured sky, and it was over. The Sons falling back, their godlike master banished from sight.

When the tale was finished, Promeus felt the heat and ice of the twin avatars flow from his body, and he was glad of their departure. He replayed their last moments in his mind, seeing again the agony of Magnus, the fear in his eye as he quit the field of battle.

Again.

Wolf and dragon, biting and clawing.

Again.

Golden lightning. A whipcrack of displaced air. A sliver of gold, a breath of old air.

Again.

Fear in Magnus' eye.

No. That's what he wanted anyone with the wit to see to think.

Promeus turned to Abidemi. 'You saw him retreat? Magnus? You saw him fall back with his Legion sons?'

'I did,' said Abidemi.

'You're sure? Absolutely sure?'

'Yes,' snapped Abidemi. 'My eyes pierce smoke and fire better than any man here. I saw him broken and bleeding. I saw him limp back into the concealing smog.'

'Did you?' said Promeus urgently. 'I need to know you saw him retreat.'

'I did,' said Bjarki, standing and gathering up his staff. 'Why do you need to know if we saw him flee?'

'I think you saw what he wanted you to see,' said Promeus, turning and running from the aid station. A dreadful, gut-wrenching sensation was uncoiling in his stomach. Perhaps it was nascent radiation poisoning, but he didn't think so. His mind awash with images of Magnus in battle with the wolf and the dragon, Promeus cast his mind outward, far beyond the battle-ruined shell of Western Hemispheric.

Ahzek Ahriman had taught him how to push his mind farther than he'd ever thought possible, and the irony that he was now turning those self-same powers against them was not lost on Promeus.

He fell to his knees as he tasted the very edges of the hate, horror and madness beyond the walls. A swamp of minds broken and enslaved, an ocean of sickness with fragments of poisoned glass lodged in every heart and every eye.

Amid the millions of firefly pinpricks of mortal and Astartes lives, larger suns burned, too bright to look upon. Once mighty souls, bound to a higher purpose, and now sullied by a doom of their own making. His power was not so great as to name them or see them as anything other than impossibly powerful stars of cursed brightness.

Yet even among these damned stars, one ought to have burned brighter than all others.

'You're not there...' said Promeus.

'What are you talking about?' demanded Abidemi.

Promeus turned to face the warriors of the Salamanders and Space Wolves, looking past them to the very heart of the Emperor's fastness.

Now he understood the source of his gnawing fear.

'The Crimson King...' said Promeus. 'He's *inside* the Palace.'

They moved through the defenders like ghosts.

Like prey animals deep in the hunting grounds of carnotaurs.

The air was thick with radiation and fear.

Is this the end?

Who will look after my children when I'm gone?

The Emperor protects.

I don't want to die.

The Emperor has abandoned us.

Take him, *not me.*

The five of them moved against the human tide, heading eastward from the ruins of Western Hemispheric. Shell impacts flared overhead, amid streaking contrails of missiles and atmospheric detonations. They mimicked the leaden gait of the wounded or traumatised who simply wandered away from the aftermath of the fighting.

As if there could ever be an escape from the grinding slaughters enacted every day.

Magnus looked down at the warplate of his sons, Ahriman, Amon, Menkaura and Atrahasis, still seeing the proud red and the pale serpentine circle emblazoned on their shoulder guards. A symbol that marked them as bound to the service of the Warmaster.

But I...

To any who looked upon him, Magnus was now cloaked in the illusory guise of a loyalist warrior of the line: sturdy Mark IV armour and a chipped shoulder guard bearing the winged blood drop of the IX Legion.

He felt his sons' discomfort at seeing their gene-sire as one of them.

'It disturbs you to see me thusly?' asked Magnus.

His voice was calm, soothing and confident, but devoid of its usual commanding power.

+As it would any of your loyal sons, my lord,+ sent Ahriman.

'Speak aloud,' warned Magnus. ***'The hunters will be alert for psychic anomalies within the Sanctum Imperialis.'***

'Apologies, my lord,' said Ahriman, 'but I find it hard to reconcile the image of an enemy with the knowledge that he is my primarch. Even the greatest magi of the Athanaeans would balk at psychic manipulation on such a colossal scale.'

Thousands of enemy surrounded them: loyalist Astartes, Army, Mechanicum, civilian and migou workers, but none of them truly saw the Thousand Sons in their midst. The dull minds of mortals and their once-brothers pressed in on Ahriman's consciousness like a polluted ocean rising to swallow an island paradise.

'This host does not care about us,' said Magnus. ***'They think only in terms of the minute-to-minute horror they feel, their fear of pain and what they can inflict in retaliation.'***

'You are my primarch,' said Ahriman. 'I have seen your power bear an entire city across the galaxy, but *this*... How is it possible we walk unseen in the lair of our enemies beneath their telaethesic shield?'

'Look up,' said Magnus. ***'What do you see?'***

'A rippling sheen of petrochemical light refracting through the aegis shield.'

'And?'

'Patterns. Chaotically evolving fractals where the shield is failing,' said Ahriman, and Magnus felt his focus drift as it followed the endlessly dividing spirals of variegated light. 'I sense deeper meaning might reveal itself if only I had time to divine it.'

'Careful,' warned Magnus. ***'Do not leave the fifth enumeration.'***

Ahriman pulled his focus back to that most fickle of the golden steps.

'What do *you* see, my lord?' asked Menkaura.

'I see light,' said Magnus. ***'Reflected light that touches the retinae of everybody around us. The wondrous complexity of the human eye's biological mechanisms transforms the photons into electrical***

signals to be interpreted by the brain. Under normal circumstances, were their brains to read those signals correctly, the defenders would perceive our true forms. But I am convincing the brains of all these people to ignore those signals. We are visible in forms I choose for them to perceive.'

'I have only ever performed so elaborate a deception on a single person,' said Amon. 'But to compromise the neurological belief systems of so many psyches at once…'

'It helps that these men and women are utterly exhausted,' said Magnus. *'Their mental faculties have been ground down almost to the level of servitors after weeks of constant horror. All of which makes it easier to manipulate so many minds without triggering the psychic watchdogs of the Inner Palace, though I use the word "easier" guardedly.'*

'Not every mind here is so blunted,' said Menkaura, his venerable gaze sweeping the faces of the Imperial soldiers.

Magnus nodded. *'Yes, there are some gifted beyond baseline norms, ones with latent sparks that might have been nurtured to greatness with but the slightest care. As much as their dulled sensibilities make it possible to shield us, it saddens me to know that none of these minds will ever reach even a fraction of their true potential.* That *is what we will change when this is over, when we can build out the psychic genome properly.'*

Magnus caught a flash of a memory from Ahriman, quickly suppressed, but there was little his sons might think that he would not know.

A battered Storm Eagle gunship, its hull plates a dull ochre colour.

A fleeting moment of connection snapping his head around.

A singular mind within…

'Lemuel Gaumon,' said Magnus, and felt Ahriman flinch at the mention of the man who had dogged their footsteps since before the Warmaster's rebellion. *'I too felt his presence. His flesh held a fragment of my soul. How could I not?'*

Ahriman hesitated before replying.

'It disturbs me that he is here, my lord. I thought he would be dead.'

Magnus shook his head. ***'We all did, but it means nothing, Ahzek. The greatest conflict the galaxy has ever seen reaches its climax, and the players in this drama must congregate. From the lead actors to the chorus, where else in this melodrama could any soul of consequence be drawn?'***

'I almost reached out to brush his thoughts,' said Ahriman, looking out over the teeming multitudes of Imperial souls. 'Even thinking of Lemuel makes my grip falter.'

Magnus understood the *real* source of Ahriman's troubles. It touched him too.

'You feel them all, yes?' said Magnus, letting his eyes drift, unfocused, over the doomed defenders of his father's Palace. ***'Their minds. All their thoughts and fears.'***

'I do,' replied Ahriman. 'Nobility and wretchedness, and everything in between.'

'The realisation of mortality brings out the best and worst of humanity.'

The woman who visits underground gatherings of one they call the Saint and dreams of being lifted into the sky on her wings of silver and gold.

The man who sleeps with his commanding officer in hopes of being posted to an unengaged part of the wall.

The man who murdered his wife and volunteered for Western Hemispheric, wrongly thinking his dying will somehow atone for the deed.

The boy who thought this fight would be a grand adventure, but who has now discovered the truth of war's lie.

So many minds, so many thoughts.

Truth be told, Magnus was enjoying the sheer hubris of this venture.

Bjarki had commandeered a vehicle by the time Promeus had sent word back to the Bhab Bastion of the Crimson King's intrusion. When Promeus emerged from the aid station, he saw Bjarki pulling up in a boxy slab of metal mounted on quad-tracks with a fore-mounted turret fitted with some kind of gatling cannon. Widdowsyn climbed aboard to man the topside gun, as the three Salamanders circled the vehicle with disdainful eyes.

The Rune Priest dropped down from the armoured side door and battered his one remaining fist against the vehicle's dusty, bullet-scarred plating.

'Look at this!' he cried. 'The man who gave me this said it is called a Taurox.'

'It's the ugliest thing I've ever seen,' said Promeus. 'Throne, is it even safe? It looks like something that's been looted by Nordafrik rad-scavvers before being looted back again by the Army, who didn't even bother to undo the damage.'

'We are none of us pretty,' said Bjarki, grinning and holding up his severed arm. 'Besides, Barek Zytos tells me a taurox is a legendary beast of their home world. A good sign, ja?'

'A taurox is a lethally dangerous beast of the Arridian Plain,' said Zytos, locking his hammer over his shoulder. 'I always wanted to kill a bull taurox one day, but I do not suppose I ever will now.'

'*Gave* you it?' said Promeus, rapping his knuckles on the battered plating. Flakes of rust drifted.

Bjarki shrugged. 'He wasn't using it, and the men it once carried are dead.'

'Oh, well that makes me feel a whole lot better about riding in it.'

'It is no Thunderwolf, but at least it is fast.'

Bjarki planted his staff and leaned it against the hull of the Taurox as Abidemi circled around to the crew door. Before the Salamander could climb aboard, he said, 'Friend Atok.'

Abidemi turned, his dark skin sheened in sweat and his eyes alight with fresh purpose.

Bjarki stood before him as Svafnir Rackwulf circled around behind, a pack-mate sealing a prey-creature's retreat. The disfigured huntsman handed Bjarki his toothed spear, and folded his arms like a gene-bred lifeward.

'We came to Terra by very different paths,' said Bjarki. 'Like the frayed ends of a long and ancient rope. But now the wyrd tells me our threads wind together, becoming one.'

Bjarki tapped the spear-tip to his breast, where Promeus saw he had carved the angular shape of what looked like a roaring draconic head into the plastron of his armour.

'You spilled the blood of Fenris to save my life, and that makes us brothers.'

He spun Rackwulf's harpoon around, resting the head just above the stump of his ruined arm, the spear-tip aimed at Abidemi's heart.

'And what is it you want? To spill some of mine?'

Bjarki laughed. 'No, brother, but we are bound together. Wolf and Drake, warriors of ice and fire. Such symbolism should not go unmarked. I will cut your warplate as I have marked mine with the symbol of the Dread Biter, the deep dragon of eternal land-thirst. Fire is its blood, yet ice its scaled hide.'

The Rune Priest eased the harpoon forwards, but just before the tip touched the deep green of Abidemi's plate, the Salamander took hold of it and shook his head.

'This plate was reforged in the shadow of Mount Deathfire, worked by the smiting hammer of T'kell himself,' he said. 'I cannot allow you to carve it, Bjarki.'

'Not even to mark our brotherhood?'

'Not even for that,' affirmed Abidemi. 'Only artificers of the Promethean cult may work the armour of a Salamanders legionary.'

Bjarki nodded and simply handed the spear back to Svafnir Rackwulf.

'It is of no matter,' he said. 'But the wyrd has shown us so marked.'

He retrieved his staff and climbed aboard the Taurox.

'Come,' said Bjarki with a grin. 'Let's run that one-eyed bastard to ground.'

NINE

Living Fire

Imperial Aeronautica strategos classified them as Doomfires, but that was simply a catch-all term for multiple patterns of retrofitted bombers capable of void operations and atmospheric work. The e-mag pulse of the atomic detonation over Western Hemispheric blew out seventeen void pylons placed along the Khat Mandau Precinct and the entirety of those rebuilt in the Saturnine Quarter after the devastating after-effects of the Phoenician's Sonance.

Pioneer crews, requisitioned dockers and conscripted longshoremen were swept up by Mechanicum work gangs to rebuild the aegis network and patch the rapidly degrading coverage. Even now, weeks into the siege, the endless bombardment from orbit and low atmosphere was still drilling down like golden-tipped spears on smoking black hafts, and gaps like this were unacceptable.

Hundreds of thousands of conventional munitions exploded against the aegis shield every day, and volleys of high-velocity macro shells painted the outer extremities of the aegis every second. Against such volume of fire, it was inevitable that dozens would blow through the gaps to pound the fortress beneath.

Entire districts and structures were smoking craters from the penetration of a single warhead. Portable void generators, intended for the protection of command-and-control centres from mobile artillery units, were daisy-chained around the inner circuits of the Sanctum Imperialis to protect the civilian populace as best they could, but such defences were stopgap measures at best.

The gap in aegis cover wasn't immediately noticed until the twin engines of an Imperial Marauder bomber, returning from a sortie over Annapurna and the shattered redoubts of Gorgon Bar, finally tore free of the aircraft's superstructure. The burning wreckage arced downwards and exhausted civilians watched as it kept on falling instead of exploding into the rippling force dome overhead.

Trailing black smoke and flames, it slammed into the upper reaches of the southernmost of the Taxonomic Towers, six kilometres east of the dome of the Hegemon. The Marauder's fuel reserves were all but gone, its munitions expended over the enemy encampments of Gorgon Bar's second circuit, so when the upper reaches of the silent tower crashed to the ground in an avalanche of twisted steel and stone, only those adepts within and those refugees clustered around its base were killed. In relative terms, it was an insignificant moment to those within the walls who witnessed the attack craft's demise.

But to those watching beyond the walls, it was so much more.

Enemy chatter passed word of a potential gap in aegis cover, and within minutes, the equivalent of six squadrons of delta-winged aircraft surged from hardened underground bunkers or dropped from low-atmosphere carriers. Imperial augurs saw them almost immediately, for they made no attempt to hide their approach or disguise their target. Close-in defence turrets and anti-air batteries on Adamant and Saturnine filled the sky with frag bursts and raking fire, but e-mag interference meant they were firing blind.

Thunderbolts and Furies already in the air were redirected almost instantaneously, their intercept protocols honed after the ferocious intensity of the air war. Even now, the sky over Western Hemispheric was lousy with blinding dust, vicious thermals that could melt plasteel and spiteful vortices powerful enough to tear the largest aircraft in two.

The engagement was fought over instruments, the obscuring, radioactive dust drawn up by the lingering mushroom cloud making a mockery of any attempt to fight visually. Pilots jinked, rolled and dived through blinding clouds that choked ports and fouled vents. Engines stalled and weapons misfired, clogged with dust and atomic interference. Pilots that fought too long died as searing air pockets melted the armourglass of their canopies or rad-squalls detonated the warheads on their missile nacelles.

Explosions painted the sky in sheets of orange flame as weaving trails of shellfire streamed like wind-blown fronds of light. Ejecting from a wounded fighter was suicide, no mortal body could survive the hellstorm of explosions, dogfighting aircraft and searing fireballs.

Only three enemy aircraft survived to punch through the aegis gap, flying below the radiation clouds and trusting to their fellows to keep the Imperial interceptors busy.

Only three.

Three Doomfire bombers classified as *Iniquities*.

Fully laden with cluster bombs and air-to-ground melta missiles.

***

The walls of Western Hemispheric were twenty-five kilometres behind them, obscured by advancing orange cloud banks threading the wide processionals that ran between the gilded structures of Imperial grandeur. Dust hung in thick veils over the thousands of refugees huddling close to the architecture of Imperial ambition, laden with toxins and poison that settled deep in the marrow.

Magnus had set a brutal pace, their perceived appearances assuring them unobstructed passage inward, but it was certain their presence would eventually be discovered. This quarter of the Inner Palace was not yet fully overtaken by warriors or muster points, but more were being drawn in from Indomitor and Sanctus with every passing hour.

Convoys of Imperial vehicles ground through the ashen thoroughfares bisecting their inward route, throwing up clouds of dust and blocking their passage as they rolled past in their hundreds.

The Thousand Sons paused as a Warlord of Legio Gryphonicus moved south to shore up the beleaguered defences of the Europa Wall, its crashing steps lifting the dust from rooftops and its howling war-horn twitching the smoke with its power. The colossal war engine was limping and drooling smoke from beneath its mighty carapace, yet it strode proud and defiant. A strutting Reaver and a pack of loping Warhounds accompanied it, supplicants to its unimaginable power.

Knights of House Cadmus marched on the flanks, their armour scorched back to bare metal and their banners hanging ragged and limp from carapace vox-masts.

Trudging columns of soldiers from a dozen different regiments followed in its wake, every eye haunted by weeks of war and cheeks hollowed by lack of sleep and malnutrition.

As he had promised Perturabo, his presence at Western Hemispheric had galvanised the Imperial defenders to reinforce the

Ultimate Wall between Adamant in the south and Bastion Ledge at the farthest northern extremity of the Palace circuit.

Perhaps that would offer up opportunities to exploit elsewhere, but Magnus cared little for his brother's grand game of siege warfare against Dorn. The spectacular failure of the Saturnine gambit had made the Lord of Iron cautious and reluctant to overreach, wary of accepting counsel from those promising quick victory. With the exception of Angron's monsters, the fighting beyond the walls had eased a fraction. The Sons of Horus were licking their wounds from so many grievous losses, and the Emperor's Children had all but removed themselves from the siege.

Each delay or diversion to avoid concentrations of loyalist troops chafed at Magnus. Time was the enemy and despite his poetic words to Ahriman, the appearance of Lemuel Gaumon at the site of their ingress troubled Magnus deeply.

He'd passed it off as a likely inevitability, a fluke coincidence, but Ahriman was too well versed in the ways of the Corvidae to ever truly believe that. A core tenet of that Fellowship was that there was no such things as coincidences, that the dance of the universe was governed by invisible music that played behind the veil of most mortals' understanding.

Some called it the Architecture of Fate, others *Akasha*. The shamans of the VI Legion knew it as wyrd. The seers of Jaghatai spoke of riding the endless storm.

To Magnus, it was simply *Thelema*, an ancient word that simply meant 'will'.

The teachings of the Corvidae were a Prosperine attempt at hearing the notes of that invisible music and learning the steps of its dance, but knowing Ahriman's old Practicus was close reminded Magnus that not even *he* knew the music as well as he thought.

Surrounded by enemy warriors, the thought was not a comforting one.

They pressed on through the cloying banks of dust, following a path that Magnus had not walked physically in over a century and a half. Here were the Galleries of Compliance, there the Heraldic Conclave, and glinting in the sickly borealis light of the aegis, were the distant silver towers of the Viridarium Nobiles.

Ahead was the blocky outline of the Hall of Weapons, and beyond its hard, martial edges, and brutalist design, their destination.

Or at least the first part of it.

The Great Observatory was raised on a stepped promontory of dark rock, the titanic structure a wonder of Old Earth even weighed against the great monoliths of its far distant epochs. Its sculpted escarpment walls of Volakas marble were two thousand metres high and veined with amaranthine. Titanic flying buttresses carved to resemble winged angels anchored it to the mountain bedrock, their outstretched arms raised imploringly to the sky.

The soaring tower that once stood at the heart of Occullum Square at the centre of lost Tizca had been part of the observatory's structure in ages past, one of the many Doric columns encircling the inconceivable circumference of its vast golden dome. The earliest colonists from Old Earth were said to have carried it with them for reasons known only to themselves. Perhaps they had intended to recreate its glory, or perhaps it was simply a means of holding on to their proud lineage.

Ancient verse spoke of the great dome outshining the sun, and perhaps it once had, but now it was cracked and gaping, the lustre of its pristine white walls black with fire and smoke damage, its angelic buttresses weeping tears of blood.

Ouslite steps, three hundred metres wide, led up towards the great entryway, their entire length obscured by sprawling favelas of temporary structures, tents, awnings and lean-tos housing the living tide spilling from within: civilian refugees from the Katabatic Plains, the Petitioner's City, and Palace outworks that were now nothing more than mud and rubble.

Trees had once lined the grand approach boulevard, silver birch and sycamore, but they were long gone, hauled up by the roots and burned in cookfires. Magnus led his sons between the craters of their uprooting, each absence like a rotten tooth pulled from a gum. He halted as he set foot on the first stair and a memory pushed into his mind like a dull knife.

The Emperor gazing up through the observatory's aetheric lensworks to show Magnus the secret births of stars and speaking in wonder of the incomprehensible voids between them. Together they had plotted the course of future crusades, and laughed as they imagined the campaigns that would one day reach out into the fathomless gulfs between galaxies.

'There is nothing impossible to him who will try,' his father had said when Magnus had spoken of the nigh-impossibility of reaching beyond the halo stars. 'No one yet alive will see it, but when humankind can fly as we fly, can see as we see, *then* the greatest prize of all will be within their grasp.'

'What prize could be greater than dominion of the galaxy?' Magnus had asked.

But his father had never given him an answer, turning away to hide His disappointment.

Memories centuries old now and ashes in his mind, but Magnus recalled them as though they were but moments ago.

'The old wounds are still fresh,' said Magnus.

'Sire?'

Magnus looked at the broken dome of the observatory and the swathes of refugees clustered around its base. Thousands of eyes were turned to face them.

'It is no small thing to walk within the walls of the Sanctum Imperialis,' he said, climbing the steps towards the observatory.

'I had not thought to be so affected. Foolish, I suppose, but it is hard to be here as an intruder after... So many memories. For so long, Terra was the centre of my existence, but this is no longer the house of my father.'

Magnus led them higher, his gaze fixed on the triumphal archway that led within. He could feel the questioning stares of every refugee upon them.

Why were five Blood Angels climbing to the Great Observatory? Why were they not fighting on the walls with their brothers? The rawness of thoughts here was hard to block: desperation, terror, bewilderment, and the beginnings of a numb acceptance that this was a battle that could not be won.

If only you knew...

He heard the name of the Lord of Angels and his sons shouted like a talisman before them.

'Sanguinius!'

'The Archangel's beloved!'

'Blood Angels!'

'Glory to the Ninth!'

The people in their path moved aside, bowing or dropping to their knees with palms together, whispered words spilling from their lips in repeating mantras.

'The Emperor protects...'

'What are they doing?' asked Atrahasis.

'Praying,' said Magnus.

'Why?'

'Because in times of woe, people crave saviours. My father is so powerful He might as well be a god, and we are His sons, avatars of a god and worthy of the same devotion.'

Yet even as the words left his lips, he knew there was something hollow, something *wrong* about them, though he couldn't say for sure what it was.

'It disturbs me to see such behaviour,' said Atrahasis.

'Why?' asked Ahriman.

'It is regression. To seek saviours is to abrogate any responsibility to enact change. If a thing needs doing, it should be done. If action is to be taken, take it. You don't wait for anyone else to do it for you.'

'Spoken like a true Raptora,' said Menkaura.

'Doesn't it sicken you?' snapped Ahriman's equerry. 'We know so much now – secrets and technologies so advanced they would appear as magic to our forefathers, wisdom and philosophy so enlightening that such wilful embrace of ignorance and superstition is inexcusable.'

'Ease your choler, Atrahasis,' said Ahriman.

Atrahasis nodded, and kept his gaze fixed on the steps as they climbed.

Eventually Magnus stepped onto the great esplanade before the observatory and craned his neck to look up towards the mighty dome. Drifts of ashen smoke obscured the circuit of columns below the dome, and only its very edge winked gold far, far above.

'It's magnificent,' said Amon, his gaze following the outline of the great archway. Dressed in agate and onyx, every stone was carved with star maps, most to places navigable from Terra, some to places most assuredly not. 'Almost the equal of the celestial chambers in the Pyramid of Photep.'

'Almost,' said Magnus with a grin.

'Yes, it is magnificent,' agreed Ahriman, looking towards a sky that was lousy with battle ejecta, e-mag squalls and flickering atomic explosions. 'But why are we here? With all the debris and shelling from low orbit, we won't see anything beyond the atmosphere just now.'

'We are not here to look up,' said Magnus, ***'but to pass below.'***

'What does that mean?' asked Amon.

'There is a hidden place here where past and future have

co-mingled since primordial times,' said Magnus. *'My father once called it a domestication of one of the materium's anomalies. A pulled thread in the fabric of time, a scab on the skin of space. We will travel the low roads that thread the liminal spaces beneath its foundations.'*

'Does this place have a name?' asked Ahriman.

'It does, a name it owned before the first men came here and raised a roof above it,' said Magnus. *'They called it the Hall of Leng.'*

The space within the observatory was so colossally vast as to defy the notion of it being an interior. The dome was fully four kilometres in diameter, its underside coffered in bronze and ouslite panels partially obscured by a trapped cloud layer that twisted like an ocean maelstrom in the twitching suspensor fields. Even to Magnus, who had designed the exacting dimensions of the Pyramid of Photep, it seemed inconceivable that such a feat of engineering could have been achieved by mortals.

Shell detonations, graser impacts and tectonic shifts from the sheer volume of ordnance landing on the surrounding landscape had cracked portions of the dome in a dozen places. Thick columns of variegated light speared down to paint the terrazzo floor and walls like reflections in a deep-water cistern. The entire circumference of the observatory's wall was carved with vivid frescoes depicting the greatest pioneers of astronomy and their myriad achievements.

Magnus saw alcove shrines and statues dedicated to Aganice, Zarkov, the Heliocentric Apostate, Hypatia, the Scanian Alchymist, Zulema, the Mother of Comets, and hundreds more: a legacy of scientific achievement without which none of them would be standing here.

The ancient ocular artefact the Emperor had wrought to scry distant galaxies swayed high above the centre of the dome on broken chains like the corpse of an enormous mantis wrought from spun silver, smoked glass and gold. The obsidian speculum in its curiously angled lens apparatus had been shattered at the first impact of weaponry, and most of the device's impossibly complex workings hung like loops of intestinal tract from its split casing.

Magnus' heart broke to see the damage, knowing that nothing else of its kind had ever existed, and never would again.

When this is all over, will the prize be worth the price paid?

Yet for all its wonder and the scientific achievements of the men and women celebrated on the walls, the observatory was now simply a place to shelter from the war.

In its day it had been a place of quiet wonder, a gathering place for seekers of wisdom and discoverers of truth, but it had become a noisome, reeking vault. Tens of thousands of refugees obscured the great star map carved into the floor, and the statues of those who had made the Imperium possible looked out over a tumultuous sea of frightened people who cared nothing for their legacies.

Magnus strode through the centre of the crowds, drawn towards a distant statue and alcove. As on the steps, the weight of expectation that settled upon him was profound.

Despite the deceptions he worked within the minds of the mortals crammed inside the Palace walls, he wondered if some deep-buried part of their brains still knew they were in the presence of a god. His image was obscured, but the human psyche could still sense that a being of great power walked among them.

They saw Angels of Death, gene-forged warriors of the Emperor's own lineage, the immortal god-warriors. But more than that, Magnus felt the presence of an insidious shadow at the edge of that belief, and now understood the strange hollowness he had felt on the steps.

'They are beginning to fear us,' he whispered.

'They are right to fear us,' replied Ahriman. 'For we are mighty and terrible, and our power is a fearful thing.'

'No, this is different,' said Magnus. ***'Once, they beheld us in awe and wonder, but not fear. It was understood that it was the duty of the strong to protect the weak. It always has been that way, ever since it was spoken of in the Iron Code. It has been a truth the best of us ought to embody.'***

He stopped before a tall statue of onyx and quartz, a grand representation of the great Kopernik and the first printed pages of his magnum opus. The way onwards was hidden here, a door only those with the wit to find it could open.

The Emperor had shown him it, and he suspected Sanguinius knew of it too. Perhaps the Khan, for few were the secret ways he could not find. Malcador and the Custodians would almost certainly know of it, but likely no others. He felt the nearby presence of the nagging stitch in reality that told him the way in was near, and lifted his hands up to tease it open with the prescribed psychic key.

Magnus looked back over his shoulder as the people nearest him backed away, eyes averted, just as the people on the grand stairs had done. But now he saw the secret truth at the heart of it: a nameless, metastasising fear coalescing in the bellies and minds of mortals.

That fear in the tales told on Terra would spread throughout what would be left of the Imperium in the wake of this war, growing deeper and darker with every retelling.

They will never trust us again.

As Magnus and his sons crossed the threshold of the Great Observatory, the three Iniquity-class Doomfires were looping a desperate course north-west, navigating by sight alone and following the Gilded Walk that ran from the Ultimate

Gate, aiming for the gap between Widdershin's Tower and the Pillar of Unity.

Imperial Lightnings chased them, hounding them with air-to-air Skystrike missiles and autocannon fire. The Doomfires were slower by far, and would normally have been easily blown from the sky like wallowing void-whales, but nearby atmospheric squalls and the sheer density of structures crowding the Sanctum Imperialis made accurate targeting supremely difficult.

The first Iniquity was taken out as it banked hard around the Clanium Library, a Skystrike warhead detonating less than five metres from its portside wing. The bomber's blazing wreckage tumbled from the sky, vanishing into one of the abyssal canyons surrounding the Hegemon before exploding.

A second unleashed nearly its full complement of ordnance over the outer precincts of the Bhab Bastion before aiming its bulk mass towards the Helian Tower in a suicidal strike on the structure's south-eastern flank. Voids took the brunt of the bomb explosions, and close-in turrets hammered the Iniquity itself, but it had too much mass and too much speed to be entirely stopped.

The bomber ploughed into the Helian Tower and split it apart.

The wreckage drove in deep like the thrust of a dagger before the last of its munitions exploded, and the tower slumped over at its middle like a disembowelled fighter. Its upper reaches fell in an inexorably slow avalanche of torn stone and tumbling bodies. Two thousand adepts and civilian staff had been crammed within Helian, a structure never intended to endure such punishment. Not even Rogal Dorn's reinforced plating could withstand the impact of so devastating a missile.

Every single soul within the tower died and, more crucially, so too did their equipment.

Cascading vox-net failure within Bhab was total, resulting in an instantaneous blackout within the Sanctum Imperialis. All strategic overview of Exultant and Annapurna was lost, and all information flowing from the military heart of Terra ceased. For thirty tense minutes, the commanders of the Imperial Palace fought alone and isolated, blind, deaf and mute, until secondary relays allowed the re-establishment of command-and-control protocols.

The net was closing on the third Iniquity as its bombardier sought a target worthy of her ordnance. Eternity Gate and the golden heart of the Palace were too well protected by batteries of mobile gun-platforms, missile stations and barrage fields. Fresh squadrons of interceptors were closing fast from the eastern hangars beneath the Dome of Illumination.

Only one target presented itself, but before the bombardier could release her weapons, bracketing fire from the Hall of Weapons' defensive guns shredded the Iniquity's fuselage to blazing fragments.

The aircraft literally came apart in an expanding cloud of superheated vapour and steel confetti, but not before a pair of spiralling munitions tore loose from the pylon mounts on its spinning port wing.

Arcing down towards the Great Observatory.

Menkaura was the first to feel the blinding stab of prescience.

He dropped to his knees, hands pressed over his mirrored helm, a powerful psychic exclamation bursting from his mind.

+The fire from above, it burns everything. *It burns everything!*+

The mental pulse was so powerfully clear after the enforced necessity of speech that it sounded like a scream in an empty room. Each of them felt the power of Menkaura's vision searing within his skull. Seconds later, they all saw it.

A sea of hungry flames, burning spectral green.

Impossible heat and retina-searing brightness.

Flooding the observatory like ocean breakers against pale cliffs.

Screams swallowed as the air in mortal lungs was instantly burned away.

Flesh melting like snow before a flamer. Bones cracking and splitting.

Magnus looked up and saw a pair of black dots in the sky, growing steadily larger as they fell. He knew what they were, could all but read the serial numbers on their casings, the words of warning stencilled on the warheads, and the sigils of spite etched into their segmented bomb casings by Neverborn claws.

'Mark Eleven Muspell-class phosphex cluster bomb,' he said.

His sons all saw them, and their psychic vision of its effects spread throughout the observatory, leaping from mind to mind like a mental virus. Heads turned skyward, but there were no screams among the doomed refugees, only a resigned acceptance of this final fate, like beasts milling in a slaughterhouse stockyard. The human capacity for terror can only endure so much before it is dulled by constant horrors. Men and women clutched each other tightly, held their children, but not one got up to flee.

What would be the point? The choice was death here or death at the hands of some other uncaring weapon of the enemy. Such blunt acceptance of fate was anathema to Magnus, but the clarity of thought surrounding him was impossible to ignore. Yes, this was death, but at least it would be quick, not the drawn-out terror that ground souls to ash by constant loss.

The bright, instantaneous flash of an explosion was a far cleaner ending.

No, Magnus would not accept that.

The time for subtlety and subterfuge in this endeavour was at an end.

Magnus turned back to the invisible scar in the flesh of the world and slashed it open with a blow from his heqa staff that sounded like a canvas sail tearing. Shimmering, undersea light spilled from *elsewhere,* conjuring fleeting knives of memory, of shared joy and exploration.

A heady brew of emotions surged from the depths of his consciousness, wondrous and ripe with potential, but now irrevocably tainted with melancholy and the knowledge that such times were lost forever. A breath of wind carried the scent of polished lacquer, willow and cherry blossoms from the strange hall above.

'I have no time for such remembrances,' said Magnus, and stepped back into the observatory, looking up towards the falling bombs.

'My lord, there is nothing you can do for them!' cried Ahriman.

Magnus watched the warheads split apart, and three thousand phosphex bomblets were ejected from the main munition canister in a spiralling pattern to spread the impacts wider.

They slashed down like glowing green darts.

'We are never so inventive as when we seek to kill one another,' said Magnus.

One hundred metres above the floor the bomblets exploded in a rippling spiral of light, and the observatory was filled with falling clouds of killing fire. The deadly radiance engulfed the observatory, instantly burning the painted murals from the walls and incinerating countless scientific pioneers whose names would never be spoken again.

The atmosphere in the dome's upper reaches vanished with a thunderclap of vaporised air.

Now the refugees discovered there were terrors that might yet touch them, and the screaming began.

But just as swiftly it ceased and turned to cries of wonder.

The glowing ocean of emerald fire hung seething in the air,

churning in a borealis of killing light. It raged and howled, a ravenous monster trapped and furious at being denied its feast of scorched meat and blackened bone. It clawed and slithered like a living thing across an invisible barrier held above the refugees, a frenzied predator desperate to reach its prey.

Below it, Magnus stood with his arms upraised, his sons gathered around him.

Psychic might blazed from him as he wove inhumanly powerful forces overhead. No longer could he maintain his physical deception in the minds of those who beheld him, and he stood revealed in all his glory: a titan of gold and crimson, red of mane and ivory of horn. Lambent light that echoed the green of the phosphex burned in the cyclopean eye of Magnus. The power in that eye drank in the light and defied it.

Magnus was the Magister Templi of the Fellowships of Prospero. The formulae of the Raptora came as easily to him as breathing did to mortals, but the kine shield he held over the refugees was greater than even the masters of that Fellowship could conjure. And just as the innermost workings of the Raptora were his to command, so too were those of the Pyrae, the weavers of flame. Magnus remembered Khalophis during the Battle of Prospero, striding into battle within the god-machine *Canis Vertex*. All the fire of the world was his to command, but not even he would have dared to tame so ferocious a conflagration.

Magnus clenched a fist and drove it up into the air.

The sky of phosphex dimmed fractionally. Its light was that of the dead, a ghostly green as unnatural as it was lethal. Magnus drew on his every reserve of power, but stopped short of employing that of the Neverborn.

It was his to command, all he had to do was *choose* to take it; that awesome, unstoppable power conjured from the darkest depths of the immaterium.

But such power was the province of the fell lords of the utterdark; he could not touch it without being instantly expelled from the Palace.

The telaethesic ward was attuned to exclude such unnatural energies and had thus far kept the Red Angel, the Pale King and the Phoenician from fully entering the Palace. Their forms were too corrupt, too tainted by that power for them to tread fully within the umbra of the Palace shields. Instead, Magnus drew only from the well of his own abilities: a great and formidable power, but it was not depthless.

'My sons!' he cried as the sickly green fire slithered over the walls, tendrils of flame writhing and twisting as though searching for a weakness in the barrier. *'The seventh enumeration, send me your power!'*

They surrounded him, a mandala formation, and their power poured into him.

How long Magnus stood with arms outstretched to consume the light he could not say.

'Time is its enemy!' he shouted, drawing strength from defiance. *'Deny it sustenance and it must inevitably turn on itself.'*

Every second his sons empowered him and every second their combined power resisted its force drew strength from the attacking weapon. Slowly at first, the howling green fire began to dim, and without fuel to sustain its growth, the shrieking light turned upon itself.

Nightmarish chemical reactions devised in a madman's lab drove the phosphex to desperately cannibalise its own unnatural structure in a frantic attempt to cling to life.

But against the immense power of Magnus the Red and his sons, it could never be enough.

The last embers of the phosphex faded as the chemical bonds at its heart finally broke apart. The fire guttered and the heat of its killing light was finally extinguished.

Magnus sighed and released his grip on the kine shield.

The dead phosphex fell to the floor of the observatory in a harmless, viscous rain that immediately began dissolving into pools of inert jelly. Disbelieving cheers echoed from the walls as dimmed sparks of hope flared back to life in every refugee's heart.

Magnus sank to one knee, a splayed hand pressed hard to the napped-gem mosaic running around the circumference of the observatory. His fingers rested on the image representing the twin ichthyocentaurs bearing Venus Anadyomene from the ocean.

'Aphros and Bythos Piscium,' said Magnus.

He remembered Horus showing him the same image in the astrological text their father had given him. Twenty signs to match His twenty sons. Magnus had hidden his amusement at the primitive nature of the book, but enjoyed the purity of the memory.

He smiled to see the image on the floor, rippling light from the rent he had torn in reality making it seem as though the oceanic beasts had been given life and were bearing the renewed goddess from the ocean once again.

A hand touched his shoulder.

'We need to go,' said Ahriman.

Magnus nodded and drew himself up to his full, magnificent height.

A sea of faces drank in the light from his copper flesh, the inhuman nature of his being, but they beheld not the monster they had been told to fear, simply one of the Emperor's sons, a warrior who had saved their lives.

'My lord,' pressed Ahriman. 'Our enemies will know we are here now. We have to *go*.'

Magnus nodded, numb after so swift and violent an expenditure of power.

'Yes. Go,' he said, half turning to the secret way he had opened beneath the Hall of Leng.

Amon, Menkaura and Atrahasis stepped through to gasps of astonishment from the refugees, but Ahriman lingered.

'Why?' he asked.

'Why what?'

'Why did you save these people?'

'You would have left them to die?'

'They will probably die anyway when Lupercal takes the Palace,' said Ahriman.

'Maybe, maybe not. All I knew was that I could not allow them to perish in the fire when I could save them. In truth, until I stepped back into the dome, I did not know what I would do.'

'Perhaps proximity to the first shard of your soul is affecting you more than any of us thought possible,' ventured Ahriman.

'Perhaps,' said Magnus with a hopeful smile. *'It is the first and best part of me.'*

With Ahriman at his side, Magnus set foot on the Low Roads.

BOOK FOUR

UNDER PALACE

TEN

Predators and Prey

Light from beneath the dark lake rippled on the stalactite-clustered ceiling of the immense cavern like undersea shadows. Crystal seams threading the rocky ceiling glittered like distant stars, so very unlike the current view from Terra's surface. At first, Alivia had thought Malcador had brought her to one of the Palace's underground aquifers, but when she had seen the villas of pale stone at the water's edge, she knew this place served another purpose.

Something about the villas seemed *off*, but it wasn't until Malcador led her between them to a circular plaza that she realised what was unsettling about them. Each was scaled for beings far larger than mortals, larger even than the warriors of the Legiones Astartes. She counted twenty of them – surely no coincidence in *that* number – and the colourful mosaic forming the plaza itself depicted something geometrically abstract, like the murals popular with Achaemenid nobles.

'These villas were built for the primarchs, weren't they?' she asked.

Malcador nodded. 'The Emperor imagined they would grow here and learn the skills He needed them to possess before the conquest of the galaxy began in earnest.'

'They never did though, did they?'

'No, *she* saw to that.'

Alivia didn't need to ask who *she* was. The Emperor was the gene-father of the primarchs, but only Erda could be thought of as their mother.

A twisted, barbed-wire bitch of a mother, but still...

'Have they *ever* been used?'

'Not really,' said Malcador. 'At least, not for the purpose for which they were intended.'

'There's thousands of refugees up top you could shelter down here.'

'Both the Khan and the Archangel proposed that, but Valdor would not allow it.'

'I'm guessing that wherever we are is too close to Him for Constantin's liking.'

'That, among other reasons.'

'But there's been *someone* here,' said Alivia, walking a circuit around the plaza and feeling the presence of a past shade. 'Something powerful, something *broken*. And recently too.'

'Your abilities are getting stronger.'

Alivia shook her head. 'No, I've felt almost nothing since we arrived on Terra. Even deep beneath Molech, I could feel the Emperor's presence, but now... it's like He's not even here.'

'He is most assuredly here, but as I said, this siege is being fought in more realms than you can imagine,' said Malcador. 'Lupercal might already be seated upon the throne were the Emperor not fighting His own war.'

'So why are you and I here?'

'Do you remember when I talked about forgiveness before we set out?'

'You said it would deprive the enemy of one of their most potent weapons.'

'And so it may, but first, let me ask you something.'

Alivia's eyes narrowed. 'Why do I get the feeling I'm not going to like this?'

'Neither of us will, I suspect. Honesty is always hard.'

'Honesty hasn't always been my strong suit, but ask away.'

'Are you a good person, Alivia Sureka? Can you look at yourself in the mirror, see past the many masks you have worn over the long millennia to the very core of your being and say, without equivocation, that you are a good person?'

The question surprised Alivia. She hadn't known what to expect, but this most assuredly wasn't it. She waited for any clarification, some guidance on what he might be expecting from her, but nothing more was forthcoming.

She moved to the edge of the lake, looking out over the smooth black waters.

'Am I *good*?' she said. 'That's a pretty broad question.'

'It really isn't. And you're stalling.'

'Of course I'm stalling. I've lived a *very* long life and no one gets to live this long without having done some things they're ashamed of. I've killed people, I've killed *lots* of people, betrayed friends and lovers, lied, cheated–'

'And stolen,' said Malcador with the barest hint of a smile. 'That storybook you're carrying in your coat pocket, the one with the old fairy tales. You stole that from a church.'

'I was getting to that,' snapped Alivia, bending to stir the water with her fingers. 'What's your point? Are *you* a good person?'

'By any conventional reckoning, no. Like you, I have betrayed those closest to me, and though it has been many years since I have taken a life, I have sanctioned deeds by others that saw appalling slaughters.'

'So, we've both done bad things.'

'*Terrible* things. Things that would, were they laid before any theoretical higher power of judgement, see us consigned to the deepest hells of the ancients.'

'I'm not sure where you're going with this, but I don't think I like it.'

'My point, Alivia, is that despite all the many terrible acts we have ourselves done or set in motion, we are *within* the walls of the Emperor's Palace.'

'Wait, is this some long-winded way of saying you're throwing me out?'

Malcador gave a weak laugh and said, 'No, because for what it is worth, our many sins were committed in the name of something *good*.'

'An evil act, even when you do it in the name of something good, is still evil.'

'True,' said Malcador, lifting his gaze out over the lake as though he expected something to rise from its depths. 'But I fear we do not have the luxury of time to delve into the semantics of such a debate as deeply as it needs.'

'We don't?' said Alivia, looking around.

'No, because you were right.'

'About what?'

'Someone powerful did dwell here for a time. Or at least a portion of him.'

'Who?'

'Until recently, Magnus.'

'Magnus? As in *the Red*. The primarch?'

'Yes, and by my reckoning, he will be here very soon.'

The engine of the venerable Taurox had finally given out on the upper approach circuit of the tiered crater of the Investiary. Not that it could have gone farther anyway – the processional ramp was choked with rubble and the Weeping Fountains shed tears no more.

'You are sure this is the place?' asked Bjarki, climbing down from the Taurox as its seized motor juddered like the death rattle of its Nocturnean namesake. 'Even a wyrd-blinded *gothii* would see this is not where that power came from.'

They had all felt it: the cold stab of a monstrous psychic event deep in the heart of the Sanctum Imperialis. Yet with every kilometre they travelled, all had felt the distance between them and its source increase.

'I'm sure,' said Promeus. 'Malcador's message was clear. Make for the centre of the Investiary and wait.'

'Wait for what?' asked Atok Abidemi, unsheathing his great, toothed blade.

'He didn't say.'

It took the legionaries two hours to descend the broken steps towards the base of the amphitheatre, where the great titanoliths of the Emperor's sons had been explosively brought down. Only two of the sixteen that had been allowed to remain were left standing.

One was unmistakable, the stoic and immovable Dorn, but it took seeing the dust-covered XX on the base of the statue opposite for Promeus to recognise it was the once veiled figure of impenetrable Alpharius.

The floor of the Investiary, like the wide ramp approaching it, was filled with vast chunks of dusty marble hewn from the great mountain in Attica that overlooked the site of Miltiades' great victory. The debris might have been mistaken for the aftermath of an avalanche but for the massive chunks of veined stone clearly shaped by the hands of mortals. Promeus saw the shattered visage of a huge face that might once have been Guilliman, a hand clenched mockingly into a fist, and upon one plinth, two vast and trunkless legs that ended mid-shin.

A sword with a hawk-winged hilt lay beneath half a helmet staring up at the tortured sky, but to whom either had once belonged Promeus could not say.

Sadness touched him at the sight of the Emperor's sons brought low.

He turned to speak to Bjarki, but the Rune Priest and his brethren had already moved off, leaving Promeus alone. Likewise, the Salamanders moved purposefully through the rubble towards a shattered plinth on the far side of the arena-like space.

At first he didn't understand what they were doing until he saw to which plinths they drew near. Abidemi dropped to his knees in silent contemplation before the plinth upon which the gene-sire of the XVIII Legion had once stood. Only a single, booted foot remained of Vulkan, the rest of his body lying shattered beyond repair in the sand of the amphitheatre.

Bjarki and his brothers stood defiantly before the broken remains of Leman Russ, whose body had sheared off diagonally at the waist. The hairs on the back of Promeus' neck stood up as Bjarki threw back his head and loosed a ululating pack-howl. The plaintive sound rose as Widdowsyn and Rackwulf added their voices, and the sublime acoustics of the Investiary carried their vengeance to the heavens and pierced even the constant drumbeat of war.

The vestiges of his former life as a remembrancer urged him to secure a better look at this ritual, but if he had learned anything during his time as a hostage of the VI Legion, it was that their grief was a deeply personal thing. To intrude on it uninvited would be lethally unwise.

Instead, he sat on a shattered fragment of stone, hoping he wasn't desecrating the remains of a primarch, and waited. He rested his head in his hands, one warm and clammy, the other cold and smooth.

He seemed to recall hearing that infiltrators had destroyed the statues of the Investiary, but the tactical sense of that eluded him. To have so deeply penetrated the Palace only to wreak symbolic devastation seemed somehow... *petty*.

Perhaps it had been a message? Or a goading challenge?

He supposed he would never know, and despite the urgency of Malcador's message and the renewed rumble of a ferocious artillery duel many kilometres north on the Ultimate Wall, Promeus felt his eyelids drooping and his breathing deepen.

The crunching sound of footsteps jolted him from his doze.

'They should tear this one down,' said Svafnir Rackwulf, looking up at Alpharius.

'Why don't they?' added Widdowsyn.

'It's just a statue,' said Atok Abidemi, leading his Salamanders back to join them. 'Besides, the traitors are destroying enough of the Palace without us helping them. And a time is coming when every scrap of ordnance will be needed at the walls. How galling would it be for a gate or tower to fall for the lack of explosives spent demolishing this?'

Bjarki shrugged. 'Salamanders and their pragmatism,' he said with a grin.

'So what now?' asked Igen Gargo. 'Atok? You led us this far. Where now?'

Abidemi nodded and knelt beside Promeus. 'You told us you could follow the spoor of the Red Sorcerers. So are they here?'

'No,' said Promeus.

'Then why are *we* here?' demanded Barek Zytos, as much of Abidemi as Promeus.

He let their questions drift over him, hearing the faint sound of distant voices on the wind, channelled through the broken stonework and brought down through the acoustic confluence of the amphitheatre's high tiers. Isolated from the fighting on the walls, the din of battle was muted below – the recent artillery duel notwithstanding – but the voices were as clear as if their speakers were right next to him.

'Put fire on that outpost. Stalk-tanks in the rubble!'

'Tower Helican is down! I repeat, Tower Helican is down!'

'Push the Seventeenth Pan-Pac down there. Hold the gate at all costs!'

'KILL 'EM ALL!'

Dozens more intruded on his thoughts, the stray comments of Terra's warriors echoing down into the Investiary and scratching the surface of his mind. He rubbed his temples, feeling a pressure growing behind his eyes and a taste of tin in his mouth.

Promeus stood, recognising the sensation.

He'd felt it on Kamiti Sona, the instant before Ahzek Ahriman and his sorcerers had ripped some kind of psychic gateway through the red ruin of a madman's body.

He cast his gaze around the arena, and his growing fear eased as he saw a shimmering, golden light near the centre of the amphitheatre. It danced like an endlessly repeating image of a lightning bolt captured on a broken picter at the instant of its birth.

'Do you see that?' he asked.

'See what?' asked Bjarki, his voice sounding like it had crossed vast gulfs to reach him.

'The lightning,' said Promeus, picking a path through the rubble.

He barely felt them following. His attention was solely fixed on the lightning. It drew him like a moth to a lure, but it was the most beautiful thing he had ever seen. It wavered in his sight, like a scratch on the glass of reality – too bright to look at directly, too faint to be seen except out of the corner of his eye.

It was a beckoning call, a summons to be willingly answered.

He skirted the massive form of a primarch's sundered chest – whose he didn't know – and even through the dense stone, the shimmering form of the lightning was visible.

At last he reached the centre of the amphitheatre and stood before the shattered remains of an upraised arm, sheared away at the shoulder. Strands of rusted rebar hung like sinew from where explosives had blasted the mighty limb from its body.

The remains of what might have been a stonework cloak clung to the shorn arm, and from the carven scales upon it, the once-owner's identity was clear.

'Lord Vulkan,' said Abidemi, a low undercurrent of anger in his voice.

Split from the top of the shoulder was the titanic skull of the firedrake Kesare, a recreation of the beast slain by the primarch as a youth and wrought into his armour.

The sculptor had worked wonders on the marble, and even though the scale of it was monstrously exaggerated for the statue, Promeus shuddered to think of the beast in life.

The impact with the ground had split the skull from the marble armour and it lay like a vast unearthed fossil with its jaws spread wide. And now, finally, Promeus saw the source of the light, a shimmer of golden radiance emanating from its jaws.

A crack in the world, teased open for a fragile moment in time.

'A passage to the Underverse,' said Bjarki, his psychic senses now aware of the light.

Promeus shook his head. 'No. That's not what this is.'

'Then what is it?'

'What do you both see?' asked Abidemi, following their gaze into the great drake's maw. His red eyes narrowed, and Promeus guessed even the stolid Salamander sensed something was askew.

'It's a passage,' said Promeus, 'but not to your Underverse.'

'What are you two talking about?' snapped Barek Zytos. 'We cannot stand idle as the fate of the planet is decided elsewhere.'

'What is it you see?' pressed Abidemi.

Promeus reached out to the light, holding to the image of Malcador's face and the message that had brought them here. In response, the illumination swelled around them.

He fell to his knees, tears streaming down his cheeks.

And, one by one, the Astartes knelt in reverence as the gene-craft that had gone into their creation responded to the radiance of their maker.

The passage of the Low Roads had tested them all.

That these tunnels were no natural geology was clear. No earthly orogenic movement or tectonic compressional energies had wrought this strange labyrinth beneath the Palace.

'The Emperor did not build these passages,' said Ahriman.

'No, He did not,' replied Magnus. ***'At least I don't think so. He may have expanded them, but He was not their creator.'***

'Who built them then?' said Amon, running a hand across the strangely glistening tiled walls and leaving a faint bioluminescent sheen behind.

'My father often talked of the Men of Leng and their curious sciences that sought to unpick the weave of the universe,' said Magnus. ***'Perhaps these tunnels are theirs.'***

Atrahasis had said nothing since they had stepped from beneath the dome of the Great Observatory, but now he chose to speak: 'To walk in such places goes against the workings of the world.'

Menkaura grinned. 'Like wandering behind the scenes of a Theatrica Imperialis set and seeing that the reality presented to the world is little more than a cheap plasterboard facade.'

The words were said lightly, but Magnus felt their unease and, privately, shared it.

To warriors of the Fellowships, to see beyond the veil without the protection of their psychic masteries was unnerving to say the least. The full extent of the Emperor's telaethesic ward was yet unknown, and to travel via such arcane means without their full powers was anathema to them.

Magnus reached out, briefly touching his sons' minds to ease their trepidation.

He felt Ahriman's growing fear of the changes being wrought on the Legion. His Chief Librarian had always feared the flesh change. Little wonder since he had lost his twin to its uncontrollable hyper-mutations. The fear that their present course would inevitably lead to such a fate for them all but consumed him, though he hid it well.

Menkaura's mind was a fortress, but one with its gates unbarred to Magnus.

The seer's mind was aflame with thoughts of betrayal and the fear of what his brothers would do were they to discover his past treacheries. Magnus cared nothing for Menkaura's deceptions, seeing only a future of endless torment and flaming eyes within eyes.

Grief touched him as he skimmed the minds of Amon and Atrahasis.

He saw their deaths, but could make sense of neither.

Magnus delved no deeper into the thoughts of his sons, for he knew that to prise open their very hearts would lead only to disappointment. Even a cursory brush with their minds had revealed all the petty jealousies, resentments and insecurities their lineage and training was intended to erase.

And yet he loved them still.

They were his sons, and even after all they had endured in his name, they remained loyal.

The thought consoled him as they moved deeper into this strange network, and a prescient sense of *imminence* filled him, like the moment before a storm breaks.

Enclosed in these unnatural tunnels, Magnus had no idea how long it would take them to reach their destination, a place in which he had never set foot, but knew as intimately as if he had built it himself.

With every step he took, the more these memories that were not memories, but experiences belonging to another, began intruding on his psyche.

Another part of *him*, but also *not* him.

Memories of peace as he walked the shores of a frigid lake, of contentment as he browsed books long thought lost, and the simple pleasure of conversations with friends of old. To feel there was a portion of his own life he had not lived cut his soul with a profound sense of loss. This was a life wholly distinct from him, and yet still a part of the one he was experiencing in this exact moment.

Flying the Great Ocean had shown Magnus the truth of time's fictive lattice and its multifaceted nature. To look only upon one seam of the spiralling flow of entropy and change was to deny a soul the wonder of all the others.

And yet there was an immediacy of being so lost in the present that all else faded…

As if in response to the memory of these un-memories, the tunnel widened and the soft glow of impossible starlight brightened its walls.

'We're here,' he said, and he felt their relief at being able to step off the Low Roads.

Magnus heard the sound of icy water lapping on a shingled shore of black sand and felt the airy openness of a high-ceilinged space before him. A mingled sense of excitement and trepidation filled him, but he quelled his euphoric anticipation at being reunited with the last and best part of him.

They were, after all, deep within his father's fortress.

Any living souls they might find beyond were the enemy.

Who knew what might await them here? The Saturnine Gambit had shown that the defenders of the Palace were cunning beyond any measure Lupercal and the Lord of Iron had believed possible.

For all Magnus knew, an entire Order of the Silent Sisterhood together with a Shield Host of Valdor's Custodians might be lying in wait for them.

He didn't think so, but to prick his pride, his mind conjured the sight of Lupercal's First Captain lying in a lake of his own blood following the disastrous assault beneath the Saturnine Wall. Once so proud, but now a blade-gutted shell, Ezekyle Abaddon had been broken almost beyond repair and his soul now drifted lost and forlorn on an ocean of despair.

So many prideful warriors, so sure of their great victory.

All now dead.

He remembered mocking their supreme self-confidence as they departed.

Was he any different?

Magnus stepped into the cavern beneath the Palace, smelling the achingly sharp tang of the lake, the smell of wet rock, and bitingly cold air. The cavern roof glittered with snaking veins of crystalline light, and a series of overscaled villas were set back a little distance from the water's edge.

He recognised them, though he had never set so much as a foot within.

His fear of the Legio Custodes and null-maidens evaporated as he saw that no such army of ambush awaited them.

Two figures sat at a table by the lake, a man robed in black and a woman wearing a military flak coat. The woman was unknown to him, but he felt echoes of the great span of time to which she had borne witness within the labyrinthine pathways of her guarded psyche.

Had he the time, hers would have been an interesting mind to explore.

The black-robed man was as familiar to him as a brother – more so, for he had more in common with him than the brothers bound to him by the gene-craft of his father. They had shared minds, flown the secret paths of the Great Ocean, and learned the wondrous secrets of its deepest reaches together.

Once they had shared a bond deeper and more resonant than any biological one, but time and tide had forced them to opposite sides of the great schism that now sundered the Imperium.

The woman helped the man to his feet as they stepped out, an unnecessary labour for his veneer of vulnerability was just as illusory as the nature of time in the Great Ocean.

He felt their fear, their awe, and their... *what... hope*?

The black-robed man smiled in welcome.

'Welcome home, Magnus,' said Malcador.

ELEVEN

Blind Man's Mate

Home.

The word sent a jolt of pain through Magnus.

To a being unbound by the laws of the physical realm, the word was almost meaningless, or so he had thought until it flew from Malcador's lips to pierce his heart like an arrow.

Prospero had always been Magnus' home, ever since he had been cast from Terra as a youth. Isolated from the species' birthrock, that distant world was also home to a remote sect of scholars and seers whose lives were spent in development of their nascent psychic potential.

Even as an orphan adrift, his powers were greater than theirs.

Prospero had been a dream, a place of joy and light, where he had grown to become the best and brightest of them all.

But now he saw it for what it truly was: a hiding place.

There he could grow and develop without fear of being eclipsed in glory, in a place where he would never be outshone or think his accomplishments cheap in the face of another's greatness.

One word had unlocked that understanding. One simple word.

Malcador was too canny not to have known the effect that word would have upon him, and it unsettled Magnus to realise how easily it had passed his guard and how deep a chord it struck. Even now, Malcador was playing his mind games.

Magnus pushed away painful thoughts of Prospero and strode across the black sands.

So like that of Isstvan V.

He had not fought at the explosive inception of Lupercal's war, but he had lived it through the psychometry of others. He had trod the blood-soaked fields of the Urgall Depression in ways more vivid than even those who had fought and died there.

'It's the Sigillite,' said Atrahasis in disbelief. 'We should kill him.'

'No,' said Magnus. ***'There is to be no killing but on my word.'***

The Thousand Sons spread out before him, a four-man echelon with their bolters aimed unerringly at Malcador's head, though the Sigillite seemed unperturbed by the enemy legionaries moving to surround him. From the woman, Magnus sensed only surprise, not the fear he might have expected. The table between her and Malcador was laid with a silver ewer, a platter of fruit and a classic, circular regicide board. A simple set with only the most basic wooden representations of the pieces.

Magnus scanned the board in the blink of an eye, running through the myriad permutations of future moves and likely counters.

'You are one move away from defeat,' he said.

Alivia watched the primarch of the Thousand Sons approach with prideful strides, feeling her heart beating wildly in her chest. She had met four primarchs in her long life: Horus

Lupercal, Guilliman, Corax, and one whose name she had sworn never to speak.

None of them affected her quite like Magnus.

To look upon such beings – she refused to call them demigods or any such nonsense – was to see the terrible power of science and magic unfettered by any notions of ethics or caution. The birth of the primarchs was the power to create monsters.

She had been awed by their abilities, but she had always seen past their mythologising. They were mighty, yes, but they were not immortal. They were not unkillable.

Magnus was something else entirely.

His body had long since surrendered to the metaphysics of his creation, neither wholly flesh and blood, nor yet something of the immaterium. An amber haze drifted up from the flesh of his limbs, like heated ingots removed from a furnace, and the red of his hair was so vivid it hurt to look upon. The moulded plates of his armour gleamed with reflections without source, and ghostly images slid across the slick surfaces of his horned breastplate.

Alivia felt his infinite gaze sweep across her, and the sense of the terrible truths behind that baleful eye sent a spasm of nausea through her. She remembered defiantly meeting the gaze of Horus beneath Molech, but where the Warmaster had embodied raw strength, Magnus was an ocean of limitless ferocity contained by a lone, straining dam of fraying humanity.

'You are one move away from defeat,' said Magnus, and even his voice was heavy with the sense that, but for his restraint, it might obliterate her with a spiteful syllable. ***'I believe she is positioning her Divinitarch for a Blind Man's Mate.'***

'It looks that way,' agreed Malcador, 'but my Tetrarch stands ready to spring a Traitor's Gambit.'

'Risky,' said Magnus. ***'Very risky.'***

Malcador smiled. 'Indeed. And against a more ruthless opponent I would not attempt it. No offence, Alivia.'

'None taken,' she said, struggling to keep her voice even. 'I prefer cards anyway. Way easier to cheat.'

'Your name is Alivia?' said Magnus, turning his attention to her. She flinched at the intensity of his gaze, but only a little, feeling like a paralysed gazelle before the hunting lion.

She nodded and said, 'Alivia Sureka. I don't need to ask who *you* are.'

'What strange fate leads you to be playing Regicide with the Sigillite of Terra on the calm shores of this lake while my brothers lay siege above?'

'He asked me to come.'

'Why?'

'I have absolutely no idea,' said Alivia. 'He's not the best at giving straight answers.'

Magnus grinned. ***'No, he is not. Indeed, he is not.'***

Malcador sat back at the board and planted his staff in the sand like a banner pole. He held out his other hand, offering Magnus the seat opposite.

'What say we finish this game?' said Malcador.

'It is all but concluded,' replied Magnus.

'Nothing is certain in the late game.'

'Some things are,' said Magnus, turning his gaze upon the seat opposite Malcador. Its dimensions stretched with a groan of twisting iron as it swelled to accommodate his inhuman proportions. ***'Besides, I do not wish to play you again. Your moves and ploys are all known to me, and our games always ended in stalemate.'***

Malcador rose from the table and said, 'Then play Alivia.'

Alivia looked from Malcador to the board and back again. Before Magnus' arrival, she had been taking a beating from the

Sigillite, and now he was offering her his superior position. Victory was almost certain from here, but against a primarch…

'A mortal?' snorted Magnus. ***'What would be the point?'***

'Alivia may surprise you, she is quite gifted.'

Their arrogance irked Alivia, so she took Malcador's seat across from Magnus.

'Sure, why not? How often do you get an opportunity like this?'

Magnus regarded her with more scrutiny, no doubt suspicious of Malcador's motives. She didn't blame him; she would be just as sceptical.

'Very well, I will indulge you this last pantomime,' said Magnus.

Malcador stood behind Alivia and said, 'You studied the game I played against Dume?'

'You played against Narthan Dume?' said Alivia, craning her neck to face Malcador.

'Once, yes, in the heady days before the Panpacific descended into a nightmare.'

Magnus nodded. ***'I replayed that game in my mind for months to understand how he beat Dume. In the end I was forced to conclude that Dume's genius had already fallen into madness by the time he made that last desperate gambit with his Empress. Now, I will play your game, but enough with symbolism and deflections, you know why I am here.'***

'A number of possibilities suggest themselves,' said Malcador.

'Such as?'

Alivia reached out to move one of her Citizen pieces forward, an inconsequential move, a delaying tactic.

'Vengeance for Prospero?' she suggested.

Magnus slid his last remaining fortress across the board to counter Alivia's opposing Primarch. Another delaying move in an irrelevant portion of the board. Scanning the pieces, she saw that only the movement of the Ecclesiarch and the Tetrarch in the Widdershin's section of the board was of any importance.

'Would I be unjustified in such a motive?' asked Magnus. *'I did nothing wrong, and my world was razed, my sons butchered by Russ' dogs, and a wealth of learning burned to ash.'*

'That was not my intent,' said Malcador, and his sadness was genuine. 'Nor was it His.'

'Your intent is meaningless,' snapped Magnus. *'You are still responsible. You sent Russ and the Custodians to my world with blades bared. What did you think they would do?'*

'Perhaps you could ask Horus,' said Malcador. 'His hands are stained red with the blood of your sons as much as mine. I say that not to pass any responsibility, I own that decision, and the doom of Prospero is entirely my burden to shoulder. I sent the Wolves. I gave them their orders, but I did not foresee how their mission might be co-opted by a single word.'

Magnus shook his head. *'The small perturbations we miss or ignore, the tiny flaws we regard as inconsequential... they have far-reaching consequences. Didn't you teach me that?'*

'I did,' said Malcador sadly. 'If only you had truly understood what it meant.'

Malcador raised a palm to head off Magnus' anger.

'Do not mistake my meaning,' said the Sigillite. 'We failed you utterly. We didn't tell you all you needed to know. We gave you the tools to forge your own reality, but didn't make clear what the cost of crossing certain lines would be. The failure is ours entirely, mine and the Emperor's, not yours. But it doesn't change where we stand now. What matters is what happens here, right now in this moment.'

'What is the point of this confession, Malcador? Do you want my forgiveness, is that it? My Legion was all but destroyed, and the dread powers that even now hollow out Horus like a wasting sickness gather like carrion around my sons. Around me.'

'My words were not a confession.'

'Then what were they?'

Malcador leaned heavily on his staff with a sigh, and Alivia saw to the true heart of the man. Despite everything, despite all the power he possessed, all the grand stratagems measured in the spans of millennia, he was *tired*.

His long life was almost at an end and he knew it.

'It is a last attempt to speak to the Magnus I knew before this age of madness,' said Malcador. 'You were always the best of us in so many ways. You had vision none of your brothers ever came close to matching. Each of them embodies greatness in his own way, but none could see as far or conceptualise the infinite possibilities of existence as you were able to. Not even I could envision the things you dreamed.'

'And yet here we are,' said Magnus. ***'Enemies.'***

Malcador shook his head. 'That clay is still soft, not yet fixed in shape, and the heat of this kiln has yet to render any transformation permanent.'

Magnus turned his attention to the game. Alivia did likewise and was surprised to see the configuration of the board had changed. They had been moving pieces instinctively, neither fully aware of the act or in full conscious awareness of their closing stratagems.

The Traitor's Gambit was no longer possible, but neither was Blind Man's Mate, the necessary pieces scattered and dispersed, with the portions of the board Magnus had dismissed as irrelevant now assuming far greater importance.

In this new alignment, the white Primarch faced off against the black Emperor, and all other pieces had faded into the background, like the singers of the chorus, melting into the curtained shadows of the wings, leaving only the leading actors in the spotlight.

'The next move of the Primarch piece will decide the outcome of the game,' she said.

'You're right, she is gifted,' said Magnus. *'And so the late game reveals itself.'*

Alivia held her breath. 'It's your move,' she said.

'Do you think **this,**' said Magnus, placing a finger on the Primarch piece and sweeping his other hand around him, '**any** *of this means anything? You both know this game is meaningless. It is nothing more than childish symbolism engineered to prime my thought processes, fire certain synaptic connections within my psyche, and not-so-subtly arrange the levers in my mind to your purposes.'*

'I admit to a certain level of theatricality,' said Malcador. 'But its message is no less true.'

'And what message is that?'

'That it's not too late to alter the course of the game,' said Alivia, placing a fingertip on the head of her Emperor piece. 'That the next move you make will decide whether this Emperor falls or retakes the board.'

Magnus nodded and removed his finger from the Primarch. He sat back, coolly regarding Alivia. Looking past him to the armed warriors at his back, Alivia felt their impatience as they watched their gene-sire parley with their sworn enemy like an old friend.

'You said there were a number of possibilities as to why I had come here,' said Magnus, abruptly returning to an earlier moment in their conversation.

'I did, yes.'

'Alivia here suggested vengeance for Prospero was one, what are the others?'

'The missing piece of your soul.'

Magnus snapped his fingers. *'There it is. Yes, the missing piece of my soul,* **the last and best part of me.** *When Russ broke me across his knee, I cried out to my sons, and together we cast ourselves into the Great Ocean in search of refuge. It*

cost me everything to save them from the Wolves, but I had already paid the greatest price when I tried to warn my father of Horus' treachery.'

'I know what that cost you,' said Malcador. 'But do you know what it cost your father?'

'Tell me,' said Magnus bitterly. ***'What did it cost Him?'***

'Everything.'

'After Prospero, my soul was sundered like glass upon stone...' said Magnus.

'I know,' said Malcador. 'I spent a great deal of time conversing with the soul-shard who dwelled here. In those moments I could almost forget the terror of the war raging across the heavens.'

'He dwelled here?'

'He did, in that villa there,' said Malcador, pointing to a nondescript building of pale stone with a glassed atrium and a high veranda overlooking the lake.

'I remember...' said Magnus, and Alivia was reminded of the old men whose minds frayed at the seams and forgot the faces of their loved ones. ***'I read the eight books of Aenesidemus'* Pyrrhonist Discourses *there.'***

Malcador nodded and said, 'He and I spoke of a great many things, but most of all we debated the nature of his existence many times. He wondered if he were the real Magnus, or whether any one of the many shards he felt throughout space and time were viable separate entities. He told me he felt real, and I believe he *was* real, but even he knew he was something shorn from a greater whole.'

'He is the best part of me,' said Magnus, reaching down to the great grimoire at his waist, and Alivia felt a sick revulsion at the power she felt within it, the unmistakable power of planetary genocide.

Morningstar...

The significance of the name was lost on Alivia, beyond its

appearance in the old religious texts, but she sensed it was as much a terrible curse to Magnus as it was a... a *weapon?*

'And that best part will be one with me again,' promised Magnus.

'You're wrong,' said Malcador. 'In that he was never the *good* part of you, he was just a *part* of you, no better or worse than any other. Each broken shard of you clung to a memory of part of you, but they were all simply a microcosm of the great soul you always were.'

Alivia saw the disbelief on Magnus' face, and also a great and building fire within as whatever certainty he had brought to this cavern crumbled in the face of Malcador's words.

'No...' he said. ***'I felt his goodness, his purity. From across the gulfs of space, even in the Great Ocean, I*** **felt** ***it. It was shorn from me before Horus poisoned the well. It is the best part of me, uncorrupted by... all of*** **this.'**

'I am sorry, Magnus, but you are wrong,' said Malcador. 'And you are too late. He is no more.'

Magnus surged to his feet, overturning the table and scattering the board and its pieces into the water. Alivia was hurled backwards by the force and speed of Magnus' motion, the suddenness more shocking than the pain of the table edge slamming into her chest. She spun through the air, landing face down in the sand ten metres away.

Alivia coughed and spat the grit from her mouth. Blood mingled with the sand, and she cried out as she felt broken ribs shift within her chest. From the frothed blood on her lips, she knew a shard of bone must have pierced the soft tissue of her lung. She coughed up a red wad of gummed fluid and pushed herself painfully onto her side in time to see Magnus with his fist around Malcador's throat.

He held the Sigillite three metres off the ground, his life there for the taking.

The warriors Magnus had brought into the Palace backed away from him, as fearful of their master's fury as Alivia.

'I need** him!'* roared Magnus. ***'What am I without him? A beast no better than Angron? A slave to desire like Fulgrim? If he is no different from me, and I no more or less than him, then all I have done is...'

'Is part of who you already are,' finished Alivia, and the nearest red-armoured warrior turned his bolter towards her. She pushed herself upright, stifling a cry of pain as the breath wheezed in her throat and the sharp stab of bone pierced her heart.

'I will not be like my fallen brothers, I will* not,'** said Magnus. ***'Tell me where to find the last shard of my soul or I will end you right now.'

'He is gone,' gasped Malcador, forcing his words out as Magnus' grip closed off his airways. 'Beyond even your power to reach.'

'What did you do?' demanded Magnus.

'What needed to be done...' gasped Malcador, '...to save the last son of Prospero.'

The wisps of smoke rising from the primarch's skin billowed in darkness and swirled around him like living things. Alivia could feel the heat radiating from him, and knew that any hope Malcador had of reasoning with Magnus was gone.

She stumbled back towards the villas, knowing there was no hope of evading any pursuit, but driven to escape by the basic animal urge to flee, to survive. She had suffered greater wounds than this and lived, but never from a being as powerful as Magnus.

Alivia fell to one knee as breath failed her. She felt a horrid, sucking emptiness on the left side of her chest. Her hand clawed the sand. Pain filled her, but she'd known worse.

She heard crunching footsteps behind her and forced herself to her feet.

Her vision blurred at the edges and she coughed up another wad of bloody phlegm.

'Turn around,' said a voice: harsh, clipped and used to being obeyed.

She almost obeyed it, *almost* reacted to its commanding tone.

'Screw. You...' wheezed Alivia between tortured breaths.

She kept going, the colourful mosaic of the plaza at the centre of the villas just visible between their walls of pale marble. If she could just reach it, at least she would be out of sight of Magnus and his sorcerers. But it seemed so far away, farther with every swaying step.

If she could only...

The mass-reactive struck Alivia between her shoulder blades and penetrated deep into her chest cavity before detonating.

An instant of fire and pain, then nothing at all.

Magnus let the anger pour from him, a fire that had burned inside him since he had first swum into being all those centuries ago and looked out upon the world with an awareness unlike any other into a face as beautiful as it was terrifying.

All he had done was in service of his father, and now, at this last moment of redemption, where his past might have been granted absolution, even that was snatched away.

He loosed a roar to the cavern roof, shaking the rock with the power of his ferocity.

He heard shouts, a single mass-reactive shot.

The fire seemed to burn for an eternity, though it had been seconds at most.

Magnus dropped to his knees as the rage began to ebb. His unleashed power flowed back along his limbs as clarity returned to his sight. He smelled the rancorous odour of burned meat, and saw smoke rising from the fiery copper of his skin.

Sound swelled, the crash of rock and crystal formations tumbling from the cavern roof in vast chunks of splintered stone. Shaken loose by the elemental power of his fury, they fell as if on a pict-reel running at half-speed. When they finally struck the surface of the water, dark waves crashed upon the shore.

Magnus saw the regicide board and its pieces pulled out into the depths of the underground ocean, the outcome of this last game forever undecided.

He looked for the woman and saw her lying face down in the sand.

Most of her torso was missing, only splintered shards of ribs and a fused section of her spine attaching her upper body to her lower. Blood spread between the outer tiles of the plaza as Atrahasis walked back towards them with smoke curling from the barrel of his weapon.

'I said no killing without my word,' said Magnus.

'She–' began Atrahasis, but Magnus gave him no chance to finish.

With a thought, he detonated every atom in the warrior's body, leaving nothing but inert dust within the clattering remains of warplate that fell to the sands.

The others reeled from Atrahasis' explosive death, fearful they too might be touched by their primarch's wrath. But he had no more wrath within him, only grief, and he closed his eye, locked in position like a frozen statue.

How long he remained like that he could not say, but eventually a wary voice penetrated the fog enveloping his mind.

'My lord.'

'Ahzek…'

'My lord,' said Ahriman, with greater confidence and force. 'We must withdraw.'

'Withdraw?' said Magnus. ***'No…'***

'We must,' repeated Ahriman. 'What you sought is gone,

but we have struck a great blow to our enemies. One that will turn the tide of the war.'

'A great blow...?' said Magnus. *'I don't understand...'*

And then he saw.

Still clutched in his iron grip was the Sigillite, but never again would he play regicide; never again would he stand in the presence of demigods and speak to them as equals.

Never again...

Malcador's corpse was a char-black skeleton of heat-fused bones and roasted meat. His fleshless skull lolled on the last remnants of sinew and spinal cord, the meat of his once great mind oozing from the molten bone of his skull.

'No!' cried Magnus, rising to his feet and releasing his grip.

The Sigillite's skeletal remains dropped to the shore of the lake where the ebb and flow of the new tide twisted and rolled them in the sand. His tall staff of office now served not as a banner pole, but a grave marker.

Two more deaths to add to an ever-growing tally.

'Sire,' said Amon. 'Ahzek is right. We should withdraw before the Custodians come. That they are not already here is a miracle. The Sigillite's death will have been felt, and the Emperor's golden warriors will seek to avenge him.'

'This was never my intent,' whispered Magnus, and his own words echoed back at him in his skull, mocking him.

Your intent is meaningless. You are still responsible.

'How could we not have seen this?' wondered Menkaura. 'We are the greatest seers of the Corvidae, and none of us saw even a *sliver* of this future? The death of so significant a soul as the Regent of Terra, and *not one of us* saw this moment in our visions?'

'We are not withdrawing, we are going to the very heart of Terra,' said Magnus. *'Nothing of what happened here matters. I saw every secret thing within Malcador, every hidden path and cordon within the Palace. And I know what I have to do now.'*

'Sire?'

'We are in the heart of the Sanctum Imperialis,' said Magnus, as singular purpose crystallised within him. ***'Within sight of what Alpharius failed to imagine and that which Horus Lupercal dares not even dream of.'***

'What do you intend, my lord?' asked Ahriman.

'I am going to kill the Emperor.'

TWELVE

The Hall of Victories

Magnus led them to the plaza at the centre of the forsaken villas.

He paused at the body of Alivia Sureka, and knelt to place a hand upon the tattered remnants of her gore-spattered flak coat. Still warm, she lay in an expanding pool of glistening red that spread from her ruined torso like bloodied wings and put Magnus in mind of a fallen Valkyrie.

'I did not know you, but I am sorry this was your ending,' he said, wiping away a red tear from her glassy, dead eye.

'Atrahasis was Raptora to the core, brutal and direct,' said Ahriman. 'Yes, he disobeyed you, but he did not deserve to die like that.'

'I said there was to be no killing,' said Magnus. ***'Do my sons now pick and choose which of my orders are for obeying?'***

'Of course not, my lord, but–'

'I saw him die as we approached this cavern,' said Magnus. ***'I could make no sense of it at the time, for it was a death such as only a handful of beings in this galaxy could inflict. It never even crossed my mind it would be at my hands.'***

'And the rest of us?' demanded Ahriman. 'Did you see our deaths?'

'No,' lied Magnus, rising to his full height. ***'I did not, and before you condemn me for your man's death, look to your own guilt. Where is Hathor Maat? Did*** **he** ***deserve to die?'***

Ahriman flinched at the mention of his former brother's name.

Did you think you could restore my soul and I would not see within yours? sent Magnus so that only Ahriman would hear. ***I know what you did, and I know why you did it. So I do not condemn you, but it is my fervent wish you could have been spared that burden. Every step we have taken since Prospero has been in the service of others, and you gave up your brother for me. Just believe that all I have done since then is for the good of my sons.***

Ahriman nodded stiffly and followed as Magnus moved to the centre of the plaza, where the confluence of the abstract patterns worked into the mosaic finally converged.

Magnus turned in a slow circle, trying to imagine which of the dwellings had been intended for which of his brothers. He could discern no differences between them enough to judge, but some of his kin had spent time here, that much he could feel.

'What might it have been like to have shared these spaces with you, my brothers?' he said. ***'Would it have been glorious or would we have squabbled and fought for the scraps of our father's attention as we did during the crusade?'***

Briefly Magnus considered exploring the villa in which his soul-shard had dwelled, but rejected the notion. What would be the point? Nostalgia for events he had not truly experienced? Reacquaintance with a life he had never lived?

No, better to leave that wound untouched.

Besides, they had only a short window in which to act.

Even now, the Custodians were likely en route, perhaps even some of his loyalist brothers.

It was a mystery to him why they were not already here. The expenditure of power in the Great Observatory ought to have drawn them near instantaneously, but that they had not yet discovered this intrusion was an opportunity Magnus did not intend to waste.

He squatted at the sigils running around the great icon of cosmic duality at the heart of the plaza and pressed a sequence he knew only from another's memory. At first nothing happened, but soon he felt a vibration through the flagstones and stepped back as a towering column of ivory rose from the ground.

Its length was porcelain smooth and apparently seamless, but moments later a curved door opened in its side and an artificial blue glow issued from within. Magnus confidently stepped into the elevator, its proportions – like those of the villas – scaled to a being of his size.

His sons accompanied him within like an honour guard, and no sooner had the doors slid shut than the elevator began a smooth descent into the depths of the planet, descending what felt like several kilometres into the heart of Himalazia.

'Do you know where this leads?' said Menkaura.

Magnus did not answer, and they continued in tense silence until the doors opened to reveal a short corridor that ended in a towering set of bronze double doors. Exquisitely carved, the twin leafs of the doors depicted a man and woman facing one another: one of the land, the other of the manufactory.

'Life and death,' said Amon, regarding the woman.

'Industry and war,' said Menkaura of the man.

'It is more than that,' said Magnus, pointing to the crossed lightning bolts of Unity hung around the man's neck. ***'It is the embodiment of my father's dream. Humanity bound endlessly to the tasks of procreation and the labours required of***

them in order to bathe in His light. He is their sun god, their Alpha and Omega, the beginning and the end. From worship of the Emperor comes all bounty. The stars around Him are us, the primarchs, the warrior angels who enforce His laws and fight at His command.'

'People of Earth: Unity is Strength, Division is Weakness,' said Ahriman, expertly translating the ancient language inscribed in the scrollwork above the doors.

The doors swung open easily, and beyond was a wide gallery, several hundred metres long and filled with displays, such as had been common within the pyramids of Prospero. Many of the gallery's cabinets and cases had toppled, their contents broken upon the tiled floor. Water poured in through a shattered section of the roof towards the rear of this stark gallery, ruining the many paintings, statues, carvings and tapestries stored there.

One of the long walls was lined with tall, lancet windows, but no light penetrated the oil- and dust-smeared glass save through portions where it had been shattered by the percussive impacts of shock waves. Glass shards littered the floor and a lingering taste of burnt ozone spoke of failed stasis fields.

Regret touched Magnus at the thought of what had been lost here.

That regret was washed away on the heels of another thought.

'How much did we lose on Tizca?' he asked, bending to retrieve the remains of a stone tablet with wedge-shaped, cuneiform script upon it. Fire and smoke had coated its surfaces in a filmy residue, already softening and obscuring much of the text.

'Incalculable,' said Amon. 'In ways too numerous to count.'

Magnus handed the tablet to Ahriman. ***'You recognise this?'***

Ahriman turned the tablet over in his hands and nodded. 'Achaemenid. From Arg-e-Bam, a fortress at the crossroads of the Silk Road. Perhaps thirty-five thousand years old.'

'And this?' said Magnus, indicating an elaborately crafted model of a magnificent galleon set upon a raised dais. The ship was rigged with sails of thin gold, its hull crafted from gilded copper and iron. From keel to crow's nest, it stood roughly a metre high.

'A child's toy?' suggested Menkaura.

'A toy perhaps, but not one for children,' said Magnus, turning a hidden key at the vessel's stern. ***'Rather, a grand plaything for some rich potentate of Old Earth.'***

High on the vessel's stern sat a crowned king, and before him on clockwork gimbals his subjects paraded on the carved deck, turning and making obeisance as the ratcheting mainspring turned within. Inside the vessel, a miniature organ played the off-kilter notes of a long-forgotten tune as iron cannons emerged jerkily from wooden hatches in the hull.

Magnus grinned as the cannons retracted and the figures on the deck all bowed to their king before the spring's energy was spent and the vessel stilled once more. ***'It is a clock and a music box rendered in the form of a galleon built to make war when control of the oceans ensured a nation state's dominance. In ships like these, the largest and most complex machines of their age, conquerors set off across the high seas to discover other cultures on the other side of the planet. To trade or make war with them. Sometimes both.'***

'And they made a toy of it?' said Amon. 'That seems wasteful.'

'Not at all,' said Menkaura, bending to examine the faceless, yellow-robed king on his throne. 'This is a wonderfully constructed object, a masterpiece of both the artificer's skill, the artist's decoration, and it displays a profound mastery of mechanics and goldsmithing.'

'What is this place?' asked Amon.

'Surely it is not hard to divine?' said Magnus. ***'It is a record of humanity's greatest achievements, each one a stepping stone***

into the future. It has all the hallmarks of Malcador, for the Sigillite was ever one to recognise the importance of preserving the past.'

He remembered Kasper Hawser, the naive conservator who had spoken with such passion on the subject of humankind's lack of foresight in considering the past. The man had constantly pushed for an audit of human knowledge and the preservation of the species' legacy to determine what was still known and what had been forgotten.

Had the man ever set foot in this gallery or ever seen this record of human progress from its Palaeolithic history to its exploration of the stars? Impossible to know, and Magnus had no knowledge of what had become of him in the wake of Prospero's doom.

Given what they had done to his mind, he was likely dead or insane.

'What would you have made of this, I wonder?' said Magnus sadly. ***'And what tears would you shed to see it all lost?'***

'My lord?' said Ahriman.

Magnus said nothing and cast all thoughts of regret and sentimentality from his mind.

He pushed deeper into the gallery, pausing every now and then to examine an object of great beauty or significance: a jade axe head, a pair of Kakiemon elephants, circuit boards from corroded husks of primitive logic engines that were no longer home to any machine-spirit, ivory chess pieces carved from the teeth of great oceanic creatures.

All embodied consequential moments that had seen humanity rise from its earliest, primitive beginnings to the lofty heights it occupied in the present, but one in particular struck him as out of place: a broken timepiece of tarnished bronze with a cracked ebony face.

It wasn't special or even particularly attractive, and at some point, it had been exposed to great heat, for the metal had softened and deformed. Despite that, the delicate hands were unscathed, lovingly fashioned from gold with inlaid mother of pearl. What remained of the clock's internal mechanisms were visible through a smoke-stained window near its base, a jumbled mass of toothed cogs that could never turn and copper pendulums that would never swing again.

'Why are you here?' Magnus wondered aloud.

'Because it marked a singular moment in Terra's history,' said a powerful voice from the end of the gallery. 'And my own, though I did not recognise it as such at the time.'

Magnus swung around, heqa staff raised before him, one hand on his great book.

His sons snapped into battle positions, bolters raised.

A hooded figure stood at the end of the gallery, swathed in a long cloak of scarlet.

The man was transhuman tall and beneath his long cloak, he wore utilitarian clothes, similar to those worn by virtually every inhabitant of Terra. A silver ring glittered on his right index finger, bearing a nazarlik symbol of warding.

Behind him was a simple wooden door, such as might be found in the ancient hall of a high castle of stone. A door entirely out of place in this stark gallery of glass and steel, and which Magnus knew had not been there only moments before.

'A descendant of Mikuláš of Kada⊠ constructed it in his clockwork palace, high in the frozen mountains of Europa. It's gone now, of course. I suspect that piece is perhaps the last of its kind, much like a great many things we once valued.'

'Identify yourself,' ordered Magnus.

The man slowly reached up and pulled back his hood to reveal a stern, but not unkind face. Unremarkable in its own way, but the man's eyes were without pupils and shone with a golden light that identified him better than any name ever could.

'When last I wore this guise I went by Revelation.'

The light of Revelation shone throughout the gallery, and all the shattered relics of humanity's ascent gleamed as though fresh from their ancient makers' hands. Dead machines whirred to life, the organ within the clockwork ship played its maritime tune flawlessly, and the clock beside Magnus chimed softly as its hands clicked to the vertical.

'You know why I am here?' asked Magnus.

The door behind Revelation opened, spilling fresh radiance into the gallery.

'I do,' said Revelation. 'But first we will talk, my son.'

BOOK FIVE

THRONE ROOM

THIRTEEN

Adrift

An achingly blue sky filled her vision, the skies of her youth, unpolluted by petrochemical emissions and hydrocarbon pollutants. The secrets of the fuels locked within Earth's body were well known even then, but the conspicuous consumption of such fuels on a global scale was millennia in the future.

The view from the mountain's summit was breathtaking: misted valleys, deep forests and dark oceans of infinite mystery.

But it was always the sky she came back to.

Alivia had seen the skies of many worlds since then, but none compared to the glory of Old Earth. Parochial perhaps, but she couldn't deny the call her home world had on her soul.

So why were we in such a rush to leave it...?

A memory of pain surfaced in her mind, but she pushed it away.

Alivia did not want to leave this place of memory and peace.

She knew it was a remembrance of the land of her birth, a vision of a time before the world had shown her its true face and bloodily revealed her own secret nature. The last time she had seen this place in dreams, it had been hijacked by John Grammaticus with a warning.

Remembering that moment, her gaze shifted down from the endless skies to the edge of the forest. The trees grew dense, only the slowly encroaching moonlight shadows visible between their claw-scored trunks.

She smiled as she saw the powerful stag once again. It grazed at the edge of the trees, its sheer magnificence no less thrilling to see with repetition. But its splendour was diminished this time, its red-gold hide patchy from some desperate flight, and its once mighty antlers snapped and foreshortened from bloody battle.

Once he had been the master of this mountain, and had led the wild hunt over the high hills and far moors, but now he was at bay and taking this moment to gather his strength.

Alivia held her breath, lest even a whisper of movement break the spell.

The stag's head came up, his nostrils twitching.

The last time she had seen the stag he had bolted for the towering peaks, a pack of red-eyed wolves snapping at his hooves, but now he walked slowly towards her.

With every step, the outline of the stag *shifted*, sloughing its shroud of metaphor and assuming the form in which she had last seen him: a tall man in the sturdy attire of an agri-worker, handsome in a rangy sort of way, with a wiry auburn beard, broad shoulders and strong arms crisscrossed with scars.

Another disguise, but a pleasing one at least.

But no matter the face He presented to the world, He could never conceal the raw power and threat behind His eyes.

'When I left Terra I told you I never wanted to see you again,' she said.

'I know, and I wanted to respect that, truly I did, but…'

His words trailed off. No explanation was needed.

'I stood watch for you on Molech, but I couldn't stop him.'

He didn't need to ask who she meant.

'I know. It was an impossible task, Alivia. No one could have stopped him. Not empowered as he was.'

'We tried,' said Alivia. 'Good men died trying to stop him.'

'But not you.'

'No, not me,' she spat bitterly. 'It's never me that dies.'

They sat in silence for a time, enjoying the view over the ocean. She'd sailed the far corners of the Earth in her long years, but never tired of watching and listening to waves on a shingled beach or crashing against a cliff.

'Why are you here?' said Alivia. 'Don't you have more important things to do? You know, fate of the galaxy, defending Terra, that sort of thing?'

He nodded. 'I have an unfathomable amount of important things to do, Alivia, and many of them are reaching their conclusion.'

'And I'm guessing your being here means one of them involves me?'

'It does.'

'Am I going to like it?'

He thought for a moment, then said, 'No, but it must be done.'

'Then to hell with you,' said Alivia. 'You don't command me, not any more. You swore the task on Molech would be my last.'

'One might argue that you failed in that task.'

'Screw you,' snapped Alivia. 'You just said that no one could have stopped Horus from going through that portal. I remember carrying you up those stairs and you telling me that I could be done with you.'

'And I meant it,' He said, reaching to take her hand. 'I still do, and I wish I did not have to ask. But let me show you what is at stake.'

She snatched her hand away and said, 'I saw Molech fall. I've been outside the walls of your Palace. Trust me, I know what's at stake. Besides, even if Horus wins, I don't think he could balls things up any worse than you.'

'You don't believe that,' he said. 'You know what's out there in the dark. You've heard the whispers of the Neverborn and you have seen what happens when men give in to the temptations of Chaos. I would not ask if there were any other way.'

'You are a liar and a monster, a manipulator and a killer,' said Alivia. 'Your armies slaughtered millions in the name of Unity and crushed anyone who opposed your rule. You made monsters from your own flesh then turned them loose on the galaxy and you act surprised when they turn on you? All in the name of a vision only you could see. You know that Magnus killed Malcador, yes?'

He nodded, His shoulders slumped. 'I felt him die. I felt his agony as Magnus ended him.'

The tears He shed were real and painfully raw, and Alivia's hatred and love for Him was so powerful it hurt her heart. Tears welled in her eyes, but she angrily wiped them away.

'There is so much blood on your hands,' she said. 'On *all* our hands. I just want it to end.'

'Then *help* me end it,' He said, offering her His hand once again. 'Let me share with you *my* Acuity.'

Slowly, and against her better judgement, Alivia took His hand.

And the Emperor showed her everything in the space of a moment.

Alivia threw back her head and screamed.

Endlessly, like the withered corpse she saw locked within the Golden Throne.

* * *

Stepping through the incongruous wooden door, Magnus experienced a momentary tug of dislocation, like a teleport flare, but deeper and more profound. A shiver travelled the length of his body as he felt the temperature gradient shift.

Wherever they were now, they were far deeper underground than before.

Revelation awaited them, His golden eyes shining even brighter.

'I have been here before,' said Magnus, and a wave of shame washed over him.

'Memories of your soul-shard?' asked Ahriman.

'No,' said Revelation, addressing Ahriman directly. 'Your gene-sire came not as a shade, nor in a borrowed memory of another piece of himself, but as Magnus the Red, a proud and loyal son of the Emperor of Mankind.'

'Is this...?' said Amon.

'The Throne Room,' finished Magnus.

Though the Thousand Sons were pledged to the Warmaster's cause and fought alongside warriors who sought to tear down every edifice of the Imperium, the shared heritage of this place was too great to ignore. It hung heavily upon them as Revelation led them deeper into the Emperor's inner sanctum.

The cavern of the underground lake had been unimaginably vast, but this subterranean donjon was orders of magnitude greater. It was filled with machinery: endless lengths of hissing pipes and cables coiled across the floor and hung from the walls like wounded serpents. Towering banks of straining equipment were set with myriad readouts and gauges, though what they measured was a mystery to Magnus.

The floor vibrated to the thrumming workings of buried machinery and the pounding of distant pistons moving endlessly in the farthest reaches of the cavern. Reeking, ozone exhalations from gigantic terraforming processors fogged the air, and coruscating arcs of power leapt between giant machines tasked with the maintenance of energy flow.

Thousands of oil-stained menials ministered to the machines beneath the watchful gaze of Mechanicum tech-priests cowled in red and black. Magnus heard binharic screeches of alarm, but instead of fleeing before these enemy warriors, their chimeric faces of metal and flesh adjudged the new arrivals to be less of a priority than the machinery they attended.

At the geomantic centre of this immense cavern was the strange and terrible edifice of gold he had seen in person, vision and dream. A gigantic, towering dais, kilometres tall and inlaid with silvery traceries of runic circuitry. It was to this arcane technology, the functioning of which not even Magnus could fathom, that every machine, above and below, was enslaved, a Gordian network of cables and pipelines that drew immense volumes of power to its mystical beating heart.

Yet it was not this that drew Magnus' eye.

Beyond this mountainous dais were vast cyclopean golden doors, their surfaces buckled by titanic impacts and forces beyond imagining. Each was so immense it could allow the greatest war machines of the Mechanicum to march through with armoured heads held high. Entire armies could pass beyond these portals, their dimensions larger than anything Magnus had seen in the Outer Palace.

Even the portals running through Colossi and Gorgon Bar paled into insignificance.

Not even Lion's Gate was equal in scale or grandeur.

Yet it was not even these inhumanly scaled portals that drew Magnus' eye.

His gaze was fixed upon the titanic throne of gold and silver raised upon the highest tier of the golden structure. Its form was layered in a patchwork of bronze and platinum, as though its inner workings had failed and been repaired many times.

Seated atop this unknowable machine, His head locked back with His eyes tightly closed, was a figure clad from head to toe in armour of burnished gold.

Pellucid ghost lights of amber washed across His granite skin in gently lapping waves, illuminating His husked pallor, the tautness of His jaw, the awesome strength radiating from Him and the pain of His suffering. The scale of the power flowing through the machine and into his father was unimaginable.

'Do I speak to Him or to you?'

'We are one and the same, but address your words to me,' said Revelation. 'The damage you wrought upon the golden doors requires my primary focus. The assaults of the Neverborn from the other side are unceasing, and the war in the webway grows ever more fierce.'

'I did that?' asked Magnus, horrified. ***'When I tried to warn you of Horus' perfidy?'***

'You did,' agreed Revelation. 'The irony of your purpose and its outcome are not lost on me, Magnus, but it has cost so much to keep the Neverborn hordes back that I find myself unable to truly appreciate it. Hundreds of thousands of lives spent fighting a numberless host of filth and corruption. Without my continued presence upon the Golden Throne, Terra would even now be a daemon world.'

'I... I could not have known,' said Magnus, gripping his staff so tight, its woven wood and adamantium core began to crack. The hissing voices from his grimoire, the victims of a murdered world, now made themselves known, emerging from its capricious pages in rippling slicks of witchfire and crawling along his arms, eager and ambitious.

'You were told,' said Revelation. 'You were instructed. You were warned, but *you knew better*.'

'I knew only what you told me,' snapped Magnus, the light of Morningstar coruscating along the length of his staff.

'And I will admit to the fault of that,' said Revelation. 'You were birthed to see further than any of your brothers, but I understood the dark and infernal and *eternal* magnitude of the warp better than you. And when I told you there were places even I was unwilling to go and lines I was unwilling to cross, then that ought to have been enough for you.'

The arrogance and presumption in Revelation's words were like a slap to the face.

'Your conceit is staggering, your arrogance unmatched,' said Magnus.

He felt his need for violence eclipse his need for answers, but fought it down for now.

Magnus looked around the chamber, unable to reconcile his continued presence and the utter lack of any protection surrounding the Emperor.

'Where are your praetorians?' said Magnus. ***'The fighting on the walls is desperate, and I saw thousands of Constantin's men at Colossi, but the captain-general of the Legio Custodes would never consent to leaving you entirely unguarded.'***

'I removed them from my presence, my son,' said Revelation. 'Even now they are attempting to break in, fearing I am about some scheme that might endanger my life.'

'And are you?' said Magnus, stepping towards Revelation.

'Very likely,' said the man. 'There is a reason why your steps led you to Leng. I hoped you would remember the secret way through the observatory. And the Hall of Victories has long been my own hidden way to walk among my people without escort.'

The implications of Revelation's words hit Magnus like a blow.

'You let me see the crack in the telaethesic ward…'

Revelation nodded. 'I did. You would never have come had I summoned you.'

'And why would you summon me?' demanded Magnus. ***'You must have known what I would do were I ever to stand before you.'***

Revelation stepped forward and placed a hand on Magnus' shoulder. His eyes were burning pools of molten gold, depthless and bright like the hearts of stars.

He shook His head and said, 'I hoped I did, my son, but I could not know the answer to that mystery until you were here, which was what made this gambit so dangerous, why I had to keep it from Constantin and all others save Malcador.'

'Dangerous? As the Saturnine ruse was dangerous?'

Revelation chuckled and said, 'Rogal's plan was a certainty compared to this.'

'Then allow me to answer that mystery,' said Magnus, ramming the tip of his staff into Revelation's chest. A torrent of unearthly fire poured along its length, unmaking his father's avatar from the inside out.

The man who was not a man screamed as the purest fire of the Pyrae consumed His created flesh, the psychic flames burning in realms mortal and immaterial. It spread along Revelation's limbs, illuminating His body and outstretched arms from within as He shrieked and writhed like a snared beast.

The light faded, and when it was gone, so too was Revelation.

Only the silver ring the man wore survived the fire, falling to the stone floor with a musical *clink*. Magnus bent to retrieve it, stirring the ashes of Revelation with the end of his staff as he slipped the ring over the middle finger of his right hand. The stylised eye carved into its flattened head was exquisitely carved.

Magnus made a fist as his sons gathered round.

He felt their confusion, their feeling of being adrift. None of them had seen this moment, not even him. To know nothing of the future was a prospect no warrior of the Corvidae relished.

'You killed him...' said Amon.

'I killed a puppet, not the master,' said Magnus, rising and making his way towards the golden dais. As he placed his foot upon the first step, he turned back to his expectant sons.

'This reunion is not for you,' he said. ***'Form a mandala, or at least as much of one as you can make with only three of you, and wait for me.'***

Ahriman stepped forward and said, 'Do what must be done, my lord.'

Magnus nodded and began climbing towards the giant figure upon the Golden Throne with singular purpose. Behind him, his sons formed a segment of a mandala at the base of the steps, bolters held at their sides as they rose into the martial enumerations.

His stride was long and driven, and though the throne atop this mountain was far distant, it took him only moments to reach the wide summit of the dais.

Though he had seen Him from afar, to be in such close proximity to his father cut him deeper than he'd expected. Not since Nikaea had they shared the same physical space, and the hypocrisy of that day still twisted in his heart like shrapnel too dangerous to remove.

Closer now, Magnus could see the visible strain upon his father's face. The canyon lines of tension, the slick sheen of sweat upon His laurelled brow. His eyes remained tightly shut, though He must surely have sensed Magnus was coming with murder in his heart.

But still He remained seated, ignoring His son's presence.

Magnus looked back to the cavern floor as he heard the unmistakable roar of mass-reactives.

Six warriors, moving in at speed. Using the vast machinery as cover.

Three in armour of winter ice, three in deepest jade. VI and

XVIII. Lemuel Gaumon followed behind, sinking to his knees behind the logic engines in awe. At first Magnus thought the Space Wolves slow and plodding, but quickly realised that the enormity of his father's presence was affecting them also.

Such fury to overcome their awe!

Magnus' gaze narrowed as he realised he knew the warriors of the VI Legion from the shared memory engrams of his sons.

'The watch pack of Bödvar Bjarki,' he said. ***'And you bring Nocturnean allies.'***

These dogs of Russ had fought his sons on Kamiti Sona and followed through the Great Ocean to assault them in the heart of the crystalline labyrinth.

There are no coincidences…

Gunfire whickered back and forth between the Space Marines. His sons were outnumbered two to one, but even without the full scope of their powers, he had no fear for their lives.

Magnus turned from the fight below. He could not afford to hesitate.

To pause in the face of synchronistic enemies, even for a fraction of a breath, would rob him of his resolve. He thought back to Prospero, to the irreplaceable knowledge that had been lost and his many sons who had died there. To the lies and betrayal at Nikaea. He thought of the falsehoods he had been assured were truths, the broken promises, and the lost hope of a shared future of exploration within the Great Ocean.

He looked into the face of his father, drawing his arm back to hurl his staff like a native harpooner with the perfect cast into the eye of a whale.

The spear trembled in his grip, forming the perfect blade.

His knuckles pressed white on its smoking haft.

Its bladed tip burned orange, brightening to molten radiance, infused with all the anguish of Magnus' fractured soul. It would be a killing strike, powerful enough to end a god's reign.

He lowered the spear, his head sinking to his chest as regret threatened to choke him. The rage and power suffusing its god-slaying blade was snuffed out like a candle at dawn.

'I loved you like no other,' wept Magnus.

A blur of motion snapped his head up as a form his equal in stature smashed down hard on the summit of the dais like a thunderstrike. A shock wave blew out in a ring of force, and flames ripped from nearby machines as arcs of overloading energy erupted like geysers.

Magnus shielded his eyes as furnace heat rippled the air, staring in disbelief at the form emerging from the dissipating cloud of superheated vapour and bleeding light.

A kneeling colossus in green armour rose slowly from the crater his landing had buckled in the metal floor. A burnished cloak of umber scale was clasped to a mighty draconic skull at the shoulder of the finest warplate known to the Imperium, and monstrous gauntlets snarled with blue-hot energies.

His skin was midnight dark like polished obsidian, and his eyes were the red of a sunset at battle's end. One hand was clenched into a brawler's fist, while the other held a mighty warhammer of indestructible iron and bronze named *Urdrakule.*

'So the rumours were true,' said Magnus. ***'Vulkan lives…'***

FOURTEEN

A Precursor to Change

Mass-reactives exploded in the air before Ahriman. Instinctive kine shields caught some and Corvidae foresight allowed him to evade the others. Pyrae fire detonated warheads and Pavoni biomancy altered the chemical composition of explosive cores to render them inert.

The mandala, such as it was, combined their power, a well for each warrior to draw upon.

'Who are they?' cried Amon, rising to the fifth. 'Custodes?'

Ahriman scanned the space before them: too many approaches, too misted by machine breath and strobing with crackling electric bleed. His bolter tracked his gaze as he caught flashes of war-scarred plate, ice blue and earthen green.

He tasted the wet, animal reek of snow-blasted skin. Of bone beads and matted beards, caustic liquor and meat ripped raw from the bone. A feral stink filled his nostrils, cold with magic drawn from the primal heart of a far-distant world, a world where life was held cheap and blood was the payment for land-thirst.

'It's not the Praetorians,' said Ahriman, recognising this power. 'It's Bjarki.'

'The Wolf of Nikaea?' asked Menkaura, an edge of panic in his tone.

Ahriman half turned to face him, sensing a spike of fear in the seer's aura. His concentration slipped and a deflected bolt shell clipped his shoulder guard. Robbed of force enough not to penetrate by impact alone, it detonated a metre from his head. Shrapnel slammed his helmet. His vision fogged red.

The howl of a hunting pack echoed weirdly throughout the cavern.

But how many throats gave voice to it?

His warplate registered a sudden, catastrophic drop in ambient temperature.

'Brace!' yelled Ahriman as a storm of ice roared towards them, a blitzing hurricane of razored shards. It battered them, sliced the skin and threw off their shared aim. Ahriman brought up a kine shield, too late. A thousand needles of ice shattered against his armour, sliced his exposed skin, and threw him from the enumerations.

A shrieking ululation clawed his mind, raw and seeking his prey reflex.

His limbs tried to lock in fear, but Ahriman shook off this blunt assault on his senses.

'I know your power,' he said, dropping to a crouch and snapping off shots at the shadows moving in the mist. They were fast, *too fast* for heavily armoured warriors. But where they moved the percussive thud of bolters immediately followed.

Amon fell back, three rounds cratering his plastron. Menkaura's silver helm gleamed in the winterlight. More shells shivered the air around him, displaced air rocking him back.

The roar of gunfire was too intense, too sustained for only three warriors.

'They're not alone,' shouted Ahriman as a shape reared out of the mist. Ahriman rolled and snapped off a pair of shots that took his attacker in the hip and torso. The first ricocheted away, the second tore the leather wolf-shield totem from his ice-blue chestplate.

A monstrous axe with a crackling, rune-etched blade swung down and slammed into the ground, splitting the rock floor where Ahriman had stood a fraction of a second before. So swift was the assault that Ahriman's foresight was all but useless.

Another blow came at him, too fast to avoid.

He lowered his shoulder into the blow, forced to take the impact on his pauldron.

Ceramite split and the impact hurled him backwards. He landed hard and rose to one knee in time to face the berserk charge of a barrel-chested legionary with a forked beard. The Space Wolf howled, and there was madness in the sound, a mind lost to his Legion's savage soul.

Ahriman pulsed a lance of terror into the warrior's brain, but whatever red mist was upon him cared nothing for the fear of death.

'Your maleficarum is powerless against me!' roared the Space Wolf, his axe cutting towards Ahriman's neck in an executioner's strike. Prescience had already shifted him back, and the killing edge passed the breadth of a finger from his gorget.

Ahriman stepped in and rammed his bolter into the warrior's side.

'Powers or not,' he said, 'I am still Astartes.'

He pulled the trigger, and at such close range, the damage was horrific, two shells tearing through the layers of ceramite and plasteel to the body below. The first ricocheted downward from his rib-plate, travelling the length of the warrior's cuisse plates before exploding in the centre of his knee.

The second gouged a tunnel through his midsection before blasting out of his backplate.

Ahriman's pleasure at the wounds was short-lived as he saw the warrior's next blow coming a second before the blindingly swift reverse stroke hit. The axe smashed into his chestplate, biting deep and smashing him into the ground.

The pain was horrendous, the bone shield of his chest shattered into an archipelago of floating fragments. His primary lungs collapsed, obliterated by the concussive pressure wave of the axe's impact.

He tried to draw breath, but couldn't. His secondary lung kicked in with a rasping lurch, unfolding within his chest with a wet sucking sound. It was grossly inefficient in the crucible of combat, designed only for survival in low-oxygenated environments. The fury of close-quarter battle demanded far more than it could deliver.

A plume of Pyrae fire behind him illuminated the cavern and a portion of the storm's ice boiled away into superheated steam. Ahriman tried to focus his thoughts, his Corvidae insight seeming to slow the passage of time.

He saw Menkaura fighting a burning huntsman armed with serrated spear as Amon traded blows with Bjarki himself. A storm of psychic energy surrounded them.

Amon was one of the greatest sorcerer lords of the Thousand Sons, but the drag factor of the telaethesic ward was hampering his powers. It seemed to have no effect on the one-armed Bjarki, who shrugged off all Amon's attacks as though he were but a neophyte.

He had no time to think. The berserk axeman was upon him again.

His breath was liquid fire in his chest, his lung straining at the limits of endurance to keep him alive. Ahriman saw a vision of his block failing an instant before he lifted his ebon staff, saw the axe smash it aside and continue on to bury itself in his throat. It would be cataclysmic damage, a killing wound. An end to his wyrd, as Bjarki would say.

Instead of blocking, he lunged forward, taking the fight to the axeman.

It was not his way. Ahzek Ahriman did not trade blows like a common pit-fighter.

Except now he was. Now he was *forced* to.

They slammed to the ground, too close for weapons, rolling and clawing at one another like barbarians. The Space Wolf slammed his head forward. Ahriman lowered his to meet him, and their skulls crashed together in a ferocious hammering of bone. Ahriman reeled, his vision a blazing starburst of dazzling light.

His prowess in such brawls was no match for the lusty killing power of the Space Wolf.

The warrior roared in his face, blood-flecked spittle spraying Ahriman's visor. The Space Wolf's fist thundered down, hammering his helm again and again, driven by lunatic fury and base savagery. Ahriman twisted his head to lessen the force of each blow, but it was hopeless.

The Space Wolf was going to beat his skull to bloody mulch.

The metal of his helmet buckled, collapsing inwards. Smashed armourglass sliced open the skin over his eye. Deforming metal broke the bone in his cheek.

He reached down, fumbling at the heavy rope tied around the Space Wolf's belt.

Where is it…? Your kind never goes without…

His fingers closed around the leather-wrapped grip of a broad, gutting knife. Oversized, exaggeratedly so, its serrated blade was crudely wrought.

But it would suffice.

His helm split and the frozen touch of the ice storm rushed

in. Blood filled the socket of his left eye. His mouth tasted of tin, and the hot stench of the Space Wolf's breath made him gag.

Ahriman wrenched the Space Wolf's blade from the loop on his belt. A reinforced fist arced back to finally drive itself through his skull. He screamed as he rammed the gutting blade up through the wound his bolter round had gouged in the Space Wolf's flank.

The eighth enumeration empowered it, his muscles burning with righteous fury as he drove the blade up and under his foe's bone shield. The jagged edge tore through the Space Wolf's lungs and heart, but Ahriman kept going, working the blade side to side like a lever to wreak as much bloody havoc as he could. The knife ripped up into the warrior's throat, Ahriman's arm elbow-deep in his enemy's body.

A flood of gore spilled from the Space Wolf's mouth, drenching Ahriman's face.

He gagged and spat as the dying legionary struggled for life. The Space Wolf was dead, but wouldn't die. He kept fighting, weakly punching Ahriman with the last of his strength before collapsing on top of him. Gagging on blood, Ahriman struggled out from beneath the Space Wolf's corpse.

He looked up, seeing three warriors in jade-green armour begin the long and arduous ascent to the golden dais where Magnus had climbed to face his father. They moved as if into a great and invisible force, the sheer power of the Emperor's psychic might seeking to press them to the ground in obeisance.

He tried to rise into his powers, but the pain was too intense, too all-consuming.

The mandala was broken. He saw Menkaura on his knees before the fire-blackened huntsman, spitted on his serrated harpoon. The dying Space Wolf tore the shaft from Menkaura's body, its reversed barbs dragging out looping coils of intestines in a red flood. Menkaura clutched his belly, hauling at his innards as if he could somehow repack them inside his gutted body. Not content with that wound, the huntsman spun on his heel and rammed the spear through Menkaura's chest.

When the spear was wrenched out again, Menkaura toppled over, an ocean of blood surrounding him in a red lake. Moments later, the huntsman fell to his knees, the psychic fire guttering and dying as the Space Wolf's life was spent.

Near where Menkaura lay, Amon was on his back, his head turned away from Ahriman. The side of his helmet was a shattered ruin where a bolt-round had blown it out.

Ahriman could not tell if he was alive or dead.

He reached for his heqa staff, lying close by, but a booted foot stamped down on it, snapping it in two before kicking the pieces away. Blinking away sticky runnels of blood from his eye, Ahriman looked up into a face he had last seen on Nikaea.

The same hawk nose, ragged beard over lean features, and grinning eyes.

But those eyes were not grinning now.

'I told you your wyrd would end badly,' snarled Bjarki.

Magnus expected to see hate in his brother's eyes, but he saw only great sadness.

He brought his staff up once more, expecting a furious charge, but Vulkan did not attack. Instead, he lowered his mighty warhammer and hung it from a clawed hook at his belt.

'Brother,' said Vulkan.

Another single word to the heart. Another word that bore great power, but this time said without subterfuge, only the stoic honesty for which Vulkan was known. In times of old, he might have embraced his brother in a clatter of warplate, made some aloof comment on his dull pragmatism, or counselled him to lift his gaze from the forgefire once in a while.

But these were not times of old, they were the new days of war and death.

What could he say to a brother who thought him a monster?

'I have a memory,' he began, his voice as cracked and broken as his soul. ***'A faded scrap of a memory, but a memory nonetheless. I stood vigil over your body with one of your sons. I do not know his name, but he held fast to his belief that you would walk among us again. I saw a white flame eternal. A mountain of black smoke and world-ending fire. I did not know what it meant at the time...'***

'That son was Artellus Numeon,' said Vulkan. 'It is only thanks to his courage and faith that I live again. And it was thanks to you he was able to bring me home to Nocturne.'

'I don't remember that, not fully,' said Magnus. ***'But I saw your corpse, cold and lifeless. How is it that you are alive?'***

'In truth I do not know,' said Vulkan. 'The ancient fire priests of Nocturne would say that the ur-drakes who dwell in the world of my birth brought me back. They would say the great drakes breathed the unbound flame into my soul and ignited the fire in my heart once more.'

Magnus smiled at Vulkan's words and cast his gaze around the vast cavern.

'I admire the poetic turn of phrase, but this is the world of your birth. Of all our births.'

'Our father crafted the iron of my soul and the stone of my flesh here, but it was Nocturne that *made* me. Just as Prospero made you.'

Vulkan took a step closer, and Magnus tensed, but his brother's intent was not violence.

'This war has taken so much from us both,' said Vulkan. 'The Imperium is sundered by the flames of war, and nothing ever returns from the fire unchanged. No matter the outcome of the fighting above, the Imperium will never be the same again.'

Magnus nodded. ***'I am no master of hearth and forge like you, brother, but the fire strengthens some things, does it not?'***

'In the hands of a skilled smiter, aye, it can,' agreed Vulkan. 'But the fires burning all across Terra are those of a blind apprentice. Nothing good will come of it.'

Warming to his theme, Magnus said, ***'The transformative nature of fire, though clearly destructive, is often a necessary precursor to change. Perhaps, in the grand scheme of things, that will be a good thing? The enemy of progress is stasis, and all things have in their nature a tendency towards complexity. That tendency has carried the universe from almost perfect simplicity to the level of magnificence we see all around us.'***

'Always the teacher,' said Vulkan with a wry smile.

It was a rare enough thing that Magnus felt the rest of his meta physical argument dissipate entirely, but as pleasant as it was to stand face to face with his brother, Magnus knew he was an unwelcome visitor in his father's great sanctum. He was much diminished, but Vulkan, for all that he had apparently died, seemed mightier than ever.

'Do you intend to stop me?' said Magnus.

'That depends, brother,' said Vulkan. 'Do you still intend to cast that spear of yours?'

Magnus looked down at the spear and its form twisted, transforming from a weapon of war to the crook-topped staff of a master of Prospero's Fellowships.

'I… I don't know any more,' he said. ***'When I followed Revelation, I was singular in my purpose, but now…? I have wandered far, but I am more lost than ever before…'***

'You are not lost, my son, you are exactly where you need to be.'

Magnus looked into his father's eyes as they opened in golden fire.

* * *

Tizca.

Magnus drew in a breath as he beheld the City of Light in all its glory, flashes of sunlight glittering like noonday stars from the polished glass of the great pyramids. The sky was the perfect shade of cornflower blue, and the scent of recent summer rain was like honeydew. Clouds ran in thin lines of purple over the mountainous horizon, and the salt-tang blowing in from the ocean was a scent he thought he would never smell again.

Tears came to him, and he let them flow for the loss of his home world.

'It was so beautiful,' he said, sensing an unmistakable presence behind him.

'It was,' agreed his father. 'I remember the day I first set foot on Prospero. You had made a paradise here, my son.'

'The only paradise is a paradise lost,' said Magnus sadly. ***'It exists now only in my memory, for the reality of what has become of Tizca is too painful.'***

His father nodded. 'A wise man once said that as memory may be a paradise from which we cannot be driven, it may also be a hell from which we cannot escape.'

Magnus turned to his father, seeing Him clad all in gold, His armour too brilliant to look upon. At first glance, it could be mistaken for something ceremonial, its every plate engraved and etched with baroque carvings, studded with polished gemstones and its every fluted edge worked with the most intricate of details.

But upon closer inspection, it was clear this armour had seen fierce battle, bore the impacts of many weapons and was stained with the blood of countless foes.

He shone with an inner light that Magnus well remembered from that first meeting, when they had embraced beneath the fire of the Pyrae Fellowship's pyramid. The great god-machine *Canis Vertex* had not yet taken its place at the entrance, but the blue flame at its summit cast a cold light over the glass of its sloping surfaces.

'I came to kill you,' said Magnus.

'I know. Is that still your intent?'

'I no longer understand what my intent is,' said Magnus. ***'The variables at play in the galaxy defy any of the formulae I might divine. Even the Order of Ruin would fail to see a path in this dark forest.'***

'Then allow me to show you a possible path,' said the Emperor.

His father set off along one of the side streets, running towards Occullum Square.

They passed an ornamental garden of psychically sculpted topiary in which scholars led discussion groups, couples read together in comfortable silence, and laughing children passed a ball between them using only the power of their minds.

Magnus heard a song from somewhere, a street performer playing a melody the first psychic settlers to reach Prospero had composed that spoke of their flight from Old Earth:

Those being all my study,
The crown I cast upon the Earth.
And to my state grew stranger,
And rapt in secret studies.

The people of Tizca walked around them, as clean-limbed and beautiful as he remembered them, robed in many colours, with great minds and inquisitive natures.

It was almost too much to bear.

'Why did you bring me here?' asked Magnus.

'I did not,' said the Emperor. 'You did.'

'That's not what I meant. Why did you bring me to stand before you? If Malcador wasn't lying, then you **wanted** ***me here, right now. In front of you.'***

His father nodded. 'Malcador spoke true. It was the last thing he did.'

Magnus hung his head in shame. ***'I did not mean to kill him.'***

'I know, but his death was a sacrifice he knew he might be asked to make. He knew that and accepted it. Another death in a grand procession of them. Painful in its own way, for he and I have shared a journey longer than most men or gods can dare reckon. Yet, in the macro of what our species faces, his death is irrelevant.'

'I always forget how cold you can be,' said Magnus.

'It is not coldness, it is reality. What might be gained by his sacrifice will be of far greater worth than a single life. A thousand lives would still be a price worth paying for what you and I might achieve.'

'You and I?'

'Yes,' said his father, and the promise of that word was the first light of dawn.

'I don't understand.'

'I wanted you here before me so there would be no mistakes, no misunderstandings, and no way for the Ruinous Powers set against me to twist my words or intent. I wanted you here before me so you could look me in the eye and understand the truth of what I offer.'

Magnus' breath caught in his throat.

His father turned to face him, and Magnus met His terrible gaze, feeling the inhuman power that lay at His heart. It was power that could strip a man down to atoms in a heartbeat and breathe him anew with an exhalation. That power had endured uncounted millennia, growing with every passing century and honing its edge for the age in which it was needed.

'And what is it you offer?'

'The chance to stand at my side once again,' said his father. 'Forgiveness.'

FIFTEEN

Blood of Ur-Drakes

Tizca's light fell away from Magnus, and now he was flying.

Adrift in the Great Ocean, he was unbound from all physical limitations, a being of mind and memory. He was thought, free from required form and mundane function.

He soared past binary stars, plunged into their nuclear hearts and basked in the secret light of their cores. He saw the birth of species unknown to mankind and the doom of those upon whose ruins and bones men and women had built.

Nor did he fly alone.

His father burned at his side, a gleaming comet of power and might.

Magnus had flown the Great Ocean since his inception, but the Emperor had known it since earlier epochs of humanity. They circled the great singularity at the heart of the Milky Way, slingshotting out to the halo stars to bathe in the light of distant galaxies. They followed the arcs of migratory comets, explored the nurseries of newborn stars, and shaped the destinies of cooling protoplanets.

Magnus was a child again, a fresh mind shepherded through the Great Ocean and shielded from its deep water predators by his father. The Emperor's light drew them, but He laughed as He destroyed them or turned them against one another.

Time was meaningless here, for this was the galaxy's infancy and death all in one.

Their course spiralled back towards a pale blue dot in the western spiral arm of the galaxy. An insignificant world, a world no different from tens of thousands of others just like it, yet this one possessed a destiny no other would share.

Terra.

They plunged towards it, falling through its atmosphere to see a world Magnus had never known, a beautiful expanse of blue oceans, silver mountains, swathes of green forest and endlessly swaying fields of gold.

Not Terra then, but Old Earth.

And just as they had seen ancient civilisations rise and fall out in the galactic depths, so too did they bear witness to the growth and collapse of countless cultures here. The sudden and catastrophic doom of Ancient Assyriu, the rapid expansion and slow break up of the Grekan and Romanii city states, the land of the Prusai, Albyon's Great Empire, and countless more: Tolosa, Dal-Riada, Byzantion, Tsernagora, Sabaudia.

The litany of vanished empires was endless.

Magnus thought of those ancient kings and queens, seated on their thrones and hearing tales of ruined civilisations. He pictured them laughing at the foolishness of these dead kingdoms, never once imagining that such a fate might one day befall them.

He looked at the incandescent brightness of his father.

Was He now facing that same moment?

The green-and-blue world became one of steel and stone, its once clear atmosphere burned with toxic fogs and its polluted oceans rising to reclaim the land. Wars of land-thirst grew to engulf entire continents, then spread ever wider as competition for resources led the global super-blocs to turn on one another.

Spasms of self-destruction flared and burned across the planet's surface, and time and time again the world's populace grew to unsustainable proportions before shrinking back to walk the knife edge of extinction.

Through it all, Magnus saw patterns endlessly repeat, moments of significance rhyming all through the course of human history. The same mistakes, the same wilful ignorance.

The same hubris.

Expeditions were hurled into space almost as soon as technology allowed, colony ships, terraformers, holy pilgrims, fleets of conquest. A centuries-long migration into the stars began, a gloriously foolhardy expansion into the unknown depths of space or a golden age of exploration, it was hard to say for sure.

It seemed humanity was done with its once blue world, that it was to be abandoned now that it was all used up and had nothing left to give.

But then came Old Night.

Even in this phantom form, Magnus felt the screams from all across the cosmos. He wept as he felt pain and loss like never before. Even in the wake of Prospero's razing he had not shed so many tears.

But again, just as it seemed that humanity's time was done, it endured.

The time of nations fell away, and the age of the techno-barbarian tribes began, a savage aeon of ethnarchs and despots, of barbarous kings and bloody priests. It seemed as though mankind must extinguish itself by cutting its own throat, yet even now, Magnus detected the first hint of a guiding hand, shaping the species' destiny in ways both consequential and seemingly minor. So careful and subtle was this hand, he wasn't even sure it was there, like a whisper in a thunderstorm.

And from this age of darkness came a light, finally revealed.

He bore many names, but only one that mattered.

Emperor.

One by one, the warlords of the past were destroyed, and a new empire grew from the ashes of the old. Into this Age of Unity was born the Imperium, the greatest empire the galaxy had ever seen.

Magnus watched events unfold in ways he had studied as a callow youth as the rapidly unspooling history of Earth finally caught up to events he had lived through. He saw the Expeditionary Fleets launched from the Field of Winged Victory within the Emperor's Palace, a place he hardly recognised, such was its tiny scale compared to what sprawled over the mountains now.

One by one, the lost cradles of civilisation were brought back into the fold, the forgotten branches of humanity spliced back into the body of the Imperium. His heart clenched as he waited for the moment where everything went wrong, when Horus fell on Davin.

But it never came.

The Legions reached the edges of the galaxy, and Magnus swelled with pride as Horus Lupercal and his Sons of Horus raised the Emperor's lightning-bolt banner on the last world to be brought to compliance.

This never happened, he said, his mind one with his father.

+No, but it should have. It so very nearly did.+

Magnus' mind flew back to Prospero, and he saw the world he knew and loved, its people flourishing, even passing on what they knew to visitors from all across the Imperium. His mind circled the planet, seeing fresh cities and arcologies, wonders he had never known, structures that bore all the hallmarks of Perturabo's wondrous designs.

Where am I? he asked, not finding himself within the Pyramid of Photep or any of the other cities of glass and gold.

+Look to Terra,+ said his father.

Back to the birthrock he flew, and there, deep in the heart of the world, Magnus found himself in the great cavern of machines, sat upon the same Golden Throne upon which he had so recently seen his father.

Fear touched Magnus as he remembered seeing a vision of this, his physical body ravaged and husked out by the unimaginable cost of maintaining the portal.

I have seen this, he said. ***It will kill me.***

+Look closer, my son.+

The vast doors before the throne were open, and a beatific light issued from what lay beyond. This was not the vision of his doom he had been shown, for here his face was serene and vacant, merely a vessel of flesh and blood. His subtle body was entirely absent.

His father felt his confusion.

+Your spirit is by my side, as it is now. We fly the Great Ocean as explorers of the furthest reaches of consciousness. Masters of time and space. As we always dreamed.+

Why show me this? It never happened, and only twists the knife of regret deeper.

+The past is set, but not all futures are lost, no matter how broken they appear. This future, or at least a *version* of it, can still come to pass.+

It is too late for that.

His father's amusement washed over him.

+Do you think I would show you this if that were so?+

***

Magnus opened his eye, feeling the familiar weight of spirit returning to his body.

Their shared vision-space experienced time on a cosmic scale, but an instant only had passed in the cavern beneath the Sanctum Imperialis. Vulkan stood at the Emperor's side, the tension of his stance betraying the expectation he felt.

His father's eyes still burned gold, his last question still hanging between them.

'How?' asked Magnus. ***'How could such a future come to pass?'***

'It is a simple thing,' said the Emperor, and Magnus saw the tremors of strain at His brow, a measure of how much psychic effort it was taking Him to communicate so directly. 'Swear your oath of fealty to me once again. Take your rightful place at my side and our combined powers will drive the betrayers from Terra. We will destroy them, and usher in a new era of crusade.'

'I thought you always hated that word?'

'I did,' admitted his father, 'but that was then. Our first endeavour was carried forward on hope, a venture to reforge a galactic culture that Old Night put asunder, to locate and rebuild our lost sons and daughters. *This* will be a war of vengeance and cleansing, a scouring of worlds and a ruthless doom to all our enemies.'

'And you want me to be part of this?'

'I do, my son,' said the Emperor, and His eyes shone even brighter. 'I *need* you by my side, because your soul is still your own and is still ruled by the better angels of your nature. I saw what you did above in the Great Observatory. You could have left all those people to die, but you did not. You *could* not. Unlike your brothers beyond the walls, you are still my son. Your mind was always the strongest of them all, but Chaos has wormed its way too deeply into their hearts and minds to ever be removed.'

'The Red Angel, the Pale King, Horus Lupercal, Lorgar, Curze, Alpharius, and the Phoenician, they are truly monsters now, but I still count Perturabo as my brother, still as your son. He is too stubborn to ever abase himself before powers he considers inferior. His soul is clad in cold iron.'

'And that is why he is lost to us,' said Vulkan. 'Perturabo has pledged himself to Horus, and you know as well as I that his word, once given, is unbreakable. He will not go back on that, not now, not ever. His ambition to humble Rogal consumes him.'

Magnus wanted to argue and defend his closest brother, but he knew Vulkan was right. To bring down the greatest work of Rogal Dorn was the Lord of Iron's sole obsession. Now the Emperor's offer had been stated so boldly, Magnus realised that *this* was the missing piece of his soul. No sliver split from the whole would restore him, only belief in a higher cause and the urge to belong to something greater than himself.

To have *meaning.*

That was the last missing piece.

Then why do I hesitate?

'There's a price, isn't there?' he said at last. ***'No matter what the poets say, forgiveness isn't free. It always comes with a price.'***

'It does,' agreed the Emperor. 'And it is a heavy price, but a necessary one. *Your* mind and body are still your own, but the warriors of your Legion are damned. In truth, they were damned the moment the first signs of the flesh change became manifest. Their bodies carry the seeds of their own destruction, and no gene-craft of mine nor the Selenar can undo it. You can come back to me, but your Legion cannot.'

Magnus felt a cold hand squeeze his heart, but his father was not yet done.

'But I will build you a new Legion, a mighty host of warriors greater than any now living. Plans are already in motion to bring about their inception. Soon, you will command warriors the likes of which the galaxy has never seen, whose flesh will be flawless, whose fists are steel and whose hearts are armoured in adamantium!'

'You would give me a new Legion?'

'I would, and they will be the pride of the new Imperium.'

Magnus said nothing, picturing this fantastical new future, one in which his Legion sons were free of corruption, free of the fear that dogged their every step. Free from the dark shadow within them all that threatened to consume them.

And he at his father's side, leading these new warriors on a new crusade to reconquer the stars. This time they would not repeat the mistakes of the past. This time they would reshape the galaxy as it was meant to be.

It was all he had ever wanted... *And yet...*

'How could I fight at your side, knowing I had condemned my sons to death?' he said. ***'I would look upon these new warriors and see in them the faces of my betrayed Legion. What kind of father would I be were I to forsake them? How could you ask this of me?'***

'It is the only way, Magnus. In truth, your sons are already dead. Within no more than a few years rampant mutations will overtake even the strongest of them. One way or another they will die.'

'I... I cannot abandon them, father,' he said, his hands clenching into fists. ***'Their fate is not yet set. I will find a way to save them. I*** **must.'**

'Please, brother,' said Vulkan, taking a step towards him. 'Come back to us, I beg you.'

Magnus turned as he heard the clatter of legionary warplate, and the ratcheting of boltguns. Three warriors clad in the livery of the Salamanders Legion crested the summit of the great golden dais. Magnus felt their joy at seeing their gene-sire, but at first sight of the Emperor, they instinctively fell to their knees in adoration, all but overcome by His incredible presence.

Magnus turned back to Vulkan and said, *'Would you sacrifice them? Would you betray even* one *of them for your own desire?'*

'I could not,' he said, his deep tones heavy with grief and his right hand sliding down to the warhammer *Urdrakule* at his belt.

Magnus felt the end of his staff transform, becoming a bladed spear-tip once more.

'Then why would you believe that I *could?'* he roared.

They moved at the same instant.

Magnus' arm drew back to cast his staff at the Emperor. It was the perfect throw, his aim true and deadly. All his fury was bound into this strike.

Fury that his father had put this awful choice before him.

Fury that He believed it was an offer Magnus would ever accept.

But most of all, it was fury that he almost *had.*

Abidemi watched the burning spear fly from the Crimson King's hand, a lightning bolt cast by the arm of a demigod to slay the king of the gods. He could barely move, barely *think.* To be this close to the Master of Mankind all but robbed him of any independent thought or will. How could any man, Astartes or mortal, dare to move under such a gaze?

Vulkan's hammer swept up and smashed the spear from the air in a single blow. It spun away, but like a comet on its return orbit it arced back around again. Magnus snatched it back into his hand as Vulkan charged his fallen brother with a look that was a dreadful mix of hate and sorrow.

The two slammed together with the deafening thunderclap of god-engines at war.

Abidemi dragged his head to the side and met the gaze of

Barek Zytos. He too was held pinned by the might and majesty of the Emperor.

'What do we do?' he said.

'I don't know,' replied Abidemi.

Vulkan and Magnus tore at one another, one with thunderous, deafening blows from his hammer, the other with tearing slashes of a burning spear. For them to come between warring primarchs would be suicide.

'This is what you saw, brother,' said Igen Gargo, his voice a whisper over the vox-bead in his ear. 'The drakes in fire. You have steered us true.'

Abidemi's hand closed on the hilt of *Draukoros*, picturing the stern, uncompromising features of Artellus Numeon. *He* would have known what to do.

Vulkan smashed his hammer into Magnus' hip, crushing bone and tearing muscle. In return Magnus buried the tip of his spear up through Vulkan's shoulder guard. It did not stop for the strength of the plate, but sliced cleanly through. Blood squirted but Vulkan gave no sign he even felt the wound.

'You are liars all,' screamed Magnus. ***'You promise forgiveness then make its acceptance impossible.'***

'You're wrong, Magnus,' retorted Vulkan. 'Your arrogance blinds you.'

'No!' roared Magnus, his hands wreathed in fire as he spun around Vulkan's every blow.

Abidemi had seen his primarch in battle before and knew he was a sublime close-combat specialist. Yet against Magnus, he moved as though hopelessly outclassed. Every feint was ignored, every killing strike turned aside with his spear, dodged or easily blocked.

'The sorcerer sees our father's every move before he makes it!' cried Gargo.

Abidemi wanted to rise, to charge to fight at their primarch's side, but his muscles would not obey him. For now, he was a mere observer to this struggle.

Magnus spun around Vulkan, and rammed his spear into his back. The flaming tip gouged his backplate before sliding clear. Vulkan made a quarter-turn to the left and Magnus cracked the butt of his staff against his brother's helmet. The metal split and spat sparks. Vulkan ducked the blade's return stroke and swung *Urdrakule* up in a pistoning blow.

It took Magnus under the chin and snapped his head back. His cheek imploded and he spat teeth and blood that was too vivid to be real. Vulkan barged inside his guard, pounding his hammer against his chest as though demolishing a wall.

The bronze of Magnus' breastplate buckled, one of the yellowed horns snapping off where it met the armour. Milky blood streamed down his chest, chunks of leather and metal flying from every impact. Magnus grinned, spinning backwards.

Vulkan followed as strips of gold and steel tore loose from the deck plates. Magnus hurled them at Vulkan, buckled girders, sheet steel and looping lengths of cabling.

His hammer smashed them all aside, pushing through a hurricane of psychic force.

Magnus laughed, his hands extended to either side as he ripped steel cabling from the ground and machines of the golden dais. They whipped through the air, lashing around Vulkan's wrists and ankles. He fought them, but that only pulled them tighter. Magnus clenched his fists and the bindings drew taut.

The Salamanders knew Vulkan's warplate as the *Draken Scale*, legend-forged by the master smiters of Nocturne in their secret halls beneath Mount Deathfire. It had withstood the fury of Isstvan V and the violence of Konrad Curze.

But now it buckled.

Flames billowed from Magnus, the spectral heat of his witch-powers. His outline wavered, as though he fought against some inexorable pull from beyond.

Vulkan strained against his living bindings. Ceramite and steel flakes spalled from his armour as it crumpled under the force of Magnus' might. His skin was sheened like polished onyx, streaked with sweat and lined with pain as he took step after ponderous step towards Magnus.

The spear of Magnus lifted into the air, its tip too bright to look upon.

'If I must be damned with my sons I will be full damned, brother.'

The Crimson King nodded and his spear leapt forward like an unleashed Marauder from the launcher of an embarkation deck. It punched through their sire's breastplate, tearing through his chest, heart and lungs before exploding from his back and arcing high into the air. Vulkan did not cry out or flinch. He kept going, pulling taut at the steel cutting through his armour and crushing the bones within. Step by step he persisted.

Abidemi screamed and surged to his feet, whatever spell had held him down broken at the sight of his gene-sire so mortally struck. His rising freed his brothers too, and Igen Gargo rose to his left, with Barek Zytos on his right a second later.

'Free him,' said Abidemi to Gargo.

Draukoros roared to life as Abidemi flanked their primarch. A blizzard of sleeting steel fragments surrounded Vulkan. It scored Abidemi's armour like the caustic sands of the Burning Walk across the Pyre Desert.

He reached Vulkan's outstretched right arm and swung *Draukoros* as Gargo hacked with his long-bladed spear. The black teeth bit through the steel hawser in a single blow, and the Lord of Drakes was free.

Like a storm front unleashed, he hurled himself at Magnus, his hammer striking for the sorcerer lord's head. The corner of its killing face struck the primarch on the shoulder, but so titanic a blow was it, that he reeled and all that was kept aloft by his power fell in a metallic rain.

Blood masked his face, his single eye alight with power.

Vulkan's arm pistoned forward.

Then, like a lightning bolt from the heavens, Magnus' spear slashed down. Aimed unerringly at Vulkan's skull, it was a treasonous blow to end his legend in an instant.

Abidemi saw it a second before it struck, and his heart turned to ice.

Barek Zytos saw it even before that.

The giant Salamander rammed into his father, like a bull-drake on the charge.

Not even Vulkan himself could resist that ferocious impact. He rocked forward.

One step only, but life and death had hung on less.

Magnus' spear clove through Zytos, its fire splitting him from collarbone to pelvis. Blood exploded from his shorn halves as he fell, and Vulkan cried out to see his son taken from him.

He roared and swept up the hammer still gripped in Barek's hand before it hit the ground.

'No!' cried Abidemi.

Even Magnus looked shocked at Zytos' death.

Vulkan had only a fractional moment to seize the advantage, and he did not waste it.

Twice armed, hammer blow after hammer blow rained down on the Crimson King.

The first crushed his shoulder guard, the second buckled the moulded surface of his breastplate. The last of its curling horns splintered under his reverse stroke.

Vulkan spun low and a third blow destroyed Magnus' knee.

A fourth slammed into his side and shattered his ribs.

Magnus reeled, forced back in the face of this relentless fury.

Flames exploded from Vulkan's fists as he smashed his brother in the face again and again. He drove him to his knees. Magnus' crimson mane erupted in flames, his skin charring to black. Bone gleamed whitely as his flesh sloughed from his skull.

Abidemi and Gargo hacked at Magnus in vengeance for Barek Zytos.

Draukoros rose and fell, tearing scraps of radiant meat from Magnus, and Igen Gargo drove his spear in deep again and again as the enemy primarch roared in agony. His great eye was filled with blood, and it wept scarlet tears as the Salamanders cut him to pieces.

Magnus raised his hand, and Abidemi hacked it from his wrist with a looping stroke of *Draukoros*. It tumbled away as Gargo tore open his guts with a twisting thrust.

Milky white blood that could not possibly be blood sprayed from the wound. It poured from a score of mortal hurts and filled Magnus' throat. A gout of the stuff vomited from his mouth, and he looked up at Vulkan through his blood-filled eye.

'Is this the end?' he said.

The words were slurred and wet, spoken through a broken jaw and cheek, through shattered teeth and a gouged tongue. Through all the terrible hurts that ought to have killed him thrice over.

'It didn't have to be,' said Vulkan, genuine regret in his voice. 'You could have stood with us. You could have been my brother again.'

Magnus shook his head.

'The price was too high.'

'A thousand sons?' said Vulkan, still pleading with his brother. 'A thousand already damned sons for the sake of the Imperium?'

'Even one was too many,' said Magnus.

The Crimson King grinned and tipped his head back.

But this was no gesture of surrender, no baring his throat to an executioner.

His blood-filled eye swam with an eldritch sapphire light, and his limbs ignited with blue and pink flames as his ruined body was lifted high into the air. The flames billowed like a pair of vast feathered pinions spread behind him.

The many grievous wounds he had suffered closed up in an instant, the skin reforming whole and unblemished. Bones reknit, severed arteries and veins spliced together once more, and immaterial flesh reformed all across his body.

The shards of his armour flew back to him, clamping fast to his body in a form as seamless as it had been before the fight began.

The last sliver within the Crimson King that clung to the material realm was finally obliterated, his body willingly given to the infernal masters in the darkness of the warp.

He looked down upon the Salamanders, his eye pulsing with the sickly blue light of cancerous stars, poisoned light from worlds entirely given over to the Neverborn.

And with the deepest truth of his powers finally unleashed, the irresistible pull of the telaethesic ward plucked Magnus from the dungeon and banished him from the Sanctum Imperialis forever.

His last words hung in the air like a curse.

All is dust.

Far below, a lone wolf's howl echoed through the cavern as the bodies of the sorcerers were snatched away in a storm of sapphire flame. Bjarki howled in grief and anger as the malefic light faded away, leaving him alone with the bodies of his two pack-mates.

He howled for all the dead he had lost, and for all who were yet to die.

Behind him, Promeus approached. Warily, he laid a hand on Bjarki's icy shoulder guard.

The killing lust still strong within him, Bjarki bared his fangs.

'His name was Olgyr Widdowsyn, the shield bearer,' said Promeus. 'His name was Svafnir Rackwulf, the finest Woe-maker of Tra. Their deeds were many, and I was honoured to witness many of them.'

'This is not the place to give warriors of the *Vlka Fenryka* a sending,' warned Bjarki. 'And there is no one here to listen to their tales.'

Promeus looked up at the golden light shining down on them from above.

'Yes,' he said. 'There is.'

SIXTEEN

Never Forgive, Never Forget

She awoke with the same scream on her lips.

Stars wheeled above her, glittering pinpricks of light, swirling like a time-lapse of the night sky. She coughed blood and tried to sit up. It was harder than she imagined it would be.

Then she realised she was stuck to the ground, lying in a pool of dried blood.

Her blood.

Almost all of it, judging by the extent of the pool.

Like she always did at moments like these, she waited, listening. She had no idea how much time had passed since she'd last opened her eyes. Darkness, silence.

Was it night? No, she was in a cavern far below the earth. She heard the washing in and out of a tide, the splash of objects falling in the water.

An underground cavern. Magnus the Red… A game of regicide. Malcador…

Alivia pushed herself upright, wincing at the flare of pain

between her shoulder blades, the tightness of new skin, the unfamiliarity of new organs, new bones.

Alivia got her legs under her and stood, her balance still off, a little unsteady.

She stood at the edge of the plaza between the oversized villas, except now there was a thick ivory tower at its centre. Still unsure of her balance, she slowly circled the tower. If it was an elevator shaft, there didn't appear to be a door.

She turned to the shore and walked back to the water's edge. The table and chairs where she'd played regicide against a primarch were scattered and broken over the shingle. Deep footsteps surrounded it, and she saw the brass casing of a single bolter shell.

Bending to pick it up, she sniffed the acrid propellant within.

Projectiles designed to kill legionaries made a horrifying mess of a baseline human.

The boltgun was a weapon designed by a psychopath.

Next to the shell, partly buried in the sand, was the smashed half of the regicide board and a trio of its carved playing pieces. She smiled as she saw which ones they were.

The Primarch, the contoured portion of its upper carving split away. Next to it lay the Emperor, the piece she had been about to move. It too was broken. Still whole, but the detail and subtlety of its workmanship was lost.

And lastly, the white Divinitarch, split in two.

Alivia clasped this last piece tightly, tears spilling down her cheeks.

She looked out over the water, looking for any sign of Malcador. Dust and rocks still fell from the roof of the cavern, and she wondered how much more it would take to bring this entire edifice crashing down. Whatever damage Magnus had wrought here had broken something fundamental to its structure, and now the endless bombardments from above were working to finish its destruction. The waters of the subterranean sea glowed with sunken lights, but she could see no sign of Malcador.

But then she saw him, his husked and shrouded body washed up farther along the shore onto the black sands. His stick-thin limbs jutted like the blackened branches of an old tree struck by lightning, gnarled and burned from the inside out.

His hairless head lolled on his shoulders, turning to face her, and his eye sockets were black and empty.

Alivia moved along the beach towards the Sigillite's corpse and knelt beside him.

'Damn you,' she said. 'Damn every single last one of you.'

The tide threatened to carry the body out again, but Alivia grabbed the edges of Malcador's robe and dragged him a little farther up the sands. There was no weight to his bones, and she laid him down beneath his staff of office.

Alivia knelt beside him as the pain and horror of the Emperor's Acuity filled her once again. She wept bitter tears, cursing that she was part of its perpetuation. She wanted to walk out into the ocean until her strength gave out, until she sank into the darkness and her lungs filled with water.

But what would be the point?

She was cursed to return again and again, to live yet another evolution of this life.

Alivia tried to push the Emperor's visions aside, but they kept coming. Furious ages of war, tides of xenospecies wreaking untold carnage, a vast and soulless regime – as bloody and cruel as it was possible to imagine.

But the alternative?

A universe of horror, of torture and disease, of wanton cruelty and bloodshed. It would be unending, torment from which the human race could never escape, for its enactors were no mortal foes, no psychotic empire that must inevitably fall. No, this was a time of immortal monsters wrought from the tortured psyches of the very people who suffered within it.

What the Emperor had shown her was little better, a dark future that was as horrifying a nightmare as it was possible to imagine, a time when human lives were all but meaningless, ashes of bone ground between the gears of history.

But at least they were *lives*. Even in this bleak reality, men and women still loved one another, still raised their children as best they could, still served something greater than themselves. They still clung to one another when the darkness closed in, and endured the unendurable, because that was what people did.

They lived, they survived, and they persisted.

But most of all, they *hoped*.

Amid all the cataclysms still to come, there were yet embers of light. She had seen a time when heroes long thought lost returned, when those embers took flight and began a final conflagration that made this spasm of rebellion look like a frontier brushfire war. The outcome of that future war was unknown, but that humanity would fight back was enough.

Alivia dug into the pocket of her blood-stiffened coat and pulled out the chapbook of stories that had been her constant companion for as long as she could remember.

Despite all Alivia's reprimands, Vivyen had marked her place by turning a page corner down. She had been reading *The Nightingale*, and the thought of her and Miska and Jeph sent a wave of grief through Alivia that threatened to break her there and then.

'My beautiful girls,' she sobbed. 'My brave man.'

She folded up the corner and flipped through the pages until she reached the story she sought. It was a good one. They all were, but this one had always been one of Alivia's favourites.

She hadn't known why until now, and a thin smile creased the corners of her lips.

'In the forest, high up on the steep shore and not far from the open seacoast, stood a very old oak tree,' began Alivia. 'It was just three hundred and sixty-five years old, but that long time was to the tree as the same number of days might be to us.'

As she read, she felt the cold that never left her bones ease, and the tiredness that was her constant companion start to lift. As though by speaking the words aloud, she too felt the joy of the Ephemerals, the playful insects who lived out their entire existence around the tree in a single wondrous day. Though their time was short in comparison, they experienced the myriad joys of their lives in moments that were fleeting, yet no less miraculous.

A tidal warmth flowed from her in a gentle susurration, loosening itself from her bones and carried away in the river of her words. It felt liberating and comforting, like being slowly lowered into a cleansing bath.

Alivia then spoke of the old oak tree as it fell into its winter slumber and dreamed a most wonderful dream.

'It saw the knights of olden times and noble ladies ride through the wood on their gallant steeds, with plumes waving in their hats and with falcons on their wrists, while the hunting horn sounded and the dogs barked. It saw hostile warriors, in coloured dress and glittering armour, with spear and halberd, pitching their tents and again taking them down; the watchfires blazed, and men sang and slept under the hospitable shelter of the tree. It saw lovers meet in quiet happiness near it in the moonshine, and carve the initials of their names in the greyish green bark of its trunk.'

The book grew warm in her hands, its ancient binding rippling as if unseen currents ran through the ink and glue and pressed fibre of its pages. The words began to blur before her, as though they were becoming unmoored from where their wily old author had set them down.

Alivia thought of all the countless lives she had lived, the many deeds of which she was ashamed and the greater number of which she was proud. In ancient cultures, a soul's eventual fate was judged upon its entry to the afterlife: on a weighing scale against a feather, by some omnipotent deity, by kings of hell, or by some other esoteric means. A life was a ledger of deeds, both good and evil, generous and selfish, and Alivia just hoped hers was at least balanced a little in her favour.

The lights in the cavern dimmed, and she had to hold the book closer to her face in order to keep reading. In the old oak tree's dream, it saw the joy and happiness it had experienced over its long existence, but still it yearned for all those around it to rise up and know that same joy.

And so it spread its branches, to pass the potency of its vitality to those around it.

'And the old tree, as it still grew upwards and onwards, felt that its roots were loosening themselves from the earth. "It is right so; it is best," said the tree. "No fetters hold me now. I can fly up to the very highest point in light and glory. And all I love are with me, both small and great. All are here."'

She paused in the retelling, blinking and trying to remember what she was doing. There was a book in her hands, the blotched, liver-stained hands of an old woman, but the words on the page were a blur.

Alivia's eyes drifted closed before she reached the end of the story, where the old oak tree finally fell, its three hundred and sixty-five years ended like the single day of the Ephemera.

She floated between sleep and wakefulness, swaying on the shore until the book fell from her hands. The sound of it landing in the risen tide of the ocean awoke her, and she felt a hand at her elbow.

A voice spoke to her, the words muffled and pained.

'I wish…' said the voice, but grief overcame it before it could finish.

Alivia looked up and saw the face of an old man, thin-cheeked and weighted by some great concern. His eyes were so very old and so very sad.

She leaned into him, feeling the sharp angles of his thin body under the black robe he wore. They were wet and cold, but he was warm beneath them, and Alivia felt his arms enfold her. He held her tight as the sight of two small girls laughing and playing before her appeared vividly in her mind.

She smiled to see them, and tears filmed her eyes as they beckoned her onwards.

'All I love are with me,' she whispered. 'both small and great. All… are… here…'

Alivia Sureka closed her eyes for the last time.

They watched over the fields of fire surrounding the Palace from the Mercury Wall. Black smoke and purple flames obscured the jagged-toothed ruins, but here and there towers of silver still stood amid the destruction.

Blazing storms wracked the horizon, and gibbering voices drifted on the burning anabatic winds carrying the stench of fyceline, blood and filth up from the traitor camps that sprouted like sores on the surface of the world.

Together with the surviving men and women of *Vulkan's Own,* Atok Abidemi and Igen Gargo stood in the shadow of the shell-battered wall's towers with Bödvar Bjarki, waiting for the next hammer blow to fall.

Three days had passed since the confrontation beneath the Sanctum Imperialis. Three days of enduring the incandescent fury of Constantin Valdor and his Custodians, three days of enduring demands to know how they penetrated the most secure portion of the Palace, of how they had evaded the patrols of his golden-armoured warriors.

They had no satisfactory answer to give him, and were only allowed to once more take their place in the battle lines when Malcador returned and ordered their release. The Sigillite had always borne a heavy burden, but something had changed within him, some soul-deep wound that would never heal, a debt he could never repay.

Valdor protested, insisting that he be made aware of any gap in his defence, but Malcador assured him that the weakness exploited by Magnus the Red was no more.

In the end, necessity won out.

To keep Astartes from the walls, even so paltry a number as three, could not be countenanced, and they were given tasking orders to the Mercury Wall. Malcador gave them the names of two others they might seek out, fellow lost and Legionless warriors with whom they might find common cause.

Vulkan remained below with the Emperor after taking their oaths not to reveal his presence beneath the Palace. Of Promeus, they had seen no sign, and his fate would forever remain unknown to them.

'I had hoped to return this blade to Nocturne,' said Abidemi, gripping the hilt of *Draukoros* tightly as shapes began to move in the toxic smoke ahead of them. Towering shadows, monstrous in form, and howling with madness. 'But that is a foolish hope now.'

Bjarki only nodded. He had said little since their release. The grief of his brothers' deaths still hung heavy upon him, as did the final escape of the Thousand Sons sorcerer.

'It is your blade now,' said Igen Gargo. 'Artellus Numeon is dead, and it now falls to you to kill in its name, to earn the right to bear its wrath.'

Abidemi nodded. 'You're right,' he said, reaching out to snap one of the black teeth from the sword's blade. Gargo's eyes widened, but he said nothing as Abidemi handed it to Bjarki. The Space Wolf took the razor-edged drake tooth with a puzzled expression.

'You once said we were bound together, Wolf and Drake,' said Abidemi. 'You wanted to cut my warplate to mark that.'

'And you told me only artificers of your Promethean cult might work the armour of a Salamanders legionary.'

Abidemi looked out over the hellscape before the Palace.

'You said your wyrd showed us so marked.'

'So it did,' said Bjarki.

'Then mark us,' said Abidemi. 'For Barek Zytos. For Olgyr Widdowsyn. And for Svafnir Rackwulf.'

Bjarki nodded, and with swift strokes carved the angular symbol of a roaring drake head, the Dread Biter. He turned to Gargo and raised an eyebrow.

Gargo nodded and Bjarki cut the same symbol into his armour, just over the heart.

With the inscription complete, Bjarki tucked the sword's black tooth into a leather pouch at his waist and grinned wickedly at his two newest brothers.

'Now we are wyrd-marked,' he said. 'And when the fight here is done, we will hunt down those who escaped our wrath together.'

First he took Abidemi's wrist in the warrior's grip, then Gargo's.

They all turned at the sound of approaching footsteps.

Two Space Marines drew near, clad in silver and with the look of hunters.

Men with a purpose yet unfulfilled.

The first was a wolf-lean warrior with tanned, weather-beaten skin, close-cropped hair and a face of scars. Across his back was a murderous greatsword and at his waist was sheathed a standard-issue chainblade and a gladius that bore a chipped cobalt Ultima at its pommel.

The other legionary was pale-skinned and patrician, broad of shoulder and with a great eagle at his chest with singular aspect instead of the customary two. He too carried a hulking blade at his back.

'I heard you did our father a great service,' he said, his accent cultured and precise.

The first warrior stepped forward, his eyes moving from Wolf to Drakes.

He nodded, seemingly finding them worthy.

'I am Garviel Loken,' he said. 'And this is Nathaniel Garro.'

It wasn't supposed to be this way…

Magnus knelt before the crazed looking glass that had once stood in a far corner of his war-pavilion. Now it was alone amid the ruins of what had once been the Palatine Tower. The din of artillery surrounded him, and propellant fumes washed through the remains of the tower in stinking clouds. Cackling, daemonic things slithered in and out of perception, but Magnus ignored every distraction.

All his attention was fixed on the mirror and the broken-glass reflections it returned.

Since his ejection from his father's presence, he had not moved from this place, as immobile as the statue he had climbed the mountains of Prospero to see in his youth.

It had long been a source of frustration to him that the mirror was incomplete, a symbol of his fractured nature, but now that it was whole again, he longed to take it up and shatter it upon the rock of this lightning-struck tower.

The transition from beneath the Palace to the ruins beyond the walls had not been gentle and had almost ended his already mortally wounded sons. Menkaura and Amon's lives had hung by the slenderest thread, and required the arts of his greatest Pavoni adepts to save.

Ahriman had needed only the skill of the chirurgeons, but something in his favoured son had broken within the Palace. Magnus could not yet tell what it was, but feared for what it might mean for the future.

His mirrored reflections stared back at him, but where they had once shown him his myriad faces, the aspects of his soul in all their varied splendour and horror, now they showed but a single visage, the one he had worn since his refusal of his father's offer.

At the centre of the looking glass, a single, teardrop-shaped shard of glass had been missing from the frame, but in its place was now a daemonglass flect that fit the gap, but which Magnus knew was wrought from material inimical to this world and all within it.

Sickly colours smeared across its surface like a film of promethium on water, and thin strands of that impossible light flowed slowly along the cracks between the shards. The reflected images closest to this new addition were already stained by this creeping power, and it would not be long before the entire mirror was tainted by the shimmering warp light.

Strangely, the thought did not displease him.

A figure entered his peripheral vision, a legionary in the livery of the Sons of Horus, with a crest of feathers across the chest of his sea-green plate. Magnus felt his wariness at approaching so close to a wounded primarch, but his soul was a dutiful one, maliciously loyal and brutally effective.

'My lord,' he said. 'My name is Kinor Argonis, equerry to the Warmaster.'

'I know who you are, Argonis Unscarred,' said Magnus, finally turning from the immaterial mirror. ***'What do you want?'***

'I bring word from the Warmaster,' said Argonis. 'He sends for you.'

'And what does my brother want? What is the intent behind his summons?'

Argonis paused, sensible enough to know a lie would be dangerous.

'A new front opens in the war, and Lupercal wishes to know if you are with him.'

Magnus rose to his full height, and Argonis stepped back, awed and not a little afraid of this new and terrible form of the Crimson King in his aspect of war.

'Go to him, Argonis,' said Magnus. ***'And tell him I am with him until the very end.'***

ABOUT THE AUTHOR

Graham McNeill's extensive back catalogue includes the Horus Heresy novels *The Crimson King* and *Vengeful Spirit,* and the *New York Times* bestselling *A Thousand Sons.* Graham's Ultramarines series, featuring Captain Uriel Ventris, is now seven novels long, and has close links to his Iron Warriors stories, the novel *Storm of Iron* being a perennial favourite with Black Library fans. He has also written the Forges of Mars trilogy, featuring the Adeptus Mechanicus, and the Warhammer Horror novella *The Colonel's Monograph.* For Warhammer, he has written the trilogy *The Legend of Sigmar,* the second volume of which won the 2010 David Gemmell Legend Award, and the Warhammer: The Old World novel *Lords of the Lance.*

MORE FROM BLACK LIBRARY

THE LION: SON OF THE FOREST
by Mike Brooks

The Lion. Son of the Emperor, brother of demigods and primarch of the Dark Angels. Awakened. Returned. And yet… lost.

For these stories and more, go to **blacklibrary.com**, **warhammer.com**, Games Workshop and Warhammer stores, all good book stores or visit one of the thousands of independent retailers worldwide, which can be found at **warhammer.com/store-finder**

An extract from
The Lion: Son of the Forest
by Mike Brooks

The river sings silver notes: a perpetual, chaotic babble in which a fantastically complex melody seems to hang, tantalising, just out of reach of the listener. He could spend eternity here trying to find the heart of it, without ever succeeding, yet still not consider the time wasted. The sound of water over stone, the interplay of energy and matter, creates a quiet symphony that is both unremarkable and unique. He does not know how long he has been here, just listening.

Nor, he realises, does he know where *here* is.

The listener becomes aware of himself in stages, like a sleeper passing from the deepest, darkest depths of slumber, through the shallows of semi-consciousness where thought swirls in confusing eddies, and then into the light. First comes the realisation that he is not the song of the river; that he is in fact separate from it, and listening to it. Then sensation dawns, and he realises he is sitting on the river's bank. If there is a sun, or suns, then he cannot see them through the branches of the trees overhead and the mist that hangs heavily in the air, but there is still light enough for him to make out his surroundings.

The trees are massive, and mighty, with great trunks that

could not be fully encircled by one, two, perhaps even half a dozen people's outstretched arms. Their rough, cracked bark pockmarks them with shadows, as though the trees themselves are camouflaged. The ground beneath their branches is fought over by tough shrubs: sturdy, twisted, thorny things strangling each other in the contest for space and light, like children unheeded at the feet of adults. The earth in which they grow is dark and rich, and when the listener digs his fingers into it, it smells of life, and death, and other things besides. It is a familiar smell, although he cannot say from where, or why.

His fingers, he realises as they penetrate the ground, are armoured. His whole body is armoured, in fact, encased in a great suit of black plates with the faintest hint of dark green. This is a familiar sensation, too. The armour feels like a part of him – an extension, as natural as the shell of any crustacean that might lurk in the nooks and crannies of the river in front of him. He leans forward and peers down into the still water next to the bank, sheltered from the main flow by an outcropping just upstream. It becomes an almost perfect mirror surface, as smooth as a dream.

The listener does not recognise the face that looks back at him. It is deeply lined, as though a world of cares and worries has washed over it like the river water, scoring the marks of their passage into the skin. His hair is pale, streaked with blond here and there, but otherwise fading into grey and white. The lower part of his face is obscured by a thick, full beard and moustache, leaving only the lips bare; it is a distrustful mouth, one more likely to turn downwards in disapproval than quirk upwards in a smile.

He raises one hand, the fingers still smeared with dirt, before his face. The reflection does the same. This is surely his face, but the sight sparks no memory. He does not know who he is, and he does not know where he is, for all that it feels familiar.

That being the case, there seems little point in remaining here.

The listener gets to his feet, then hesitates. He cannot explain to himself why he should move, given the song of the river is so beautiful. However, the realisation of his lack of knowledge has opened something inside him, a hunger which was not there before. He will not be satisfied until he has answers.

Still, the river's song calls to him. He decides to walk along the bank, following the flow of the water and listening to it as he goes, and since he does not know where he is, one direction is as good as the other. There is a helmet on the bank, next to where he was sitting. It is the same colour as his armour, with vertical slits across the mouth, like firing slits in a wall. He picks it up, and clamps it to his waist with a movement that feels instinctual.

He does not know for how long he walks. Time is surely passing, in that one moment slips into another, and he can remember ones that came before and consider the concept of ones yet to come, but there is nothing to mark it. The light neither increases nor decreases, instead remaining an almost spectral presence which illuminates without revealing its source. Shadows lurk, but there is no indication as to what casts them. The walker is unperturbed. His eyes can pierce those shadows, just as he can smell foliage, and he can hear the river. There is no soughing of wind in the branches, for the air is still, but the moist air carries the faint hooting, hollering calls of animals of some kind, somewhere in the distance.

The river's course begins to flatten and widen. The walker follows it around a bend, then comes to a halt in shock.

On the far bank stands a building.

It is built of cut and dressed stone, a dark blue-grey rock in which brighter specks glitter. It is not immense – the surrounding trees tower over it – but it is solid. It is a castle of some kind, a fortress, intended to keep the unwanted out and whatever people and treasures lie within safe from harm. It is neither new and pristine, nor ancient and weathered. It looks as though it has always stood here, and always shall. And on the wide, calm water in front of it sits a boat.

It is small, wooden, and unpainted. It is large enough for one person, and indeed one person is sitting in it. The walker's eyes can make him out, even at distance. He is old, and not old in the same way as the walker's face is. Time has not lined his features, it has ravaged them. His cheeks are sunken, his limbs are wasted; skin that was once clearly a rich chestnut now has an ashen patina, and his long hair is lifeless, dull grey, and matted. However, that grey head supports a crown: little more than a circlet of gold, but a crown nonetheless.

In his hands, swollen of knuckle and weak of grip, he holds a rod. The line is already cast into the water. Now he sits, hunched over as though in pain, a small, ancient figure in a small, simple boat.

The walker does not stop to wonder why a king would be fishing in such a manner. He is aware of the context of such things, but he does not know from where, and they do not matter to him. Here is someone who might have some answers for him.

'Greetings!' he calls. His voice is strong, rich and deep, although rough around the edges from age or disuse, or both. It carries across the water. The old king in the boat blinks, and when his eyes open again, they are looking at the walker.

'What is this place?' the walker demands.

The old king blinks again. When his eyes open this time, they are focused on the water once more. It is as though the walker is not there at all, a dismissal of minimal effort.

The walker discovers that he is not used to being ignored, and nor does he appreciate it. He steps into the water, intending to wade across the river so the king cannot so easily dismiss him. He is unconcerned about the current: he is strong of limb, and knows without knowing that his armour is waterproof, and that should he don his helmet he will be able to breathe even if he is submerged.

He has only gone a few steps, in up to his knees, when he realises there are shadows in the water: large shadows that circle the small boat, around and around. They do not bite on the line, and nor do they capsize the craft in which the fisher sits, but either could be disastrous.

Moreover, the walker realises, the king is wounded. The walker cannot see the wound, but he can smell the blood. A rich, copperish tang tickles his nose. It is not a smell that delights him, but neither does he find it repulsive. It is simply a scent, one that he is able to parse and understand. The king is bleeding into the water, drip by drip. Perhaps that is what has drawn the shadows to this place. Perhaps they would have been here anyway.

Some of the shadows start to peel away, and head towards the walker.

The walker is not a being to whom fear comes naturally, but nor is he unfamiliar with the concept of danger. The shadows in the water are unknown to him, and move like predators.

+Come back to the bank.+

The walker whirls. A small figure stands on the land, swathed in robes of dark green, so that it nearly blends into the background against which it stands. It is the size of a child, perhaps, but the walker knows it to be something else.

It is a Watcher in the Dark.

+Come back to the bank,+ the Watcher repeats. Although its communication can hardly be called a voice – there is no sound, merely a sensation inside the walker's head that imparts meaning – it feels increasingly urgent nonetheless. The walker realises that he is not normally one to turn away from a challenge, but nor is he willing to ignore a Watcher in the Dark. It feels like a link, a connection to what came before, to what he should be able to remember.

He wades back, and steps up onto the bank. The approaching shadows hesitate for a moment, then circle away towards the king in his boat.

+They would destroy you,+ the Watcher says. The walker understands that it is talking about the shadows. There are layers to the feelings in his head now, feelings that are the mental aftertaste of the Watcher's communication. Disgust lurks there, but also fear.

'Where is this place?' the walker asks.

+Home.+

The walker waits, but nothing else is forthcoming. Moreover, he understands that there will not be. So far as the Watcher is concerned, that is not simply all the information that is required, but all that is available to give.

He looks out over the water, towards the king. The old man still sits hunched over, rod in his hands, blood leaking from his wounds one drip at a time.

'Why does he ignore me?'

+You did not ask the correct question.+

The walker looks around. The shadows in the water are still there, so it seems foolish to try to cross. However, he has seen no bridge over the river, nor another boat. He has no tools with which to build such a craft from the trees around him, and the knowledge of how to do so does not come easily to his mind. He is not like some of his brothers, for whom creation is natural…

His brothers. Who are his brothers?

Shapes flit through his mind, as ephemeral as smoke in a storm. He cannot get a grip, cannot wrestle them into anything that makes sense, or anything onto which his reaching mind can latch. The peace brought about by the song of the river is gone, and in its place is uncertainty and frustration. Nonetheless, the walker would not return to his former state. To knowingly welcome ignorance is not his way.

He catches a glimpse of something pale, a long way off through the trees, but on his side of the river. He begins to walk towards it, leaving the river behind him – he can always find it again, he knows its song – and making his way through the undergrowth. The plants are thick and verdant, but he is strong and sure. He ducks under spines, slaps aside strangling tendrils reaching out for anything that passes, and avoids breaking the twigs, which would leak sap so corrosive it might damage even his armour.

He does not wonder how he knows these things. The Watcher said that this was home.

The Watcher itself has been left behind, but it keeps reappearing, stepping out of the edge of shadows. It says nothing; not until the walker passes through a thicket of thorns and finally gets a clearer view of what he had seen.

It is a building, or at least the roof of one; that is all he can see from here. It is a dome of beautiful pale stone, supported by pillars. Whereas before he had been finding his own route through the forest, now there is a clear path ahead, a route of short grass hemmed in on either side by bushes and tree trunks. It curves away, rather than arrowing straight towards the pale building, but the walker knows that is where it leads.

+Do not take that path,+ the Watcher cautions him. +You are not yet strong enough.+

The walker looks down at this tiny creature, barely knee-high to him, then breathes deeply and rolls his shoulders within his armour. He presumes he had a youth, given he now looks old. Perhaps he was stronger then. Nonetheless, his body does not feel feeble.

+That is not the strength you will need.+

The walker narrows his eyes. 'You caution me against anything that might help me make sense of my situation. What would you have me do instead?'

+Follow your nature.+

The walker breathes in again, ready to snap an answer, for he finds he is just as ill-disposed towards being denied as he is to being ignored. However, he pauses, then sniffs.

He sniffs again.

Something is amiss.

He is surrounded by the deep, rich scent of the forest, which smells of both life and death. However, now his nose detects something else: a rancid undercurrent, something that is not merely rot or decay – for these are natural odours – but far worse, far more jarring.

Corruption.

This is something wrong, something twisted. It is something that should not be here: something that should not, in fact, exist at all.

The walker knows what he must do. He must follow his nature.

The hunter steps forward, and starts to run in pursuit of his quarry.

II

He flows over the ground, each step sure and certain and placed to perfection. Walking is second nature and not something about which he has to think, but running awakens something within him. This sense of urgency, this sense of a goal towards which he is striving; it provides focus and clarity, and makes him not only more aware, but also more aware of his own awareness. He realises that he perceives the forest in a new way: not as a homogenous landscape, but as terrain. The ground on which tracks will be left, the plants that will show the signs of a body passing, the thickets where a predator might wait in ambush and those in which lurking would lead only to becoming a meal for the plant itself: these things are as clear to him as words upon a page.

This *is* his home, and nothing can hide from him here.

The scent leads him onwards, as distinct as a wrong note in a symphony, and strengthening as he closes on it. The Watcher is forgotten, as are the king in the boat and the shadows in the water. He is hunting beasts through the trees, just as he used to long ago, back before…

Back before what?

The hunter slows, his focus disrupted for a moment by

another flash of something that is not even memory, but perhaps the shadow of one. He does not remember what came before, but he remembers that there was something to remember, which is both welcome and infuriating. All he knows is that he hunted like this in the past.

He shakes himself. Memory will return when it returns, *if* it returns. For now, he still has a quarry to chase down. He presses on, still following the scent of corruption.

The hunter is not certain when the forest begins to change character, for there was never before any way with which to mark the time except by counting his own breaths or heartbeats. However, at some point he becomes aware that the mist is thinning. The light around him has a source now, high up and to his left, and he can feel the heat of this sun upon his scalp; it is a thick heat, a wet heat, the type that reaches into the throat and threatens to clog the airways. The trees are different, as well: they are still tall, still towering, but this is no longer a world of massive, low-hanging branches. Now their crowns splay out far above him, and their trunks are bare apart from the climbing plants that seek to scale their neighbours to snatch a glimpse of light for themselves. The air is alive with the chittering of insects, and the hunter can no longer hear the song of the river. He pauses and reaches down into the ground once more, this time coming up with a fistful of mouldering leaves. They carpet the ground, thick and brown, and do not easily give up the prints of those who have passed over them before; not like soft earth does, the tracker's friend.

The hunter does not know where he is now, any more than he truly knew where he was before, but he knows that this is somewhere else. He is no longer home.

The scent of corruption is still strong, though. Stronger, even. The hunter is drawn forwards, pressing on through this new undergrowth: purplish ferns, pale roots trailing down